Also by David Allan Cates

Hunger in America
X out of Wonderland: A Saga
Freeman Walker
Ben Armstrong's Strange Trip Home

TOM CONNOR'S GIFT

(mad grief, mad love, and a crooked road home)

To Sarah

What a pleasure to
get to Know you —
Good luck and see
you next year —

BP Bangtail
Press

Published in the United States by

Bangtail Press
P. O. Box 11262
Bozeman, MT 59719
www.bangtailpress.com

Cover painting by Dean Gazeley. A detail from "La Planchadora."
www.deangazeley.com

For O.B.

When you left
you took almost
everything.

I kneel in the nights
before tigers
that will not let me be.

Charles Bukowski
From "For Jane."

TOM CONNOR'S GIFT

(mad grief, mad love, and a crooked road home)

one

the bear

Morning and still no trace of dawn. I shuffle out the back door past the stacked split wood on the porch toward the outhouse. I don't make it. In the dark I stop and bend my knees and pull my underwear aside and urinate on the frozen ground, the puppy running circles around me. I smell myself and smell the trees and the cold wind from the canyon. The air makes the skin of my legs taut, and I shiver and feel a strange resolve to do this every day for the rest of my life, get up while it's still dark and walk outside and squat like an animal and smell the air while I let my urine out. Didn't some widows in some cultures pull out their hair or mat it in dirt or smudge their faces with ash or cut stripes on their breasts and keen for three straight nights?

I stand up. The stars show above the canyon wall and the moon glows from somewhere behind it and my boots make pretty prints in the dusting of new snow. As I walk toward the wood pile for an armload, it occurs to me that I am walking because I am not sleeping, whereas just a few minutes ago I was sleeping because I was not walking. Don't try to make sense of that. My legs below my robe and above my unlaced leather boots are bare and cold but the air feels good, as though I'm breathing through my skin, my cheeks, my eyelids. I know there were dinosaurs around here hundreds of millions of years ago and because I can't understand what *hundreds of millions of years ago* means, I eliminate those words from my head. I walk and feel and what I feel is there are dinosaurs around here *right now.* The wood pile is nineteen steps away through a grassy meadow dusted with new snow and spaced with big pines and truck-size rocks that have fallen from the cliff. Hidden dinosaurs make the moon shadows of the trees and rocks more interesting. I wonder what's under each of the rocks and wonder if a woman is. She'd have been out for her morning pee a thousand years ago, and she'd have heard the crack above her as the rock broke free, then heard nothing as it fell. I hear the same silence she heard moments before her death and the same river in the canyon below. I hear my breathing and the sound of each step on the frozen ground and try to breathe with my stride, once for every two steps, but that's not quite right, and by the time I've arrived at the wood-pile of stacked pine between two ponderosas I've got it: three steps, one inhale. Three more steps, one exhale.

At the woodpile, I grab sticks of split pine and lay them across my left forearm. The thick robe keeps the wood from scratching my skin. In each of my twenty-four days here (one day for every year of my marriage—but this is a coincidence) I've marveled at how I could have survived almost five decades on this earth with rice paper skin. Almost everything I try to do outdoors pinches or scratches and I have more nicks on my body than I ever have had. I remember counting them on my husband's body when we were young—this little cut on the back of the hand from the barn door, this on his knee from the corner of the baler, this on his elbow from something un-der the car. His body a map of his days, and looking for nicks and cuts and bruises was a way of knowing him. At five or six sticks the weight is enough so I wrap my right arm under as well and turn to carry the wood back to the cabin. My fingers are suddenly so cold I'm making fists and my biceps are burning with the weight. It would be nice to have the arms and shoulders and back of a man. My son when he was teenager told me he wanted his muscles to burn with fatigue every day and I know women in other cultures carry a lot of weight so maybe it all comes down to living too long without burning biceps, or maybe just living too long.

Loaded with wood, I breathe once every two steps. I try to breathe through my nose very Zen-like but start to suffocate so open my mouth and get a full lungful and then start thinking about the bad taste in my mouth and how I'll try to drink a full pint of water when I get back into the cabin, as yesterday I started drinking coffee immediately and forgot about water or juice or anything like that. Then, just after lunch, I felt so thirsty I drank almost a quart of water in less than fifteen minutes. I felt my stomach bulge out to bursting and that's when I thought, why didn't I feel thirsty before this was necessary? Why did the thirst just lie back like that all morning and then suddenly start shouting? I hadn't even been craving it, but suddenly I felt like a madwoman trying to gulp down enough water. Which is a sideways journey into thinking about sex, because then to amuse myself while my arms are burning and my mouth is tasting bad, I wonder if drinking a lot of water has any meaning in the big picture? Could there be a particular time we drink water when it would be very meaningful and could there be a time we drink water when we say, oh, it meant nothing? And that amused me even more. Carrying wood back to the cabin under the still starry sky, my untied boots crunching on the frozen ground and the skin of my bare legs tight and clean against the cold air, I think, some people say all sex means something but those are people who have never taken part in meaningless sex. Or won't admit it. Which is just another way of thinking: how do we decide which sexual act means something and what sexual act does not? I mean, does it mean anything if something is meaningless? And, if you feel bad afterward does that mean it meant nothing or is that proof that it must have meant something? My husband Mark told me he fell for me because the first time we lay in bed together and he touched me I looked at him in a way that made him know he was into some *deep shit*. Those were his words, of course, and they were figurative. Just so the record's straight. He had sex with two other women during the time we were married—two that I know of—and he told me they meant nothing. That touching them meant nothing. And I believe him, somehow. But what I can't seem to understand is why, if touching them meant nothing, if he was able to make that decision—and of course, I've made that decision about sex, not when I was married, but before I was married, I had sex with boys that meant nothing—so why if he tells me that, and I believe it, then why did they mean something to me? So much so that I was mad at him for years. Years I'll never have back, years I lost being angry. During which, who knows? Maybe he had sex with even more women, women who weren't angry with him. Who could blame him? Me, I suppose, because even thinking about it makes me mad again, even now, carrying wood in the dark on the far side of the Great Plains. Suddenly I'm burning mad at all the wasted time, and at him for dying and for making me mad again long after I thought I was over it. My fists are clenched as anger floods my neck and face and oozes out my pores and feels somehow like the only true thing I have anymore. It's the only thing that makes sense or nothing does. I feel I am going to split with this truth, so big and hard and beautiful and irrelevant.

I've arrived at the back door of the cabin already, and I need to turn around with my armload of wood and use my hip to bump the door but it has latched and won't open. Irritated, I turn a little too sharply and try to lift the latch with my hand even though I've got both arms supporting the wood and my cold fingers balled up in fists. I can't seem to do it, and finally I have to let the wood drop. I should have bent down and let it roll off my arms but because of my anger I just let it go and try to jump back—a trick I don't quite manage, as one of the pieces hits my shin on the way down. I unleash a string of cuss words at the top of my lungs. My shin is pounding in pain and I know I'll have a bruise and probably another bleeding scrape, but I find the echo of my voice off the cliff weirdly amusing.

I cuss again, just to hear it again, then bend to pick up the wood that has scattered around my feet. Crazy grief is a good drug, bending the banal to strange. Things like peeing outside, drinking water, and cussing off canyon walls get interesting fast but it's all a distraction. The fact is I'm so sad since Mark died I don't know what to do in the world of human beings. I don't know who I am beyond a woman bending in the pre-dawn darkness to pick up the firewood she's dropped. I bend and feel the cold sticks with my cold hand, and I concentrate on that, and think as I lift each piece, this is real, this is real, this is real, just *that*, just *this*—which is when I see the bear.

I'm trying to be truthful so although that slipped out—*which is when I see the bear*—I have to stop because it's not true. What is true but harder to write is that's when I *feel* the bear. But I don't know how I feel it. Hadn't I been feeling dinosaurs in the air earlier? Wasn't I breathing dinosaurs, feeling them on my skin? I didn't feel the bear like that, or maybe I did, but I didn't feel its breath or its claws or its heat. While on my knees picking up wood I simply felt the air change, as though lightning were going to strike—but even as I say that I know that's something I've heard about, never felt. So maybe I smelled it—the bear was so close, I must have smelled it. But I can't say what the smell was. Only that it made all of the tiny hairs on my body stand and from my knees even before I lifted my head I knew what I'd see.

But that's not true, either. I didn't know what I'd see. I only knew there was something there, and even knowing something was there—a dinosaur?—I was still surprised to actually *see* it. I have a puppy (where did he go?—from running circles around me when I stepped outside to suddenly long gone) and once I walked the puppy past a statue of a bear in a park, and the puppy trembled and wouldn't go near. He'd never seen a bear in his life, much less been hurt by one, and yet he knew to be afraid of the shape of that statue. I marvel at that, but here I am, on my knees smelling a scent that has my hair standing up—and when I look up there's his head turned around the tree looking at me from no more than a few steps away, as though he's been there since I came outside and peed and walked to the woodpile. I want to tell you he had an engorged tick on his chest and his fur silver tipped and ragged and wet on one side, and he had two toes on his left forepaw and details like that but it was dark and I could see only how he was standing upright with his head turned and his face trained on me. He looked like a big cartoon character with tiny eyes reflecting the light of the heavens—or more likely absorbing the light from the heavens, because even so close I couldn't see his eyes. What I saw was their lack, their empty blackness. I might have stopped breathing then. At least long enough to become aware of my heart trying to jump up my throat.

I force myself to begin again. First a gasp and then a real breath. Another and another. And with each new breath and the hard, cold feel of the gravel under my knees, I become more aware of my body as prey, the bear not fifteen feet away—tall, so very tall, like a hairy giant. A monster, and that's what I think as I carefully breathe through my nostrils and begin to gather the wood that I dropped—again?—five sticks of split pine. I tuck them up and hold them against my chest. Why do I bother? Why don't I ignore the wood and stand up and step back safely through the door into the cabin? I don't even need the wood to start a fire. There's plenty of wood stacked on the porch. But this is my obsession, not using that porch wood, or if I used it to replace it immediately, because if the stack on the porch grows smaller—and I'm sure it's at least three days of wood—but if it gets smaller my reptile mind's convinced I'll freeze to death in a blizzard. Just two nights before I lay in bed after using wood from the porch to stoke the fire before I went to bed, used a couple of pieces, and as I listened to the crackling stove and felt the coziness of my bed, I forced myself to get up and go outside (with the bear?) to replace the porch wood I'd used. So on my knees now with the bear looking at me, I gather up to my chest the last of the pieces and that's when I hear him growl. Low and horrifying. How many times when I was little or my children were little did we imitate the growl of a bear or a lion or a dinosaur—and I'd even heard such growls at the zoo before (not dinosaurs, of course) but when the bear makes that noise deep in its chest or deep in the middle of the earth I feel my bones soften and my flesh turn to jelly. I stare at the earth under me just barely lit now by what must be a paling of the eastern sky. I feel my neck bending forward, stretched and exposed, not my throat but my neck like a woman awaiting the sword. My god, nothing like a bear so close to make everything morbid. I stay as still as I can but my breathing and my heart seem out of control and I know the bear can smell my fear, and I'm sure I can, too. And then I get tired of something, I don't know what, tired of the rough weight of the firewood in my arms or my knees against the frozen gravel and it's only me, now, only me and my obsessive idea that I don't ever want the pile of wood on the porch to get smaller even by one stick, only me and the little blood that trickles from the throbbing scrape on my shin, me and the tiresome smell of *die-sores* as my son used to call them, me and the hole in my heart where my husband used to be. I push up to my feet. When I look back to the tree she's—*she*? I don't know—when I look back to the tree the bear is gone.

I manage to open the door behind me with an armload of wood, and I step backward and into the kitchen. I hear the growl one more time as the door bangs shut and my legs give out and I sink to the dirty wood floor with my back to the door that suddenly feels too thin and flimsy to keep a bear out. It's while am sitting in the dark like that, trying to catch my breath, that I feel the wet under me and realize that despite the pleasure I took in peeing on the ground outside, I apparently saved a little for the bear.

I get up and change my underwear even before I barricade the door, which I notice now is broken. I mean it won't quite latch properly. I push a stool under the knob to hold it closed and keep the bear out. *A stool? To keep the bear out?* I don't think about that. I start a fire in the wood stove, pour water from the storage barrel under the sink into a caldron that I cover and set on the propane burner. I put some water in a smaller pot to heat for coffee, and soon I have just that, a beautiful cup of coffee and a basin full of warm water, and a warm-enough cabin to strip my clothes off and stand to bathe by the kitchen sink. Through the window looking east I see the wide sky over the plains fire to pink, red, orange and yellow, and in a few places where the river bends the water mirrors the colors of the sky. I'm dripping in warm water now, standing in the low light next to the hot wood stove. The river starts high in the wilderness behind me and races through gaps in a series of massive parallel ridges before being held for a while behind a dam and then breaking out here onto the plains. I wrap myself in a towel and stand at the window and look for the puppy and the bear but see only a pair of swans. They lift up over the still green cottonwoods in the canyon and follow the bend of the river eastward until they disappear into the first rays of sunlight. The bear is the first bear I've seen in the wild and I wonder how long I'll feel afraid, how long before I can begin to absorb the sadness and climb out of my cave. Home feels like a long shot but I know I can't stay here forever. On my first trip west, a million years ago, on my first night sleeping out on the plains, I saw the northern lights. I was sixteen years old and in love with a wild and troubled boy, not the one I married. Something tells me the answer begins and ends with Tom Connor's story. Back then I was *ooh sooooo frightened and I was ooh sooooo brave.* I'm standing here at the window in the cabin actually singing it. That trip west was the first time for a number of things.

the best part of traveling is the people

"It's this country," the driver said as he flailed his long right arm toward the green fields and red barn passing out my window.

I flinched. Tom laughed in the backseat. I glanced around to shut him up but he wasn't looking at me.

"You nervous or something?" the driver asked.

"About what?" I said.

"How should I know? This year's Super Bowl match-up? The financial future of the Metropolitan Opera?"

I stared at the road. At least Tom didn't laugh this time. What kind of boy would make his girlfriend sit in the front seat next to a drug addict? But he wasn't like other boys. For one thing, he was wearing a canary-yellow tuxedo with pants and sleeves about six inches too short for him and a checkered-flag nametag sewn onto the shiny lapel that said *"Tommy!"* And maybe I wasn't his girlfriend, either. He was on his way to Montana to see his mother, who was dying in a hospital, and I came along because I loved him and he asked me to, and because I was afraid I'd never see him again if I didn't. Maybe I should have told him that. What I said was I'd never seen mountains before.

"Just because I stopped to snort a little H?" the driver said. "Is that it?"

"No," I said, even though it was. Just ten minutes before he'd pulled into one those clean little waysides Wisconsin has on its highways, and with a nice family having a picnic at a table right in front of the car, he unwrapped some tin foil and snorted a brown powder he called Mexican Mud. I was afraid of how he'd drive after that. He slowed down, actually, slipped the Cadillac into cruise control at an even fifty-five.

"Listen, you ever heard of low-level Alpha particles?"

"Who hasn't?" Tommy, smart-alecky, from the backseat.

The driver didn't notice. "They travel in waves," he explained.

Tommy blew a bubble off his tongue that floated over the back of the front seat, all the way to the dashboard, where it landed, sat for a moment, clean and beautiful with the blue sky behind it, and then popped, leaving a shiny wet circle about half the size of a penny.

"It was the low-level that killed the buffalo," the driver said.

"That's funny," Tommy said. "I thought it was the high."

"Myth," the driver said. "Sixty million buffalo? Tell me exactly how *high*-level waves could kill that many?"

Tommy sent another bubble forward. It landed next to the driver's leg on the front seat but he didn't notice.

"Let me give it to you straight," the driver said. "Everybody's looking for where the waves and particles meet, right? Which is why the black race will never be successful in this country. Their systems are set up for a different combination of waves and particles like you'll find over there in Africa."

"And they're so super successful in Africa?"

"Excellent point," the driver said, sniffing. "But hey, you ever hear of the Black Death?"

"Everybody's heard of the Black Death."

"Half of Europe in the fourteenth century. Dead. Like that." He snapped his fingers. "The survivors survived. That means there was a purification process underway. Which is not inconsistent with good wave-particle theory. It means half of the white Europeans, because of their wave-particle ratio, had to be eliminated. I'm not saying I don't feel bad for the Jews and all, killed by the Nazis? Terrible. On a human level, I mean. But cosmically speaking? Hey, the Jews were never that happy in Europe anyway. You know it. I know it. They knew it. I'm just saying Hitler was the first person to propose a systematic solution to a problem everybody else was afraid to acknowledge."

He looked at me when he finished. Of course I thought of my mother and the ghosts of her family, and of course I worried I was a coward but I didn't say a word.

"Hitler was a hero, if you stop to think about it," he said, and kept staring at me as if to make sure I was thinking about it.

Yes, I nodded *yes.* I couldn't help it.

The driver breathed as if relieved that was settled. He actually looked very happy at how he'd tamed horror with a theory. He continued, "Oh, *Das Fuehrer* was brute, don't get me wrong, but the universe calls for brutes from time to time. He did the work that was in accord with the natural laws of particle-wave theory."

A semi-truck passed slowly, and the noise of the eighteen wheels through our open window silenced him. After it had moved well ahead, Tom said, "So what did you do before you became a scientist?"

I put my hand over my mouth and pretended to cough to cover up my laughter.

"Insurance," the driver said.

My cough turned into a coughing fit. I was bent over my knees and couldn't seem to stop laughing so I just kept pretending to cough until I felt Tommy's hand on my back. Finally, I relaxed and little, and sat up.

"You all right?" the driver asked.

I nodded. I was afraid to look back at Tommy, though. I

wanted him to keep his hand where it was, on my shoulder and neck, but after a while he gave me one last pat and sat back again in his seat. I looked out the window at the rolling grass hills scattered with clusters of oak trees. We passed more farms and billboards and hundreds of cars and trucks going our way, or the other. Before long, Tommy fell asleep, which is why he'd insisted on the back seat. He laid his head against his balled up jean jacket and closed his eyes. The car smelled of cologne, denim and vinyl, and even though we'd only left Chicago that morning, I felt gross down to my bones. The driver took it out of cruise control and speeded up to 65, then 70, and I tried not to think.

"I lived in the suburbs with my wife and three kids," he said. "I worked every day to make ends meet, but my wife liked to spend money and we fell behind anyway. I complained about it at work and my buddy says, *Hey, just make more money!* So I got into dealing. Seriously, though, I figured 99 percent of the time you're selling to junkies. You're not selling to kids on the playground. That's a myth. I sold to people who never should have been here in the first place, who probably could only be happy in Africa. I knew it. They knew it. Which is why they were junkies."

I didn't answer. We passed another hitchhiker, a boy with long blond hair and cardboard sign that said WEST. I was hoping we'd stop, but we drove right by.

"Then I went to prison," the driver said. "And now I'm out and on my way home. The H is just to keep me up, keep me going. I feel good and I don't want to stop, see, because I miss my kids bad. Lately I've been thinking about one time when I took my youngest to church and then skiing. She was five. We're sitting in the big crowded ski lodge, and she looked around at all the people and she said, Did all the people from church come here to ski? Blew me away. I mean the way kids see the world. All the doors and window blown open. I'd like to see it like that sometime. Anyway, that little girl? She's twenty years old now."

Saying that seemed to make him sad, and then it made *me*

sad. I wondered what my life would have been like if my dad—instead of spending his days worrying about clients and their cases and his nights worrying about me and what kind of trouble I might be in—what my life would be like if he'd been in prison. Easier, maybe, I thought, but that just made me sadder. I leaned over against the door and closed my eyes and tried to sleep but couldn't, so I faked it the rest of the way across Wisconsin to Minneapolis, where the driver got a hotel room right on the Interstate. He said we were welcome to stay there while he checked in on his ex and kids. If things went well, he'd be gone all night and the room was ours, paid for, on him.

The wave-particle ratio must have been right—for he never came back. I showered that night while Tommy slept, and in the morning we showered together. He was happy and kept playing games with the soap to make me laugh. For all his craziness, he could look so adorable. Sometimes when we kissed I'd think I needed nothing else on earth but his face right up next to mine—as long as I could adore it and kiss it I'd be happy. We dressed and ate waffles in the restaurant, then strolled out to the highway with our packs. He wore the same yellow tuxedo and, as absurdly as it fit, it looked pretty in the morning sunshine. He struck a gallant pose with his arm extended and his thumb out.

"The best part of traveling is the people, right wench?" he said, and winked, but I got him to promise he wouldn't make me sit in the front seat alone again with a man driver. Within ten minutes we got a ride in an old rusted Oldsmobile from a man with a big head of curly red hair and a red beard he fingered constantly. The backseat was loaded with junk so we all three sat in the front, me in the middle. We accelerated up onto the highway and drove out of the city heading west. Red Beard was going to Seattle, so we figured we had it made all the way to Montana. We couldn't believe our luck and kept smiling at each other and holding hands. The driver told us he'd lived all over and when he was about our age he spent a year roller-skating around Denver. He said he'd built luxury hotels in Hawaii and train bridges across the Yukon, but the thing he'd remember until the day he died was the first time he hitched across the country and got a ride with a man who was going to Canada to ditch the draft.

"The guy was all torn up, but I couldn't really see it at the time," the driver said. "Understandably, he didn't want to go fly across the ocean and kill people in a war he thought was wrong. He wanted to do the right thing, but the right thing meant he'd be an exile. The right thing to him—the brave thing—meant his family and everybody in his hometown would think he was coward. I was only a few years younger than him, and I'd just run away from home—so being an exile didn't seem all that bad. I hadn't a clue what to say. I remember we went about thirty miles per hour up Loveland Pass above Denver in this old beater of a jalopy. He stopped the car and told me he had to take a leak. There we were at the top of the Rockies. Three hundred and sixty degrees of snow-covered peaks. The dude walks off the shoulder into the snow, behind some rock, and—Boom! He shoots himself."

"What did you do?" Tommy asked.

The driver squinted and tugged at his beard. He shook his head as though trying to remember. "I don't know, really. I guess I freaked out."

"Did you flag somebody down?" I asked.

"I don't really remember," the driver said. "But I don't think I did. I know I walked around behind the rock and found him. And I know I drove his car down to Denver and ditched it."

"You mean you left him there?"

"I did."

"Wicked." It was one of Tommy's favorite words. After a long pause, he said it again.

"I don't know what I figured. Maybe I thought he'd done something brave but I knew nobody else would understand. Somehow it comforted me to think if they did find him, they'd think he'd been murdered. Maybe his parents and friends would like him again. I don't know. I was young. In Denver I got a job delivering newspapers. That was the year I took up roller-skating. Sometimes you do things, sometimes you feel things. The meaning of it all? Hey, you're asking the wrong Jimmy Callahan. *Where are you? What's the next thing to do?* As far as I'm concerned, *those* are the big questions."

"Agreed," Tommy said, and I think he really did. He came from a rich family but when he was thirteen his dad dropped dead right in front of him. Heart attack. Now his mom—who'd moved to Montana just a couple of years later, leaving Tom with an old aunt in Chicago—now his mom was dying, too, and he didn't seem to be afraid of anything. He probably figured, what could be worse? It's obvious to me now why my parents didn't like him, why they suspected he was missing something you need to build a life with, and why they were most likely out of their minds with worry for me at that very moment. But how could I know anything about that then? I only knew I held Tommy's soft hand on my lap and remembered his warm breath in my ear last night, the sweet taste of his mouth. I only knew I was a long way from home and he made me feel brave.

We passed miles and miles of sunflowers, of corn, of soybeans. We drove over hills and green valleys, along lakes and over river bridges, past signposts, exits, ravens clustered on a dead deer. First the mackerel clouds moved in from the northwest, and then lower, more solid ones followed. We drove and drove, and west of the Missouri the flat green fields broke into a strange landscape of brown cones and deep ravines. The sky turned leaden from horizon to horizon, and when the sun set and the sky grew dark only a very occasional ranch light twinkled across the broken land.

"Pick a spot," the driver said. He was talking to me because Tommy had fallen asleep against the window.

"What do you mean?"

"A direction. Point your finger."

I pointed past him to the southwest, to where the thin silver line of horizon was all that separated the sky from the dark land.

"Okay," he said. "Now if I stop the car and make you get out and walk that way, how far do you think you'd get before you go mystic on me?"

"What?"

"I mean, take away these roads connected to distant cities, and take away our wheels and all you have is yourself and the earth and the sky, and tell me, how long before you throw yourself face first on the ground and start calling for a witch doctor?"

I shrugged while my stomach tightened with dread.

The driver laughed. "Don't worry, I'm not stopping." He tugged on his beard and pushed his foot down to the floor and the old car shuddered with new speed. "We don't deserve this country, did you know that?"

I wanted to pinch Tommy's leg to wake him up.

"We stole it," he continued, "and we don't deserve it, and without our machines it scares us witless. Did you know that?"

I managed to shake my head.

"Well, now you do," he said. And we drove on into the night and I stared out at the stars and the vast sweep of land scooting by us at eighty miles an hour and I thought of Tommy's mom dying somewhere in the Rocky Mountains, and I didn't sleep at all. I remember wondering if no matter what else happened in my life, if this might be one of the things I'd always remember, this first long night crossing America.

And so far, these many years later, it still is.

Because, like I said, there were other firsts, too, starting with the car breaking down just over the Montana border. The clunk-clunk started on the edge of a little town, and the driver said uh-oh and then the motor stopped and he took it out of gear and we glided silently down a sleepy main street and came to a stop right in front of the only light. It was a bar, of course. We all went in and while the driver tried to figure out what to do, Tommy and I started drinking. I had a glass of wine and he fought off his grogginess with shots of tequila and before you know it we were laughing and drinking more. After a while Red-Beard headed off to sleep in the car but Tommy and I stayed and I switched to tequila, too. Everything seemed suddenly amazing. The car breaking down where it did was like a boat crossing the ocean and starting to sink right when it came to an island. Could we have planned it any better? At bar time we took our packs from the back of the car and walked up a bluff at the end of the main street. With the little town behind us, we stared out over the plains and felt as if we were on a beach looking out at the sea. Even in the dark we could see forever. We zipped our bags together and with Tommy over me, something else happened that had never happened before. I felt wave after wave of a wild pleasure break under my skin and wash the colors of love up under my eyeballs. Just when I'd think it was over, I'd feel it gather again, and I'd squeeze and surrender all at once, and feel it lift and toss me again and again, and all of that while looking past his shoulder at more stars than I'd ever seen in my life.

Afterward, we lay on our backs next to each other and listened to coyotes yipping madly past the edges of our vision.

"*Yeeeee-ha!*" he kept saying before he fell asleep. It was funny because first he was shouting and then it got quieter and quieter until it was only his breathing as he drifted into sleep. I couldn't believe I was out on my own, lying on the big heart of the world with a boy I loved sleeping next to me. Whenever I've heard the expression *one with the universe*, it's that night I think about, and about how and why it happened. Sure I'd taken the first step. I mean, I'd said yes when he asked me to go, and packed my clothes in the night and snuck out before dawn. We'd hiked together up the ramp onto the Eisenhower heading north, all thumbs and backpacks. But after that, well, it seemed it had been all waves and particles. Of course we didn't deserve this land. What possible feat of greatness could anybody do to deserve such bounty? Such love and beauty? Nothing that I could imagine. And if all of that wasn't enough to turn me into a quivering ball of pitiful flesh, dissolved in my gratitude, something even more unpredictable happened. In the hours just before dawn, pale light began to spread upward from the northern horizon and wave like a gauze curtain in the wind. It grew to cover almost half the sky and turned the softest of yellows and greens and blues. I'd never seen the northern lights before and I nudged Tommy awake. He kept saying *awesome, awesome,* until finally he fell asleep again, and I lay awake and speechless, shivering with wonder and the precious ache of his hand in mine.

Not quite speechless, though, I said, "Tommy, I love you."

Is this what was called *going mystic?* Did somebody need to call a witch doctor? Didn't I already have enough reasons to remember this first long night crossing America?

He didn't answer. I probably should have gotten him to speak, to say something, but I was very young and had run away from home with a boy I loved and I just needed to tell him. I was scared because I knew he didn't love me like I loved him but he moved to show he heard me, and he held me in his arms and his breath in my hair made me feel it was okay, I was going to be okay.

the only thing I care about is losing majors

Inside the warm cabin, I'm sitting in front of the big window, my back to the woodstove, my feet up on a table. The stool is wedged under the doorknob against the back door that now hangs crookedly from its hinges. The screws are coming out of the soft woodwork, and I try to imagine what Mark would do, how he'd fix it, and feel some despair at my capacities. Then I quickly take reasonless comfort in the fact that at least the *front* door closes and latches and locks. Outside, smoke like ragged pieces of fog blows from my chimney past the near trees toward the river and the mouth of the canyon. The puppy has returned, thank goodness. He's asleep on the couch, but no sign of the bear. Listen to me: *no sign*. Just over three weeks here and I sound like an old trapper. What I mean is, from this chair looking out the window, I haven't seen him again. He's sleeping. He's eating. He's walking around sniffing and doing bear things. Mark used to say he wanted to be a lion. What great fun to sleep twenty hours a day and wake only to mate with females and eat the meat that the females killed. He recognized, of course, that like all male lions it would also be his duty to chase off hyenas, but because we lived on a farm in southwestern Wisconsin, he didn't anticipate hyena chasing would take much time.

In the six months since he died I often hear his voice so quiet and so loud I lose my breath. I want to grow my body huge, spread my arms and legs until they are big enough for all of the wild feelings to be able to stretch out and lie down and rest for a minute or two or five or ten. Is that a craving for death? I don't know. I wonder if I had a really long orgasm if I'd feel better, but the amount of blood in my veins seems inadequate to the task—and I don't even want to imagine what I mean by *task*. So maybe it's my imagination that's crippled and bent and withered by grief. I hear the wind shake the cabin. It's been gusting for days. I breathe deeply, try to take some of that big air into my body. I lean back and stare at the sky through the window and breathe air from up past the invisible cliffs, suck it down from miles above my head, breathe it down from the clouds themselves. "This is living," I say, and lean back in my chair and feel my body deaden with the numbing weight of sadness. Mark worked outside his whole life. He smelled of the outside. He smelled of horses and cows and grass when he was younger and when he was older, he smelled of his woodshop. His apron is still there, I'm sure, and the sawdust, and the light through the row of south windows. When he knew he was dying and his strength was shrinking and his pain growing, he would to go out to his shop and use his lathe to make wooden spheres ranging in size from golf balls to volleyballs, but most of them like softballs, perfectly round and smooth. He made them from oak and walnut, from mahogany and teak, and from woods I'd never heard of before that he'd collected over the years and been storing in the shed for some special project. When I asked him why he was making spheres he shrugged and said he wanted to. I didn't ask him again. He'd been making things for other people his whole life and now he was making things for himself, beautiful and perfectly useless round wooden balls. He decided he was going to make as many as he could before he died. As his illness dragged on, the number grew and soon they lined the long windowsill in his shop and filled boxes and crates and baskets like so many smooth, earth-colored eggs. I liked to hold them, feel their weight, and run my fingers around their sanded curves. His rough hands could make the surface of wood as soft and smooth as velvet.

Sometimes we walked in the evening. He'd hold my hand. It was as intimate as he had the strength for. Then I'd go to bed and he'd sit up and look at the fire and smoke marijuana—something he hadn't done in years but that he started again in those last months. He savored moments of quiet wakefulness. He told me he didn't want to spend his last hours sleeping. He wanted to spend them conscious. He told me he had come to understand that he loved consciousness. It was an odd thing to say. *I love consciousness.* He said ever since he was a little boy and he remembered looking at himself in the mirror and breathing and moving and making faces, seeing himself alive in the glass, feeling himself alive, being *conscious of his being alive*, he had been a little bit in awe of consciousness. If we all get a certain number of moments in which we are truly conscious of our life, of living, he enjoyed those moments as much as anybody else I know. Once, near the end, the cancer spread all over his body, death looming—he had been sitting in the den and when he saw my shape in the doorway—he looked up and spoke.

"Doctor," he said. I paused. "What?" It was a game we played. The room smelled, and I stepped past him to open a window. He waited, and when he had my attention again, he said, "Two very important health questions from your number-one patient." That wasn't true. He was never my patient. I learned early on that I couldn't be his doctor and his wife. "You ready?" he said. "I am," I said, and sat on the arm of the couch. He made his face very serious and took on a kind of puzzled expression.

"Where do farts come from, Doctor?"

"You," I said, "mostly."

He nodded thoughtfully. He looked around the room and blinked and blinked again in the sweet soft light of early evening. Along the far wall were the last stripes of sunlight. In the corner where he sat, the dark shadows of evening.

"And the second question?" I asked.

"Does it all go away?" he asked. He lifted his hands as though to hold it all. His eyes were deep pools—truly curious, wide awake. "*Everything?*"

I shrugged. I suddenly couldn't see him for my tears. I put my face in my hands. See why I couldn't be his doctor and his wife?

Late at night I'd hear his steps on the stairs and then in the bedroom. I'd hear him fuss with his clothes and feel the bed sway as he lay down behind me and got under the covers. I'd lie still and listen to him breathe and settle in, and then often I'd feel his fingers graze my cheek, move gently down my neck, my shoulder. His skin was hard but his touch light and I would be wearing only my underwear and he'd let his fingers trace my side down to my hips and then come around to my stomach and then, sometimes, if he didn't think it would wake me or keep me from sleep, up to my breasts. I'd make a noise so he knew it was all right, and he'd hold me. One night near the end, he came to bed and I pretended I was asleep because the sadness had gotten so heavy I didn't know what to say or do anymore. I felt his weight on the mattress and his heat behind me and then more movement and his heat above me. But instead of his hand, I felt his pot breath and then the tip of his tongue on my cheek, very gentle. He was tasting me. Trying to taste my skin without waking me. Then he pulled back and lay on his side again and I felt the bed begin to move slightly as he began to sob. Twenty-four years of marriage and he'd cried only three times as far as I knew, when his father died and when the twins were born and when our daughter was married. I moved over in the dark and put my arm around him, and he let me, and we both cried then. We held each other and sobbed until we were exhausted and we were dry and red and couldn't anymore. Then, for some odd reason, right about when we were done with all of that, the defective smoke alarm in the living room went off—making that high awful whine—and then, as if to harmonize, from the floor at the foot of our bed our old dog sat up and started to howl. We rolled over onto our backs, our mouths salty with each other's tears and tried to make sense of what we were hearing. The defective alarm downstairs—it had gone off before—and the excited dog there in our room. We stared up into the darkness and started to laugh. He'd be dead within a few days, certainly no more than you could count on two hands, and I was going to be alone, and then after a while—months, years, decades, what did it matter?—I would die, too. It struck us—or me, at least—that long after we were both gone there would always be stupid stuff like this, malfunctioning alarms, dogs howling madly. Things like that are all that's immortal—why hadn't anybody ever told us before? We held hands and lay on our back in the dark and laughed. People go crazy in this life looking for meaning. Anything for meaning! Love, work, exercise, gambling, drinking. My brother likes whores. *I deserve a blowjob every day,* he told me once. I think of his earnest broad face and big blue eyes blinking madly when he told me that, and it makes me laugh. Tiger Woods said in an interview, *The only thing I care about is winning majors.* Well, he cared about sex, too, thank goodness. Why is it that most people liked him better when he pretended he was a golf robot? Hey, but don't listen to me. Everything I've ever learned has the stink of loss. Without it, I'm sure I'd never have had a thought in my head.

Maybe you're thinking: *Oh my god, she's going to be unbearable.* And I might say in response: *The only thing I care about is losing majors.*

The day before Mark died I helped him walk outside and up the hill behind the house and sit down on the grass. We held hands and then the twins walked up the hill and we all sat quietly and felt the spring wind and looked at how the grass in the valley had turned candy-green overnight. In the next few weeks, the green would darken and move slowly up the hill and the yellow and red buds on the oak trees would pop into tiny pale leaves that grew until full summer turned the edge of the forest into a dark green wall along the far side of the sloping pasture. Mark squeezed my hand. He looked pale and drawn and only his eyes glimmered. I put my arm around his bony shoulders. I rested my head there. He stroked my hair. I shuddered and the world disappeared except for the flutter of bird wings in the air. Crows. Mark was watching them. He used to say they were magic. That was years ago. We sat on the hill together and felt his dying and spring coming, and I don't know that the world ever looked so beautiful. Cody and Kate helped their father to his feet and I sat alone until they made it down the hill and disappeared into the house. When the screen door slammed shut I felt the beginning of a dry emptiness that would fill me to the brim after he died. By the time I walked down the hill and followed my husband and grown children into the house I felt as if I were walking in ether, breathing water, a fish pretending to be a mammal.

Okay, here's what I know: I've been well loved, and that love has given me more strength then I ever thought I could muster, and since Mark's death six months ago I have worried and wondered and felt frightened and sad and weakened by the prospect of a life without it. So less than a month ago, I walked off a shift in the emergency room and left the Wisconsin farm we'd lived on for more than two decades, and I drove all the way across the plains to a friend's cabin where the Sun River spills through the Eastern Front of the Rocky Mountains. What am I looking for? Maybe a place where the shell of my body will crack and the cold dust inside will blow away in the wind. It seems all I've done since Mark's death—and too much of what I did before—is protect myself. So besides the big bear outside the cabin that has me either scared to death or reckless beyond belief every time I go outside, the big dramatic question of my life is a mad one: *what happens if I blow away in the wind?*

Also, my grown daughter and son, from opposite corners of the earth, want all of us to meet back home on the farm for Thanksgiving next month, an experience I can't even begin to wrap my mind around.

All of us?

Suddenly a big gust collides with the wall of the cabin and sends the stool that's been jammed under the doorknob crashing to the floor. I feel the cold and look up, expecting to see the bear in my kitchen but the back door has merely pushed partway open in the wind. It sags on the bottom hinge. The top hinge has pulled completely out of the rotten woodwork and the screws hang ugly as long, brass teeth.

who in their right mind would make such a choice?

A t dawn on the Great Plains after all of those firsts, Tom and I rolled up our sleeping bag and walked down the bluff into Wibaux, Montana. We found Red Beard's car still parked in the same place, but we didn't find him. Tom said maybe he'd taken up roller-skating again. We strolled down the main street under a big blue sky puffed with fairy clouds. Bright gusts of wind touched chimes on somebody's front porch. I thought we'd be heading for the Interstate again, but Tom veered the other way when he saw the freight train that had paused sometime during the night. We crossed the street to the tracks and he walked to the train office, which was in a little tower. I hung back as he opened the door and started up the stairs.

A man's voice shouted down, "What the hell you want?"

Tommy tilted his head back and his little brown patch of chin hair caught the light from the top of the stairs. "When's the westbound leaving?"

"Who's asking?" said the voice.

"A traveling man and his wench."

I heard laugher. Then, "You and your wench probably got time to head across the street and eat breakfast."

So we had eggs and toast at a café with cute yellow curtains and matching booth upholstery. Tommy kept making faces at me, or not at me but the little girl who kept peeking her head over the booth behind me. She liked his yellow clothes, she said, and he said he liked her yellow hair—and wasn't it a rule that you had to have something yellow to eat at this yellow place? Pretty soon he had us both laughing. He told me last summer he passed through a little town like this, stopped for gas, and when he paid, he asked the woman behind the register what people did to keep from getting bored. She took a step backward toward a door covered with a curtain.

"We love nature," she said, and looked at him. But he didn't get what she meant until she said, "And we use our personal resources."

He stepped behind the counter and followed her through the curtain.

I said, "Really?"

He nodded and grinned gleefully at what life had handed him. The thing about Tommy was how he could tell stories like this even as he was making the little girl laugh by sticking out his tongue, and as much as I loved him and should have been jealous, I somehow wasn't. In fact, I liked it when he told me these stories. Weird as it sounds now, they made me feel particularly close to him, and special, as this boy four years older than I, who had so many choices, had chosen me. I got some change and tried to get him to call the hospital where his mother was and see if he could talk to her, but he said he wanted to surprise her. I told him she might not be in the mood for surprises, and he said, a little too dismissively, "Well, I am."

While we ate, we kept looking out the window at the train yard, ready to bolt if the train started but it didn't, and not even for a couple of hours after breakfast lying on cardboard in the shady corner of a boxcar, open on both sides. Tommy stuck his head out when he saw a brakeman pass.

"Let's get this train moving," he said. "The hobos are getting restless."

The brakeman grinned and said, "Soon enough, Mac," and just then we heard the clanking of the couplings work their way down the train to us, and we jerked into motion. The sun was already high—it must have been noon. The train pulled out of town and followed a river for a while, the light green leaves of the cottonwood rustling in the breeze. Later, when it stopped in the middle of nowhere, we jumped out of our box-car and ran ahead to a flat car where we could climb up onto a stack of plywood and catch some rays. We were thirsty, but like the miracle that the whole trip had been so far, we found a jug of water wedged between the plywood stacks and also a leather jacket with a can of Copenhagen in the pocket. We couldn't believe our luck. Not only were we not going to die of thirst but Tommy loved snoose and both of us had some, and it made us dizzy and we spit off the car onto the cinders and laughed.

"Thank you, Makka Allah!" he said, throwing both hands in the air in thanksgiving to what he called the god of beveraging and strapping and chewing.

The train started again and we lay on our backs and counted almost fifty little puffs of white cloud scattered across the biggest and most terribly blue sky I think I'd ever seen. I'm sure it was the slowest train in the world, but we were way up high and in the open so that was okay with me. Tommy was so excited to have found the water and the chew and to be on the move he wanted to have sex way up there, but even though we couldn't see another person for miles across that empty grassland, I felt too exposed. I told him I'd barely slept last night and as much as I loved being on the train, I felt too dirty, and not in the way he liked. So I got him to sit cross-legged next to me, and I know it wasn't easy for him, but I made him hold my hand and sing for me. He knew all the words to a lot of songs. His singing was sweet and almost immediately I wanted to change my mind about the sex and I felt bad for a long time that I never told him. I wondered if that might have changed what happened, how things turned out, and because I hated the idea of my powerlessness, I spent way too long the next year feeling certain that everything would have been different if only I had been more generous or ready or willing.

Afternoon thunderheads grew magnificently in the west and we admired the billows of white that seemed to touch the heavens. As they got closer, their black bellies churned with turmoil and the wind picked up and we held each other in anticipation of the storm. I was thrilled by the smell of the air and by the first bolts of lightning on the western hills, and by the time the sun went down the gentle world we'd been traveling in all day had blown apart. Darkness came fast, ripped open by lightning and then the rain and wind had us tucked down in the narrow gaps between stacks of plywood. Freezing and wet, we hung on for warmth, screaming at each new jagged bolt and just about when we thought we might die like that, we wouldn't, and another ragged and brilliant explosion would rip open the sky. Finally the rain stopped and the thunder grew distant and we managed to dig from our packs the few clothes that weren't soaked. We put them on but still shivered together through a miserable half sleep as the train went into the mountains and came to a stop in a night fog so thick we didn't know which way to walk when we finally hopped off the flatcar and out of the train yard.

We thought we heard cars on a highway, so we headed across a wet field to where we could finally see the lights of a truck stop. I sat at a table and drank coffee, still bone cold and shivering. I held the cup to my face and felt the steam. Tom went to a phone booth to check the book and find out where we were, and on his way back to the table I could see his brown eyes smiling and his little mouth turned that cute way it did when he was going to say something smart-alecky. I wanted to kiss him right there in the restaurant.

But what he said was, "I hope there'll be some good movies or concerts or something for you to do while I sit and watch my mom die."

I hadn't really forgotten but I almost had. I'd gotten so caught up in my magnificent journey that his sad one had kind of faded away. I felt about two inches tall.

"Don't worry about me," I said.

We went to the hospital right after breakfast. We didn't have a lot of money and the breakfast was an emergency splurge after that rough night, but Tommy wanted beer too, so we got some at a convenience store and he drank five in the time it took me to drink one—this was just on the mile or so walk to the hospital—and while we walked and drank our way through the sweet dry dawn, warm, too, the shape of the mountains became clear through the fog and put us both in better moods. Tommy was telling me about his mom—about the two or three nice things she'd done in her life. It seemed he was trying to put himself in a good, brave, loving mood to see her. Which was all in vain, anyway, as when we got to the hospital, she was gone. Checked out two days before. Apparently she wasn't so bad off after all, and after calling Chicago to tell him she was dying, she'd made a miraculous recovery. This should have been good news but it didn't feel that way for some reason. We called her home, and a house-sitter told us she'd gone down to Costa Rica. This was back before anybody had heard of Costa Rica so he may as well have told us she'd gone to the moon. It's very strange, I know, but by not dying, she'd broken his heart more than if she had been. He'd worked himself up to making this surprise, heroic visit, and he'd worked his way toward grieving her, maybe even to forgiving her—and then she left him once again. These are all of my thoughts now. I didn't have a clue then. I'd been so caught in my love for him that I'd almost forgotten everything else, and if you haven't already suspected, if the past few days had been a good dream, what followed was a bad one.

After hanging up the telephone with the house-sitter, Tommy still didn't want to leave the hospital. He stood at the check-in counter of the hospital and started picking out the candies in the bowl on the desk and tossing them over the receptionist's head. She smiled at first, as people tended to do when Tommy did something playful but semi-obnoxious. After all, he was wearing a yellow tuxedo with a checkered-flag nametag.

But he threw another candy and another, just tossed them up over her head, and then more like *at* her head. He started making seal noises and clapping his hand together between throws, which is when the woman's face turned red and she started to stand up. I'd never seen Tommy mean before. But here he was, tossing candy at the receptionist and making seal sounds and laughing a big, ugly laugh.

"Excuse me, sir?" the woman said, shielding herself. I grabbed his arm and it's funny but I remember smelling the boxcar on him, which even though we didn't do it there, reminded me of sex. I guess everything about him reminded me of sex, even at that perverse moment. He shook me off and I hit the wall next to the elevator and almost fell down.

"Tommy," I yelled, but he was yelling, too, and then he wasn't just tossing individual candies with two fingers, but he reached in and got a handful of hard candy and threw it as hard as he could against the wall.

By this time the receptionist had fled and Tommy began what I can only describe as a meltdown. He wasn't just throwing candy now but everything. He tossed a plant the size of a cat against the wall and the pot made a cracking sound and the soil went everywhere. The waiting room had cleared out behind him and I remember how red his face was and how he grabbed a stapler and threw that and lifted a stack of magazines off a table and threw those on the floor. I was in the corner screaming his name over and over again. I was worried about him, sure, but I was worried more about us. *Things have been going so great,* I wanted to scream. *Don't ruin it!*

He was tackled by a couple of security men and I watched his chin hit the tile floor, and I couldn't believe his face didn't break. I was crying so hard I couldn't stop, so I don't know exactly what happened next. I don't know why they let us go, but they escorted us the front door of the hospital and sent us on our way. Didn't even give Tommy a bandage for his chin. A hospital, for crissake, and he had to hold his yellow sleeve to his chin to stop the bleeding. We didn't have much money but it was raining and we had to re-assess so we went to a hotel that night, a cheap one on the gulch. Now what? First a shower, after which we made love and I kissed his chin and his face a thousand times, and after the magic of what seemed an unending orgasm I cried and cried. I felt as if something had broken open inside me and now was pleasantly spilling. He held me tight and cried, too, and it seemed to me that together we shuddered in our glorious and heroic love that could endure anything. I felt brave and wanted to risk everything for this boy. Before birth control and modern hospitals, some absurd number like one in ten women—each having multiple pregnancies, of course—something like one in ten women died in childbirth. Which is to say that for all of those thousands and thousands of generations of women before birth control, sex really did mean a good chance of death.

Who in their right mind would make such a choice?

One madly in love, of course. For sex and love made meaning where before there had been none—and once we feel that meaning, once we feel connected to the big and the grand and mysterious, well…anything might happen and something always did. In my case, what happened was I was lying in bed glowing with post-coital bliss. I lay there with my head on the pillow listening to Tommy finish up in the bathroom—and making a lot of noise doing whatever he was doing—first peeing very loudly and for what seemed forever—how could he hold so much water?—and then messing around with the fixtures, it sounded like, for I heard metal and a bump—anyway, while all that was happening, my glowing cheek on the pillow, I was thinking how those freaks who claim to see auras could probably see mine a mile away. I closed my eyes and remembered the northern lights, thought of them as our aura—Tommy's and mine—as if the earth were glowing from the orgasmic heat of our bodies that night on the Great Plains. It was a thought that so excited me, I wanted to share it with Tommy (which as I write I can say is a euphemism for wanting more Tommy) so from bed I called his name. I knew he was sad because of his mother. And I knew he'd lost it and was awful there at the hospital, crazier and meaner than I'd ever seen him—but isn't that what love is? Seeing the bad and loving anyway? I thought, hey, he was a little drunk and certainly disappointed. Who wouldn't be mad? But our good love making and my happy words could make him better, make him hopeful and playful again, and brave, too. And so I wanted to share all of that with him and feel him in me again, his body so eager and willing I wanted to cry—and I'd make him smile afterward and pull him back into bed with me and hold his sad head in my arms.

I called to him again but heard only silence now in the bathroom. Which seemed odd and too sudden. For about five minutes all of that noise and now nothing? I got up and approached the bathroom on tiptoe. I didn't want to embarrass him if he was doing something embarrassing, but I also wanted to jump in and surprise him. Maybe he was in the bathtub on his back with his ears underwater. I wanted to kiss his mouth all of a sudden, his lovely slippery mouth, and I wanted to tell him about the light of the world we made with our fire, and to tell him everything was going to be okay, everything was going to be beautiful and we would live a life so full of color and heat we'd cook ourselves blind. I was going to just open the door but made myself knock. No answer. I still felt joyful and wanted to share it. I didn't feel any dread. Remember, I'd just risked my life; I'd just turned my life into the dangerous life of a woman in love with a man. I turned the knob and opened the door.

What I saw was Tommy with a cord around his neck, hanging from the ceiling fan. He'd put on his yellow tuxedo, again, I remember that. And I remember his bloated red face, eyes skewed. I screamed, I'm sure, but I also threw myself at him, lifted him somehow. He wasn't a big boy, and somehow, even with him on my shoulder, I reached the sink and the scissors he'd used to cut the cord to a manageable length. I'm not going to tell you I remember how I got him down, exactly, but I did, and remarkably fast for somebody who I'm sure was screaming at the top of her lungs. I lay on top of him, straddled his chest and pried my fingers under the cord and I loosened it and watched the blood flow from his head. I opened his mouth and breathed into it, and breathed into it, screaming for help as I did so, screaming and breathing, and suddenly he opened his eyes and looked at me with almost horror. Except he suddenly closed his eyes again and just lay there rubbing his neck. People were pounding on the door now and I got up and started to answer it but Tom sat up and shook his head and finger no, no, no, and so I just yelled through the door that I'd stubbed my toe and knocked my nail off. Are you okay? somebody asked, and I said, yes, yes, I'm sorry I made such a fuss, and whoever it was walked away from the door. I turned and looked at Tommy. He wouldn't look at me.

"Are you all right?" I asked.

"Too many low-level particles," he said.

"Should I take you to the hospital?"

That made him laugh. "You think they'd like to see me again?"

Just then the door opened and a security man came in. "What's going on?"

a million years of everything all lined up just right

I brace the back door of the cabin closed again with the stool and think I'll have to think about what else to do to keep it closed, but not now. Despite the bear, I don't want to sit inside all morning. I don't care how gusty or cold it is. I don't feel like walking yet, although I might later in the day. What I feel like is sitting outside in the wind and smoking cigarettes. I smoked when I was young and I bought a pack at the first place I stopped for gas on my drive west. I smoked all the way out here, and I've been smoking a couple of cigarettes in the morning with coffee and a couple at night after dinner, and I can't believe how after thirty years I still love it. I step out the front door of the cabin and feel the breeze blow my hair wildly so I reach into my pocket and take out a Green Bay Packer stocking cap. I put it on, unfold a plastic lounge chair, wrap the blanket around me and sit down. I'm close to the cabin, my back to the logs, so I know the bear isn't behind me. The wind is so loud I keep hearing things around the corners of the cab-

in but I satisfy myself with the fact that if the bear comes from
either side I'll have time to reach for the bear spray. I light the
cigarette and when I exhale the smoke disperses wildly down-
wind. Maybe it will scare the bear from coming from that way.
I take another drag and the nicotine gives me an immediate
sense of well-being.

A few years ago, when our twins graduated from college,
Mark and I rewarded ourselves with a trip to Chile. It was a
country he had read about for years. We rented a condo on
the seventh floor of a high-rise on the edge of a city. That first
afternoon we stocked it up with snacks and wine and made
plans for our excursions but sometime after dinner an earthquake hit and the building began to sway. We were going to
make love, and I was on the toilet, actually, and I stood and
pulled up my underpants and braced myself against the wall.
Even managed to stumble out and under the threshold, my
hands on both sides. Mark was lying on his back on top of
the bed. I said, *Earthquake*, and he said, *You think so, Doc?*
and while the earth groaned and the building swayed and
cracked and everything I thought solid turned jelly before my
eyes—the roads outside, the window, the floor, my flesh—I remember surrendering to the great earthquake gods. Call them
what you want, what was certain was they were bigger than
us, even bigger than both of us. We were bugs, and bugs that
might soon be squashed, but it was still more terrifying this
morning to see the bear alone than to stand bracing myself in
that doorway for forty seconds—and forty seconds lasts forever—wearing only my underwear, my breasts going around and
around as the building swayed and shook, my eyes locked on
my husband and his locked on me.

Then it ended, and the world hadn't swallowed us whole.
What I remember first was the quiet. I let my hands cautiously
slide down from the sides of the doorway. I couldn't believe the
floor felt so still. I think once you feel a floor move like water
beneath your feet, you never take solid for granted again. Mark
was still lying on his back looking at me, a grin on his face.

"You feel the earth move, baby?"

The radio had gone off, the lights. Every surface was cracked—there was broken glass on the floor from a water glass that had slid off the counter. I turned back into the bathroom and turned on the faucet. We still had water. When I came out, Mark was up and I leaned against him and put my arms around his waist by the window. We stood looking out over the city and felt each other shaking. Some buildings had tumbled, but most were still upright. The streets were beginning to fill with people and would fill with more in the next few days as people were expelled from buildings that were deemed unsound. Ours turned out to be okay and they let us stay. We spent two more weeks there without electricity and with no ability to leave. No flights, no trains, and no unbroken highway out of town. But we had a place to sleep, food and water, and something to do. Mark served soup, set up cots, and built latrines at a temporary shelter. I saw patients. The seriously ill and injured were being treated at the hospital, so what I saw were minor injuries and common sicknesses, ankle sprains, puncture wounds, headaches, sore throats—little to do with the earthquake but suffering is suffering. What I will never forget were the stunned faces of children who had lost parents and of parents who had lost children. No medicine for that, but in the evening we'd come back our hotel room and sit on the balcony and drink wine. I remember one night, the city just beginning to electrify again and a few lights were blinking on below us. The ocean beyond that still held the pale glow of the day. I looked at Mark's face and felt such a strong sense of well-being it almost embarrasses me to try to describe. We'd fallen in love again. Who would have thought? As though our life was beginning again and the barely-covered stresses and irritations had shaken away and collapsed around us, inside us. I had a feeling that no matter what, that whatever happened, we'd be all right. Floating in the pool of our love, I could live in the world without fear. We were a marvelous team—we'd raised children together! We'd survived an earthquake! We could get by with little and still be helpful, still be happy, as long as we had each other.

Now I have cigarettes. I hold one tenderly in my right hand and watch the ash grow. I dangle my left hand, my good hand, close to where I set the bear spray. A couple of times I reach for the spray, slide off the safety, aim and—How fast could I spray it if I had to? I don't pull the trigger because I don't want to waste the spray, but I'd like to see how far it goes. I'd like to know how easy it is to aim and hit what you're aiming at but I'm tucked against the leeward side of the cabin and I can feel the swirl of the wind so I know if I used the spray, the pepper would swirl, too. I'd probably be just as deactivated as the bear. We'd both be on the ground snorting and coughing and rubbing our eyes.

So I smoke and content myself with quick-drawing the bear spray, aiming, and quick drawing again. The activities amuse me. I watch the low clouds spill out of the canyon, thin and open, and just the tops of the jagged cliffs, one thousand feet above me catch the yellow light from the east. They look like tan spires growing out of the cloud. I hear the honk of geese and the occasional break and fall of rocks from the cliffs. A magpie flies over and lands in a fir tree. It's late October, but still summer and already winter. An unusually warm fall has kept the aspen and cottonwood down by the river at the base of the cliffs in full green leaf, but last night the temperature dropped into the single digits and a light snow fell. It blankets everything this morning. No, it dusts everything and swirls in the wind. Collects in the crannies on the cliff, covers the ground in the meadow but not the tall clumps of grass. It nestles in the needles of the scrub pine and fir and bursts into swirls when the wind shakes the trees. It's enough to highlight the color of the rock, and make the fast moving patches of blue sky bluer and the green trees greener. The sun suddenly lights the blond grasses in the meadow and on my patchy blond cow dog puppy. I can hear the sound of the river through the canyon like wind. I hear a distant rifle shot, and another, deep in the mountains. My puppy leaps through the grass and buries his nose in the snow. Lifts it, snorts. Looks up at me, looks this way and that, twitchy—he's vole hunting. His fox-red ears up and flicking, his eyes look and look. We hear more rocks break loose and fall from the big cliff. I look up but can't see anything falling even though the sound of the bouncing rocks makes a hollow crack, boom, that fills the canyon with its sound. I explain to the puppy that the rock has broken loose because of tiny amounts of water expanding to ice in the cracks. I explain that the skirt of small rocks that extends from the meadow in front of us to almost halfway up the cliff is there because of all the rocks that have fallen over all of the years since the cliff was made new, scratched out by a massive river of ice and left naked when the glacier melted. The dog doesn't pay attention. He bounds off after another vole in the tall grass. Upriver a couple of miles into the canyon, there is a ten-sided log lodge with a woodstove in the center and a big stone chimney rising up to the peaked roof. Drinking there are guides and guests and camp cooks and hunters in from the big wilderness up river from here. It's a scraggly bunch of folks who find shelter there. Folks like me who have washed up from the plains and others who have come out of the mountains. I know because I've been there, quite often last week, and I know because I'm sure I'll go there again. But for now it's me, the puppy, the bear, and all the things in my head. I am forty-nine years old and you'd think I'd no longer be so surprised by the fullness and emptiness of all things, by the essential paradox of truth. But I still am. For even as I grieve my husband's life, even as I know I loved him more than any man has a right to be loved by any woman, and I was loved equally in return by a man whose heart only grew as our time together grew—and even as it became clear our time was ending and his heart just kept growing—even knowing all of that—it's not *his* letters that I gathered in a shoe box and hauled across the plains with my cigarettes and bear spray and firewood obsessions to this cabin. What I've brought are the letters that Tommy sent me.

Tommy's letters were really more like stories. He was a writer, although unpublished for the most part, and I read the letters aloud to Mark as I received them—so they were never secret. And when I was young and studying to be a doctor, and

Mark and I were working hard, trying earnestly to be married and to raise our children, I often had no clue as to how to think about the strange, sometimes moving, and often irritating letters Tommy sent from what may as well have been the dark side of the moon. Tommy wrote to redeem his life—the life I saved in that Helena motel room—and as a way of fighting his way out of the darkness into the light. He knew the big questions at an early age, questions that in my charmed life I'm just getting around to. Like *how do we endure suffering? And how—when life has flung us far and wide—how do we get home again?*

I'll answer the way he might have—ironically, I suppose, considering the way he lived and died. *Start with where you are,* he'd say. Begin with the feel of your feet on the ground or your bottom on the chair. Begin with the fresh air on your face, the smell of your cigarette smoke and the wood smoke from the cabin chimney, and with the feel of the warm wool cap pulled down low over your hair. The wind has suddenly calmed and you hear geese honking upriver. They seem to be getting closer but you can't see them yet. Sit back and tuck in your blanket and tilt your head back to get a good view of the high cliffs and the patch of blue sky. See how suddenly a line of snow geese have flown out of the cloud and into the blue sky and how the sunshine makes them flash an almost translucent silver like ghost birds coming to visit from who knows where.

It's a miracle: this chair, this blanket, this canyon, this day. I know eventually I'll have to think about other things—like the broken back door, like what I'm going to actually do—but for now what I want to think about is how a million years of everything lined up just right so I can sit here and watch the geese head southeast across the plains, watch until they are a line of dots that I can't see anymore, that I can only imagine flying forever into the sun.

you always let your 'ho talk like that?

He told the hotel security that he'd fallen in the bathroom and knocked himself out. The hanging had changed his voice a little but maybe that was just him keeping his head down so the red cord line didn't show. I confirmed his story, good-old-credible me, and they didn't take him away to the nut house, as he called it. But because I was a minor, they did call the police, who called my parents, and my parents told them to put me on a bus the next day heading east to Chicago. While I waited for what seemed like hours in line to get on that bus, Tommy and I hugged and kissed and hugged and kissed but everything was different. For one thing, I begged him to come home with me and he wouldn't even talk about that. And for another, well, how can I say it without revealing my selfishness? I felt betrayed. I refused to feel his despair, only my disappointment. I wish I could chalk that up to being a child, but I felt something similar many years later, the last time saw him. The bus station smelled like something disgusting and I couldn't believe we had to wait so long just to get on a bus. Two black guys about my age were standing next to us in line talking too loudly and calling each other *nigga* so many times I wanted to scream. Luckily Tommy had bought some wine, which we drank out of a water bottle so nobody would know, and he told me he didn't see any bright light or hear any happy voice calling him or any of that bullshit, so he didn't think he'd try it again. I shouldn't worry. He said he'd be heading south of the border—and eventually to Costa Rica. He said he was suddenly so *not* pissed at his mom he couldn't believe it. Hanging himself had given him a new perspective. She hadn't known he was coming out here, he said, so how could he blame her for not dying?

I loved him as much as I had the day before but he somehow seemed unreal to me now, not the same immortal flesh of yesterday. I kept thinking how he felt cold and waxy when I first got him down. I didn't know what to say and after a while he stopped talking, too. I'd saved his life—saved his life with my love, I thought—and that probably embarrassed him. Or the fact that he'd tried to kill himself embarrassed him. Either way, I resented having to tiptoe around his embarrassment. We were having such a great trip, I thought, and he'd ruined it. If we weren't standing in line with all these other people around, I might even have yelled at him. I was suddenly that angry.

The black teenagers next to us kept calling each other *nigga* and it was getting on my nerves. We had a teacher in our high school who showed us pictures of lynched black men hanging from trees and crowds of white people around them with happy faces and you just know what they were saying, so every time I heard that word that's what I thought. And thinking of hanging men, of course, I couldn't help but think again of Tommy hanging, and his red face, and the weight of his body, but instead of making me feel tender, it made me even madder. Tommy seemed very tired. He had a flat look in his eyes and a dead touch that felt cold and clammy and magnified the depressing elements of the bus station: the smell of bad food, the mysterious sticky spots on the floor, and really old drunk people. The two black guys had moved from calling each other *nigga* to calling somebody they both knew a *nigga muthafuc-ka*. My god, if nobody else was going to say it, I was.

"Do I have to stand here and listen to you two foul-mouthed boys talk your trash right into my ear?"

I said it loud, and the boys turned and stared. In fact, the whole bus station turned. It got quiet fast. My ears burned, my cheeks, too. I had a sense I'd done something wrong that I didn't fully appreciate. I mean, for once I wasn't too cowardly to tell jerks to shut their mouths. But the way the world works is because I'm a girl standing next to her boy, I'm not the one taking the real risk. Poor Tommy. Of course he knew the doo-doo I'd stepped in, and to his huge credit, he didn't back down when the black boys' eyes looked quickly past me to him. They looked insolent and wise, and stepped right past me to Tom-my, one on each side of him. He told me later that his stom-ach shrunk into a hard little ball, and in his head, he thought, *Okay, I guess I'm going to get beat up now.*

"You always let your 'ho talk like that?" one of them asked, the bigger one, I couldn't help but notice.

"He doesn't *let* me anything," I said, stepping up close to the clump of them. "I talk when I want to. And I'm not a 'ho."

Something about the way I said that made them laugh. But they quickly stopped and looked back to Tommy again. The tall one extended his arm straight at me, palm at my face, and said to Tommy, "You hear anybody talking? I don't hear no-body talking."

"Crazy 'ho talk," his buddy said, and hearing that, Tommy and I looked at each other. *Crazy?* Did they have any idea? And just like that we started slugging the both of them. Talk about going crazy. I'm shrieking while I'm punching and I see both of them slugging Tommy, and I'm wind-milling away but they don't even seem to feel my fists. They both stink like I don't know what when I get in close, and then one of them turns and hits me hard in the face with his fist. I had no idea fists were so hard. It was the first time anybody ever hit me with one. When I told Tommy that later, his face all puffy and purple—but at least not dead, the baggage man broke up the fight before he got killed—his broken face broke up in laughter. "What a precious little life you've had!" he said. He looked really joyful when he said it, and sometimes when I think of him, I think of that face.

I didn't get on the bus I was supposed to get on but I got on the next. We hugged and kissed, and then I climbed up on the bus and got a seat. After all we'd been through, saying goodbye was anticlimactic. I'd saved his life in the hotel then put his life in danger by starting the fight. His face was swollen, but I had a fat lip, too, so he hadn't taken *all* of the punishment for me standing up for what was right—even though he'd taken about ten punches and kicks and I'd taken one. He seemed okay with that. I think he felt glad actually. I thought that I couldn't have imagined a better thing to happen as long as we had to say good bye. It's a perfect example of how you can't plan things. They happen however they happen, which hardly seems profound. Waves or particles. Who'd have thought? I lay my head against the window, pressed my face to the glass and I pressed my hand to the glass, too, and Tommy waved back. I thought about our rides and our first night, and I listened to a Down's Syndrome couple making out behind me, and telling each other they loved each other over and over again. Then the bus pulled out and he was gone. I stayed like that for a long time as the bus wound though the city, my hand pressed to the window, my face close, as though there were something out there I was still trying to see and touch. I thought of how my face might look to somebody outside the bus. Would they ever guess what happened? How I fell madly in love for the first time and how I'd risked everything and how my mad boyfriend suffered and how I saved him? How I got a fat lip and how Tommy was heading south to Mexico and beyond to see his mother? How he was troubled, sure, but it was trouble that would pass—and when it did, he'd come back for me?

I thought about that in the dark through the mountains on the bus, and still at daybreak across the plains and all that day and all the way home. How even with my fat lip, Tommy would remember me and come back for me. How he loved me so.

what's for dinner?

I'm cold outside, even with the blanket. The sunshine high on the cliff never descended. The wind roars again through the canyon and trees and around and around my head. It makes me think I hear things. I think about the bear, of course, and so I keep my eye on the dog. This morning when the bear came, the puppy ran away. So I figure if I see him run off again, I'll know something's up. Regardless, I stand up with my blanket to go inside. At least I stayed outside for a while, my brave little achievement for the day. Most days I can be shocked almost senseless with the demand to comb my hair. As long as I'm going in, I get another armload of firewood. The wood is heavy but I *big-girl* it. (Mark's expression. I used to hate it so he stopped saying it, and then, a half-dozen years later, I started to use it with my daughter, who liked it. Oh well, what mysteries we are.) I *big-girl* it all the way to the cabin, and go in the front door. I kneel down and put a couple of pieces in the stove, and a couple more in the box behind. I start looking around for tools, screw drivers, whatever, and finally I find one in the closet but it's got the wrong kind of head and even if it didn't, there's no way those hinge screws could ever get a grip in that soft wood around the door-frame. I look for wood putty to put in the old screw holes to make them tight again, but I don't see any. I find some dry spackle in a bag and wonder about that. I put the bag on the counter, prop up the door as straight as I can and wedge the stool under the knob again.

It's suddenly warm in here, deliciously warm. I sit on a chair and get distracted by a picture of a painting on the wall of the cabin. Somebody years ago saw it in a magazine, tore it out, put it in a frame, and hung it up. It's a painting of a windy day at the seaside, and a boy walks in the foreground with a red balloon on a string blown almost horizontal by the wind. A white dog with a black spot runs out ahead of him, its tail up like a sail. The boy has his head down as though he's looking for shells. Behind him is a couple sitting on a blanket, fully dressed. The woman is wrapped in a yellow shawl and she has her head on the man's shoulder. The man wears a tall black hat pulled low so his ears stick out. At first glance it's a picture of the peace of an ancient day at the seaside. The boy and his dog. The couple in an affectionate pose that brings to mind the way the expression "make love" was used in the nineteenth century. But something in the picture draws my eyes toward the horizon and way out on the gray waves something that looks like a capsized boat bobs against the blue-gray sky. The people don't seem to notice it. Except for the wind, the day looks pleasant, and the people and the dog look very much alive in their own pleasant concerns—the boy looking for what he's looking for, the lovers filling the world with their feelings. And yet this mysterious capsized boat is out there beyond the breakers, and I have to look at the picture a while before I see the next thing, which is tucked into the shadow of some bushes up at the head of the beach. When I first see it, I think it's a rock or maybe a cave in the sand, but after a while I can tell it's a body. Fully clothed but blurry enough so I can't tell if it's asleep or dead, although I instantly suspect it has washed up from the distant capsized boat.

Suddenly the picture gives me a sense of dread mixed with a strange sympathy—not for the dead man—but for the family. The dog will find the body and this lovely day will end for this family. Oh, it's possible that next week the family might come back and enjoy the beach again. The air and light. The shells. The warm shoulder of a lover. What's not to enjoy? Somebody died and somebody is grieving madly, but that's invisible. It can't be painted, except in how it might change the colors, even make them more beautiful, perhaps. Which makes me think of something else as well, how suffering is invisible, how people drown and bodies get washed up on the same beach where others find shells and make love. How the living keep living.

During particularly sad parts of my husband's treatment, as I stood next to him holding his hand, I'd think of how just outside the wall of this exam room, the sun was shining on grass and birds sang and dogs played and children ran and shouted in the schoolyard and people drove by in their cars on their way to work, going shopping for dinners, listening to beautiful music. When he was first ill, these kinds of thoughts were like salt in my wound—the world so unfair that we are here suffering while others laugh and play miniature golf. But as the cancer progressed, and death became imminent, the thought that there were others—the woman walking down the sidewalk with her red high heels, the man standing in his garden with a hose, the girls riding their bikes to school—the fact that we were surrounded by people who were completely oblivious to our dark dread became a balm for our pain. In fact, we'd laugh about it. Somebody, somewhere is eating ice cream, we'd say, which was a reference to something Mark would do to make our kids and their friends laugh. He'd stand in front of the kitchen freezer and ask, "Do you know why *ice cream* is better than *no ice cream*?" His audience would look at him, waiting. "Okay," he'd say. "This is *no ice cream*." He'd pause and mime a long, exaggeratedly sad face. Then he'd pivot neatly, open the freezer, grab a half gallon of ice cream and dig out a chunk with his finger. "And this is *ice cream*!" he'd say, and plop the chunk into his mouth, and mime a smile as exaggerated as his frown.

My daughter Kate and her husband Spencer live in Kuala Lumpur; he's a diplomat, and she's a young and beautiful diplomat's wife with a degree from Stanford in biology. My unmarried son Cody lives in Montreal, where he's just started medical school. He's studying every night until midnight. It's his first year. I remember that well. I became a test-taking machine. My world narrowed. My son is that way now. It was at the funeral they made this plan to come home to the farm at Thanksgiving—but Thanksgiving is now just weeks away, and our family together without my husband and their father seems like a rare and terrible disease that I still can't bear to think about. I like thinking about my son's tender head bending over his books, though. I like thinking of Kuala Lumpur and of my daughter's face, her pretty hands—of her flesh in the both exotic and banal world of matrimony. I hope she's happy. I hope she takes pleasure in breathing and eating and the small interactions of her life. I hope she likes her nights next to her husband. I hope she grows to like saying those words— *my husband.* She admitted to me at the funeral that she isn't used to them yet, doesn't like the way they sound coming out of her mouth, and I was able to reassure her. I remember that strangeness with the words but I grew to love saying them. *My husband. My husband, Mark.* The syllables in my mouth felt warm and full, yet I know how it might be a horror, too. I have in mind a story but I won't think of that yet. I have other things to do. For one, the cabin is dirty so I reach for a broom leaning against the logs in the corner and I begin to sweep the floor. I sweep the kitchen and around the counter to the living room, where the wood stove is, and when I am done I go to the sink and the water tub and I use a wet rag to clean the counter and just keep going and do the kitchen walls and the broken back door, where it's dirty all around the knob and up and down the door-frame. I empty all of the kitchen shelves, scrub them as well, then put everything back.

No, actually, that's a lie. I do all of that in my head, but I don't budge from my chair. The place is a mess and I don't even know how to start. The floor, but also the kitchen counter, the bags of groceries, the dirty dishes, the leftovers neither covered nor put away. When I look at the kitchen I want to cry but I can't seem to budge. I look away and feel better. I close my eyes and imagine the counter is cleared and wiped, the dishes are washed, the floor is swept, and the door is fixed. That's a good thing. I'll just pretend that it's done. Or I'll get to it later. In fact I make a promise to myself that I will get to it later and for a moment that reassures me. It's late morning and it's nice to have a plan beyond reading Tom's letters, which are still jammed, unsorted, in a shoebox held together with tape and twine and tucked into my suitcase. Out the window I can see the branches of the pine trees waving in the wind. I can hear the wind in the metal chimney. I can see it lifting the shingles on the cabin across the meadow toward the river. With no phone or computer here, I have not heard from either my son or daughter in twenty-four days. Part of me feels guilty for not being in contact with them—shouldn't we be grieving together? What I want, frankly, is just one clear thought past the pain. Maybe that's why I came here. Where, I wondered, would my mind go if I dared a quiet place? (I didn't anticipate this wind!) Where would my mind go if I dared a place without distraction? (I didn't anticipate the bear!) *We strive we strive we strive,* Tom wrote me once. *And sometimes we're just one big bucket of hurt, and we ask,* Now what? *We ask,* What for? *And as the light fades at the end of the day and still nobody has bothered to answer us, we ask,* What's for dinner?

In my case, it's not even lunchtime. Eleven o'clock. I go to the refrigerator and get out some rice and beans and an egg. I fry the egg and warm the rice and beans and I roll them up in a tortilla and sit down to eat.

maybe he thought I looked like a pig, too

My parents met me at the Chicago bus station, and if they imagined my love for Tommy and his for me, they weren't as impressed by it as I was. When they saw my puffy lip and the little cut on my cheek, they thought he'd hit me. My mom started to cry and my dad's face turned sour and awful. I told them, no, they were wrong, that what happened was we got in a fight in the bus station and….

Of course that explanation didn't make them feel any better, so I didn't even bother trying to tell them about the attempted suicide. Things were unpleasant enough, and because I didn't understand myself the enormity of my confusions, I focused all of my feelings into the one I did understand: I thought I would die of a broken heart. I mean, not that I thought our relationship was over—not that—but simply being away from him made me feel broken. I didn't know what to do with my days. I lay around and stared out the window. I slept late and bathed forever and had no interest in calling friends. This made things at home a little strained, although Dad was always at work, and when he came home, he didn't want to talk about my love life. He'd ask what I did today, and I'd say nothing. He'd say, I hope that was fun, and I'd say a riot. He'd kiss my head and tell me he loved me. I thought he was clueless.

With my mom things were more complicated. She knew I was suffering from a broken heart, or at least a strained one, and she'd try to talk to me, touch me, cook good food for me. She actually tried to make me feel better. But the problem is I didn't want to feel better. For one, I didn't think she really understood love like I did. And for another, I just plain wasn't interested in feeling better. I was interested in suffering, and in trying to recall my happy memories of the trip, which was really the same thing as suffering. For when I thought of how brave and glorious I'd felt on the road with Tommy—well, at home I felt a lot less of both.

I thought about Tommy all the time, day and night. His face but also his body. I would lie on the couch and just imagine his physical weight pressing me down into the cushions, and it was just about then that Mom came in one day and said, "Janine dear, what are you thinking about? Tell me?" Like she wanted to have a girl-to-girl talk.

But how could I tell her what I was thinking? I just started to cry. She reached for my hand but her touch suddenly repulsed me. Not that her fingers really felt bad, but how was I supposed to be comforted by my mother because I couldn't be having sex with my boyfriend right now, on this couch, like I wanted? It was all just too weird. So I pulled my hand back and that hurt her feelings, and she got up and stomped out and I lay crying and shouting, "I'm sorry, Mom! I'm sorry I'm such a grouchy wench!"

"A what?" Her head peaked out from the kitchen. She looked mildly amused. That's one thing about my mom, she could be very angry and then not.

"A wench," I said.

She stepped closer and sat down where she'd sat down before. "A wench," she repeated, and I could tell it was a word

she'd hadn't said before, or a word she hadn't said in a long
time.

"That's what Tom calls me," I said, and just saying his name
made me cry. I couldn't see her anymore, I had so dissolved
into tears and covered my face, but I love her when I think of
the sweet and curious tone of her voice when she asked, "Tom
calls you a wench?"

I must have nodded. But what was most important was
what she said next.

"You love him, don't you?"

After that it was better around the house. Still, I didn't hear
from Tommy for weeks, then months. No letters. No phone
calls. The longer it went on, the more certain I was that I would
die of a broken heart. And I think I half wished I would. But
I didn't. I got on with my life. I started my senior year of high
school—and when I heard about my friend's crushes or journeys into sex in the backseat of a car somewhere, I'd think
of Tommy and me, and I'd think, oh, if they only knew how
small their adventures are they'd be embarrassed to tell me
about them. It all felt very shallow and juvenile compared to
the glory of my love.

I'm sure I was a jerk about it. I had convinced myself that
this was all a test, a love test, and that he still loved me but was
on a journey. In school we were learning about myths and the
soul journeys of heroes, and wasn't that what Tommy was on?
He had to go out in the world and test himself, and he had to
find and confront his mother and resolve that before he could
come back a man. When he came back, he would come back
for me. But I waffled between feeling like a saint, all into my
noble suffering, and a jaded sister. One moment I'd be heroical-
ly carrying my heavy burden, and the next I felt the opposite,
weightless, flying, as if none of it mattered and I was completely free. Didn't I live on earth with all of these other miserable
people? What made me think I was any better? I felt hurt and
alone and older and wiser, goddamnit, and none it mattered.
We were studying one of the uncountable times in the history
of the world when one group of people ganged up and killed

another group of people—and I remember one particular sentence written by a Nazi, something like, "Well, judge me however you need to judge me, but if you do not live in a time and place where you are forced to go after your neighbors, or your neighbors are forced to come after you, consider yourself lucky." I don't know why that sentence affected me so much, but it did. And twisted as it sounds, I used it as an excuse for seducing my friend's little brother, and then some guy I met at the store shopping with my mom. Right under her nose I let him know what he could have and then came back later to give it to him. Then a week later I wandered off with another boy I barely knew during a party with my stomach bloated with beer and feeling about as gross and un-sexy as possible in the bushes just out of reach of the light from a bonfire our class had made at homecoming. I remember slithering back into the crowd afterward and him going his way and me going mine. That might have been it but I could see him clearly across the big fire laughing with his friends and he looked, I thought suddenly, exactly like pig—and so I wondered—I couldn't help it, it was a bad feeling, but it was the bad feeling I was after—and so I wondered if when he looked across the fire at me, maybe he thought I looked like a pig, too.

That's how the long dark senior year unfolded. Love. Love lost. Random bursts of reckless sluttiness. Good scholarship, though. Math had always been easy, but despite knowing about the holocaust since I was in diapers, I'd never paid much attention to history before. Maybe my own broken heart and nasty behavior allowed me to understand or to imagine better what other miserable lives felt like. That and the fact that I wanted to get out of Chicago and to go college and I knew my parents would help if I kept my grades up. What I do know, and what keeps this story going, is that the first Saturday in June, when I was seventeen years old, almost a year to the day that I left for my wild trip west with Tommy, a year of changing from a girl to a woman, a year of suffering and misery and learning, a year in which I'd moved through all of the stages of grief from denial, to anger, to depression, to acceptance, I received from him the first of what would become almost a hundred and fifty letters sent to me over more than thirteen years. Apparently he'd been in Mexico and beyond since I'd last seen him. Apparently he hadn't mourned me long because apparently he'd been engaged. But that had just ended, so he picked up a pen and wrote me a letter that began with these words. *"Dear J--Fortunately I did not tie the ol' nuptial knot with my bonita chiquita—not to say this or that about why or what but more or less it's mo' better than mo' worse."* No introduction. No how are you? No sorry I haven't written in so long. No I hope your life hasn't spun out of control.

I got the letter from Guatemala just before I was to get picked up to go to the stadium for graduation. I remember trying to read it in the car but with my friends talking and asking me things, I couldn't concentrate. My heart was knocking and my hands were shaking. I sat through the ceremony with the letter in my hand, dying to get alone to read it. To read the rest of it. I don't recall a single thing that was spoken. I only remember the feel of that letter in my hand, and then, when I needed to use both of my hands to cross the stage and get my diploma and shake hands with the principal, I tucked the scratchy paper under the waistband of my skirt under my gown. I remember I felt as if I was walking across the stage with my letter, me and my letter, me and my Tommy, who'd ditched whatever nasty *chiquita* he'd thought he loved and was now reaching out to me. I smiled and waved at my parents and I don't think I had smiled at them so happily in months. They were floored. The year had been awfully hard on them as well, and when I smiled and waved from the stage I could see even my dad was crying.

the bear again

It's after lunch and after a nap, and I've gotten out the shoe-box and pushed aside the mess on the table and set it down. Just opening the box and looking at all of the letters in their different-colored airmail envelopes makes me begin to panic. That and the wind that again rattles the back door and the stool wedged under the knob. I get up and slide a big stuffed chair from the living room through the kitchen and up against the door. Then I finger the ragged wood on the molding where the screws have pulled out, pick up the bag of spackle and read the directions. Just add water. Like pancake mix. So I get a little jar and mix the white powder with water and spread it over the soft place in the wood where the top hinge was con-nected to the door-frame. I do it with a spoon. It looks solid and smooth when I finish and I'm briefly pleased with myself.

I go back to the table and the letters but my heart starts beating faster and I decide that before I begin reading, I'm go-ing to put them in order. I want to read them like that, as I received them, as they were written, but the tactic also helps me delay.

The first week here I took long walks and read crappy novels. The second week I hung out at the canyon lodge and drank too much wine and ate too many bad salads and good steaks. And this third week I've been a little sick with a virus, my throat scratchy, and I picked up this mutt puppy that I haven't even named yet from a woman giving them away outside the grocery store in town. It's not that I am dreading reading the letters. I am dreading being finished with them. Reading them has been my purpose for weeks and after I've done it, I'm afraid I won't have anything to do or any reason to do it. I keep imagining reading them and then just staring out the window thinking about Tommy and his tragic story and feeling only worse. More empty and alone than I feel already and with nothing particular to do. We can endure loneliness and emptiness as long as we have things we have to do. Work to do. Children to clothe and feed. That sort of thing. The cabin where I'm staying is an old friend's and she and her husband never use it, so it's mine, really, for as long as I want it, and reading these letters is the only thing on my *schedule*. The word makes me laugh. How odd not to be busy. How unnatural it feels. For years my life was a schedule I was perpetually behind on. My husband waited for me. My children waited for me. The hospital built a waiting room for all of the patients who waited for me. I could go back to work, and I want to be able to go home, but even the thought of being back at the farm on Thanksgiving—three and half weeks from now—freezes my insides. I suggested to the twins that we meet some other place but they wouldn't have it. They want to tie this loss they are feeling to something real—to the farm at Thanksgiving without their father—but I'm far from convinced I'm going to do that. I'd meet them anywhere else in the world. I calculate my savings plus the value of the farm if I were to sell it, and the doors of the world start to swing open, all of them leading to strange and ridiculous rooms. I could go north to Canada and ski at Banff for the winter. Or south to Chile again and eat grapes. Or Antarctica. When I think of these places I think of snapshots of me in these places. Not really being there. Just being seen there. Just having proof that I was there, by myself, or with fun people I meet and that I never see again. My life no longer a schedule but a series of albums posted on Facebook. My mind blows with ideas, all of them mildly amusing and equally empty. I could go to England or Spain or China. Why not? I have literally no obligations. I could help my son with med school and still I'd have enough money to take cooking classes in Paris for a few years. I could take trains and ships around the world numerous times. I could take a riverboat down the Amazon. Ride a horse across Mongolia. I could make these adventures as dangerous or as exotic as I wanted. I could get in shape and climb Everest. The variety of things I could do is staggering, but at the moment they all feel equally empty and sad. My mind rebels against such a concept that the world could offer so little. Poor little rich girl. It's pathetic and makes me angry at Mark for taking everything with him. *Ah, love,* he'd say, quoting his favorite poem, *let us be true to one another*—even when he wasn't always. And then he died. Like the period at the end of a novel. Only a blank page to follow. Ugh, now what? Has the world really neither joy, nor light, nor love, nor peace, nor certitude, nor help for pain?

What a bastard that he could die and take all of those things away—even my desire to see our children at Thanksgiving. And what a fool I was to think—when he asked me if it all goes away, *everything*—that he was talking about himself.

I begin to feel the need to pee. Talk about logistics. But this one is problematic from the start because when I look up from the table and out the window of the cabin I see the bear again. That and twenty below is why they invented chamber pots, and I do have, even in this simple cabin, a pot to piss in. But it's not twenty below, it's forty above. And what's good about this bear sighting is that it's just that: a sighting. No surprises. The bear is about two hundred yards away and rooting around on the grassy slope leading down to the river. It's early afternoon and the clouds have come in heavy so it looks darker than it should be. The wind is still vibrating the walls and the metal chimney and keeping the branches of the pine tree out the window in constant motion. This time I'm determined not to wet my underwear, but I wait so long it's close before I go to the front door and step outside. I can't get the puppy to follow. It's cold and windy and my ears are full of air. About ten feet from the door, I stop, unbutton my pants and squat where I can see the bear. He's still a couple hundred yards away, across the grass to the north and just at the tree line, and when he catches my scent he turns and looks. We look at each other. He's still as a stump and I am too. My stomach tightens and despite the cold, every pore on my body seems to open. By the time I finish, wipe with a Kleenex, stand and pull up my pants, I'm ready to run the ten yards back to the cabin door. But I make myself stand still for a moment. I suddenly want to watch the bear move again. I want him to move first. We stare at each other and I'm waiting for him to blink. The wind is strong and cold and my eyes begin to water. I have folded the Kleenex over and am gripping it in my hand, which is when I realize I don't have the bear spray. Not that I need it, as I'm close to the cabin door, but I still feel scared. I don't move. The bear doesn't move. On the road by the river I hear a truck, see the dust blow away behind it as it heads west across the last quarter mile of the Great Plains toward the canyon. Both the bear and I wait until the truck has wound into the draw and disappears, and we wait until the sound of the wheels on the gravel has been swallowed by the wind and the big rock walls of the Rocky Mountain front, and then I get a strange feeling. It's as though the bear is telling me he is not going away. That he is going to win. That I cannot stand here as long as he can stand there. I don't want to get weird here, but with each breath I have a sense of my mortality like I have never felt it before. The wind is suddenly stronger, the big gray sky suddenly flatter, and the cliffs rising up at the mouth of the canyon behind the bear make an entrance into a world so big and ancient that my puny mind can't begin to hold it. The bear doesn't seem troubled by these thoughts. He stays still and stares, lifting his nose slightly. I remember reading that bears are almost blind but that their smell is a thousand times stronger than ours, so while I look at him I imagine him smelling me and wonder what I smell like to him. Urine, probably. He thinks I'm a big walking puddle of urine—no wonder he's curious.

The silliness of that thought finally makes me blink. I mean, I move first. It feels like all the surrenders I've made in my life. It feels as if I'm falling. It feels like the earthquake felt, like the world has me in the palm of its careless hand and this bear is a reminder. I step backward and pivot toward the cabin. I am about to go in without wood but I haven't surrendered that much. To hell with the bear. I walk another twenty yards or so to the woodpile to get an armload from the stack. When I turn to walk back to the cabin I can see the bear still hasn't moved. I give it the finger, like I used to give Mark the finger, the only person I ever gave the finger to, because it would make him laugh. The memory makes me sad, and then even madder.

"Fuck you," I say to the bear, my words puny in the wind.

I go into the cabin through the front door with the wood and feel the heat, stack the wood in the little box behind the stove, except one piece for the fire. Then I walk over to the table and sit down in front of the box of letters. The bear is still in the same place out the window across the meadow at the base of the woods, but he's turned his back now and has resumed rooting around on what must be an old log. I pull the box of letters closer and begin to take out the envelopes one at a time, look at the strange stamps, and the postmarks, and begin to lay them out in order. First I'll pile them by years, then by months. The gods may not like a plan, but I do. I get busy and a few minutes later when I look out the window again, the bear is gone.

two

Tomás Joad

I finally got to read Tommy's letter in the bathroom after the graduation ceremony. I locked the stall door and pulled the envelope out from the waistband of my skirt and opened it to slip out the folded pages. In the stall next to me I listened to a girl puking. I couldn't decide if she was drunk or bulimic or legitimately sick, and I didn't ask. Even if she'd been shot and a growing pool of her blood was seeping under the stall wall, I wouldn't have said a word now that I finally had a chance to read this letter. I unfolded the pages and spread them on my lap. After that eye-opening first line about his broken engagement to the *bonita chiquita*, he wrote, "What in tarnation you doing this summer, wenchie? Life guarding at the country clubbie? Saving expensive lives-ie? You tasty suburban girls are such squares. I say you should just let all of us dead sink to the bottom of the pool and we'd be a visible warning to all the happy surface swimmers. Why don't you rip the old man off for some scratch, slip a couple a thousand cc's of kickin'

Harley between your legs and make like a dirty Panamanian whore and blow that suburban scene right off the map, dig? There's more to life than sloppy sunscreen and 3-minute radio songs, Mommy-o! There's more to life than riding around in cars with boys."

His words took my breath away—nasty, yes, but I loved the wild tone, his tongue-in-cheek, smart-ass play. But sad, too, the oblique reference to my saving him. Reading it made my blood pump and my head feel light. The sound of his voice! Nobody was like him. Nobody I had ever met was like Tommy.

"On the serious side," Tommy wrote, "I'm in a cute little poor country where all the happy tourists eat peanut butter and granola, and we are next to a pretty blue lake with a *papier mâché* green volcano on the other side. We sit around rough tables at night under strings of lights hanging from tree branches and drink beer and assess whether we might be able to recreationally screw each other, and then, regardless of how that works out—and it doesn't matter in the least—regardless of how that works out, in the morning we sit on the veranda and watch the soldiers go by in jeeps and trucks and some unlucky ones have to actually walk, and they follow the dirt road and the trail around the lake and all the way over the toy volcano where they then get to finally get out of their jeeps or stop marching. *Finally, a village!* they say. *Finally we get to buy beer and tobacco chew and have a party.* But no. Some grumpy officer tells them this ain't no party, this ain't no disco, you're here to do the oldest work in the world: massacre natives! So they go to work killing villagers because the villagers don't want to be feudal serfs anymore, the greedy injuns! Our happy old— did you know he was a movie star?—president calls them commies and sends money to the soldiers, so that's what the poor young soldiers have to do—what soldiers do everywhere, *sí?* They take the money and buy nice boots and guns and gas for their jeeps and crappy green uniforms and heavy steel helmets and they go up into the mountains and chase enemy women and children and old folks who want to build roads and schools and bio-digesters, and other bad commie shit. When they catch them, they make them dig pits and stand in them. The soldiers shoot them right there so they fall into their own graves and really, it's just a lot less work. First the natives are doing it to each other so that's one fewer thing we Americans have to do. Teach a man to fish, I always say. Second, the logistics are sweet. I mean, I like to think how some bright boy got the idea: *Man, it's just so hard killing people. Afterward you have all of these heavy and messy dead bodies. We should get the soon-dead to dig their own graves.* He probably got a promotion. He's the bright guy who was in your class and you thought, what a bright guy he is, such great ideas! Well, here he is putting his god-given wit to some practical use, by golly. Or probably in the States he's figuring out how to program a computer to get robots to do the killing, which is even better, because with killer robots all of these solders could hang back at the barracks playing ping pong or watching movies and saluting the flag or doing other fun stuff to give each other patriotic boners instead of out here in the dusty road marching and sweating. But until the killing robot is perfected we'll just have to rely on these poor brown boys who have nothing else to do, no good scholarships or career opportunities, so hey, at least in the army they get tortillas and beans! At least in the army they get to do the shooting. Remember the wave-particle dude? I think of him often because he'd know why all of this is happening. Why I'm sitting on the balcony of my hotel looking across that pretty lake I told you about at that toy volcano and watching the soldiers return from their dirty work. Maybe not enough rest but plenty of good exercise and fresh air so they look tired but strong and healthy. Very normal types, good boys, probably, which makes me think the one thing universally true about men is how we fall into killing as naturally as we fall into fucking. Women? I'm not so sure. They like to breed with men who kill—that's certainly true, especially if he's got a uniform! But the only *other* thing that seems universally true about women is that once they get to know me, they lose interest.

"Oops. Poor me! You'd think I was the one the soldiers were

shooting at. Speaking of, I wonder why I don't throw myself into the path of the marching soldiers and say *Stop! Do any of you know what a bad thing you're doing? What would your mothers say?* I used to think I was brave until I came down here. Or I thought it was a question that hadn't been answered yet. Now I know it has been and the answer is *No.* (Although I keep telling myself I'm going to change that. That being a coward isn't permanent.) Partly what gives me hope is I wonder why I tried to kill myself in good old Helena, Montana, before I ever saw this kind of shit (because by weird accident, *I have seen it. . .*) and now that I have, I don't want to kill myself. I keep thinking I've got to stay alive because nobody else around here seems to notice how fucked up everything is. You should hear them talk. I mean the other travelers, tourists: *Have you been to* this *cool place? To* that *cool place?* Like sitting in a nightclub in Berlin in 1942, all your mom's relatives being rounded up at gun point out in the street while the hep-cats sit in the night clubs listening to music, going, *Wow, I dig this scene! What crazy music!*

"But to be fair, it *is* crazy music. That's a fact. I love to sit on the front porch and smell coffee and exhaust, see the sparkly yellow and green hills, feel the cool air, warm sunshine. Sometimes I watch the maids hang up the sheets. First they wash them in the big red sink. Then they bring them over to the lines and lift the sheets up to drape and all I can see are their fingers over the wire and their bare pudgy brown feet and ankles under the hanging sheets. When the wind blows sometimes the hanging sheets wrap around their lovely bodies and I choke with desire. That's the good part about this place. The bad part is many of us cheapskate guests share a big room and my bunk mate is a lunatic who is always accusing me of stealing something—his socks, his comb—even his toothbrush. Which I could bear but not after this morning when he sat down next to me on the front step and said, *This might sound like a stupid question, but are you gay? Because it seems like every six hours somebody is wagging his do-jiggy in my face. You ever feel that way? I just want to know if you're going to do*

it so I can get ready. I hate it when I'm not ready. I hate it period
but I really hate it when I'm not ready.

"Maybe I can stand a partial lunatic but this guy is cracked
wide open, so I'm going to catch a bus to the next murderous
country, if you please, wherever the poor people are getting
uppity and want to change their lives and are getting kilt for it.
Wherever that is hap'nin'—with our tax dollars!—you'll find
me. Ol' Tomás Joad. I'll write you from there. I think of your
serious pretty face and that makes me want to write. In case
you are wondering I did make it where my mom is, but that's
a whole other story for another day. Keep studying. You're
smart. I try to talk to people here but most are idiots. They
say, *Go to Roatán, dude. You have to go to Roatán.* Or some
such place. Every time I turn around somebody's telling me
what I have to see if I'm going to really tourist this place right.
People dying right and left and all anybody can talk about is
Roatán, dude. Yesterday I decided I'd fucking die before I went
to *Roatán.* It was a simple decision.

"Love, Tomísimo"

ticket to the human race

Despite the terrible things he described, my brain never really got past that first sentence, the part I read before I even left home to go to my graduation: *Dear J— Fortunately I did not tie the ol' nuptial knot with my* bonita chiquita—*not to say this or that about why or what but more or less it's mo' better than mo' worse.* Sure, families might have been forced to dig their own graves, soldiers might have shot them, but my mind was still trying to stretch around the idea that Tommy had met a *bonita chiquita* and asked her to marry him. Or if not asked—I couldn't believe he proposed—they'd come to some sort of mutual agreement to marry (probably when they were naked). And then (probably when they put their clothes back on again) they decided not to.

But even reduced like that, his engagement was a lot to handle—and even more difficult because he didn't write anything more about it. Unless you count where he said that after they get to know him, all women lose interest. So I went to work on those few words. Did the chiquita eventually lose interest? Is that why they broke up? Did he think I must have lost interest in him, too? And if not, did he think I didn't know him well enough to lose interest in him? I was almost five years younger so maybe he thought of me as girl and not as a woman. He wrote that I was smart, but people say that about dogs and kids. I admit I felt betrayed and disgusted at myself for feeling betrayed. We hardly had a promise between us. But when I thought of how I'd grieved during this last year it hurt me that he hadn't seemed to. How could he have let somebody in so fast? Maybe I'd never taken up much room in his heart.

I recoiled at that notion, so there in the bathroom stall of my high school, still wearing my graduation cap and gown, I kept reading and re-reading the beginning of the letter. I zeroed in on the words, *but more or less it's mo' better than mo' worse,* and took comfort. The only thing as bad as him marrying somebody else would be if he didn't marry her but had his heart broken. So I re-read the letter with an eye toward whether he sounded that way. The pure awfulness of me pining for him and him pining for somebody else would have killed me. By the second time through, I came to the conclusion that he wasn't heartbroken in the least. The *chiquita* hadn't really touched him. And while he sat on that balcony thinking of what he'd seen in the mountains and what happened with his mother in Costa Rica—what girl came to his mind? *Moi.* So maybe he still loved me. He signed it *Love, Tomísimo,* hadn't he? Even I knew that was a stretch but I didn't care. I went so far as to think he was suffering because of me. (Massacres? What massacres?) That he felt so hollow and empty because he'd tried to replace me with the *chiquita.* (How could a mere *chiquita* plug up a *ME*-sized hole in his heart?) It wasn't even fair to try, and so at the last minute he'd set her free. He was that good of a person. In fact, he was way better than me, because while it seemed my heart had grown hard and wrinkled, his had opened up. Of course he'd failed—how could he not have failed?—but at least he'd tried. There was something heroic about that, something I admired, especially in such a dangerous place. I know this was foolish thinking but what do you expect? I hurt much more then he apparently did and I was trying to forgive him for that.

It's suddenly evening at the cabin and I sit at the table and watch the country out the big window darken to gray. The meadow, the cliffs gone—even the bear, who I can't see anymore. On the table in front of me are the letters sitting in neat stacks, sorted by year and by month. I trace the corners of the top one, the first one, the one I read in that stall on graduation day. The past is a deep ocean and our stories little rafts to float on. One thing that separates me from my colleagues in medicine—not *all* of them by any means, but from too many—is that I know I'm a doctor by chance. Most people who work hard for success tend to tell you how they imagined a straight line and had the balance and skill to walk it. To hear them talk about their lives is to hear their hands go *pat pat pat* on their own backs as they recount their hard work and sacrifices. I don't know. Maybe it's just too crazy-making for any of us to fathom all of the chance happenings that make us who we are, but my point is that as hard as I worked—and I did work hard to become a doctor and to be the best doctor I could be—I've never been able to pat myself on the back for all my good decisions and the good life that came from those decisions. I can't do that because I know that sitting in that stall, reading that letter from Guatemala—I know that if Tommy had seriously beckoned, I'd have been gone the next day. To wherever he was. Just like that. I'd have dropped all of my plans, borrowed all the money I could, and left immediately. I'd have been next to him on that balcony looking at that pretty lake and that pretty volcano and feeling the awful injustice of the world and girding myself for a brave and tragic life. But he didn't ask. So I worked that summer as a lifeguard, as he assumed I would. Only instead of a country club pool, I took the bus downtown to a rowdy public beach on Lake Michigan where I used my already proven abilities to yell at strangers to behave. I sat in the sun writing smart and sassy letters to Tommy in my head. I got a tan and grew beautiful but my beauty was like a magic wand that I wanted him to see but didn't care if anybody else did. That's not entirely true. Occasionally when I was bored I liked to pick it up and wave it around and get everybody to look at me, but after a while that would make me equally bored and I'd toss the wand down and resent people for still looking. In a letter later that summer, Tommy mentioned that he was thinking about being a writer. Inspired, I sometimes composed sentences describing my love for him, sentences of such beauty they'd make me cry, sentences that I knew if he read would make him love me as much as I loved him, but sentences in letters I couldn't send because he was always traveling and even though he wrote me every few weeks, he never told me where he'd be.

My only consolation was that I was becoming a more compassionate person. I mean, my heartache over Tommy seemed to be my ticket into the human race. It started when I was crossing the stage to get my diploma and I saw my parents' faces and knew how they'd been suffering. It was like a door opened in my heart. I don't mean I spent much time contemplating the massacre of villagers. That was still beyond my powers. But for the rest of the summer I'd look at all the people I saw during the day—literally thousands—and I'd think how every single one of them had a story at least as sad as mine. In the evening after work I'd take the bus home, microwave a cold dinner and sit on our screened-in porch and smoke cigarettes and read great nineteenth-century novels. I'd feel the air blowing across the gardens and grass of that green suburban world and convince myself that each breath I took was full of the same molecules of yearning and hope and despair and emptiness as the air these characters had breathed more than a hundred years before. I'd smell my flesh and wonder if I had as much blood in me as Natassya Fillippovna in *The Idiot*. I could easily believe some of us are destroyed by our lives, like Anna Karenina. Yet when Estella finally sees Pip at the end of *Great Expectations* and she tells him that suffering has been her teacher and that she's been bent and broken, she hopes, *into a better shape*, I could easily believe that too. At night I'd dream of Tommy and by day I'd wait for his next letter, and his next—prepared to leave, I was always prepared to leave. But he didn't ask, and so in the fall I got a ride up to Madison with a friend. I enrolled in college and then, eventually, med school. One life happened and another did not. I met Mark in med school while doing a family practice rotation at a clinic in Baraboo. So that's when we started, the two of us. That's when the life we lived together began.

his suffering artist days had passed

While waiting for the spackle to dry on the kitchen door-frame so I can try to re-attach the hinge—with what? I still haven't found a screwdriver—I've pushed not just the heavy chair and the stool over there, but also added an end table from the living room to my little barricade. It makes me feel better. There's also the front door, which thankfully latches and locks, and the big front window and the small one over the kitchen sink. It's dark outside and in the yellow lamplight I see my reflection in the big window but nothing outside. I stand up and lean into the glass, cup my hands on each side of my face and see moving shadows of the pine branches and dark shapes even farther out in the meadow, but I don't see the bear. I wonder how close he'd have to be for me to see him. I wonder if he'd come right up to the window and if bears ever break cabin windows and come in. I've heard of them breaking car windows to get food at the national parks and this window would be easier to break than a car window, but the cabin has been here for years, and as far as I know so have the windows. I slip off the pepper spray safety and let my forefinger slide to the trigger and practice aiming. This way, then that, I spin, squint, and aim. My still un-named puppy is curled up on a chair next to the stove with his nose under his tail. "Are you a bear killer?" I ask him. He doesn't even open his eyes. His day is over. If anything's going to happen bear-wise, I'm on my own.

There are fourteen stacks of letters on the table. In front of the stack on far left is a sticky paper on which I've written 1982. On top of that is the letter I read on graduation day; it was written May 20. Next to that stack is 1983, 1984, all the way to the far right stack marked 1995. Thirteen years and three months of a mostly one-sided correspondence that over time I received with fewer and fewer expectations. While I was in college, his letters mostly amused me—his quirky personality, his strange and funny insights into culture, the dangers of war and politics. But as I studied my way through med school, they entertained me less. His weird experiences never seemed to lead to anything, only to another odd feeling, another odd thought. Most I read with only mild curiosity, on the city bus or in the library or sitting at the Union Terrace. *Who was this man I'd fallen for so hard?* Only a handful of years had gone by, but the passion I'd had for him felt like a dream. By the time I was doing my residency in North Carolina, their strangeness often disturbed me. For one thing, I barely had time to read them. Mark and I were already married, we had twins, and I was working horrendous hours. Some of the letters got tucked away into the shoebox without even being opened. Then after we moved back to Wisconsin, to the farm, and the twins were growing and Mark started farming and woodworking and I began my practice—well, frankly sometimes the letters just plain irritated me. Sure Tom's weird stories could make us laugh—some even moved me to tears—but he showed so little interest in me or my life that privately I felt miffed and sometimes wondered if he'd put the wrong letter in the envelope.

Self-centered, I used to think, and dismiss him. But I see something else now. At their most basic, they were notes from a lonely man who for some reason wanted to share with me (or with some idea of me) his awe and glee and terror and confusion in abundance, a man who struggled to find his place in the world and who wrestled openly with his demons. In giving me a running play-by-play account of his own soul in conflict with itself, he was giving me an opportunity to be aware of my own. It wasn't something I always had the time and energy for.

His last letter was a postcard dated September 3, 1995, and it's one I memorized because for years I had it taped to our refrigerator door on the farm. There's no greeting or sign-off, just this:

Should we have stayed at home and thought of here?
Is it right to be watching strangers in a play
In this strangest of theatres?
Oh, must we dream our dreams and have them, too?

Only years later did a friend of Mark's recognize it as lines from a poem called "Questions of Travel," by Elizabeth Bishop. Not that that mattered. It seemed a natural expression for what he'd experienced, and just the right words to end with. For I think he knew he'd never write me again. Certainly as time went by after I got that last poem and realized I was never going to get another letter, I felt some relief. But also sadness—which probably explains why I had it taped to the refrigerator for so many years. Apparently when he stopped writing me, he stopped writing altogether, so those fourteen years comprised his writing life. "The bloom of my youth," he called it much later—the last time I saw him. "And more of a vice than a career." For he never finished a novel to his satisfaction, and he published only a few short stories. He wrote occasional news articles for the wire services or national magazines—even a handful of cheerful travel pieces (never on Roatán). When he sent me the poem, he was already on his way back to the States to start business school in Florida. Over the next few years, he called occasionally. We'd talk briefly. Or rather he would, just to fill me in. I didn't think about this at the time—it would have felt too pathetic and sad—but I may have been the only person in the world who had an interest in the next chapter of his life, the only person who knew him. He got his MBA and worked a string of jobs as diverse as selling custom-built yachts around the world to distributing cigarette advertising materials to convenience stores. He married a beautiful woman from Monaco who could barely speak English. He couldn't speak Italian or French. He said he found this very funny, especially when they had two children, a boy and a girl, and his family would be chatting away over dinner and he wouldn't have a clue what they were saying. Eventually he worked his way into teaching and held a string of posts at small colleges from Miami to Seattle. In those years, he began to telephone me late at night. His calls grew less frequent, once every three or four months, but they lasted longer. He always called to tell me how lucky he was to get this great job, what a lovely setting it was, and how smart the students were, how much fun he was having. How he loved watching his son and daughter grow— although they and their mother were taking longer and longer visits to Monaco—how much he loved teaching, loved training dogs. Golf. Some beautiful but obscure new business idea. This went on for a few years. The calls were infrequent enough that for the most part I'd be glad to get them. But then one night when the phone woke me after I'd been working two nights in a row, I heard the familiar sloppy slur in his voice, and I knew I'd had enough. Although he might be feeling cheerful and enthusiastic about Ethiopian food or fly fishing, I knew I couldn't pretend to be. I told him to please not call me if he'd been drinking. I don't regret that I said that but I do regret that he never called me again. Well, he did once.

I PUT THE BEAR SPRAY down and pour myself a big plastic cup of wine, then take an assorted group of letters—after all that time putting them in order, I can't stand to read them that way—and sit by the woodstove and turn on a floor lamp. I have a funny feeling. It's strange to say the feeling is like a shadow but that's the word that comes to mind. It's like whatever I'm feeling now is only a chemical or radiological imprint of a real feeling I had when I read the letter for the first time many years before. I know that's ridiculous but it makes me braver.

"Dear McJanine McBean," he wrote from Managua in November 1987. "The sweat of midday starts in the manyana. Just for the breeze I walk a quick turn from my room around the block and this is what I see: the vacant lot of weeds and plaster and glass, the rummies in twos and threes, stingy old drunks in the shade of a broken adobe wall, the brown boys playing baseball in the street with a broom for a bat and a rock rolled up in a sock for a ball, the lovely shape of a woman reclining in a doorway—who teaches you lovelies to stand like that?—a granny sitting on a rock under a tree in the front yard. (If I had a dime for every woman in a doorway and granny under a tree in this country, I'd be rich. Which doesn't take much down here, I admit.) In the bombed-out park nearby are clusters of wheel-chaired young men, war wounded, passing time and staring. Not hate or envy but curiosity and bother, *desculpe*, excuse me, *con permiso*. I move through the space between pedestrians and cars and buildings, drinking OJ or Coke from a plastic bag to wash down last night's *guaro*, moonshine. Back at the 30-cent-a-night *hospedaje* I sweat in a shady hammock while the German *turistas* tan themselves in the courtyard. All the ex-pats chant with flushed faces: *Revolution!* Reagan's war makes everyone a radical. Or a wounded veteran. Or dead. On the way here, crossing the border, I didn't have any money left. I'd been robbed on the highway and I made the mistake of telling the Honduran border guard that I'd been robbed by a Contra. (And I wasn't even lying.) But it made him angry. He said it must have been a Sandinista. I argued with him for a while until I bloody well (a habit from traveling with Brits) realized he was serious, and wasn't going to let me pass. He locked me in a cell by myself for hours, which certainly helped focus my mind. Especially because I wasn't quite by myself— there was a dead man lying on the floor in the corner. At first I thought he was asleep—I admit I'm slower than the flies—

but after a while I figured it out, too. I'm not kidding. I was locked in a cell with a dead man and I wanted to get out but stubbornly refused to surrender completely to the idiot guard. I mean, I had my principles...at least until the heat made the dead man start to smell. So I thought for a while and came up with an absurd compromise. I pounded on the door until the guard came back and I told tell him he was right, indeed, the robber had the heart of a Sandinista but the clothing of a Contra. Which was fine with the guard, apparently, because the next thing I heard is the key in the lock and the door opened, and he gave me my passport back and let me walk away—out of the jail and across a bridge, across a gorge, across the border. Wow. Explain it however you want. To me it was a miracle. And I'm not talking about being let out of jail but making it across that bridge. Rotted planks suspended by fraying cables, ropes—vines? And while I'm halfway across, a truck full of Cherry Coke begins to drive out as well. I want to sprint to the other side because I'm sure it's all going to crash and I'll die and they'll put me back in the cell with the other dead guy but frankly it's just too hot to run. I don't even watch as the truck drives up behind me. I can feel the tremendous sway of the bridge as it takes the truck's weight—the taut ropes whine and the planks crack. I just keep my head down and walk and sure enough, both the Cherry Coke and I manage to cross the bridge out of one hot dusty country and into another."

I'm not done with the letter but the dark window in the cabin is giving me the creeps so I get up to pull the drapes but not before I put my face to the glass again and try to see out. I don't remember where I was exactly when I read this letter. I hadn't begun doing rotations yet, so I know I still didn't know Mark. The way I met him, I was sleeping with his roommate, Eric, who I worked with at the Baraboo Clinic. It was a barely engaging romance and I would have ended it quickly but began to realize the real reason I wanted to sleep at his place was that I looked forward to seeing Mark (whose fiancé was in the Peace Corps in Africa). The first morning I slid out of bed early without waking Eric, tiptoed into the kitchen, only to find Mark sitting at the table reading the paper. He barely looked up and I had to introduce myself but he handed me a good cup of coffee and didn't make me chat. He just kept reading the paper and passing me sections he'd finished. In subsequent visits, I came to look forward to seeing him in the morning. I liked how he looked at me, playful, curious, but not too much of either. Out of the corner of my eye I liked the slope of his shoulders and how the thick blond hair on his forearms glowed in the light from the window. I wanted to run my fingers through it, back and forth, back and forth. Eric was a late sleeper and Africa was a long way away and I suppose Mark and I were both ready for something big—a miracle, maybe, a long walk across a shaky bridge. Three months later I was pregnant and we were engaged. A year later we were married.

I pick up Tommy's letter and continue reading:

"Like I say, a miracle. Which if you're unfamiliar with the term up there on the grid of the North American Midwest, is something that happens every day down here. Well, maybe not that often for me, but I did have a kind of mystical experience yesterday. It started when I saw a pretty teenage girl get off one of those over-packed buses with people hanging off the sides and riding on top. She just kind of plopped down and stood waiting for something or someone. It was one of those not-uncommon scenes. The sidewalk in chunks, the wall she leaned against cracked, the tiles in the roof behind her broken or missing. But she looked good. I mean, she was the only thing in sight that looked put together correctly. And not just her tidy body, but her shiny black hair combed into a ponytail held with a pretty yellow ribbon, and the fit of her clothes, her shoes. She looked like she'd just descended from heaven. I felt a religious calling and went over and stood next to her. I didn't talk because I didn't know what to say. I just wanted to stand there for a while. But of course me standing there for so long looking out in the street and not talking made her uncomfortable, so finally I spoke. I asked her if she was waiting for something or somebody. She said no, she'd just taken the bus here to see what would happen. 'Really?' I asked, amused. She nodded, very serious. I shrugged and said, 'Me, too.' We both stood there for a while until I got an idea. I looked at her but she wasn't looking at me. Still, I liked my idea. I wondered if she'd like it, too. *Yes,* I thought. *No,* I thought, and back and forth like that until finally the drama got too much for me and I had to ask. 'Want to step around the corner with me and kiss?' She looked up at me. I looked down at her. She didn't speak or smile, just nodded, real subtle, just enough, and so we stepped around the corner of the broken wall into a shady spot where we kind of gently made our way into each other's arms and started making out big time. We did that for a long time. She didn't want to go any farther. Every time I tried to move my hand to a strategic spot, she slid it gently back up to her shoulder. I said, 'Hey, what if a bomb goes off and both of us die in our clean clothes? What a tragedy!' She didn't seem to think so. (Or else I just said it badly in Spanish.) Regardless, I sweated and grunted around trying to touch her and finally, to distract me, she began to teach me a prayer—I swear this is true. She had me sit down next to her on a piece of cardboard and lean back against the wall and repeat a prayer her grandmother taught her. She said her grandmother had a sad life. Lost four children when they were young, and her husband recently come back from the war a little loco. She said this prayer gave her grandma great comfort. Did I want to learn it? What could I say? Of course I've already forgotten it but by the time night fell in that alley, I had it memorized. How could I not? We were sitting surrounded by every piece of broken crap you could imagine, broken fans, broken hoses, broken car parts, broken windows, everything messed-up and broken but her— and we held hands and prayed together. I have no clue what I was praying for but I knew it was as holy as it gets."

In the cabin, I still haven't pulled the drapes. Through the window I see the dark shape of a pine tree in the yard, its branches waving frantically in the wind. The tree must have been broken when it was younger because the main trunk splits into two trunks about five feet from the ground. Both grow out horizontally for about a foot and then curve to grow upward for another fifteen feet. In the faint light from the window, with the wind blowing, the tree looks like a man squatting and holding his arms up toward the heavens beckoning answers. Howling. The chimney moans. The barricaded kitchen door is quiet but the roof creaks. Speaking in tongues. As holy as it gets. Which reminds me of a funny story. It was a long way between Tom Connor and Mark Kraemer—a long walk on a swaying bridge, just to stick with the metaphor. I already mentioned the sundry hook-ups my senior year of high school. Freshman year in college, I specialized in drinking to excess as a means of keeping boys away. Not a conventional way to stay safe, I'll admit, but I often drank so much I'd puke, which even college boys didn't think very sexy. When I was a sophomore I started hanging out with a boy named Josh Stevens. He was from Rhode Island but lived briefly in Denver before coming out to Madison. He had long hands and fine fingers—good for playing the guitar, he told me—and his thin lips and translucent skin made me feel tender just looking him. He was the first boy who made me feel that way after Tommy. He always had pot and we'd sit in his room smoking until late every night listening to music and I'd listen to him talk about the music scene in Denver, which was much more honest, he kept telling me, and not so corrupt as in Madison. His friend Sam had a band there. He made me listen to examples of Sam's recordings and then recordings of local Madison bands. I can't say I knew what he meant or heard what he heard but I liked his passion and felt honored he was sharing it with me. He was serious about the guitar but seemed to like to talk about it more than he liked to play it. I'd lie back on his bed—we'd both be on his bed—maybe our feet would touch. It was all very casual and brother and sister-like, but I didn't feel that way. He could make me want him just by the way he dipped his head and pushed his hair away from his eyes. I'd stretch and make noises but couldn't get him to really look at me. I would have thrown myself at him but just the thought paralyzed me. We never did anything but talk and smoke and talk some more. Or he'd talk and I'd listen without understanding, and then I'd leave late at night so hollowed out with desire I could barely breathe.

At the end of the semester, Josh announced he was moving to back Denver. His friend Sam and his band mates needed somebody to stay in their apartment while they played in Europe. I could tell he wished Sam had invited him on the tour, but apartment sitting for the band would have to do. Josh thought he'd probably transfer and start school out there as well. He was done with Madison. Suddenly he seemed very unhappy. I was flabbergasted and sad as well. We told each other we'd write, and we did, but after Christmas when I got his first letter I resolved I'd go see him at spring break. I was determined to force us across the line we hadn't crossed, even if it meant knocking on his door naked. It turned me on to think about standing at his door naked, though the fantasy never got to him actually answering the door.

When vacation started, I hitchhiked to Denver by myself through a March blizzard in Nebraska that had me delayed briefly in an Ogallala motel room with a woman and her two children. She was friendly and glad to have me with her, she told me too many times, and then tried to show it by climbing into the shower with me once she got the two kids into bed. Oops. A misunderstanding, we both pretended, and I made it to Denver safely just two and a half days after leaving Madison. I wasn't naked when Josh answered the door, but when I saw his pretty face I was hoping.

"Oh my god!" he said. I'd surprised him. He was happy and it made me optimistic as I threw myself into his arms. I let my head fall back so he'd kiss me but he didn't seem to notice, keeping his face tucked down against my neck. Was this a brother-sister hug? His hands stayed on my back. I couldn't stand the ambiguity anymore and pinched his ass. He jumped back and laughed. He invited me in and fed me and talked in a way he'd never talked before about his new life, his new school. He was very animated and happy. He didn't even mention music. Apparently his suffering artist days had passed. I wasn't sure what I felt about that. I liked that he was different, but I'd liked him before, too. Suddenly, after dinner, he said, "I have a surprise for you."

My stomach dropped. I had to look to the floor. I thought, he's been waiting for this as long as I have.

"I want to take you to my church," he said.

"What?"

"I want to show you what's happened to me since I've been home."

"Home?" I said. "But you're from Rhode Island."

He smiled at me as though he felt confident I wouldn't always be so clueless.

His church was in the back room of a neighborhood body shop. The preacher had long hair, wore a colorful South American–style vest, and played an electric guitar. The entire sermon he was either grooving on his guitar or cajoling people to get down and give themselves up to the Holy Spirit. By the end of the service, I was the only one who was still in her seat. Everyone else—fifty, maybe, it was a small congregation—everyone else was writhing around on the floor babbling in tongues. Including Josh, who knelt at my feet, his arms raised and his face tilted back and that mouth I'd thought of kissing so many times filled with the weird sounds of the Holy Spirit.

Afterward I didn't know what to say. My hopes for a romance with him were over—he made it clear his new religious principles were so strong he could not imagine having a girlfriend who didn't share them. He explained all of this while we walked back to his apartment. Of course I nodded at everything he so patiently explained—and part of me envied him, part of me admired him—but an even bigger part of me held out some small hope that he'd backslide. He didn't. He told me I could have his bed but he matter-of-factly laid out a sleeping bag for himself on the couch. I think he saw my stunned face. I mean, it had been a long trip out there and would be a long trip home. I probably looked like I was about to cry. He sat down, patted my hand and said, "I was a terrible *terrible* sinner, Janine. The church has helped me feel right about myself again. Don't begrudge me that."

I was confused. "A terrible *terrible* sinner?" I said. All I could think he'd ever done wrong was smoke pot, which I was disappointedly beginning to understand was something else we weren't going to do here in Denver. "What sins did you commit?"

He looked at me long and hard with big watery brown eyes so sad and hopeful I wanted to swim in them. "Lust," he said very carefully, as though he enjoyed the feel of the word on his tongue. "My worst sin was lust."

I think I might have stopped breathing altogether. I don't know for how long. But when I started again, I gasped. He looked concerned. "Lust?" I practically screamed. "When? With whom?"

"With you," he said.

"Shut up!" I said. I wanted to punch him. I did punch him with both fists in the chest. "You never touched me!"

He caught my fists and held them between his hands. He kept his beautiful stupid eyes on mine. He said, "In my head I did. I worshipped your flesh and was dooming myself to hellfire. I was obsessed with you. I ravished you over and over again."

I did start to cry then. I was ashamed at being such a loser, for one thing. Ashamed for having blown it again, for having made nothing of such a big feeling for a boy. What was my problem? Didn't other girls have regular boyfriends they took long walks with, watched movies with, ate popcorn with, had sex with? Why was my love life so weird? First it was a matter of life and death with Tom Connor, a crazy boy who left me for his mother (and apparently for every other *chiquita* he met along the way) and then it was a matter of eternal damnation with this fanatic who'd apparently ravished me over and over again and never bothered to tell me.

the bear is not a metaphor—or a
grizzly, I don't think

I wake with the letters on my lap and it's dark. I don't remember turning off the light. I reach for the standing lamp and almost knock it over but manage to turn the knob one way then the other. The light doesn't go on. I stand up and shuffle blindly across the room to the switches by the door. I click them but nothing happens. Outside the wind is still gusting so I figure a power line has gone down somewhere. The dark seems particularly thick. I stand still and realize there is a faint glow through the crack around the door of the wood-stove and I make my way that way and open the box. The fire is almost out. I reach for a piece of wood and build the fire up again, leave the firebox open so the light of the flames flickers across the floor and far wall. I sit down again and think of that last letter, the poem that Tommy sent me. In the years after he stopped writing, I never asked him about his disappointed ambitions, and he never mentioned them. Maybe I should have asked. Maybe I should have asked if he was ruining his life by drinking so much. It's a pretty simple question. I just didn't think about it. I was too busy thinking how self-centered he was. He told me on the phone that when he turned forty-five he marked the day by going to his friend's cabin with his wife and young children and drinking forty-five beers. He shot forty-five bullets with his .45 caliber pistol. Taken a bath in the creek. It had been great, he said, just what he needed.

"Gee, Tom," I said. "I'll bet your wife and kids enjoyed it, too."

He said they hardly noticed. He said his wife called him *Thomas le Terrible* and his kids called him either *Le papa* or *Waaaaaaah!* He said they were huddled in the cabin having a diaper picnic in Euro baby talk.

I pretended he was exaggerating, pretended amusement. It was only after I was already off the phone with him, already ready for bed, standing in the kitchen, Mark reading in the living room, did the reality of forty-five beers begin to sink in. *Forty-five?* If a patient of mine had told me he was going to drink that much, he would have had my full attention, even without a gun. I might have asked a question or two. I might have told him what I know about what happens to people who drink that much in a day, who *can* drink that much in a day, who need to. But I didn't say anything. It was like I was still a girl in my relationship with him. I stood in my kitchen and wondered if he was looking for some kind of truth from me and that I'd just let him down by not calling his bullshit *bullshit*.

That's the way to guilt, though, and for the most part I've got too much of my mother's Jewishness and too little of my dad's Irish Catholicism. So I didn't stand there in the kitchen after that phone call and rub my temples and feel guilty for not saying *What? Forty-five beers? Are you kidding?* What I felt first was my mom's pessimism, "the certainty of the persecuted," she used to call it, a shrugging knowledge that suffering and death were close and inevitably on their way. But I also felt anger—that's how my daddy shows in me—and I thought, what a prick of Tommy to think I might be his moral rudder or his health guide. Me, the girl who let him have her...*and* have her...*and* have her again. And then cut him down from the light fixture in the hotel. Now he wants me to be his doctor? I slammed my hand down on the counter. From the living room behind me, Mark asked what was up. I said I'd just smashed a spider. He said poor spider.

Now, sitting in the cabin and watching the flames in the woodstove grow to flicker on the far wall, I see Tommy wasn't looking for doctoring. In fact, he probably wasn't even thinking anything about me at all. He was just using me to create a little spin for himself. Forty-five beers was extreme but if he could say the words so casually, well, maybe it wasn't a big deal. Forty-five years, beers, bullets, and a .45 caliber pistol, as though it were a fun numbers game, a neat trick and a bath in the creek for good hygiene. The story was downright bright for what it left out: the thousands of empty bottles before and after those, the crawling puking terror, the night sweats, waking, pacing, the out-of-control descent. His wife and children taking sanctuary where they could. When I thought about it more, his world was always darker than he let on. In his letters and in his calls, he put his best foot forward, his best handsome face and bright, clever mind. That was maybe what he wanted from me, somebody to tell a-not-quite-so-dark story to. His stories often showed me something that I could not make a lot of sense of but didn't feel I needed to. I can see now that their meaning didn't lay neatly inside the strange details of his startling juxtapositions—the fixed-up girl in the broken world, the make-out session melting to prayer—forty-five beers, forty-five bullets, and a bath. Their meaning lay outside those scenes in the big darkness beyond. His stories were points of light that illuminated a little halo of mist. But what he was really writing about was neither the point of light nor the little halo of mist. His subject was what that little halo suggested, what you had to imagine: the immense night fog blanketing the land beyond, the dark, dark world.

Or at least I can feel and imagine it now. The darkness of the cabin suddenly has me claustrophobic, so I take refuge in staring out the window again. I see the dark shapes in the distance, and closer, the pine again with the two arms waving at heaven. I remember I had a professor in college who said reading poetry was like staring out a window at night. There's something out there, but what? A good poem will make you look for a long time. And even after looking for hours you may still never know exactly what it is you see, but it will only grow more compelling, more real, so you won't be able to look away. I see something moving out in the meadow that looks like a bear but I don't think it's him. It's probably a bush in the wind. The professor would say the bear is a metaphor. Which is probably true but before he's a metaphor he's still a bear. And I know this for certain because just as I start to think about it, I see him again. This time he's only a few feet away through the glass and he's staring right back at me. I recoil, even cover my face. I imagine him leaping for me through the glass. But when I look back, he hasn't budged. If it weren't for the glass, I could almost reach out and touch him. He's not a grizzly, I don't think. He's a black bear. I'd like to say I can tell this by his size and by the shape of his face or whatever—but mainly I think I know because last week when I was spending a lot of time at the lodge, a man asked if I'd seen a very big old cinnamon-colored black bear nosing around these cabins. I said no, and I hadn't, not yet, should I be worried? He said for your puppy, maybe, but the bear won't hurt you.

   Nevertheless I stand paralyzed with fear. All I can do is blink but when I open my eyes again, the bear is still there, still looking in at me through the window. I know that man at the bar has vast gaps in his knowledge about the world—he's just like anybody else that way—so how can I assume he knows everything about this old bear? I blink again. It seems it's my only tactic in this stare-down game with the bear. Just keep surrendering. I try it again. I blink and blink and finally—*voilà!*—the bear is gone. He's disappeared from the front window. I pull the drapes and stand still and just about when I've convinced myself I might have been seeing things, inventing things, I hear him nosing at the front door. The noise is worse than the sight, but at least this time I don't pee in my pants. He makes a snort as clear as can be—a snort like a giant pig, actually. The puppy has awoken and is sprinting loops in the L-shaped cabin from the kitchen under the table around the woodstove and couch and back again, whimpering slightly as he runs. That sound, as much as anything, breaks me out of my freeze. I find the bear spray and stand by the front door, put my ear to it. I can hear him breathing, even with all of this wind and the crazy running dog, and what strikes me is how slow his breath is. Such a long inhale and long exhale—I can feel the weight of his body in the sound. I slide the safety off and slip my finger onto the trigger. I lift the latch on the door and open it a crack and point the tip of the canister out and spray a burst into the swirling night wind. Then I quickly close the door but I guess not fast enough because my throat suddenly feels like I breathed in a tiny fish hook and my eyes burn. A little bit of the pepper must have blown back, and I'm amazed at the power because it drops me to my knees struggling to cough out the fish hook and squeeze back the tears. I'm also still afraid of the bear, so even on the floor as I spasm with coughs and slobber, I keep my body leaning against the door to make sure it stays closed in the wind. For the second time in a less than twenty-four hours the bear has me feeling pretty humble and I know that sometime I might think this is funny but right now I can't stop coughing and crying, and even when I finally do, I still feel a little thing that makes me want to clear my throat over and over again. I manage to stand up and stay quiet long enough to listen and I can't hear the bear anymore. When I finally get my eyes dry I can see the door is latched shut so I step sideways to look out the window and I can't see the bear, either. The puppy must have breathed some pepper too, as he's making a strange snorting sound though his nose even as he's still running frantic circles. I collapse in my chair. My heart is beating like mad and I'm damp with sweat and I don't know how I'll ever get to sleep again tonight. Mark used to say all the good things in his life happened when he was sweating and his heart was beating fast, but *screw him*,

I think, *he's dead and I have to live like this.* I know something about this situation is comical but—sorry, Mom—apparently I don't have good enough character to do anything but clench my teeth in bitterness. I feel my own thin skin and the immensity of the world in the roar of the wind, and I know I could walk out the door and with or without pepper spray the bear would probably run away. I could walk for days and weeks and months into the mountains or across the plains and no beast would eat me. But neither would anybody care. I mean, in all of that land, in all of that space—Mark is dead, Tommy is dead, and my children are a long way away and looking in other directions—in all of that space only the wind moans. The puppy whimpers as he runs. Something rattles in the chimney like a lunatic bird. I could open the door and walk in a straight line until I died, and when I think of the immensity of the sky the idea seems suddenly beautiful. Yet I'm afraid of the dark. And also afraid to turn on my headlamp. I don't want the bear out there to see any sign of me in here through the window. I know none of this makes sense, but if you were sitting in the dark sweating and hyperventilating with a snorting puppy running crazy circles at your feet, would you make sense?

I switch on my headlamp—I surrender, I'm a tiny light in the darkness and *blah blah blah.* The headlamp and the darkness are not metaphors either. It just gets too dark at night. And I have all of these letters to read. I hush the dog, get him to come over, and pet his head until he's calm. "Puppy, puppy, puppy," I say. Then I shuffle through a stack of letters and find a long one that I remember exactly where I was when I read, one that disturbed me deeply and also (I remember, I admit) turned me on.

Zochee the Wonder Woman

Dear Wenchísimo Jenísimo,

She was pretty, short hair, looked like a dancer, big black eyes, but I didn't look. People who sit at bars often times want to talk, but I'd chosen that exact spot after walking up and down the various wings in the airport looking for a place where I could watch the Olympics, see how Bernie, this buddy of mine from Lake Forest, would do in the gymnastics. Either the televisions were on other channels or there were no empty stools until I found this one, so I'd ordered a big tall beer and a shot of whiskey, which I was sipping while settling in, getting ready for the drama. It was 7 p.m. and I'd been in the airport since about 1 o'clock and I still had four hours until my flight to Tegucigalpa.

She ordered something to eat, and I watched television. Eventually—too many ads, or maybe it was the smell of the fish tacos she ordered—I looked over as her plate came and she looked at me. We said hello and she started to talk. With some people it's that way. Once you say hello, they tell you everything. In her case, she was going to Paris to begin a program at Sorbonne in psychology. She'd been working for a few years in Portland teaching brain-damaged patients how to do simple things like walk or brush their teeth. When I told her how depressing I would find it to not be able to use my body, she frowned and said, as though it were something she'd read for a test, 'It takes about five years to find other ways to keep the darkness away, but people do, and once they do, they are often as happy as they were before the accident.'

Well, I thought. So that was that. Actually, I was thinking how happy *she* must have made the men. A beauty visits them every day, lays *hands* on them, hey, sure they stand! And while I'm thinking that—wondering if I should say it, flirt like that—she's suddenly on to talking about her roots. Slovenia, where she was born, and then to Miami as a child. She grew up there and went to college in northeastern Ohio before coming here two years ago. She said all of this like she'd said it too often, spinning out the quick story that took her from Slovenia all the way to this bar stool on her way to Paris. She said she'd just started getting used to Portland but still didn't like it and was glad to be leaving.

Too WASPish? she said.

You asking me?

I don't know.

Well, what do you mean?

She shrugged.

Too white? I asked.

That's not it, she said, and explained that she'd lived in eastern Pennsylvania in the summers during college, which was even whiter. But different, and she liked it a lot more than here. She said she wasn't even exactly sure what she meant by too WASPish.

Too smug? I asked.

She grinned and nodded. Yes, she said. That's it.

I'd impressed her, and for my prize she turned to half-face

me—she wasn't paying a lot of attention to the fish tacos, in fact she'd taken a carrot from her purse and begun to eat that instead—and while she crunched away at that she began to tell me about Pennsylvania, living in a tent for a year with somebody named Sara. I kept looking up at the television, or else at her pretty white hand gripping the fat carrot. Back and forth. The floor ex had started. I wanted to watch and she noticed and apologized for distracting me. She had too-short black hair—about an inch and a half all over and it stuck up or lay down in kind of a tough modern city girl look—but she had shy black eyes full of yearning. I said no, really, it was me who should apologize for watching TV when she was talking. It was just that I'd been waiting all day to watch this event. I told her she wasn't intruding, which was all she needed to hear, because she plunged onward with her story. Apparently Sara was a genius and could do anything, like program computers, raise dogs, grow vegetables, and build a cabin in the woods with no power tools. My friend Bernie wasn't up yet, so I kind of half watched and half listened. I heard her say trans-female. Trans-female this and trans-female that, which eventually, I couldn't help it, made me turn and look at her. I had to ask, What is a trans-female?

A man who is on her way to becoming a woman, she said.

I looked at her. I didn't know how to react because I hadn't heard who was a trans-female. I only hoped she wasn't. Bernie was going get his turn soon. We were friends when we were kids. In fact, we both started gymnastics together. He stayed with it, and although I barely saw him in high school, I admired him completely. He was at the gym all the time, practicing all the time. The rest of us fucked around in the parking lot, or made plans to do this or that, and he was actually doing it. Eating right, sleeping right, training hard. He inspired me, because when we started gymnastics together he wasn't really much better than I was, and now he was the U.S. champion, about to tumble in the Olympics. It made me think, hell, if Bernie could do that, then I could do something great as well.

But Zochee had my interest with this trans-female thing.

What does *on his way to becoming a woman* mean? I asked

On *her* way.

What?

On hormone therapy.

I cupped my hands in front of my chest, and raised my eyebrows.

She nodded

And? I pointed to my lap.

Zochee finished the carrot and smiled coyly at her fish tacos.

I waited a beat. I was afraid to ask, but the time had come. Who exactly are we talking about here?

She looked at me, amused.

Sara? I asked.

She had all of my favorite parts, she said.

I couldn't take my eyes off her. What was I going to say? Just about when Bernie was ready to go, the coach and the camera getting in his face, this beauty Zochee is telling me about her romance with a trans-female. Oh, I said, because I suddenly remembered how she'd said Sara was a genius. Sara had run away from home and lived in the woods and could make a cabin with her bare hands. Zochee loved Sara, Zochee lost Sara. Her eyes were brimming tears.

Isn't this your man? she said, and nodded up at the TV.

Grateful, I looked up. Bernie had stepped onto the corner of the mat. Immediately I was nervous as hell. It looked distractingly bright in the arena and then the camera zoomed in on his face. Very cool to see someone like that who you've known since you were six. He turned his gaze inward, stood still for a moment, and then suddenly sprang forward for his first tumbling pass. The camera backed off and he did a front handspring to back, a single front with a twist, a double, I don't know all, but my god he got high in the air! And then he came down wrong. At the end of that first run. His ankle turned, and he fell forward, out of the square, which was big-time point dockage. The ankle twist looked bad at first, and my stomach fell, but he stood up right away, nothing broken, nothing damaged, even. He stood for a second looking down at his foot though as if he'd seen a ghost. What horror! What happened? I'd been waiting for this all day—and now this?—but think of how long he'd been waiting, working, waiting! And now nothing. He was out of it. Even if he did absolutely perfect the rest of the routine, which he practically did, it didn't matter, because in the first three seconds he'd fallen—he was out, and it was over—and now that he was out, who cared about the rest of them? I didn't. And the suddenness of that loss—of caring and then suddenly not caring—left me feeling empty and burned, and I resented how I'd spent all day in the airport waiting. Waiting more for this than for my midnight flight. And the last hour trying to find a TV and a stool to watch—and finally finding one—and now it was over. The Olympics are full of sports like this. I like sports like hockey or basketball where you can play terribly for a while and still win, still come back. That's my kind of sport. I hated gymnastics. I hated figure skating and ski racing. In fact, I suddenly hated all sports where you had to be perfect to not let anybody down, where you had to be perfect to win.

All that ran through my head in about five seconds. I felt disappointment like a hole in my stomach but when I turned from the TV, there was Zochee still heartbroken and mourning her Appalachian lover. Two years in smug Portland teaching people how walk again, or how to learn to live in a wheelchair, but it wasn't enough. Here she sat in an airport bar dabbing her tears in front of a complete stranger.

I'm sorry, I said. You were talking about parts?

It was the right thing to say. She laughed. Her napkin was pretty soggy so I handed her mine.

I can tell you this—she said, dabbing away—because you'll never meet her, but Sara's penis wasn't much more than a tease.

Good to know, I said. I finished my whiskey and took a drink of my beer. Because if I by some fluke I do meet her, I won't expect much.

Again she laughed, and the laugh quieted into a smile. She'd stopped crying and the napkin was a ball in her hand.

She had taken no more than a couple of bites of her fish tacos. She shrugged and told me the story again. Sara ran away from home in Maine when she was sixteen and learned to do everything on her own. She fixed cars. She built solar panels. She'd just dig in and figure things out. They lived together in a tent up in the hills for a year while Sara built them a cabin. But soon after it was finished Sara told Zochee she was too conventional for her. Sara wanted to be *alternative,* and Zochee was a student, a scholar, and had a bright grad-school, clinical, and research life ahead of her. Zochee was a Wonder Woman, Sara told her as she was dumping her. She needed to go off and live the Wonder Woman life. Sara was going to stay in the mountains. Sara was not going to leave her cabin. Sara was going to have her penis removed. Zochee started crying again when she said that. She gave me a look that appealed to me to understand her—and I might have—I don't know, the grasping, the yearning, the mystery of herself and her dissolving passion. She suddenly switched the subject and told me she felt lost. Happy to be going but feeling as if her life were spinning out. No anchor. Just one opportunity after another.

I'll live and study in Paris for a while, she said. I'll learn French and get a Ph.D. It'll be amazingly great—but so what? What does amazingly great mean? When the fellowship is over, I'll apply for jobs and some other place will make me an offer, and I'll go there.

My turn to shrug. I thought about the millions of people in the world living in squalor, working all day every day in sweatshops, living on tortillas and salt, rotting away in prisons, young women carrying water from a dirty well to a dirty husband and dirty children in a dirty shack or washing clothes in shit-ridden stream, dreaming, dreaming, dreaming.

I said, Amazingly great is better than amazingly shitty.

She laughed. You got a point there.

She didn't really know what I meant but I knew what she meant—or I thought I did. We live in a weird world where nobody is allowed to say the obvious, but Christ, she was a 29-years old woman. What she wanted was a good man to love

her madly and fuck her madly and give her mad children...
and then to still love her more. *More* was the key. The first was
easy. She was living an amazingly great empty life. Enduring
connections? She didn't have any. Or enough. I'm sorry, super great fellowships in Paris aside, what matters to a woman—what she'll talk about and live for and think about until
the day she dies—is who goes into her vagina and who comes
out. (Strange that I would say that—son of my mother, forgotten lover of too many—but hey, the exception proves the
rule.) Zochee stared at me. I turned to feign interest in the rest
of the gymnasts on television but couldn't. Who cared about
amazingly great Olympic medals? I took some large swallows
of my large beer. I'd let it sit too long and it was warmer than I
like. I took some more large swallows. I finished it and ordered
another. Another whiskey, too, which I drank fast, and then
pointed for another. I offered to buy her one but she shook her
head. I could feel her lost self still reaching out to me, a man
next to her at an airport bar. But as pathetic as that sounded,
I was tired enough—or after the second whiskey, anyway, just
buzzed enough—to feel touched. Of all the thousands of people in this airport, I was the one she climbed on to keep from
drowning in the swirl of random questions. Why was she going to Paris for this prestigious fellowship? Would she be going
if she didn't have a prestigious fellowship? Maybe she'd be going to _____ instead. What had she ever done that had any value at all beyond building an impressive résumé? She knew she
must have done something—she'd loved a trans-female who
rejected her for being too conventional. But how unfair! What
kind of conventional Slovenian immigrant girl lives in a tent
in Pennsylvania for a year? She hadn't even a clue how to argue, what to say. All she had—all any of us have when it comes
to love, unique as we think we are—is conventional language:
See me love me touch me and let me touch you, yes, I surrender,
oh oh oh , let's build a cabin—and of course—*neverletmego . . .*
      Come to bed with me, I said.
      She looked surprised—who wouldn't be?—and kind of half
smiled. Frowned and stared. Was I serious? I kept my face

blank, my eyes on her. I can't say for sure how serious I was when I asked it—the words, conventional words, just popped out, really, maybe as much a way out of the heaviness of her story, the sludgy sticky sadness of her questions. But when she asked me if I was serious, I looked at her mouth and her soft cheeks and I suddenly wanted to see her face up close and kiss her. And when I looked at her hands with too many rings and wrists with too many bracelets, I wanted to see her naked. I was tired of thinking, too. I wanted to do; I wanted to feel.

Go to bed with you? She seemed to be teasing me for my choice of words, my conventional choice of conventional words. The conventional nature of our barstool hookup. She wanted to get ironic, to rise up in the air and smile wryly at where we were.

I wouldn't go there with her. I said simply, There are motels near the airport.

She quickly looked down, sniffed, looked at her plate and her hands and then she pushed the plate with the rest of her fish tacos over to me. I don't want the rest, she said. Do you?

I nodded and began to eat her food with my fingers. She watched. The bartender, who had tried to sell me some food with my drinks, watched. I wonder how many strangers sat down and started talking and one of them finished the other's meal. It was intimate. I looked up at Zochee and she was looking at me with my mouth full and it was as though we'd already had sex. And it's that look that I remember when I think about her. Very open, curious, raw. Her skin gleaming in that light, the colored light of a barroom. Her lovely neck and shoulders, breasts, waist, her dark purple, almost black pants, these little black ballet shoes with no socks, one tucked under her round ass on the barstool—how can women sit that way? I could tell by her bright eyes—I almost felt I could have fallen in love with those eyes—moist and black, smart and funny—I could tell by her eyes that she was struggling with what as each second passed without an answer became more and more of a certainty. I mean, as each second passed without her saying no, the more certain it was to happen. I should have insisted she say yes, rather than nothing. Not that it would have changed my life, or we would have been together any longer than we were, but at least, I think, it would have been a little less melancholy for her. Personally, I don't mind melancholy—it's what things are, really, and I just wade through the darker waters and sometimes get to think the thoughts that fly away in the light. I wanted her for the reason men want strange women. So I could know something I didn't know before. But a woman usually needs more than that. She isn't necessarily in it for the knowledge—she's looking to be stirred up, transformed, and she needs a reason why she's letting this particular man do the stirring. And Zochee—I could see as she stared at me eating—really, I think all of this was going on in that two and a half minutes it took for me to devour her fish tacos and drink another whisky—she was trying to come up with a reason. She wanted something she could tell herself—even if it was only that she needed the physical sensation and thought I was just the man for that. But judging by her face, she couldn't even come up with that one. I mean, she asked for the bill and signed the receipt, put away her card, and looked at me as if to say, *Okay, ready?* But it was like her move to Paris. She hadn't a clue why she was going. Apparently just having the offer was enough of a reason. That and the fact that she hadn't been all that happy where she was.

We got a cab at the airport. It was raining and I held her hand in the back seat while she stared out the window at the blurry, bendy lights. At the hotel, I held an umbrella for her so she could get into the lobby dry. Maybe I was still trying to give her a reason. I felt her next to me, slightly behind me, while I checked in. I felt her hand on my shoulder. In the elevator to our room we both got out our itineraries to see exactly how much time we had until our flights—I had three hours, she two and a half. I held the door of our room for her and she rolled her suitcase in, I rolled in mine. She twirled, did a little curtsy. I closed the door behind us and bowed. It was one of those moments when you are trying to locate yourself in what is happening. It was one of those moments when you know sex means something—even if you don't know what—because of how it makes you feel, just the idea of it—a little giddy—and then of course you immediately start wondering bigger things, things that are only peripherally related to sex—questions like, *who is this person?*

But as soon as I had her clothes off—she suggested I take them off as she stood passively in front of the bathroom mirror watching as though still wondering who she was, where she was, searching for a clue as to why she was—as soon as I had her clothes off—and she was more beautiful naked than I imagined, so beautiful she made my legs weak and I dropped to my knees at her side to kiss the curve of her hip, worshiping that sweet swelling—as soon as I had her clothes off she went limp. But more than limp. I mean worse. She went from a quivering mass of smart, funny, feeling young woman to a dull, flat, tired young woman. Her eyes—something I never could have imagined two minutes before—dulled as dry as sand. She leaned—a terribly lonely gesture, as though her sigh was the last breath of her life—she leaned forward to put her hands on the sink in front of the mirror, and she said, *Okay,* as though to say, *I'm ready,* or *Go ahead,* or *Now.* Obedient, I stood up behind her and I looked at her flat dry eyes in the glass looking at me. At first I thought she wanted to know who I was, this man she was pulling inside her. But then I began to understand the question wasn't who I was but who she was: *Who am I sharing my body with this strange man?* she seemed to ask.

I feel as if I should say now that it was a horror, that the weirdness was more than I could handle, and that I could not finish—or something like that. But it wasn't like that. I found her passivity—except for her ringed fingers gripping the edge of the sink and those muscles in her well-braceleted wrists and forearms tense—I found her passivity, her eyes flat and empty, their weak searching like the weak reach of a dying man for something both invisible and out of reach—I found the whole thing suddenly, bizarrely erotic. I felt sucked up into her nothingness—and I liked it. I plunged onward with tremendous energy. I closed my eyes and pictured myself a small person, tiny, but with a huge cock wedged inside her—trapped inside her. I imagined I was hanging there like that, my feet not even touching the floor, and I quivered madly for what seemed like minutes while I ejaculated.

When it was over, I dropped off her like a bug. I staggered back against the bathroom wall and slid down to sit on the floor. So it was from that sweet angle that I watched her stand straight and take a deep breath, blink at herself in the mirror, and bend to pull up her panties without so much as a wipe, much less a shower. Then she reached for her bra and put that on, and then the rest of her clothes. She didn't speak and neither did I, and I started to wonder if she was even going to acknowledge me at all when she suddenly bent down to put a dry kiss on top of my head, said thank you, even though her eyes said something different, more complicated, something like, *okay, now we've both looked for ourselves in each other and found nothing.* I guess it was a real sharing of feeling even if the feeling was nothingness. Did it make me feel more alone? Yes, it did. She'd taken the handle of her rolling bag and pulled it out of the hotel room into the hallway and left, let the door close, even as I was still sitting naked on the bathroom floor. I waited a few seconds like that and then scrambled to my feet and opened the door but by then she was well down the hallway, just another pretty young woman on her way to Paris.

Okay, this is all more than you want to know, I'm sure. A little tale of my empty little life and sad sex with a stranger. True, true, all true. But you're the only one I could ever tell this too, and especially this part: *I liked it.* I mean, it made me *glad.* After Zochee left I became more aware of my breathing. More aware of my skin. I didn't want to shower either, I wanted to keep her scent on me, and even hours later on the flight south I could still smell her on my hands and my face, and when I thought of her on another plane, her body resting against a soft seat and her face reposed in sleep, I wanted to kiss her again. I had planned to drink heavily on the flight—I can't sleep on red-eye flights unless I do—but with her all over my skin I didn't have to. I felt content despite the sadness and loneliness and whatever else. I had a big vacuum inside me and I liked it, just as I liked that she was flying five hundred miles per hour through the night sky to Paris with my semen inside her. Semi-aroused for the next few hours, I didn't want to sleep. The music from the headphones was lighting fireworks in my head. My entire life I'd never had an opinion about classical music but on that dark flight with my head leaning against the window, I got a picture of the cold universe, a pattern of stars that went out forever with no love or hope between them but this wild, swirling music, these notes so beautiful and sad and infinite, they filled the darkness and made me mad with joy. Whatever happened between Zochee and me—judge it however you want—she could have gone off and had my baby, I could be flying away with a disease—but here's how I saw it: because of her—her what? her beauty? her cunt? her heartbreak?—because of her and that wild music (Bach—when it ended, the man said it was Bach) I fell a little bit more in love with the world.

–Me

lemmegoyoubastard

I turn off my headlamp and sit in the dark cabin and stare at
the yellow flicker of flames in the woodstove. The letter dis-
turbs me. I wonder what poor Zochee felt, flying away to Paris
that night? I wonder if she fell more in love with the world, or
less. Whether instead of feeling more of something, she felt
only more numb. Who knows? Nobody but Zochee herself,
and she flew off alone and never wrote me a letter. I wonder
if she got pregnant. I wonder if she ever figured out a reason.
What a dreamlike way to live. It makes me dizzy and unhappy
to think about. Yet Tommy's emptiness and joy seem to swallow me—and the precariousness of his life has my stomach
in knots. I think how he lived there, *here,* with that feeling,
this feeling, an empty feeling in an empty place—no love nor
light nor hope nor certitude nor help for pain—and for a long
time. He had to find his pleasures and some joy there in that
empty place. He was a depressive I'd cut down from a light fixture in a hotel bathroom, and he was still looking (and finding

and writing to me) reasons to live. At least until he couldn't anymore. Zochee was a Wonder Woman. She saved him for a while, as I had, but there can't be a Wonder Woman every time you need one. Eventually you've got to get good and drunk to go to sleep.

I stand up and tap the box of red wine I'd set on the counter and pour myself another big cup. The letter distracted me enough to forgot about the bear. Now I'm tempted to pull the drape aside but I resist and kneel before the woodstove and wedge in another log. I wonder if I'll sleep. I want the wine but also hope I don't have to pee before morning so before I sit down I set the cup of wine on a shelf where I can't reach it. The Zochee story seems different from his other letters—less smart-alecky—but also it feels like a complete story. It occurs to me then that maybe it didn't really happen, that maybe it's a short story he wrote and instead of sending it to a magazine, he sent it to me. But the first time I read it I didn't think about that. I was on Picnic Point—a curving finger of land that extends from the University of Wisconsin campus about a quarter mile out into Lake Mendota. I remember the sandy beach, the wind, hair in my face and the smell of sunscreen. I remember the motor boats and sail boats out in the big green waves of the bay. The blue sky with puffy clouds. I remember lying on my back and closing my eyes and letting the sun heat my body through my swimsuit and mix colors behind my eyelids. I felt a wild exuberance in my belly, both mean and tender. I don't know. It seems pretty clear now. It was August. My roommate was about to drop onto my belly a letter from Tom Connor about Zochee the Wonder Woman. Something was going to change.

I'll start at the beginning of that day, though, I mean the very beginning when I woke to the sun streaming in my third-story window and a breeze carrying the smell of recently cut grass. From the outside, it might have looked like the highpoint of my life so far, that morning, the morning I got the Zochee letter. I'd finished college in three years and been accepted to medical school right here. So I actually knew what I was going to do, stay in Madison, become a doctor. I knew I should feel like the happiest person in the world. I liked Madison, Mad Town. Mad City. I had three wonderful years behind me and a bright future in front of me. What more did anybody need? I also had a boyfriend, a secret fiancé, actually, as we agreed we'd be married after my first year of med school. He was from the Chicago suburb near mine—and we had a lot of friends and acquaintances in common up in Madison. His name was Pierre (Peer, like the capital of South Dakota) Malone, and he was president of the college Republicans, a club I'd drifted toward in part because of my crush on him. He was tall and handsome and I was comforted by his certainty. He loved me and wasn't afraid to say it, and frankly that felt good, like having a big truck in the driveway in case I needed it.

The phone rang too early that morning, waking me. It was my mother, of course. She'd been calling almost every day. I know she was trying to share her joy but I'd been up late the night before with Pierre and didn't feel quite right. She kept saying how hard I'd worked for it. How happy and relieved I must be to finally have it all figured out. I don't know why her words bothered me so much. I *had* worked hard and I *was* glad to have graduated quickly and be headed for med school right here. But the more she said it, the worse I felt. For one thing, she'd been calling so often and saying the same thing so many times that I'd begun to feel as if she was really talking about herself. How hard *she* worked. How relieved *she* was—as though a great big weight had been lifted off of her, raising me, and now she could finally relax. But if she could relax, I couldn't. Just under my happy skin, I was very nervous about starting med school. I didn't know if I was smart enough. I was nervous about getting married next year. I didn't know if I could be a good wife to Pierre. I didn't know how hard any of it would be, only that everybody always said med school and marriage are *really, really* hard.

"Of course you're relieved, Mom," I said, "You don't have to actually go to med school!"

It was silent for a second. I could feel her taking the time she needed to ignore my childish tone. "You'll do fine," she said. "It's everything you've worked for and I know you'll do fine."

My mother didn't exactly have an accent. She'd been fourteen when she came from Poland. But she didn't speak like everybody else, either. So when she said "everything you worked for" the *r*'s were a little too pronounced, as was the *k* in worked. It always made me feel sorry for her. Anyway, it softened my tone. I said, "Mom, I didn't work any harder than anybody else. I had lots of friends who worked really hard and didn't get in." This wasn't exactly true. I had one good friend, Lisa, who'd worked harder than me, and she didn't get in. Just couldn't get a high enough score on the MCAT.

"I'm lucky," I said. "For some genetic reason I take tests well. And other things just kind of fell the right way."

She didn't like that. She'd had the good luck (everybody must have told her so) to be visiting an uncle in Chicago when the Nazis went into Poland in 1939, separating her from her family forever, so she'd never been a big fan of the word *luck*. It struck me that it must have been one of the first English words she learned, and here in America where we tend to confuse luck with virtue, the word would have seemed grossly unfair. She was a girl swimming in anxiety and sadness, and she grew to be a woman still afloat in both of those pools. Nevertheless, my mother was innately kind.

"Okay," she said, "call it what you want. Your father says you have the world by the short hairs. I never understood that until this morning. Have you heard other men say it? We're happy for your success. You deserve it. Enjoy it."

I suddenly felt too queasy to argue. Besides, Pierre was at the door, back from his early work out at the gym, so I hung up. He was handsome in the morning light and I felt rescued from a conversation that was making me feel worse by the second. I must have hugged him too tightly—he just showered and smelled clean—because he suddenly wanted to have sex again. But my stomach was turning and my breasts felt tender, and with my mother's voice still in my ear (and after how many times last night) I just plain wasn't in the mood. Also,

I was beginning to feel that no matter how much I wanted it, he'd always want it more. It made me tired even to think about, and grumpy, too, especially after we did it again anyway right there on the couch and he was so happy and suggested we go to Picnic Point to hang out. We brought beer and sandwiches, and drinking the beer—a whole half a bottle—seemed to hit me wrong as well. It made my face feel heavy and numb and my head ache. Even the sun and the happy blue waters and the joyful shouts from the windsurfers seemed to conspire to get on my nerves.

And then I got the letter. My roommate Sandy brought it to me and dropped in on my belly. I sat up. I didn't like the way Pierre looked at it. Or how he asked who it was from even though he knew. I normally would have read it in private, but his prying eyes provoked me so I opened it enthusiastically and read it right there on the beach. I wasn't in love with Tommy anymore, but I was eager for a distraction, and the story was certainly that. Tiny Tommy with the giant cock. The naked and sexy and vulnerable Zochee. It was funny, too. *Who goes into her vagina and who comes out.* I thought of Tommy saying such a thing, thinking such a thing and wanted to laugh—even share it with somebody, but when I heard Pierre say, "What'd he say?" I felt my jaw clamp shut.

Pierre asked again. "What'd he say?"

I didn't have a clue how to answer. There was a long P.S. that I was too distracted (and irritated) to read and would save for later. I lay back down again and closed my eyes and let the sun melt into colors that swirled across the dark underside of my eyelids. I was going to go to med school because that's the way my life had played out, that's the way things had gone. I got along with school and school got along with me, and as I said before, I had the right genes to take tests well. Like Zochee on her way to Paris, I felt suddenly detached from my own life, as though none of it had been my will. Why did I even come to college? Because Tommy never asked me to go down to Central America. Why did I even apply to med school? Because my mother's mother, killed by the Nazis, was a doctor, and so

Mom had always wanted me to be one, too.

Pierre took on a lighter tone, "Hey, what's that Connor up to now?"

I stayed quiet until he'd given up on me and I could open my eyes just enough to peek at him. He sat next to me in the sand, leaning back on his hands, staring out at the lake, trying to be patient, I suppose. I'd been trying to figure out if I could live with him, but I had the sudden premonition that Pierre was the one that was going to have a hard time living with me. I was going to be very busy. I wasn't a cheerful person. We weren't sexually compatible. I thought of Tiny Tommy again, dropping off the back of pretty Zochee onto the floor. Of Zochee bending to put a dry kiss on his head. I tried to think if I knew what Bach sounded like. I thought of Zochee and Tommy, their scents on each other, flying off to different parts of the world. I thought of Tommy semi-aroused all through the night. I felt the hot sun on my body through my nylon suit and realized I was turned on. But when I squinted my eyes again to look at Pierre, I felt cold. There was nothing wrong with him, nothing at all, but Tommy's letter—all of that empty space, all of those stars!—his letter had focused my mind. *What went in and what came out.* Could I *talk about and live for and think about* Pierre and Pierre's children for the rest of my life?

"Pierre," I said.

"Yeah, babe?"

I was still lying on my back. I'd closed my eyes again. I was impressed by how Tommy wasn't afraid to just say the words— *Will you sleep with me?*—just to see what would happen. Why not? If he felt it, he said it. I determined to try to be just as honest.

"Pierre," I said.

"What?"

Say it, I thought. Just say it. I opened my eyes and peeked at him. He was smiling as though I must be teasing him. I took a deep breath and closed my eyes again. It was easier that way. "I don't think I love you," I said.

"What?" he said.

I opened my eyes again. He was still smiling. "No," I said. "I'm serious about this. I've thought about it a lot. *I don't think I love you.*"

Confused now, he wrinkled his forehead. It was his thinking frown, and he made it until he believed he had an answer. It never took him long. "Janine," he said. "What the fuck did Connor write you?"

"Nothing," I said.

Now his face was angry. "Lemme see that letter."

"It's mine," I said.

"That bastard." He tried to grab it but I wouldn't let him have it.

"No," I said. "He has a girlfriend. Her name is Zochee."

"Her name is what?"

"Zochee the Wonder Woman."

Because he couldn't grab the letter, he picked up sand with both hands, squeezed it in his fists. "Zochee the Wonder Woman," he said. "That figures."

I wondered how that figured but didn't say anything. I didn't know what to say. I felt as if I had said it all. Then I thought of Tommy's letter and said, "With you I'm just too far from *I surrender*. I'm just too far from *neverletmego*."

"Jesus!" he said, frustrated. "What's that mean?"

I wasn't sure myself, so I said—as much to myself as to him—I said, "Think about it. Just think about it."

We had a big fight later that evening on the front lawn of my house. He'd followed me home and kept asking if I was happy, and I said I didn't know. He asked how could I not be sure about something like that? I cried, feeling like an idiot—he was right, how could I not know the answer to that simple question? But I didn't, and when he approached me to comfort me, when he tried to take me in his arms, I panicked. I knew for sure that was the last place I wanted to be. I slapped him and ran away. I'd never slapped a man before and my hand stung. In the dark it felt as if I was running faster than I was. He wasn't chasing me, but he shouted my name over and over again, and as I heard his voice get fainter and fainter, it seemed to give me energy. I ran all the way to my friend Lisa's house on the lake shore. She rented a room in the basement. I knocked on the door but nobody answered. I went around the side of the house and walked out to the end of the pier. I love the way footsteps sound on a pier at night. I sat down and dangled my feet over the water and caught my breath and thought of Tommy's stars and it was a stupid shock to realize the stars I could see up over the lake were the same stars. *Tommy? Where was Tommy? Wandering the world having sex with strangers. What did he have to do with my life? Nothing.*

Lisa came out the pier behind me and sat down. I felt her hand on my shoulder. Lately I'd been the one comforting her about not getting into med school, so this was a change. She seemed to know exactly why I was there. My roommate probably heard the shouting in the yard and called her. I told her the story of not wanting to be in Pierre's arms, of being just plain sick of his arms and chest and body. I told her I slapped him hard. This seemed to amuse her. She liked to play what I thought of as a tedious game and she did it again now.

"Which would you prefer?" she asked. "To be in stud man's arms? Or to swim in a pool filled with vomit?"

I told her the pool. She said, "Oh, baby. Would you like a husband who didn't like you to hold him?"

It took me a moment to realize she was dead serious, that she'd suddenly veered from the game.

"What?" I said.

"Would you want to be married to somebody who didn't want you to touch him?"

I shook my head. Lisa was the only one who knew we were engaged and at that moment, I was grateful I'd told her.

"Well." She shrugged. "Then poor Pierre." She said it with all of the syllables. "Don't you think he'd maybe like to have a wife who *likes* him?"

"I *do* like him," I said. "I just don't *love* him."

She almost laughed. "Then offer to take care of his dog when he's out of town or something. Don't marry him."

At that moment, sitting on the pier and looking at her face

in the night, I suddenly thought I knew something as clearly as I'd ever known anything. And true to my new honesty of blurting out what I was thought I knew, I said, "Lisa, do you love him?" And before she could answer, I said, "Is that why you're telling me this?"

I'd caught her off guard by the question, and her face snapped back as though I'd slapped her as well. She'd wanted to go to med school but didn't get in. She'd been brave about that. She'd even let me comfort her, although my long faces on her behalf must have been difficult to bear. And now it turned out I had a fiancé she loved.

"Fuck you, Janine McCarthy," she whispered, and I remember she said my last name like that, my whole name, and it felt like a spear through my heart. She stood up behind me.

"Lisa," I called, but her only answer was her footsteps on the pier. I wanted to apologize. I called her name again but she stepped off the pier and onto the dewy grass and left me in silence. Well, not quite. I listened to the crickets. I listened to the lap of waves against the shore. The night was dark and the lake was dark and I felt suddenly very lonely.

I BROKE UP FOR good with Pierre later that evening. Considering the fact that I thought I was doing him a favor, I was surprised at how hard it was. First of all, when I went back to where he lived, he thought I'd changed my mind about him and decided I not only loved him but wanted him like crazy. He opened the door and hugged me—I let him hug me, it happened so fast, and within five seconds he was already ready for sex. I had to peel him off to tell him that's not why I was there. I was there to tell him that *not loving him* meant we'd have to break up, that it was only fair, and that's when he started to cry. It totally floored me. Suddenly this big man's face was shiny with tears and he was begging me to give him another chance. I felt terrible. I also felt resolved. I told him it wasn't about chances. I wanted to hold his head and comfort him but I kept my distance. I just said what I said, matter-of-factly, and when I started to turn away he stopped me. I felt his hand on my shoulder. He turned me and I could see that just that fast his tears had dissolved to self-pity.

"Gimme a last little bit," he said.

"What?" I shook my head, irritated.

"You owe me that much, at least."

"You've got to be kidding," I said.

From self-pity, it's only a short hop to meanness—I could see it in his face as he moved in close and took my shoulders with both hands, took them too hard, actually.

"No," he said, "I'm not kidding."

We were in a basement—the house where he lived, that he shared with his friends—where he had a bed right next to his work bench. I started to panic, or to almost panic. I started thinking he could do whatever he wanted and if I screamed, nobody was home so nobody would hear. And then I thought something else. I thought, *if he tries something, I'll kill him.* I knew it as surely as I'd known anything in my life. If he tried, I'd grab one of the tools on the work bench—a hammer, a crow bar—and hit him over the head until his skull cracked. I thought this so coldly I shocked myself. If, according to Tom Connor, men fell into killing as easy as they fall into fucking, for me, killing would even be easier. Pierre must have felt my homicidal resolve. I must have been giving off killer waves. I think he knew that if he messed with me, he'd die.

"Lemmegoyoubastard," I said, and he did. He let go of my shoulders. His big hands fell useless at his side. He stepped back and then turned sideways because I think he was starting to cry again. This time I didn't have to stifle any desire to comfort him. I said good bye and went up the stairs and through the empty living room and outside. Earlier in the evening I'd been feeling such peace and strength, then just a moment ago, in the basement of my boyfriend's house, terror and vulnerability followed by a homicidal certainty and strength.

If he had gone any farther, I would be a killer right now. Because he didn't, I am not. If somebody were to ask me today, *Why did you become a doctor and not a killer?* I'd say, *Luck.* What would you call it?

I could smell the grass and the black walnut trees in the yard, and the lakes just blocks away in either direction, and I walked all the way back to my place where I sat on the front steps to think about things. I knew my mom would not be upset. She was worried about me starting med school with a boyfriend, and the idea of starting it alone made me feel calmer as well.

I still had Tommy's letter in my pocket, so I got it out and by the porch light read the postscript I'd been too distracted to read earlier.

"P.S. Morning and out the window bright sun and a beach below like a long white stripe between the water and trees. The plane landed in San Salvador and filled with men wearing sunglasses and Guayaberra shirts and I imagine them killers who fly from country to country. They drink coffee or booze or both, just like me, and incline their heads toward the window, just like me, do their jobs, just like me (although I don't really have a job, but hey, a guy can pretend). They do theirs from behind the tinted glass of a Range Rover picking up live people and dumping off dead ones late at night on deserted roadsides—and then back to the airport in Guat City or Teguc. They board the plane and smile at the stewardess, they bring presents to their sons and daughters, sure they do. They may even be happy, which bothers the small part of me, especially because I don't know if I am. I know I like sitting on the sidewalk with a *compañero* sipping *guaro* and lime, *salsa* music jumping through the walls of the cantina behind us, watching the setting sun bright up the white alley wall, the orange roofs, the green cypress in the yard. This is what I want to remember always and knowing soon I'll forget only makes me want to remember it more: the all-night cafe in the center of the city and counting my coins to know I can't afford anything but coffee even though I want *guaro*, too; the clean light and the old man sitting in the corner signaling the waitress that he will pay for me, so I order coffee, a shot of *guaro*, and a piece of cake! I nod my head to thank him and feel the hairs on my neck rise. I want to remember, too, the young mother and her two toddlers coming right up to the window next to my table, the window which is not glass and opens right on the sidewalk, a pretty young worn-out woman looking for a place to stay the night. Three a.m. already, and I want to remember dropping my remaining coins through the window into her sweaty hand and her *Diós te bendiga*, and I don't want to forget any of it and so at dawn I'll be back sitting on the steps of my room listening to birds in the trees across the street below, listening to a dog bark next door, writing a letter to you beneath a door light on the steps of a *pensión* in a foreign city, watching a man in a sleeveless white shirt walk by with a radio on his shoulder playing big band dance music. The streets are empty. I tap my foot to the music as it fades down the block thinking of home, of love, of where and when I might die. I stare at the few heartachy stars hanging on as the sky brightens to dawn. I watch the last of them twinkle out and only then go inside and feel safe enough to sleep soundly and forget until I see it all again the next night, too."

IN THE CABIN I fold the letter and put it back in its envelope just as I did more than twenty-five years ago on the steps of my apartment house in Madison, Wisconsin. I kneel before the woodstove and toss in another log. The wind is still blowing, a flood of cold air washing down the mountains and through the canyon to spread eastward across the plains. The cabin shudders but stays intact. It must be built for this, I think. It can't have stayed built all of these years only to break up in pieces when I'm here. Just in case, I take my big cup of wine off the mantle and sit down again, this time to drink. Maybe I'll give up men forever. My aunt was a nun, a wonderful, intelligent woman who taught grade school, and I think of her and her mind blissfully undistracted by who went in and who came out. But it's too late for that. I sip the wine and close my eyes and remember sitting on the steps that night and staring at the sky and thinking of Tom Connor on the steps in another city thousands of miles away. It was as if we shared a soul window, or whatever you'd call it, looking out at the Big Empty and feeling the universe expand. I remember the night was balmy with August heat. I remember I tried to smoke a cigarette but it made me sick to my stomach. I remember thinking Tommy could have a baby over in Paris. I remember thinking he could be carrying a disease. But I also knew if he showed up right then and there—if I happened to turn my head on that night and saw him standing in the yard—well, he could have bit me open like a truffle. I could fall into loving him as easily as I could fall into killing Pierre and I didn't know what any of those feelings meant about me. I thought of tiny Tommy falling off Zochee and I thought of failing every test in medical school and what would it matter? I don't know why those thoughts amused me but they did, and I felt suddenly grateful to whatever swirling farting hiccupping power in the universe had flung my mother out of Poland, her doctor mother into the ovens, and me to that place, to that city, to that front step, listening to that whippoorwill in the night. I even tried to say a prayer of gratitude, which was just me closing my eyes and trying again to feel it all—more than I could name and as much as I could bear. I wanted to thank Lisa for helping me know what to do, and I would've been much sadder if I'd known that although we'd stay friends for many years, we'd never again be as close as we were before that night.

I'm sure I thought of a lot more things in the hours before dawn. Most I've forgotten, but reading the letter again here in the cabin has made me remember—and not without shame when I think about the lack of grace I showed him at the end— how on that evening in August 1985, because of Tom Connor and the beauty of his words, I too fell a little bit more in love with the world.

just please don't steal my little ear

As it turned out, I had more than just a big feeling inside me. I was pregnant as well. Of course it was Lisa who had to tell me. It was about a week later and over the course of the last few days she heard me complaining about my nausea and sore breasts and sensitivity to smells in between my complaints about my mother and the terrible heat wave and the party boys next door, and she got right in front of me one day out in front of my house and she stopped me—I was in a hurry to go somewhere, anywhere, I don't know where, I was restless—but she got in front of me and gave me this long, flat look.

I stopped on the sidewalk. "What?"

"Don't ask me," she said. "I'm not smart enough to be a doctor." She wasn't being pathetic—it had become our game whenever I asked her a question. So I said, "Better ask me, then, because I am." That too was part of our game. She said, "Well, Doctor, when was your last period?"

"What?" I said.

She shrugged and just kept giving me that look.

I felt my face flush with blood and the beginnings of a desperate little something flutter in my abdomen.

"I'm late," I told her, trying to sound calm. "But I'm often late."

I know it sounds unbelievable now, but the thought had not crossed my mind. The little fluttering in my stomach stopped. Or if it didn't exactly stop, it was minor in comparison to the feeling that somebody suddenly dropped a car on top of me. I was stunned, breathless. The fluttering had become a weight inside me. My womb—I don't know that I'd ever thought those words before, but they came to me then—*my womb* felt suddenly too heavy. I looked for a place to sit down. I did sit down, right there on the sidewalk. I crossed my legs and covered my face.

"Janine?" Lisa said.

But when she got me inside and sat me on the couch, made me a cup of tea, and brought it to me steaming hot—*Lisa was kind! My mother was kind as well! Why wasn't I kind?*—and asked what I felt, all I could say was I was embarrassed. Embarrassed that she'd seen all the bad news first—*you are not in love, you are pregnant*—and embarrassed that I'd let it happen. Since I was in high school, I'd been the one to get and supply all of my friends with condoms, even birth control pills that I got from my cousin. I felt as if I'd been caught doing something really, really stupid. Something that everybody knows you don't do—have unprotected sex. Yet that wasn't even true. I'd been on birth control, I didn't miss taking my pills. So then what I felt was injustice. I knew girls who were always forgetting, but I never forgot—why had this happened to me?

Of course I couldn't ask the questions, and even if I had, Lisa would have been unable to answer. She just kept saying poor Janine, poor Janine. I will always love her for not asking me what every other person I knew would have asked me at that moment: What are you going to do?

I retreated to my room and didn't come out for days. I lay in bed and got up to puke in the mornings as loudly as I could—

not stifled little pukes like I was doing before Sandy had gone on vacation. Mainly I just lay in bed. I didn't read. I didn't watch movies. I listened to the birds out the window. I didn't know which call came from which bird, but I tried to hear how many different birds there were, how many different sounds I could keep track of and distinguish. I gave each song a different name in order to help me keep them separate. If you had come to visit me, you would have seen me lying in bed, almost comatose, and you would have thought I was terribly depressed and you might have thought that I was thinking, "To be or not to be?"

But in fact I was most likely listening very carefully to a bird call and thinking, "Is that a Rosie-roo-REE? Or a Rum-tum-TEE?

When my mom called, I pretended nothing was different. I answered the phone in the morning from my bed. When I sat in just the right odd way, with my head tilted and as high as I could stretch, I could see Lake Monona out the window. In the morning I could hear the ski boats. I told her I was learning to water ski. A few days later, I told her I'd learned to drop a ski and was now doing slalom. A few days after that, I told her I'd learned to drop the second ski and had skied barefoot, skimming across the lake surface early in the morning. I told her it was exhilarating. It was oddly liberating to tell such bold lies to my mother, especially at a time when my body kept telling me I was her and she was me. It was almost as if I knew she'd forgive me. I knew she'd know exactly why I should be forgiven. I felt two things very strongly, and with more certainty than I'd felt anything in a long time. The first was that I had something inside me that I wanted out of me as fast as I could motivate myself to get up and get it done. And two, a tremendous weakness, a terrible inability to move, a tenderness that made me want to weep at the beauty of the sound of the mourning dove out the window.

My father was raised Irish Catholic and my mother Jewish and although that may seem like a lot of religion, in order to keep the house from being saturated, they over-compensated and the house had none. Having a Jewish mother makes me officially Jewish, (especially a Jewish mother whose mother died in the holocaust) but we never went to synagogue, never sang a holy song on the Sabbath, never lit a candle at Hanukkah. I know my parents believed in sacred things, but I don't know what. I suppose they settled on money and nice things. My mom had her ghosts, of course, and my father had his—what Irish ex-Catholic doesn't?—but a testament to their power is how they were never named or spoken of out loud.

I think I *lay in* for almost ten days. It secretly amused me to be like the woman in nineteenth-century novels. If those women could take to their beds, why couldn't I? No birth control back then, so they were probably all pregnant as well. Lisa came to visit every day. She brought me food but she didn't linger, she didn't sit on my bed and pass time. What I know now was happening was she was beginning to have sex with Pierre. I don't think I would have minded, but I am glad she didn't tell me. She'd end up married to him by the end of the year, and after four children in six years, he'd leave her for another woman—a dozen other women, probably.

Mark told me men like Pierre were doomed to irritate their wives with their libido, doomed to feel the attention of other women who wanted them for the same thing that was driving their wives to take cover. I suppose Mark was talking about himself as well. I didn't think that at the time, but I was young. He apologized once to me, just once. He said his eyes were always on me—they never left me, and underneath my pain, I knew it was true. Regardless of whatever brief consolation he'd taken, his eyes were on me. I also know there were many days and nights I wished they weren't. I didn't like all the time to be the center of his affections, and so although my body stayed faithful, there were long gaps—days, weeks, months—during which I didn't care to look very carefully at him at all.

IN THE CABIN, I push aside yesterday's toast and the open jelly jar and a dirty dish from who knows when, eye the growing furniture barricade at the back door, and reach for Tommy's next letter. It's the one that finally got me out bed and on with my life but I don't remember what the letter said. In the light from my headlamp, I notice my Big Gulp wine cup and I stand up and reach for it and take a sip, then another, and then, finally, a big gulp. There. I look through the 1985 stack on the table to find the letter. At first I think it must be the wrong one but the date is right, fifteen days after Zochee. I skim through the first part. He was on a rant about what he called the American religion. He said religion is not necessarily what church you go to but what you worship. Carved stone, corn, buffalo, oil. It's anything you'll kill and die for. But he said for Americans, killing and dying—but especially killing—*is* the religion. We say we're killing and dying for freedom, but in reality our killing and dying have become disconnected to any actual freedom. Did we really think Vietnamese peasants were going to come over and put us in chains? He said our wars are more religious spectacle than they are a true fight for survival. We sacrifice our soldiers and countless foreign soldiers and civilians to our *Freedom god* just as the Mayans sacrificed virgins to the *Corn god*. The causal connection is specious but the spectacle makes us feel good about ourselves. Nothing like a little bloodshed to strengthen our resolve. Whereas a medieval peasant looked for succor from pain and suffering and death in the stories and pictures he saw in church, we look for the same thing in the stories we see in our movies. (*Did you know our president was a movie star?* he asked again.) And one of the central, comfort-giving stories our American movies tell us is that in some faraway place (and sometimes right there in your city as well) our good guys are making the world a better place by killing all of the bad guys—Indians, Nazis, Japs, gooks, terrorists, crooks—*every single one of them.* In other words, our stories tell us over and over again that war—violence—makes the world a better place. Past wars made our lives good. Current wars are protecting us right now. And future wars will make the world brighter for our children.

Curious about how or why a political rant would have gotten me out of bed, I turn the page and read on:

"A beggar man wearing only shorts, old-looking, wizened, approaches an old gringo wearing a peach *Guayaberra* shirt standing on the curb with his foot on a case of empty beer bottles, smoking a cigarette and waiting for a ride. The beggar puts his face very close to the face of the old gringo and pantomimes smoking. The old gringo takes a drag on his cigarette and tries to look past him. The beggar decides he's going to make this impossible, so he leans even closer, his face just inches away from the old gringo. He pantomimes smoking again. The old gringo endures this as long as he can. He can't just walk away because he's got the big case of empty bottles and he's waiting for somebody. He tries a few more drags on his cigarette but they're no good anymore so finally he just gives it to the beggar, who puts it in his mouth, rocks back, steps around the old gringo and continues down the street. I don't know why I write that—maybe because that's what I'm looking at as I'm sitting in this café, that and at my waitress with the skin like chocolate pudding, a *Guanacasteca*. She's wearing a white blouse and white pants and I'm trying to avoid looking because what I'm really looking at are her black panties and black bra showing through the sheer fabric of her clothes. Her body is smooth and tight, and whether she's taking an order, clearing a table, or carrying food, she looks as if she's got a slow dance going on under her skin. Really, it's the most suggestive stroll I've ever seen, and over and over again it says, *Come hither, dude.*

"Then she stops walking and sits down at a table and uses the palms of her hands to spread dried red beans across the wooden surface. Her blood-red fingernails click and sort, click and sort, looking for little pebbles in the beans. When she finds one, she picks it up between her thumb and forefinger and throws it on the floor. She asks what I want without taking her eyes off the beans. *Casado con bistek y resbaladera*, I say, and she calls out *Casado con bistek y resbaladera* loudly so the people in the kitchen can hear, still without taking her eyes off the beans. I decide that conscious or not, everything she does is foreplay. I don't care if she's sixteen years old, her every move is a step in the dance that will keep the human race going, thank goodness. She owns the world. She'll be pregnant within the year. She'll make a life with that body. She'll sustain a life—what else is there? What else has any meaning? A career in finance?

"At the very moment I'm thinking this and about to throw myself face first onto the ground—what am I but an insect in comparison to the light of the world in her blood?—I hear a woman screaming in the street. I look out the open door. A woman is walking with the old gringo and he's carrying the crate of empty bottles. About a half a block behind them is a little girl, maybe eight, maybe ten, and while the drunk mother and the old gringo walk away, the mother keeps turning to lob all sorts of insults back over her shoulder at the little girl. She's saying terrible things to her, calling her one nasty name after another. The little girl kind of hangs back, right outside where I'm sitting. Maybe I'm super-sensitive to mother abandonment, but you should have seen her face. Crying miserably—and I think maybe I should invite her in, this little girl. Buy her breakfast, because…I say to myself, *you want to change the world? Well, here's your chance!* But when I look up, she's still following her mother. Of course she is! (Do I identify, or what?) She's too young to leave her. But in two or three years she'll be picked up by one of the village raptors, won't she? He'll take her away. Buy her some clothes. And part of the horror is she'll think she's been liberated."

I put the letter down and take another big gulp of wine from my Big Gulp cup. Out the window, I can see a bear-less meadow in the first light of dawn. No fog today— too windy. The unending sound of it is beginning to get on my nerves but the sky is the palest of pale blues where it has begun to turn day. I'll have to take a walk today. I'll have to go to sleep, and then get up and take a walk. Past the first line of trees, tucked along the inside of that blue curve of river, is a pasture with a lot of horses. I'll take a walk down there. The horses have been in that grass for weeks and no bear has come and chased them and killed them. A horse pasture seems to me to be a civilized place, a safe place.

I know that Tommy's letter had nothing to do with my decision. I'd made that almost the first moment I realized I was pregnant. But after ten days in bed, the letter did have something to do with my resolve.

I put down the cup and pick up the letter again. Here's how it ends:

"Strange as it might seem, I met the old gringo the next day sitting in the same café. His name was Paul and he told me he was rich. I said, well you're drunk, too, so buy me a drink. He did, and when I had it safely in my hot little hand, I asked him about the little girl yesterday. He tells me, sure, she's definitely fucked. I say if you're so rich, why can't you help her? He says he could if he felt like it. He said he could get her in school somewhere, says he'll even grant—like God, he will *grant* things—he'll even grant it's a good thing to reach out and rescue a child off the street.

"But, he says, what about the other billion?

"I don't know what he means.

"Don't you see? he asks.

"No, I say.

"It's meaningless, he says.

"What is?

"It's like you and your writing, he says.

"What? (I'd unfortunately told him I was writing a novel.)

"Don't deceive yourself, he says. You can art that moment. (He really said that—*art the moment*—and I was impressed.)

"You can make it social like you say you want to do and maybe you'll do it so well a hundred years from now a reader will get goosebumps and feel moved, but when the goosebumps are gone and the feeling's blown away, so what? The little girl—or a thousand million like her, will still be fresh prey.

"I wanted to ask him how all of that fit together, but I also wanted to drink some more. Still the blood was rushing to my face as I fought to keep the words down. I must have started to speak because he raised a hand to say let's stop this right here. Then he took an ear out of his pocket. I swear to god. It looked like a dried apricot. It wasn't until I felt it between my fingers that I knew it came from a human being. His face brightened as he watched me hold it.

"I've carried that since Vietnam, he says, just to remind me.

"Remind you of what? I say, handing it back to him.

"He shrugged. Just to remind me, that's all.

"He put the ear back in his pocket and ordered another refreshment. One of many fine beverages we drank long into the night. I had to help him back to his *pensión.* The whole way back he kept saying, Don't steal my ear, okay? Just please don't steal my little ear. I lay him in his bed and he patted his chest pocket to make sure it was still there. He seemed very grateful it was. He said, Two good things about commies is you don't steal much, and you know how to drink.

"Wenchita," the letter concluded. "I'm glad you're also on this weird wide world, but this is how weird the wide world is. (Say that ten times fast.) Or maybe just how weird I am, because I'm glad even for the horror. I'm glad for that ear and for how happy the old geezer was that I didn't steal it. I left him there in the room grinning and patting his pocket and the night outside suddenly bloomed possibilities. I felt like General Patton gazing out over a battlefield bursting with flowers, green grass, and the burned and bloated bodies of the dead.

"I love it, the General says in that famous line from the movie. God help me, I do love it so."

call it the river of suffering

Lisa's sister counseled me through the process. She told me it was a myth perpetrated by right-wing nuts that women feel sad and guilty after having an abortion. She took me by the hand. She walked me into the clinic. She got me the appointment and made sure I got there and waited and drove me home in a car she borrowed from Pierre, of all people, who thought she needed it to drive to Milwaukee for a Brewers game. I remember feeling the ache inside me and thinking *yes, this is me, a woman now, this is me no longer a girl blown by the wind but a woman who has decided she's going to become a doctor.*

Afterward, I did feel sad, though I never bothered to correct Lisa's sister, and the sadness was a sadness I absorbed over time into my cells, and it made me bigger, more compassionate, braver. Sacrifice gives our lives meaning, so going to medical school suddenly had a meaning it hadn't had before. Of course, having the child would have also given my life a meaning it hadn't had before, but I did what I did—and if I didn't exactly feel guilty, as though I'd done a moral wrong, I did feel ashamed, as though at my core I might not have what it took to be the kind of person I'd always hoped I could be. I also felt disappointed, as though I'd failed at something. Oddly, this disappointment made me more patient with myself, and more patient with everything and everybody else as well. I developed an odd ability to stop time whenever I felt irritated. I'd be in the grocery store checkout, or waiting to cross the street, or getting on the bus to go to class, and I could use my brain to slow things down. To become hyper-aware of my five senses. To breathe the air—and to hear it move. To see the light—and to close my eyes and feel its textures on my skin. I could feel myself awake in the world like never before. Classes were hard, but I studied like a woman possessed. Perhaps I was. Sometimes I felt as though I could absorb words off the page directly into my mind. Sometimes I could hear the instructors' words so clearly that their voices became my voice, and in my dreams I was giving their lectures. My picture of the future changed from grainy and unpleasant to sharp and hopeful. The classes, the routine, the hard work—all of it put me in touch with something bigger than me and as old as humanity itself. Call it *the river of suffering* and by studying to be a doctor, I was building my house on its banks. Does that sound too grand? Well, it didn't to me. Those lovely, focused years were about making myself better. Somebody, somewhere, was going to need me, and that's how I'd work, one patient at a time. No need to distract myself with the other billion. I had an instructor who used to say to us, *The healthy and happy people today will be miserable and sick tomorrow. Even the yet to be born will someday need your help.*

Next time, I told myself, I'd be ready.

three

he looks me over pretty good

In the morning I wake to a knocking on the cabin door. It takes me a while to realize where I am, and that the cabin door is shaking with each knock, and that the fire has gone out and the air is cold and I have to pee bad and the wind has stopped. I lie still. It's eerie not to hear the wind and it makes the next knock sound even louder. I say, "Just a second," and the knocking stops. I sit up in bed and turn my feet onto the floor and struggle with my boots. I suddenly remember the terrible, slow breathing of the bear through the door and remember shooting the pepper spray and it feels as if it were a dream. Did I really do that? Did I really have a bear right outside the door and still dare to open the door? Did I spray into that wind?

"Just a second," I say again, and stand up, grab my robe and peak through a gap in the drapes. No bear, but there's Mark, which doesn't surprise me in the least. In fact I think it's about time he showed up. After he died, I saw him a lot around the farm. I caught glimpses of him crossing the driveway on his way to the barn. I'd see him disappear into his workshop below the yard. Sometimes when I came home from work, I'd see smoke rising out of his workshop chimney. I'd burst in there out of breath only to find the room empty and the stove ashes cold and black. Sitting in the farmhouse kitchen, I'd hear his truck door slam. Lying in bed, I'd hear him pace in the living room downstairs or open the stove in the morning to start a fire. I could smell his body in bed with me. I could smell him in his office and his closet, and I could smell his marijuana smoke drifting up from the front porch and into the bedroom window.

If all of that sounds crazy-making, it was, and it was part of the reason I fled to this cabin 1500 miles away. But the nasty trick of grief is how there is no escape. You're either haunted by ghosts or you're haunted by running away from ghosts—or by failed attempts to run away.

He knocks on the door again.

"Mark," I whisper against the glass of the window.

He doesn't see me or hear me, so I take my time. He stands with his weight on one leg and hooks his thumbs in his belt loops. He has sawdust in his beard. His thick brown hair looks like he just took off his cap. He grins and waits. I can see the shadow-less meadow past the edge of the drape and the sun off the beige grass and realize it's not morning but probably past noon. I wrap myself in the red terry-cloth robe. I'm embarrassed the fire's gone out and that he'll see I'm just waking up. But what does he expect? Who could sleep with a bear nosing around the door and looking in the window? More than anything in the world I want to tell him how much I've missed him, and for a mad moment I'm overjoyed with the opportunity to try to do just that. But when I look inside myself and try to imagine coming up with the words that could describe how much I've missed him, all I feel are vast, burned, empty spaces, and all I could possibly say is, *Baby, where have you been?*

On the table amid the chaos and remnants of the last three weeks of meals are the stacks of letters, and some on the arm of the stuffed chair. For a moment I feel as if I've been doing something wrong, staying up all night and sleeping past noon, reading Tommy's letters. Then I feel a surge of anger. How dare he judge me! I'm the one that has to try to fill up the empty world again. I'm the one who wakes every morning dumbfounded with confusion. I know the world has exactly the same stuff in it—grass and trees and birds and a vast blue sky and clouds coming forever from somewhere and going forever away, nights with their endless darkness even on the nights of the five round moons since the full one on the night before he died. Five moons and all of them as dull and flat and dreary as the last, and did he have to take the moon shine with him, too?

Yet part of me hopes Mark won't wait for me to open the door, that he'll burst in on his own accord, sweep me into his arms, look at me the way he did when he loved me most and loved me best, and say my name as if to say, *Here we are!* I'd fall toward him and he'd catch me, tuck me in his arms and lift us both like a rocket into space.

I let the drape fall and head for the door. In the two steps there I remember coming out of Eric's bedroom in Baraboo one the morning—I'm sure it was for the last time—I was looking like a mess and Mark looked over his newspaper with wide open hazel eyes that seemed to take me in, all of me, and he said hesitantly, carefully, but almost as if he'd been thinking about it and trying not to say it, he said, "You are a beautiful woman." Simple, like that. I could see his mouth search for something else to say before he settled on my name. "Janine," he said. Just that. Just that statement and then my name.

"Mark," I say, almost breathless now, and swing the door open. No surprise to you, of course, but the man at the door is not Mark and not the bear. I have to swallow a lump before I can properly breathe. The man is a wiry, small man, shorter than I am. Despite the cold, he's wearing only a tee shirt. He has big thick eyebrows and the skin of his mostly hairless scalp is almost blue in the shadow. He's holding my puppy and he's not smiling, but he looks amused.

"This yours?" he says. His hands are big and his arms, one

covered almost completely with tattoos, skinny. I nod and take the dog. I'm embarrassed even though this man doesn't know what I was just thinking. The puppy is warm and he licks my neck. I don't remember letting him out, but then I do. At dawn he was whining at the door.

"Where was he?" I ask.

"On the road," he says. Under those animated eyebrows, his eyes are as green as emeralds. He looks me over pretty good. He has the look of somebody wanting to say something funny but holding it in. "I figured he might belong here."

Now I can see he's looking behind me into the cabin—at the mess and the comically large barricade against the back door. I know he's wondering if there's somebody else here with me. I think for a moment of turning and saying something over my shoulder to an imaginary companion in the kitchen, *If you're done cleaning the guns, come meet the nice little man who brought back the puppy.*

"I'm Bart," he says.

"Janine," I say. He steps back a half step and new light hits his face. He has a spot on his cheek. I think *melanoma.* I want to tell him to get it checked out. I want to tell him I had a husband who had a little black spot like that last October and it could have been this exact date we noticed it, one year ago and—

"What's his name?" Bart says.

"Who?"

Bart is looking down at the little cow-dog mutt in my arms. Tan and white and still fuzzy like a puppy.

"I just call him Puppy."

"Well that fits." Bart smiles outright for the first time. I can feel the cold air on my skin and am suddenly worried that my robe isn't wrapped well enough around my front. I hold the dog tightly against my chest.

"Hey there, Puppy." He reaches out and pets the dog's head right under my chin. "Now we all know each other. I live up the canyon by the dam, in case he gets lost again."

"Did he go that far?" I ask.

"No," Bart says, "but in case you need help looking for him again."

"Thank you." I'm eager to shut the door. I'm cold and Bart seems to be finding this more fun than it is. Also I have to pee.

"If a truck doesn't get him, the coyotes will," Bart says.

"Or the bear," I say. I didn't mean to prolong the conversation, but it just popped out.

"You seen him?"

"He was right here last night. Standing right here where you are."

"Where I am?"

I think of Mark standing there, feel disappointed, and nod.

"Right here?" His eyes sparkle and he shakes his head. I'm getting a little irritated at his mysterious amusement.

"I could hear him breathing through the door." Just saying the words brings back the fear. The long, slow breaths. The weight of the animal, the nearness. "I shot him with pepper spray."

Bart raises his great thick eyebrows in surprise. "You get him?"

I tell him the truth. Not the embarrassing and humiliating truth, not the whole truth—but I tell him nothing but the truth. "He left," I say.

I watch through the crack in the drapes as Bart studies the ground in front of the cabin, even gets down on one knee to look closer at something, a track, I suppose, and then apparently satisfied I wasn't lying about the bear, he gets back into his red truck and turns it around before driving out onto the gravel road and east onto the plains toward town. I'd seen Mark's spot on his cheek right way. I had him checked out. I did everything a doctor you sleep with should do for you, can do for you. And by spring with the new grass on old hills, baby green leaves on black twisted oaks, it killed him anyway. It was like a poison dart from the sun. What could I do? By spring I walked the pasture behind the house to the ridge orchard with my children who I'd held as babies, one on each of my arms holding me up. I felt the new give in the soil under my feet like always in the spring, and he was dead anyway. I looked up at the same set to the land, same curve and slope, smelled the same buds and blossoms like always in the spring, and he was dead anyway. The most painful mystery of all was right out there in the landscape around us. How could there be all of this feeling, all of this growth and explosion of life and still so much room for emptiness? To fill it somehow I say his name out loud. Mark Kraemer. What a great thing a name is. Say the syllables and fill the air with something besides death. Maybe Bart is a dead man, too. Maybe I am a dead woman. Saying Mark's name, I'm having a hard time caring about the answer to either of those questions. All I know is when Bart's truck is finally out of sight, I have to run out the front door and around to the back of the cabin to pee in the grass under the big ponderosa pine on the way to the wood stack.

Bulgaria or wherever

Inside, I make a fire to warm the cabin. I think about taking a standing bath again but knowing Bart is out there, even if I saw him drive away, makes me less interested. I decide to wash my face and hands at least, so I heat water for the basin and bend over the sink and scrub. It gives me pleasure to see how dark the water gets. It makes me feel glad to pour in fresh water and clean my face and hands again. Out of the corner of my eye I see dirty dishes stacked at the edge of the sink from days ago and the groceries still out in bags on the cluttered counter, and I have another short fantasy that I clean everything up this morning, put all of this food away, the dishes, make the kitchen shine with scrubbing. It's a quick fantasy, and it's over before I lift my face from my wet hands and begin to dry myself with a paper towel. While I'm doing this, I'm also heating water for coffee, and when that boils I pour it through. I look at the now-dry spackle on the door-frame and think about screwing the door hinge back in again, but without a screwdriver, well, instead I sit down on the couch and reach for a cigarette. I've rationed myself two each morning and two each evening with the belief that if I keep the habit in a box, keep it ritualistic, I won't get hooked. Finally I'm ready. I've got a dish I can use as an ashtray, my coffee, and a letter. I call to the puppy to join me. He jumps up and lies down with his head in my lap. I wish he could talk so I could ask him some questions about Bart, normal questions a woman wonders when she's all alone and the man knows she's all alone and she has no telephone and no gun. Questions like, *is he a maniac?*

I have bear spray, at least, which I have new respect for. If just a whiff of pepper made me feel like I felt, imagine a full blast. The spray can is still sitting on the end table next to the chair. I have a sudden image of Bart having parked his truck just down the road and circling back on foot, of Bart sneaking up to the house. I lift the puppy's head off my lap and get up to walk across the room to get the bear spray. I sit down again and practice sliding the safety off and aiming, sliding the safety off and aiming. Then I put it down on the floor next to my feet, reach for my cigarette, and light it. I take a deep drag. When Mark told me I was a beautiful woman, I was getting just old enough to understand how rare it is for man to say that—especially when you are fully clothed and not in his bed. I was about to turn twenty-four, and I felt as if I were aging. It's hard to believe that when a woman's that young she thinks she's aging, but she does, and especially if she doesn't have a serious boyfriend, or maybe even more so if she's sleeping with a man she doesn't particularly like. Who knows. We all have blind spots, and no matter how hard we look we can't see them, which is why they're called blind spots. They're surprisingly easy to see in others, though. My father was a wise man who by then was on the Illinois Supreme Court. He wasn't big on talking to me or Mom, but his legal opinions showed a wide and lyrical mind, capable of compassion and clear thinking in the often muddy waters where the lives of actual human beings mingled with the law. Years ago when Frank McCourt wrote a popular book about growing up in an Irish family, my dad tried to read it but couldn't stand it. The fact that McCourt wrote unblinkingly about the bad of his family seemed like a betrayal of all the Irish. He said he never met an Irish person who drank like McCourt's father. This made Mom and me and Mark a little uncomfortable. Not only because his comments ended any discussion about the book, but because they were so obviously blind. I remember thinking, here is this wise man, and look how blind he is about this subject. I remember thinking, if he is so blind to that, what must I be blind to?

One summer after we'd been married almost four years, Mark started complaining that romantically I required he hit home runs, that he peel my skin back with his words or deeds. He said, Can't sex just be playful in a casual way? It can, I said, but it just doesn't work like that for me very often. I mean, unless I'm seeing the northern lights rise up from the plains, I start to get bored fast, and self conscious, and embarrassed. I just want it to be over. It's the way I'm built, I guess. (It's what made him fall in love with me, I wanted to remind him, the way I looked the first time, how he knew he'd *stepped into some deep shit*—) All the physical technique leaves me cold unless I'm feeling way out on an edge emotionally. Unless I'm feeling crazy and touched. Mark said, Hey, I'm a man, I look at my wife. You're pretty. I want to touch you. But when I reach out, you practically flinch. What do I have to do, wait for another friend of yours to get married at a country club, where I can dance you to exhaustion and then take you out on the golf course in the dark, lift your dress on the 18th green?

Maybe, I said, and tried to smile playfully. He only looked sour.

While we were having this conversation—an ongoing talk we had over the course of months—Mark was carrying on with a dancer visiting her cousin down the valley. He felt bad and didn't want to feel bad and somehow if he could get me to concede over and over again that I wasn't enough for him, he'd feel better, or at least not so bad. All those conversations I thought were about us, about me, were really about him. Somehow that felt like the real betrayal, especially as he'd inspired

me to try to be more playful, at least until I found out about
the affair in September, soon after it was over, soon after she'd
gone to Bulgaria where she had a Fulbright teaching dance.
In the months that followed I'd look at Mark from a distance
and try to remember what I loved about him but feel as if the
actual tissue of my heart had been scorched. It hurt like that.
*What had happened? The little birds of trust that used to sit so
safely on our shoulders had flown away. How do we get the birds
to come back? Why would birds ever land on us again?* At work
I seemed to be able to put it aside. I could go from patient to
patient all day long and listen to their stories with more compassion than ever, but at home I left the atlas open to Bulgaria
on the coffee table in the living room. Mark closed it a couple
of times but I opened it again. I'd never thought of Bulgaria
before in my life and now I thought about it every day, every
time I passed through the living room. It *was a scorched and
barren place,* I thought. A land of gypsy women who danced
other women's husbands into bed.

But blind spots are more about what we don't see in ourselves than what we don't see in others, so who knows what
mine are. The one man who knew them all is dead. I lean forward and squash the cigarette out in the dish and pick up a
letter from the stack on floor. I scan the cutesy and tedious
salutation and the fact that I was ever amused embarrasses me.
My mouth tastes ashy. Thinking of smoking is sometimes better than actually doing it. Maybe I'll save the second "morning" cigarette until evening. So far those haven't disappointed
me yet.

Costa Rican comfort

Dear McJanine McBean, Bonita Wenchona,

We're sitting in a deserted San José barroom at 3 a.m.: Juan Carlos the Costa Rican poet, Fernando the Salvadoran tool salesman, Javier the Marxist Spaniard, and me—the American journalist. The fluorescent light shines off the white Formica counter, and when I squint, the rows of colored bottles sparkle nicely along the wall. Our table is scattered with glasses, an empty jar of the house rum, and a bowl of melted ice.

Javier, a photographer, pulls some prints from his leather folder and passes them around. One is of a young woman in fatigues, sitting on a log, a semi-automatic rifle strapped over her shoulder and a coffee basket on her knee. The pose is already Nicaraguan kitsch, but there's something else in her face. Javier says she's a medical student (like you!) and in the army reserve. She lost two brothers fighting Somoza and two more fighting the Contras.

I examine her lips, the corners turned upward slightly as though she were hearing an old joke told by a friend. Her smile is both clean and dirty. It's pained and brave and fun. I want to marry her, and say so.

Javier curls his lip and pulls the picture away. Save your promises, he says. The world has heard enough from gringos.

Juan Carlos the Costa Rican poet kicks me under the table but pretends to be dozing when I look at him. He's trying not to laugh. He thinks Javier's a riot.

Nobody really believes Cuban lies, Javier says, head forward, eyebrows raised, giving me that all-knowing, continental look. He's lean and blue-eyed and arrogant. But American lies? He shakes his head disgustedly. People actually believe them!

Then, out of the blue, Fernando the Salvadoran tool salesman, who lost a tooth and a half up front when hit by the rifle butt of a suspicious Salvadoran soldier, says, Well, as long as we're showing pictures, what do you think of these?

He slips from his wallet two photos of his girlfriends back in Salvador. He passes them around and asks which we prefer, *La Negrita* or *La Otra*. I prefer *La Otra,* and point to her. She reminds me of a *bonita chiquita* I loved long ago and far away. Well, that's not quite true. You are far away but not so long ago because love is still what I feel although I made a brave and successful effort to let you go. That's what one does with the ones one loves, *correcto*? *Let her go*? (I read that on a cool poster with a dove on it.)

Seriously, though. You are a dear and good person, and in almost thirty years of living I've concluded I am mostly a thirsty one. As I wrote to you once long ago, it's more or less mo' better than mo' worse.

Juan Carlos the Costa Rican poet bumps me again under the table. Gringo son of the Great Fascist, he says. He cups his hands as though trying to hold water. Don't let it slip away, he says.

What?

He spreads his fingers and shakes his hands as though it's

already gone.

Your mind, he says, and laughs.

Juan Carlos manages to scrounge enough money to eat by digging plants in the country and carrying them into the city on a bus in a plastic bag. He pots them and sells them to businesses. We've been sharing a room at the *pensión* and know each other's secrets. I walk grooves in the floor and talk myself to sleep. His back is striped by scars he claims to have received when two Costa Rican policemen pulled him off the road, tied him to a tree, and whipped him with a cattle switch. When I asked him why, he raised his eyebrows and looked at me as if I were an idiot. Stealing, of course, he said, The police are very moral men.

The waiter blinks the light in the bar so we stand up, pay our bill, and move the discussion into the empty street. We walk together. Javier the Marxist Spaniard and Fernando the Salvadoran tool salesman begin arguing about revolutions or empty stomachs, which comes first. Juan Carlos is telling me he's come to the conclusion that although gringos are marvelous liars, it's still easier to lie in Spanish than in English. Then he says he's been thinking seriously about becoming one of the bourgeoisie because everyone else always talks about giving *The People* bread or spectacle, some god or another, Marxism or Jesus, but he only wants to write his poems and publish them.

And frankly, he says, two creases squeezed neatly across his brow, I really don't give a shit about *The People*.

Javier breaks his argument with Fernando and turns to Juan Carlos. The stupid bourgeoisie don't believe in anything but their stomachs and their cocks, he says. And since neither amount to much in your case, you'll never make a good bourgeoisie.

Wrong, Juan Carlos says, grinning. The rich and the poor believe in those things. The middle class believes in white bread and monogamy. And I would like very much the chance to get used to them both.

I like the way our voices and footsteps echo off the front of

the old buildings as we walk down the center of the street. Juan
Carlos makes me laugh—and when I laugh, if I'm not immortal, at least I'm okay. In Nicaragua I was often afraid I might
be swallowed by loneliness on long nights, or simply fall into a
pothole on a dark Managua street and come home with a limp.
So I have my refrain. I'm tired of it but say it again: *I'm okay. I
have no major scars. I walk well.*

But on the other hand, Juan Carlos says, after looking at the
pictures of Fernando's whores, who can think very straight?

Fernando slides the photos into his shirt pocket and hurries
to catch up. Juan Carlos, he says, you are a filthy pig who never
could think straight. All you really need to know is God and
you don't even know Him.

This is not the first time Fernando the Salvadoran tool
salesman has brought God into the conversation.

Juan Carlos laughs and rolls his eyes. He says, Ha! If I could
attract two pretty girlfriends with a toothless grin like yours,
Fernando, I might believe in God, too!

Fernando shrugs. He says even so, none of us have met God
yet, and God is waiting to meet the whole bunch—especially
especially Juan Carlos.

Why me? Juan Carlos asks. I don't want to meet God.

Why you? says Fernando. Well, because this one is a gringo,
and not even God understands gringo Spanish very well. And
this one is a Spaniard, and God knows that regardless of what
a Spaniard says while living, he will beg on his knees when
dying.

Javier stops, spins around, throws his long, skinny arms
into the night and says, This is all pure shit, this idea of God.
This is just exactly how good little fascists are made!

Juan Carlos is thoroughly enjoying himself, big grin on his
handsome, young face. Just to rile Javier the Spaniard, he says,
Okay, Fernando, perhaps you're right. I'm ready. Introduce me.
Let me meet this God.

We've arrived at the *pensión* where we've been staying,
where we first got acquainted, and we stand on the old, cracked
cement steps leading up from the sidewalk to a wrought-iron

gate. Juan Carlos nudges me with his elbow and says he'll be sure to ask God to speak slowly for my sake. Javier groans and mutters something I don't understand. Fernando says shut up, and then steps forward and puts his hands on each side of Juan Carlos's face, tilts his own head back and says toward the sky, God, allow me to introduce Juan Carlos. Juan Carlos, allow me to introduce God.

I look at Fernando smiling and showing the gap where his teeth should be, and I look at Juan Carlos, smooth face relaxed between Fernando's hands, mouth hanging open, eyes aimed upward. It's quiet. The volcanoes across the valley are jeweled silhouettes. There's no traffic on the boulevard and although down below shine lights from the city, the stars show easily past the branches of the mango tree.

I wait. Fernando waits, his hands still holding Juan Carlos's face. Behind them, even Javier waits.

In a just a few minutes, we'll drift off the steps to our rooms, and tomorrow to other places. Javier will pack up his camera and prints and catch a freighter to Peru. Fernando will carry his sample tools onto the bus to Panama. Juan Carlos will disappear into the hills with his shovel. Only I'll stay. In the morning I'll file a brief story with the AP on the Nicaraguan port of San Juan del Sur, then head down to the Parque Centrál and write you this letter. I have a sudden and terrible feeling that it's all slipping away for good, each precious moment of nothing into nothingness—so when Juan Carlos whispers *Mucho gusto, Diós,* pleased to meet you, God, and a breeze touches the back of my neck, I shiver.

We all feel it, and during the next moment or two, nobody speaks or even looks very directly at anybody else.

Finally Fernando breaks the silence. He says God just kissed us all—that's what we felt. Javier laughs and says if that's God's kiss, then he'll stick with women. They ask what I think and I manage to say in that in my professional journalist opinion that's a breeze, a cool breeze.

Juan Carlos says our brains must have shriveled to the size of raisins to bounce so dreamlessly inside our skulls. He says what that was, was comfort. Costa Rican comfort. He says to remember it, because for one brief moment in our measly little lives, longing grew wings and flew away.

So that's how it goes with me.

Love and pretty white doves,
TeeCon

yesyesyesyesyes, he said

I put the letter down and get up to make myself a peanut butter-and-jelly sandwich. I find both the peanut butter and the jelly jars still open and a knife that looks as if it's been used for peanut butter and jelly sometime in the last few days, and I find the bread—white, Wonder-ish bread—in one of the still unpacked grocery bags. I make the sandwich on a plate smeared with hardened jelly from probably the same sandwich the peanut butter and jelly on the knife was a part of. Despite this grossness, I think about how in the long arc of my days here at the cabin, not to mention the even longer arc of my life on earth, peanut butter and grape jelly is always a good sign, a courageous sign. I slice the sandwich and eat half while I stand in the kitchen. No milk, but a big glass of water is good, too. When I finish, I put on some long underwear and clean socks and dress to take a walk. I want to take a walk, and I'm going to do it in broad daylight with my puppy in the horse pasture. I'm not going to be made a prisoner because I saw a bear. People have been walking in this country for hundreds of years, thousands of years—they walked all the way here from Asia after the last ice age, and a good percentage of them were not eaten by bears.

While I dress, I eat the second half of the sandwich and drink a second glass of water. I distract myself by remembering the evening I read that letter to Mark. I'd read it a few hours earlier by myself, and I can't deny I was rocked to understand for the first time that I was the *bonita chiquita* of letter number one, that I was the one it had been *more or less mo' better than mo' worse* to break up with.

But in my naiveté I also felt grateful, because here I sat with Mark, and although we'd known each other for only four months I'd fallen fast and hard and had something big to tell him. It was winter. Snowing. In the summer I'd be moving to North Carolina to begin my residency so before I told him what I had to tell him, I thought I had to put all my cards on the table. At least that's what I thought when I was twenty-four. I couldn't stand secrets. I couldn't stand waiting for him to know.

"He loves you," Mark said.

I remember we were sitting on his couch looking out his second-story window when I finished the letter. I felt a lump in my stomach and Mark's eyes on the side of my face. Suddenly I didn't know if I was prepared to explain Tom Connor, to give him the whole story.

"He hasn't seen me since I was sixteen."

"Do you write him back?"

"A few times. Three or four."

"When was the last time?"

I thought about it for a moment. We were sitting on opposite sides of the couch, the opened envelope and the pages of the letter scattered between us. "Just before I started med school," I said.

"Not since then?"

"I don't know where to write. He never tells me. And he doesn't know where I live either. He always writes to my parents' address and they forward the letters to me."

Marked picked up one of the pages from the couch cushion between us and glanced at it, then put it down again. "He's a good writer," he said.

"Half the time I don't have a clue what he's talking about."

"You're his inspiration."

I wasn't sure I knew what that meant "He never asks a thing about me."

Mark just looked at me.

"What?"

"Has he ever told you he loved you before?"

"You mean come right out and said it?"

Mark nodded.

I shook my head. "This is the closest, what he says here." I was going to add that I didn't believe it, and that I knew what love was and that *good and dear person* was nothing compared to what real love felt like but I kept my mouth shut. We stared out the window for a while. Mark had turned the light off so we could see the snow better. There were so many falling flakes you could let your eyes glaze over or you could just focus on one flake and try to follow it swirling down to see if it landed on an oak branch. We had our stocking feet up on the low bookcase.

"That's a lot of letters," Mark said.

I let that sit for a moment. I knew he had something else to ask and I was going to wait until he asked it. To offer an answer before he asked would feel defensive. So I waited. It was very quiet in the house. No music. Nobody stirring in the apartment below. Out the window, the snow fell. Finally he asked it, "Do you love him?"

My cheeks burned. I wished he were touching me, that I could lean against him, feel the weight of his arm around my shoulders, my hand in his.

"A long time ago," I said. "I did. Now I love you."

Coming out of my mouth it seemed weak, but it was the best I could do without sounding as if I were trying too hard to convince him. I just let it sit. The little ball in my stomach grew harder and heavier. Mark was drinking wine. I was drinking water. I wished he'd say something.

"I need one more thing," he said.

I didn't answer. I had something to say to him, too, but had to get this whole subject out of the way first. I tucked in and waited.

"I need to know," Mark asked, and paused. I could feel him struggling to control his breath. "I need to know," he began again, "if someday he showed up here, would you love him again?"

"No," I said.

"I mean," he said, "if he showed up tomorrow, or ten years from—"

"No," I said, again. "This is easy, Mark, I promise," and I pushed the letter off the cushion between us and slid over to kiss his cheek through his beard. I whispered in his ear. "I was a just girl, then, and he was just boy."

I tucked in even closer. Mark tried to take a deep breath. He let it out slowly but not smoothly.

"I love you," I said, and I felt as if I'd never really known what the words meant until I said them then. "I love you and you love me."

He looked away. "I don't know," he said. "It just that that's about the most frightening thing I can think of."

"What?" I said, and almost laughed, because the idea of it seemed suddenly absurd. "Tom Connor coming here?"

"No," he said. My cheek lay against his chest and he was stroking my head with his hand. "Loving. Loving you. Being so in love."

I listened to his racing heart, listened to his shaky breathing begin to even out. I felt the warmth of his blood through his skin and wanted to stay like that forever. I wanted to climb under his skin and sleep and grow but I still had to tell him. I sat up and took a drink of water. Then I reached for his glass of wine, actually took it out of his hand and drank the rest of it.

"You don't even know how frightening," I said.

"What?"

I hadn't quite got the tone right. I was hoping to make him smile but his mouth tightened and he looked a little grim. "I have something to tell you," I said.

"You do?"

I handed the empty glass back to him and felt his eyes on me, curious, waiting.

"And something to ask."

His eyes narrowed. I could see I was scaring him. I tried to swallow but my mouth was drying fast. How had this happened to me again? I was almost a doctor, for crying out loud. I was careful and conscientious. I closed my eyes.

"I'm pregnant," I said.

When I dared to open them again, his whole face had lit up. His eyes wide as windows, his mouth dropped open like a door. He blinked and his mouth moved but no sound came out. He tried again, still no sound. Finally he managed to repeat, "Pregnant?"

I laughed. I nodded.

"Jesus," he said.

I nodded again.

"I can't believe it," he said.

"Are you glad?"

"Am I glad?" He leaned back on the couch. His face was plastered with a smile.

"Yeah?" I said.

"Yeah," he said, but who knows what he was really thinking. He was way out there. He was soaring. He was saying just exactly what I was saying.

"I just need to know," I said. "I need to hear you say yes, you're glad."

"Yes, I'm glad."

"Many times," I said. "Say it many times."

He looked at me as if to ask if I was messing with him but he said, "Yes yes yes." He was beaming.

"Good," I said, and tucked back down against his chest. I looked out the window past our feet. My chest was tight too, but it was loosening fast. I felt each new breath come easier. I looked closer at where our hands held one another on his lap. He had both of mine under one of his.

"Because they're twins," I said, and again I could hear him struggling to breathe, to speak.

"You mean?"

I took both his hands and put them on my stomach, covered them with mine.

"You mean?" He tried again. He didn't seem capable of finishing the question, so I asked my own, and once I asked one, the rest just burst out in a flood.

"So are you happy? Do you still love me? Will you love me forever?"

"Yes," he said, and started to laugh, and then I started to laugh, too, the relief rushing in like helium that filled our chests and seemed to lift us both up off the couch and out the window. "Yesyesyesyesyes," he said, and I think of us sometimes in that moment as the Eternal Couple, naked in our clothes and pregnant with our children and rising up into the cold night, delighted among the big flakes of falling snow. We laughed bravely and tucked in close to each other for heat.

"Good," I finally managed to say. "I'm glad we got all of that settled."

they shoot horses, don't they?

They say that grief makes us crazy and our path through it
will be crooked and we should avoid making any big decisions the first year but nevertheless I decide to walk straight
across the road through a meadow toward the horse pasture in
the mouth of the canyon, to take a sane walk with my dog to
the river. The air is warming up, a little breath of summer here
in late October. If it was forty when I woke early this afternoon, the dusting of snow gone, it feels fifty now and the sky is
a crisp blue. The puppy doesn't know anything about straight
lines, and he's pulled one way then the other by his nose. He
zigzags and runs circles and smells everything he can. I take
deep breaths and try to smell what I smelled when I smelled
the bear, whatever that smelled like. I can't recreate scents
from my memory, but of course if I smell them again, I know
what they are. As I walk here I can't re-create Marks's smell,
pull it out of my memory, but months after he died I could
still smell him on the mattress even through clean sheets. The

puppy circles me as I walk through the grass. His face looks like a baby face, confused and dumbfounded by all of the sensory information coming at him, by all his urges and reflexes, simultaneously stunned and alert. He sniffs and scratches and runs for no reason. He stops and chews on a stick. Then jumps up at me. I step on his back foot to make him go down and he cries and tries to chew my pant cuff but I gently kick him off. My boots and my coat have frayed places where he's chewed them. Mark told me when we got our first puppy that it would destroy something I loved, and the very next day it chewed up a sweater my mother had knit for me. I see Mark walking just ahead of me in the blond grass. But the puppy doesn't seem to. I point and say, "See him?" but the puppy only looks at my pointing finger. I shake my finger and point harder at Mark walking slowly away. "There!" but the puppy only looks at my finger again. My shaking pointing finger, then at me, then at my finger again. I raise a foot and point like a pointer dog with my nose. Do dogs understand that kind of pointing? This one doesn't. He just stares at me. I put my foot back on the ground and Mark-Walking-Away turns into a stump. The wind blows. Not hard like yesterday. Just a little breeze. Okay. A stump is a stump and a puppy is a puppy and two hawks are circling slowly, hunting the meadow. Everything seems better all of a sudden. I'm glad the puppy didn't look when I pointed to a stump. I'm glad Mark's a stump now. Even as I think this I know it's not true, but I roll with it, dance to it, this crazy music. It's my grief dance, my cha-cha, my two-step widow walk. A cloud shadow passes across the meadow. An airplane engine echoes in the canyon. River water, laughter from somewhere—from me?—and I feel a thrilling joy out of nowhere followed by a hollow despair—then both of them at the same time. All of this fullness and still so much room for emptiness. Why not? I can wear a blouse and pair of pants at the same time. I can carry joy and sadness on my same skin. Life is weather. Life is meals. I'm already looking forward to making spaghetti for dinner: just boil the pasta and open a jar of sauce, if I can find it. So what I'm looking forward to is eating the spaghetti, really, because the cooking is pushing aside the mess far enough to find the burner and light it. I'm glad, I'm not glad, I'm glad, I'm not glad, I'm glad, I'm not glad. None of it has anything to do with what anybody in the world can see. An invisible craziness, an invisible twist of despair and hope and pain and madness and clarity. Grief is in the body and the body is in the soul. The pain is the beat and the beat is the truth. *La dee dah, la dee dah dum.* Thinking all of this sends me tumbling. Sometimes I'm sure it's been a dream, not just Mark and our children, and Mark's death, but *my whole life.* I don't know who I am, or I've forgotten. I don't know where I am and never knew. Then the next moment, the very next *step,* I feel so weirdly happy and light it doesn't even matter—nothing does, nothing ever has!

I hear a car on the gravel road and I want to hide. I hope it's not Bart. I stand perfectly still. I wait for the car to come around the bend—the red truck, heading for the mountains, for the canyon. I hold perfectly still like a deer in the field. It isn't until the truck is about even, a hundred yards away, that the driver sees me and I see him. It's not Bart. It's Mark, and he lifts a hand off the steering wheel and waves in that familiar way.

"You were his inspiration!" he calls out the window.

"What?" I say, although his words are as clear as the sky.

"And mine, too!"

Mark smiles and waves again. Hello or good bye? I wave back and watch the truck accelerate toward the canyon. It's Bart. It's not Mark. I can tell because I recognize the gun rack holding a horizontal rifle behind his head on the back window of the truck. The puppy looks at me and I feel suddenly foolish so I stop waving and give the truck the finger—actually, give the dust rising behind the truck the finger. It feels like the sane thing to do. It keeps me from falling over.

The last time I saw Tom Connor, when he came by the farm on his way to Florida, he was so wobbly with booze he walked with a cane and with one of the dogs he trained, the last one, I suppose. He'd lost everything—job (he'd lost a lot of jobs, but for the first time was unable to slide on down the road and talk the dean at the next small college into hiring him) house (the bank had taken it back) and finally, his truck (rolled and totaled). His plan was to go to his ex-wife's house in Orlando. His children were there. They were 9 and 11, I think. I couldn't imagine he'd sober up. He'd go home and it would be hell for all of them. It probably wouldn't have changed anything, but I didn't say a word to him about any of it. About his drunkenness or about his plan to go home and ruin the lives of his family—or about what else he wanted that I refused to give. And not out of virtue, either, much less a promise I'd made twenty some years before, but out of stinginess, some deep coldness at my core, and a resentment I know now was born of self-pity.

A gust of wind from the canyon confuses the puppy as we make our way across the meadow closer to the river. He dashes, he stops, he sniffs, he walks cautiously. A woodpecker in a dead cottonwood startles both of us. The puppy runs back to me and jumps up and then spins and runs off into the tall grass, leaping up occasionally like a gazelle so he can see over the grass. The beauty of his little leaps makes me happy. Suddenly he stops and I watch him sniff, lift his leg, sniff some more. He twitches his head up, lopes a couple of steps, and grabs something to chew. The taste excites him so much he wants to run circles again, but what he's got is heavy and he's pulled equally between the desire to chew and the desire to run. I love to watch him in these little dilemmas. He doesn't know what he is yet. A dog with no role model. He smells things and feels things and responds to things. He wants to be with me and he wants to run away from me. He wants to chew and to run. He wants to smell, but doesn't know what he's smelling, only that it gives him lots of feelings that he expresses by running or crying or jumping up. It is an amusing thing to watch a puppy try to learn to be a dog. I say to him, "You don't know how to be a dog, do you?" He turns and looks. His little bright eyes blink. He looks happy that I've spoken. "Yes, we're a team," I say, and then correct myself: "We're a pack!" He looks away again and sprints, stops, looks back like a little boy who wants to show you over and over again what he can do. I remember squatting in the garden on the farm and Cody, when he was about five, swinging on the swing and shouting, *Look, Look, Look, Mom.* I'd say, *That's great, Cody.* He'd swing some more, he'd say, *Look, Mom, can't I swing high?* I'd say, *Yes, very high.* He'd say, *Watch me jump, Mom.* I'd look up as he landed and tumbled like a rubber boy in the grass. *Aren't I a good jumper?* he'd say. *Yes, you're a good jumper,* I'd say. *I'm the best jumper in the world!* he'd say. *You're the best jumper in the world,* I'd say. *What about Kate?* he'd say. *Is Kate a good jumper?* Kate would be helping me in the garden. She'd be digging and pulling weeds with a stick. *Kate's a good jumper,* I'd said. *She's a good weeder, too.*

"Good puppy," I say to Puppy, as I gather him in to make sure he gets safely across the gravel road on the way to the horse pasture. We've got to cross through another grove of cottonwood trees and then drop down to the flat along the inside of the river bow. I can hear the river echo in the canyon. The sun touches the rock walls and lights the grasses and the dog runs and leaps across this meadow toward the horse pasture. Mark always named our dogs. If I didn't like something about the dog, I told him. He fixed it, or he didn't fix it, but it was his job. Stay off the couch, don't chase the children. Don't chase the chickens. The dogs were always his. But not this one, who ran away when a bear came yesterday. And who ran silent circles in the cabin last night when the bear came to the door.

"Do you smell the bear?" I ask. "Does it scare you like it does me?"

I think of the joke: you don't have to be faster than the bear, just faster than the other camper. The puppy is faster than I am...I laugh as I walk. I feel vulnerable. I feel pale, elegant, sluttish. Actually, I feel none of those things but I remember the phrase from something, a movie, a book. *Pale, elegant, sluttish.* I feel as if I might pop. I feel as if I might blow away. I am suddenly very worried for my son, away in med school. His hands appear to me like beautiful pieces of art. Long, graceful fingers. He was never a worker. Mark fought with him for

while to get him to help him do things on the farm. Cody hated to get dirty. He didn't like the smells. He had allergies and
complained if he had a callus on his hand. Mark couldn't figure him out. He felt frustrated and disappointed to have a son
who wouldn't help, to have a son who would never be a work
companion. Then one evening after he'd been scolding Cody
for not doing something he should have done, something that
would have made Cody dirty and sweaty and sore, Mark came
to bed, and we both lay there and listened to the boy—maybe
he was thirteen—crying in his room, and Mark said, "Well, I
guess I can make him miserable, but I can't make him different."

And that was the end of that. Mark never again bothered
him to do farm work.

Cody is interested in research—and so I've encouraged him
to go that way. He has the personality for research. He's not a
clinician. I think about his face and want to hold him tight.
Sometimes I can't believe he is no longer in my body with his
sister, no longer small enough to hold. Sometimes I wish he
were a solder in Afghanistan rather than a student. Not really,
of course, but at least then I'd have an excuse for how vulnerable I feel when I think of him. It makes no sense, but few things
do anymore. For instance, I like not having a phone—no land
line in the cabin, no cell—because it makes me feel safer. No
way to get any more bad news. I must instinctively know that
any more bad news would break me in two, and so here, of
all places, I'm safe from bad news. I like the idea of it, safety,
I mean. It makes my blood pump just imagining it. While I
walk I say a prayer for my son. I feel bad how many hours pass
during a day and I don't think of him, don't say any prayers
for him. I think of how strong he is, his body out of mine, his
man's body, his wide shoulders and square jaw. Then I think
of the last time he was home—it was just after the funeral, the
next day, I think, and I heard him talking to his friend Nate
about a girl, Sam, they'd both grown up with. Samantha had
been to the funeral and had been hanging around our house
all week. She was one of his good friends, I thought, until I

heard him say to Nate as clear as can be, "Sam's a cunt." It took my breath away—not just the word but the casual sound in his voice. If he'd sounded angry, I might have felt different but he sounded completely at ease in his cruelty, using that ugly word to dismiss a girl he'd known as a friend his whole life. I didn't know what to say. I was in the other room so I didn't say anything. I went to bed and didn't sleep. I thought of a million things to say to him, things that didn't make any sense, like, *Think of your sister, what would Kate have thought if she'd heard you say that?* But he wasn't a boy anymore and he wasn't talking to his sister, and his father who was alive and healthy six months before and who might have had something to say that Cody would listen to was cold and mute and buried. In the morning when he came down for breakfast I hugged him and kissed him and stared at his man face, the stubble on his cheeks, his sleepy eyes. I'm sure he thought it was all about sadness and maybe it was but neither of us had anything to say so I hugged him and kissed him again.

The puppy and I step across the fence into the horse pasture. It's about thirty acres. For some freak reason I've always been pretty good at estimating acreage. One of my many talents that impressed Mark. Green pine and fir on the slope to the west, the blue river and a cluster of cottonwood to the north, and massive gray cliffs rise on the far side to hold up the sky. About fifty horses are spread out across the pasture grazing. They are used by outfitters to take people into the wilderness but for now they graze this good grass, the last of the season. Mark loved grass. He loved raising grass to feed animals. He took pleasure and pride in keeping his pastures lush and productive and he loved the look of animals standing in grass. I feel his pleasure when I see what I see, and I wonder if I always will. The dog and I walk. The dog looks back at me, looks ahead at the distant horses, looks back at me again. We're about halfway across the horse pasture toward the river when I notice some horses turn and begin to walk toward us. It doesn't seem odd because it's what horses often do when you walk in their pasture. They come over. They want to take a good look. I never spent much time riding, but we always boarded a few horses on the farm. We'd feed them in the winter and they'd graze our grass in the summer. I'd take the kids out and we'd feed them a carrot or sugar or pet their soft noses. I stop and watch the horses walk through the shin-high grass. They come in groups of twos and threes. I feel a touch of breeze on my face and the warm sunshine on my neck and for a moment feel moved. The sky, the cliffs, the grass, the beautiful horses walking. They form bigger groups—four, eight, twelve—and as they gather, they seem to gain courage and to walk faster, and the leaders, the closest ones, have their heads down, which is when I suddenly realize they are not coming over to get their noses rubbed. They are looking at the puppy, who seems suddenly aware of their murderous intent. I look back toward the fence we crossed to get into the pasture, but it's a hundred yards behind me, and the closest groups of horses now are about half that distance away. I stand frozen for a moment but the puppy has started back the way we came so I turn to follow him. These horses live where there are wolves and coyotes and bears, so they must have a no-carnivore rule in this pasture. I walk fast and hear the hooves behind me. When I glance back again, the scattered groups have converged and formed one large herd that is following us. We walk faster and the horses do, too. I think about the bear, and wonder if they've chased him as well, all the way up to my cabin. I want to shout, *Hey, this is a puppy! He eats puppy chow!* but the puppy's out ahead of me so I'm not worried about him, I'm worried about me, about the horses going over me to get to him. The sound of their hooves, hundreds of hooves behind me, sends bolts of panic through my body. I want to run but resist. Running away from a herd of horses feels like a losing option, so I keep walking as fast as I can until they've caught up to within fifteen feet of me, almost trotting by now. I turn and shout and wave my hands. That stops the lead horse, a sorrel stallion. The herd bunches up behind him, but as soon as I start walking again, they follow. I have my jacket in my hand and I spin around and whip the jacket and shout "Hey Hey!" and that stops them again. I walk backward and shout and wave my coat and pull the bear-spray out of the little holster on my belt, but I'm afraid I'll fall down walking backward so I turn again and hear them speed up behind me. I look over my shoulder and see the sorrel stallion is closer, head down, eyes wild. I spin, shout, wave my arms, and again that stops them all. I can't believe my skinny body and squeaky voice can stop tons of horses. Even in my fear I feel amazed at my power. I turn to walk away, hear the hooves approach and stop and shout again. Wave my coat around and around above my head like a lasso. All of those huge animals pile up behind the leader, their heads up, eyes rolling. I walk away fast, spin, and shout; I walk away, spin, and shout, and like that, finally, get to the fence. The puppy has run under the lowest wire, and with pepper spray in one hand and my balled-up jacket in the other, I hurl myself down onto the grass and roll under as well. I stand up just as the herd gets to the fence and spreads out along its length, their colors big and warm under the spectacular blue sky. The puppy begins to run back and forth on our side of the fence, barking.

"Shut up," I yell to him, but he doesn't mind me. He keeps barking and racing back and forth. The horses stretch their necks out over the barbed wire and breathe. My god, I can smell their bodies, feel their heat. They could push over the wire fence like paper but they don't seem to know it. Or maybe they're just as happy as we are to have it between us. I slip the safety off the pepper spray and am ready to blast away just in case. The puppy is still running back and forth and barking and as the horses watch they swing their heads in one direction then the other like fans at a tennis match. I aim at their faces turning back and forth, back and forth, and for a moment I'm Jane Fonda at her beautiful best, and I'm thinking, *hey, they shoot horses, don't they?* Actually, I'm terrified now— feel it flow into me even more than it did when I was in the pasture with them. I have never seen such aggressive horses. They would have killed the pup, killed me if I was in the way. The horses are breathing hard and I am, too. My heart is racing. I am sweating. I think of Mark saying the best things in his life happened when he was sweating, and I remember him sweating when he died, as well. Does that give me comfort? I don't know, but every now and then on my way to the cabin with the dog, I look back to the pasture and the horses are still all congregated along the fence. Behind them is the big, grassy field, and the bend in the blue river that in the morning is blanketed by fog, and the cliffs behind, and upstream the gap that leads to the mountains, that leads to the wilderness. I think I would like to go there sometime, inside there, to lose myself in mountains beyond mountains. But for now I'm lost here, on the edge, and to the east the plains spread all the way to the sky and I walk that way toward the little puff of smoke coming from the cluster of trees that surrounds the cabin. A little puff of smoke in a sky so big I'm swallowed by it, and strangely happy to be swallowed. I am nothing. I am an ant. I am an animal on earth.

"Right puppy?" I say, and he looks back at me, panting, eyes bright. He's smiling. Sure he is. *That was fun*, he seems to be saying. *Let's do it again!*

Back at the cabin I bring in more firewood and stack it in the box behind the stove. I dig around in the kitchen and find a box of spaghetti and a jar of spaghetti sauce, boil water, cook the pasta, heat the sauce and eat until my stomach is full. Give the rest to the dog, stack my dirty plate on top of the saucepan, then sit back and light a cigarette. I think a nice dinner should end in tobacco smoke. I know I'm a doctor but I hate that I live in a time when it simply isn't done. Sure tobacco kills, but a lot of things we all seem to like just fine also kill: cars, wars, horses, the sun—and I'm not talking about dying anyway. I'm talking about living, and as Tom wrote me once, if there were a way to write this so you could read it all at once, all of the words splashed on the page or poured in a big cup to drink in one big gulp instead of one sip at a time, well, if I could tell it all at once, if we could feel it all at once, the horror, the petty stinginess, the big anger and confusions, the great loves and fears, the infidelities— heartbreaking and funny all at once—like how my brother told Mark and Mark told me how my brother and his wife were visiting Beijing, and they'd been out shopping all day and it was late but his wife was upset because the beautiful (and very expensive) tea set she'd ordered had still not been delivered to their hotel room on the eighteenth floor, so she sent him down to the lobby to ask again and he met a prostitute dressed in a gray business suit (skirt and blazer) in the elevator and once the door closed she pointed to her mouth and raised her eyebrows and he said no thank you he was just going to the lobby to check for a tea set, but in the lobby he learned the tea set had not yet arrived so he took an awkward ride up again in the same elevator with the same prostitute who apparently worked that elevator all night, and back in the room he had to tell his wife the bad news and go to bed with her, and while she lay fretting and unhappy, he began to think more and more about the pretty mouth of the woman in the elevator and after all of that shopping and running around he'd done all day he thought he deserved a treat, so he told his wife he'd go back down again to check for the tea set and this time he took advantage of the opportunity in the elevator and when he got to the lobby, amazed and walking on wobbly legs, the tea set was just being delivered, so when he got back to his hotel room he was a hero, and his wife so pleased she wanted him suddenly and he had to make an excuse and roll over and stare out the window at the ten million lights that are Beijing at midnight—if I could tell all of it at once, like Tommy tried to do, if I could find life within death, meaning and beauty in words written by a man who ultimately found neither—would I know then that nothing negates nothing because it's all still here in every breath? All of it, the bully horses, pretty puppy, scary bear, the dead men I loved, children from my womb flung out across the world? If I could tell it all at once, would I know it all then? Would I be able to feel it all? Would I want to?

Tommy's letters, I think, are getting to me.

Out in the country where Mark and I lived, there was a little roadside bar. We'd go down there on summer nights to hear local musicians playing bluegrass or jazz out on the patio. The heat and humidity would have given way to a balmy breeze that cooled as the shadows grew long and hazy off the wooded hills. We'd listen to the music and the whippoorwills and have drinks while the twins—big enough, finally, for us to come—played where we could see them on the grass and stones of the nearby graveyard where Mark's grandparents were buried. We told them to play there so we could watch them but as often as not I'd sit with my eyes closed after a long day—after long years of so little leisure—and I'd feel cradled by the air, by the music, and by Mark, by being close to him, feeling his stillness, his gaze. After being so busy for so long, I'd miraculously not forgotten how to do nothing and rest. Mark would hold my hand under the table and I'd feel each breath of his, of mine, every moment a touch of grace.

Yet even as I remember this peace, suddenly in the cabin I'm sure my life is too quiet. I'm not breathing fast enough or deeply enough. I'm nervous as a junkie. I stand up and turn on the radio and spin the dial until I find a crackly polka station from Canada. I turn it off, sit down, get up, turn it on again. I find another station but change my mind and go back to the polka, then turn the radio off for good. I contemplate shaving my head, smearing pitch on my bare breasts and running outside to keen into the night, but instead I sit down at the table and examine my nails under the light. I've let them grow for the first time since college. I need a file and lots of colored polish. Thanking about that even for a moment changes my mood. I light another cigarette and sort through the letters until I find the one I'm looking for, the Big Gulp, read-it-all-at-once letter.

there is nothing sensitive to say about a massacre

Wencharoni McBeanie,

   Back in Nica from Guat City and my mattress is straw and
hanging on the underwater-green wall of my room are a Santa Claus head, three plastic dolls still in their boxes with cel-
lophane fronts, a crucifix with a dying Jesus, a pig made out
of clothespins, Winnie the Pooh embroidered on terrycloth,
a red felt Christmas stocking, a magazine cutout picture of a
baby with jar of Vaseline petroleum jelly, and another of a boy
with his dog in some place like Switzerland. I'm not kidding.
All of these things are decorations. It's as though the owner is
insane, but she isn't. It's common down here to decorate with
such random stuff. I lie in bed looking at these things and outside in the street I can hear shooting and a drunk grunting
around in the train yard. Through the window I see his wobbly silhouette. A truck roars behind him on the empty street.
I step out of my room onto a common porch and a man with

a hat steps out on the porch from the room next to mine and
he spits in the dark. He stares at me, spits again, and goes back
inside. The drunk walks like a monkey, using the knuckles
of one of his fists to keep from falling as he crosses one set
of tracks after another. The smell of piss and shit and tortillas. The rhythmic *ching...ching...ching...*of a machete being
sharpened in one of the rooms. The horror, the petty stinginess, the great love, and the betrayals in every musical note.
In every handful of earth. The blood and the sweat and the
cum. From the other side of the hotel, I hear a man scream
in Spanish, *whore, whore, you dirty whore!* And then nothing.
Silence made worse by the slow *ching...ching...ching....* Maybe
I should have stayed home. Or at least in another hotel. Maybe then I could have thought better—or better yet, not at all.
Either way, I'm beginning to suspect there is nothing smart or
sensitive to say about a massacre. I would like to write this all
in a way you could read all at once, simultaneous, swallow it all
with everything that ever was or will be, the good and the bad,
the living, the dead and the yet to be born, feel it like you can
feel a handful of dirt after you've let it fall from your fingers, or
like a fuck the morning after, feel it like you feel the sound of
birdsong or the breathing of an old man and old woman in the
dark as they sleep in the same bed, breathe it in the way you do
your own smells wafting up from under the sheets as you lie
in the dark holding tight on to yourself. I want to tell you how
their farm was a paradise—this farm of the old woman and
old man who loved each other very much and for a long time.
How they grew organic marshmallows in the wetland and jelly
beans on the hillside. I want to say something about how there
is no beauty without truth—otherwise it's kitschy and fake.
And there is no truth without beauty, because the truth always
takes our breath away. Even the truth of a murdered child huddled next to his murdered parents. Even the truth about the
old man and old woman farmers who spent the better part
of a couple of decades saying bitter things to each other. Even
the truth about how many good people in America think this
killing they are paying for down here is making the world a

better place. I want to say something about those things but don't have any new words, and the old ones make my ears buzz and my eyes glaze over.

Across the café, a fat man sits at a table sweating profusely and drinking beer. Yellow sunlight sparkles over green mountains but he raises a bottle to his shiny lips and says, "To ugly life!" I join him. After a spooky night I want to stay out of my room. The day proceeds from six beers onward. I see it all coming effortlessly toward me as if I'm on one of those moving sidewalks in the airport, and by nightfall, I find myself walking the empty and dark streets with a woman I've met, a fellow traveler, a filmmaker. Our footsteps echo, our shadows grow and shrink along the walls. The doors are all closed. She holds my hand, and when we find her place, we fall into bed. One thing I've noticed is that when there are gunshots in the streets, the sex is better.

Afterward, she lectures me. She says she's been a witness to the horror, and now she must share it with the world. Her face flushes and she pounds a tiny fist into her palm. She looks both uncrossable and also close to tears. Because she's naked, I'm feeling virtuously patient. I don't want to talk, but she asks and asks again, so finally I say I don't know what she's talking about. Maybe my tone catches her off guard, or maybe she would have cried anyway. I don't know. I tell her there are many tragedies I'd never write and others I try to write because my life feels worthless unless I try. I tell her that when I am not trying to make some sense of the heartbreak—trying to find a way to hold it all—well, I want to kill myself.

This seems to cheer her up. She wipes her tears. She puts her thin arms around my shoulder and lays her face against my chest, and by god as long as we are warm and alive we may as well go at it again. My my. I don't understand any of it, not a whit, but I'm having a much better night tonight than last night—and to think it all started at breakfast with the fat man and beer. When we finish our romp I kiss her forehead and she finally falls asleep. I slip out on my way to the bathroom and never come back. Oh well. The whole isthmus is burning and by all standards this is just a minor fire.

Actually, it's dawn, and I follow the pink sky to the edge of the lake and a little outdoor restaurant where I hear Elvis Presley. I sit and order, and soon a skinny old woman begins to shout at the man bringing me a cup of coffee and plateful of fish. She calls him shameless for serving a *gringo*. She says he's a Nicaraguan and a Nicaraguan should never serve a *gringo*. That the *gringos* killed her son. That the *gringos* are trying to kill the whole country, that the gringos should go back to *gringo* hell and he should not only not feed the *gringos* but should grow some *cojones* and shoot this particular one.

Besides my coffee and food, the man also conveniently carries a pistol under his belt. He looks at her and then at me. Maybe he's trying to imagine shooting me but can't grow the *cojones*. More likely they're plenty grown but he's not all that interested in the idea. He shrugs and puts on my table a fried fish whose head and tail hang over the edges of the plate. I'm a customer after all, and this is a clean, well-lighted place. The woman is very drunk. She has many colorful plastic bracelets on her wrists, and they've suddenly captured her attention. She takes them off and puts them on again, takes them off, rearranges them, and puts them on again. She does all of this with the saddest face I've ever seen. I eat my meal in peace and afterward buy us all rum. I want to tell the woman how sorry I am about her son. I want to say something but can't think of how to begin. So the three of us—the waiter, the old woman, and I—all three of us sit with our feet up staring at the pretty morning waves and the volcano islands, and all three of us share a drink and listen to Elvis.

Abrazos and long-range leaps and smooches—
Tomb

how do you stay married to a man?
how do you stay in love?

I put the letter down and get up and pour myself a cup of wine. The mention of the rum makes me thirsty. Does that mean I'm becoming an alcoholic? His unabashed carnality makes me something else, which I take as a good sign, although part of what I feel when I feel it is panic that nobody will ever want me again, nobody that I would have anyway. I sit back down again at the table with the wine and use my palm to smooth out the crinkled paper that the letter was written on, put it back in the envelope, then take it out again. About the only thing I know for certain about desire is how fast it can change. When my daughter was in high school she said she was staying overnight at her girlfriend's house, but she wasn't there in the morning when we called. When she came home around noon we confronted her with this inconvenient fact, and she admitted that she'd stayed overnight with her boyfriend, but they didn't have sex. She said they both decided they weren't ready for sex. I told her that was nice but if she wasn't ready for sex—wasn't ready to look at this boy the next day and know he was the first one, wasn't ready to protect herself against STDs or pregnancy (although, why would she believe me?)—then she shouldn't climb into bed with him. She thought I was being overly protective. She thought I didn't trust her.

"I want you to think about a couple of things," I told her. She snorted, but I pressed on. "First of all, you need to remember that whether or not you can imagine it or not, he could force you, and so until a girl knows a boy very *very* well, she should never put herself in a position that contradicts her intentions. Like get in bed, under the covers, in her underwear, with a boy she doesn't want to have sex with."

This made her angry. She thought I didn't like her boyfriend. She was right, but that was beside the point. She said, "Mom, we're not talking about 'a boy' and 'a girl.' We're talking about me and Jace, and he would never force me."

"Okay," I said, "Of course not. But even if Jace is a perfect gentleman, and even if you might not be ready for sex when you climb into bed with him, well, fifteen minutes under the covers has been known to change a girl's mind."

She blushed and looked away, turned away. We were having this conversation in the farmhouse kitchen. From where we stood we could see over a half-wall counter into the living room, the woodstove room. On the ceiling of that room was a ceiling fan. Every few seconds our border collie Pete jumped up at the fan. He'd get about four feet off the ground and appear up over the half wall, blue eyes wild and hypnotized by the fan. Then he'd fall back to the floor again where we couldn't see him. Then he'd pop up again.

"All I'm saying, Kate," I said, "is you have needs you don't know yet—needs that'll make irrelevant the question of whether or not you're *ready.*"

"Mom," she said. "How can you be so cynical?"

"I'm not being cynical," I said, and watched Pete jump. "It's just the way we're made."

Kate spun around and flashed me another angry look—only now she was crying as well. Pete jumped again. He'd do this silently and forever, as far as anybody knew. Nobody else in the house seemed bothered by it.

"One more thing," I said, and I tried to be gentle. "I don't think you can believe for one second when Jace tells you he isn't ready for sex."

Despite her tears, she screamed at me. "You don't even *know* him!"

I wanted to touch her but when I reached out she spun away. "No," I said, "but I know boys, and as far as Jace saying he isn't ready for sex—as far as any boy saying he isn't ready—you can be pretty certain that the moment you decide *you are ready*, he will be too."

Pete jumped and jumped again. I couldn't stand it anymore and walked out of the kitchen and grabbed him by the collar and put him outside. When I came back into the kitchen Kate was still there, slumped away from me, face down, all the air out of her. How had I made such a mess of it?

"It's just the way boys are made," I said, and tried to smile, tried to turn my tone a little bit playful. "And although it's often annoying, it's also pretty handy in its way."

How's that for a frank sex talk? Poor Kate to get stuck with a blunt mother like me. Or *struck* with a blunt mother. She had that look, anyway, as she blinked her big watery green eyes a couple of times, blushed a carnation pink, and ran upstairs to her room as fast as she could.

From the table in the cabin I look out the big window at the blue sky fading to gray dusk. I stand to check out the meadow, look for the bear but don't see him. The stove needs a fire. There are still a few hot coals from this morning and I could build it up fast with a few sticks but I think I'll wait. The cabin is so small that if I build a fire before it gets cold, the stove will make the cabin too hot and then I'll want to open the door, but I'll be afraid to do that because what if the bear comes around again?

I touch the pepper spray in its holster on my belt just to reassure myself. In case I grow any *cojones* I'll shoot a *gringo*. This thought amuses me but also reminds me of writhing around on the floor last night trying to cough out the sharp little hook of pepper spray in my throat. I decide to go outside and pee before it gets dark. When I get back—with more wood, of course, that I stack on top of the already full box behind the stove—I grab my cup of wine and sit down again with the letter. I have to admit I don't remember at all the peaceful scene at the shore of the lake listening to Elvis. I remember reading it early in the morning in my rocking chair in our one-bedroom (the twins had the bedroom, Mark and I slept on a fold-out couch in the living room) apartment in Durham, North Carolina, while I was trying to nurse the twins. They must have been less than four months old and I was back at work already doing my residency in the hospital and feeling overwhelmed. It's amazing I remember reading the letter at all, because when I think of those times, those first two years with the twins, which corresponded with my first two years doing an E.R. residency, well, frankly, the specifics of that time seem blasted away from memory by the trauma itself, the difficulty anesthetized by the passage of time. When my dad was beginning to lose his mind to Alzheimer's, he went through a stage of reading all of his papers, his letters, everything he had around the house, and he was lucky because he had a lot—transcribed interviews and many fat fragments of a never finished memoir that told the stories of his life. He read about how he'd taught and practiced law for decades. How he'd become a judge, played the piano and the guitar, raised pigeons, gardened, built a cabin with his own hands in Northern Wisconsin, and then because he wanted to learn to sail, he built a sail boat. He read how wanting to learn to sail forced him, at age fifty-six, to finally learn how to swim. Yet he was so detached from what he was reading, he'd often look up from the page to tell me something his father had done.

"No, Daddy," I'd say, "that was *you* who did that. Those are your stories. You wrote them."

He'd look at me as if I must be kidding. "How?" he'd say.

"You mean how did you write them or how did you do them?"

He shook his head, incredulous. "Both."

"You had a lot of energy," I said. "You were young. And you had Mom to help."

He nodded and smiled and I wasn't sure who he was thinking about when he said, "Yes, Mom."

So how did I manage? Two words: sleeplessness and Mark. I was young, too, just twenty-four when the twins were born, and of course there were times—especially before they were born—when I wondered if I was ready, despite the vow I'd made to myself after terminating my first pregnancy. But what I was learning then, what having children and doing a medical residency both teach (and what much later I'd try to tell my daughter) is this: what *you're ready for* and what *you need to do* are two different things, and often doing what *you need to do* makes the question of what *you're ready for* irrelevant.

Which finally brings me back to exactly where I was when I read this letter the first time: early one morning under a green light in our apartment after a day and night of work made even longer by a three-hundred-pound woman in a diabetic coma who was literally dragged by the feet (her body was rolling on one of those wheeled planks mechanics lie on when they slide under your car) into the emergency room and down the tiled hallway by her desperate husband just as I was getting ready to go home, and if that wasn't enough, they were followed by a man who'd shot himself in the head and walked in (yes, walked) just as I was getting ready to go home again. I suppose in situations like that it should be easy to focus on what is needed—but at the time I was distracted by other needs, too many needs, as my breasts were leaking even as I tended his wounds, milk soaking through the pads in my bra and wetting the front of my scrubs. I think I started crying on the way home from the hospital. I'd missed six important weeks of my residency, staying home with the babies, and in the two months since I'd been back I felt so far behind I'd never catch up. We were working easily a hundred hours a week and still I thought I'd never learn what I was supposed to learn. I was missing my babies, too. I was determined to be a good mother, and what that meant to me then, the only thing that meant to me then (the only thing I could do for my babies, really, as I was gone so much) was breast feed. The plan was I could feed them when I came back from work and feed them before I left for work, and pump milk at work for Mark to feed from a bottle the next day when I was gone. I thought I could keep breastfeeding for six months despite my long shifts and long weeks. All of the literature said it was the best thing for the babies. The nutrition, of course, but the mommy factor, as well. If my babies didn't have me holding them and touching them and talking to them, they could at least have my milk. It meant a lot to me. It made me feel as if I were there with them even though I was not.

So I arrived home leaking and tired and carrying a heavy agenda for how it was supposed to be. My husband would have the twins changed and clean and present them to me, the great provider. I'd feed them until all three of us drifted off to sleep, and then Mark would take them from my arms and put them in the crib, and lead me back to bed without waking me and hold me tight until morning, when I'd drag myself up and shower and head back to the hospital. Instead, I found Mark asleep in bed with two empty bottles on the pillow and the sleeping twins next to him. My breasts started leaking again just looking at the babies. We had a little rule never to wake sleeping babies no matter what, but we also had a little rule that he wouldn't feed the babies before I got home, that he would save that feeding for me. I picked them up and held them and they woke and started to cry and I started to let out even more milk. Mark woke too and said the babies weren't hungry, that he'd waited as long as he could but had to feed them, and now that I'd woken them up again, I could jolly well hold them again until they went back to sleep.

Pretty soon we were all crying. Well, not Mark. He just lay back down and lifted his head occasionally to shout back when I shouted at him, until finally he couldn't even do that, and his head just stayed right on the pillow and he went to back sleep. I couldn't believe it. The babies were screaming and I was pacing and scolding and he fell asleep right in the middle of our argument. I wondered if he was on some kind of drug, and that made me even madder. It was an absurd thought—Mark didn't smoke marijuana until he was dying and barely even drank—but I thought it anyway because anger was my drug and it was coursing wildly through my veins and needed to be fed. I walked with the screaming babies, one in each arm, feeling sorry for myself and for the twins for having a drug-addict father. I had the kind of sleeplessness they use to torture prisoners, and let me tell you, I would have said anything, done anything, to get some sleep. What I did finally was sit down, which is what the babies wanted, an end to the frantic jiggling. They settled down enough so I could try to get them to take some milk and they did take a little, but barely any, and then they fell asleep with their mouths still clamped gently on my nipples. I was afraid to move and too boiling inside watching Mark sleep to go to sleep myself, and that's when I noticed the letter, and that's when I read the letter—my milk crusted scrubs hiked up over my bare breasts, trying not to wake my over-fed babies, and boiling mad at my sleeping husband for doing everything he was supposed to do—that's when I read the letter.

Of course the letter made me even angrier. His description of the woman and sex embarrassed me—as though I cared who he was having sex with—and it seemed that's all he wrote about. I balled up the paper in my fist, which is why the paper's now crinkled and also why I don't recall anything about the peaceful scene at the end. Did he have the slightest idea what he was talking about? What a woman was, what she could do? I'd been stretched and torn and sewn and sore and only now perhaps healed, at least the flesh of me. I looked at Mark sleeping in the bed and tried to calm myself, but I was resenting my fatigue and my feeling of incompetence at work and incompetence at home, and most of all resenting how much I needed Mark to make it all work, and resenting him for not wanting me, and resenting the fact that the babies had taken that from us. Taken it all from me, anyway, as I hadn't had even a stirring like that in many months. Would I ever feel it again? And if I didn't, what would that make me, some kind of sexless freak? I'd cut my hair super short and start wearing sexless clothes and prattle endlessly about my babies. Mark would turn into my drone husband trailing along behind me following instructions. The thought sent me tumbling into despair. I looked at Tommy's letter. *Screw him,* I thought, *and his six-beer mornings and wild nights.* What does that have to do with anything that matters? My mother used to say the work of adulthood was buying groceries, raising children, and staying sane. Mark and I were doing the best we could. Tommy was living like a child. *Fuck him,* I thought. From anger to despair to comfortable anger again, I crinkled up his letter even tighter in my fist and tossed it across the room into the corner.

Again I looked at Mark sleeping. I'd fallen for him barely more than a year ago and yet it felt like ages, and lately like the great ice age. Thirteen months ago he lay on top of me with all of his weight, which was nothing compared to the weight of the babies he put inside me or the weight of the things I'd need to learn and the things I'd need to bear. I sat with my sleeping babies on my lap and looked at how the weight of him sagged the hide-a-bed, but after putting the twins back in their crib and shutting the door, I climbed in with him anyway. There was nowhere else to lie down. I felt him move next to me in bed, hard and trembling, felt this with bitterness, almost, who did he think I was? My breasts were still leaking milk and I hated how it made me smell, and yet I hadn't even showered yet—I'd save that for morning. I felt empty inside, completely spent except for the heat of the anger, a burning feeling focused just exactly where the tip of his penis touched my hip.

He put his arm around me. "Welcome back, baby."

I moved away, tensed for a fight, but soon heard by his breathing that he'd fallen back asleep, which I held against him as well. I envied Mark how he'd fed the babies, and I was mad at him for not waiting, and I could understand why he didn't— how would he know when I was getting home?—which made me all the more angry, how I had no control over when I left work or even any control over whether I could feed my own babies. My breasts hurt and I thought I should pump them, but I thought *fuckit, fuckit fuckit, I'm tired of that fucking pump,* and so I lay there and thought I could feel them begin to dry out, feel this gift of milk begin to ebb, and that made me mad, looking at Mark and thinking how he was making my breasts dry out, taking this life away from me, and somehow I jumped from that to how while I was holding the man with the gunshot wound to the head, wet circles suddenly darkened my scrubs over my nipples and how he just lay there and watched, eyes wide open. Amazed. Maybe it saved his life. My god. Sometimes you run to the bathroom to replace your pads and change scrubs but if you've got a man who's just shot himself in the head and you are trying to get him to calm down so you can look at his wound, and you are holding his head, and cleaning his wound and you can't run to the bathroom and change your pads and your scrub tops you might be thinking, at least for a second, you might be thinking you son of a bitch, if you'd had better aim you'd be dead and I'd be cleaned up and home by now.

Mark and I fell in love probably four times in the twenty-four years we were together, each more miraculous then the last. Each falling was a surrender into deeper levels of vulnerability, and each falling we fought with every cell of our bodies. It was a pattern in our marriage that both threatened it and saved it. We'd resist surrendering and resist and resist, and then, exhausted and in need, we'd find each other again. It was the ebb and flow of love—which even after all of these years the only thing I know for sure about is what it's not. Love is not the same, ever, ever, ever. I suppose that night was the second. I mean, the first was the original tumble and pregnancy when we fell laughing together down the rabbit hole. This time, I went to sleep feeling wounded, incompetent, scared, but so tired I somehow fell asleep anyway, and then woke in his arms, grateful he was there with me. Where did the anger and bitterness go? A good sleep does marvelous things. I remember thinking, *how did this good thing happen to me?* I remember thinking, *what did I do to make this good thing hap-*

pen to me? I remember thinking *I will love this man until the day I die.* Last night I had been so caught up in my body, the birth, the babies, my work, I hadn't really looked at him, and suddenly, there he was—

"Are you ready for this?" he asked, poised over me.

I nodded. I shook my head. I pulled him down on top of me. I hurt, I wasn't quite ready, but I needed him just where he was with a need fiercer than any I'd ever known. It woke me up and shook me to my bones. I'd been afraid of losing my anger, the chip on my shoulder. It had been my strength, kept me upright, getting up, doing what I had to do for the babies, getting me to go back to work, and now I'd have to do without it—I'd have to do it with this man, who I loved, and there was nothing scarier I could think of. My bones shook. How deep could I go? Deeper. No. Deeper. No. More. I hadn't the strength to resist. I clung to him and each time we came together it was a surrender, a falling into a place of dependency I never imagined possible. Such tender nothingness, such huge weakness, so tired, so sore, so weak. I was a wreck, I was destroyed. I was in love again. I remember pulling him toward me. I remember instead of a barrier, as it had been feeling of late, my skin felt like an opening, and when Mark touched me I lost my solid boundaries. My breasts wet and my vagina wet and my mouth wet and afterward when I cried and cried and cried, my eyes and nose were wet as well. Mark held me, held me, held me, and like that we plunged into the abyss. We'd only known each other a year and a month. How could we have come so far?

When we finished, I heard the babies beginning to wake, and my breasts let down milk and he said he'd get up and bring them to me but just as quickly I let go and let myself fall back to sleep again before he returned. I say let go because it felt like I'd been pulling a rope as hard as I could, afraid to let go of it, afraid I'd fall, but when I relaxed my grip, I didn't fall at all. Instead, whatever was on the rope floated away, but I was still where I'd always been, and I wondered why I'd ever thought the thing that floated away was so important. I dreamed I sat knitting booties in a bizarre green room with a stuffed Santa

Claus head mounted on the wall. I kept hearing gunshots and when I finally got up to look out the window into dirt road a man with a big plastic President Reagan mask was walking the length of a line of Mexican bandit prisoners giving each a jelly bean like communion wafer before shooting them in the head with his pointer finger. When they all lay dead, he lifted his mask—it was Tommy under the mask—and he blew the smoke off the tip of his finger like a gunfighter in an old Western.

I woke with the sheet twisted and the blankets bunched up at the foot of the bed. There was still an hour and a half before I had to be at work, and Mark, who'd collected Tommy's balled-up letter from the floor and set it on the counter, must have also already fed the babies and somehow gotten them back to bed, and now was on his way out the door for a run. He paused when he noticed my eyes were open. I curled up into a ball to stay warm. Without saying a word, he stepped over and spread the blankets to cover me up again.

The last time I talked to my daughter, she called from Kuala Lumpur shortly after the funeral to see how I was. I wasn't good. I mean, what was there to say? I was an empty shell and every cell in my body hurt. I told her that and then there wasn't much else to talk about. Except there was. Even over ten thousand miles I could feel the weight of the silence. I could tell she had something she wanted to ask me. Finally I said, "Honey, what is it?"

What I heard next was a voice so sad it squeezed the blood from my already broken heart. "How do you stay married to a man?" she asked, the voice of my daughter who'd just lost her father, the voice of a little girl, the voice of a very young woman living half a world away and trying to do a very big thing. "How do you stay in love?"

I was numb, exhausted, worn down by the wild swings of grief. If I'd been feeling more cheerful I might have tried to make something up or even tried to tell a dumb joke, but the fatigue and pain had made me nothing if not honest.

"I don't know, sweetheart," I said. "I really don't know."

the secret of living to 100 and the way
it looks from the bottom of a well

Dear Beanereen (me wee wencheen)—

This dusty, dirt-road, mangrove swamp port is my sanctuary. I can head east or west across borders for war stories if I need some cash, but in the meantime I have a jolly life indeed. On the way to the market every morning I pass a woman named Teresita. She calls out, Buenos días, Tomás! and I call out Buenos días, doña Teresita! One day she calls me over to where she is sitting. She is tiny, and she only has one leg below the knee, and she has a lapful of green mangoes, and she sits on a broken sidewalk in front of an open door leading into the dark, two-room apartment she shares with a beautiful grown-up great granddaughter I've noticed from time to time. There's a main room crossed by two hammocks and a kitchen smoky from an open cooking fire. A dirt floor and corrugated zinc roof held up by rough two by fours. She says she turned one hundred years old today. I'm amazed. She looks old, but 100? I tell her she doesn't look a day older than ninety. She offers me a couple of the mangoes on her lap, and I take one. I tell her I should be giving her a present. She laughs and asks if I want to know the secret to living one hundred years. I say sure, hey, maybe I can sell it. That makes her laugh. She raises one finger in the air and says in this high and shaky voice, I only had one man! Just one man! I only had one man! and for a moment I'm thinking she's going holy roller on me, which would be fine, I mean, she's a hundred, she can say whatever she wants, but I have a little feeling of boredom. Then she lowers her finger and looks at me with a twinkle in her eye, and she says, And he died...seventy years ago!

This makes her laugh so hard the rest of the mangoes roll off of her lap, and I swear she would have fallen off the rickety old chair if I hadn't caught her. I tell her I should get her a present. Does she want something like a new rocker? Some shoes. A shoe? She tells me she'd like a little bit of medicine for her hurt foot (the one that doesn't exist anymore) but what she'd really like is if I'd take her great granddaughter, Maria Isabel, out to buy her a dress for her wedding. Maria Isabel is getting married but doesn't have anything pretty to wear. I just got a little money for a story and can only drink so much of it, and beyond that, I have nobody to spend it on. We take a walk to the boutique part of the city, Teresita's pretty granddaughter Maria Isabel and me. I follow her from one place to another. She either doesn't like me or doesn't like to talk to me or be seen with me. I try to think of something bad I've done in this town, but I'm pretty new, so maybe she likes to walk way ahead of me and just look back occasionally to make sure I'm with her because she's afraid her fiancé will see her with me, or somebody will tell him that she was with me. I would have started to get bored and miserable as she dragged me through the one-hundred-degree heat from store to store if it weren't for my expert talent at simple-minded self-entertainment. For example, we went to one tiny boutique decorated with magazine cutouts, pictures of mountains and beaches, and beautiful women wearing beautiful clothes on said mountains and said beaches, and I sat on a bench while Maria Isabel tried on one dress after another until she finally found one (I won't describe it except to say it wasn't a wedding dress but just a pretty blue dress to get married in) and then she asked me if she could also get a bag. I wasn't sure, to tell you the truth, as I didn't know the word she used, but the dress was not expensive so I said yes. On the opposite wall from where I was sitting was a scale and as I sat there it seemed like a parade of young women walking by in the street would step in the store and up on the scale and weigh themselves. The store was very small, and the bench and the scale were wedged in under the awning, and when the women got up on the scale, their bottoms were about an arm's length from my face. I found this a pleasant distraction from whatever very important thoughts I might have otherwise had.

After paying for the dress, for the bag, and for some shoes, and after picking up some ibuprofen on the way back to Teresita's, where Maria Isabel finally stepped up close and gave me a *gracias* kiss on the cheek (even after all of that walking on all of those dirty streets she smelled like butter) I said *adios* and happy birthday and happy wedding, and kissed Teresita and with two green mangoes she forced into my hands, skipped happily off to the cantina and another old lady. Her name is Marisol and she's not so old as Teresita. She's still upright, still running a cantina. She's the most foul-mouthed woman I've ever heard. I could tell you some of the things she's said in casual conversation about her sex life, or the sex lives of others, but the words translated into English would make her seem like a pervert. Make her stranger than she is. Because what she is is strong and fun-loving and smart. She started out very poor, one of these barefoot urchins you see, and through hard work and good cheer and good luck, she got pretty rich, at least for Honduran standards. Lives in a nice house surrounded by her children and their children. In fact, everywhere she walks she's surrounded by a cloud of grandchildren. She often has a drink in her hand, even when she comes over to my end of the bar, or tonight to a table I'm sitting at, and sits with me for a while. She likes me because I tell her funny stories and don't complain. She says whining and complaining are the only things that really wear her down. Everybody with their aches and pains—this hurts, that hurts—until she thinks she's going to scream. She told me been married to seven men. (She didn't mean she'd walked up the aisle seven times, but lay down with seven men.) She said only two of those were worth a shit and they gave her seventeen children. She said she was seventy-two years old and *no me duele nada*. Nothing hurts me. When she said that she lifted her glass and we drank. A man behind her was shouting her name, trying to get her attention, trying to get her service, but she stayed focused on me and on her drink, and only after her glass was empty did she raise her fist above her head and flip the man off. Then she winked at me, and stood up to go back behind the bar. Janine, you should see this woman. Strong, broad shouldered, a beautiful brown, smooth-skinned face, black hair and legs and hips that a woman half her age would die for. I thought, hey, if anybody should have seventeen children, if anybody should pass on her genes in such abundance it is Doña Marisol.

So after such a wonderful day—and thanks to Marisol, plenty to drink, why when I get to bed does the nightmare still come? Not a memory exactly but a refinement of the horror. I don't know if the mind of the boozer turns bad memories into nightmares even as he thinks he's using booze to dampen the nightmares. I don't know. And I don't want you feeling sorry for me, thinking, poor man, such a bad memory, no wonder he drinks! I look at my mom, and her whole family, and I think, hey, I'd be drinking anyway. If I weren't haunted by the way it looks from the bottom of a well in Guatemala, the empty eye of heaven and only the shrieks and grunts and gunshots and laughter—yes, laughter!—while the soldiers chased down and massacred the villagers, I'm sure I'd have some other unpleasant memory. Say, the first time I learned the world was unjust when my dad and I watched the '72 Olympic basketball finals and saw with our very eyes the Russians steal—how could it be possible? How could they be allowed to do it?—we saw the Russians *steal* the gold medal from the US basketball team....

But before I get more specific about the nightmare, I want to write a memory of another day before I forget. I don't know how it fits with the rest of this letter, but who cares. When I was a little boy, I wanted to tell a story at the dinner table. I don't remember what it was about but when I finished, my dad said, "That story is like a new pencil. It has no point." I think he was trying to be playful, but it hurt my feelings and I stopped telling stories around him. Then he died when I was thirteen so I guess I blew my chance. Anyway, maybe this letter is like a new pencil. If it had a title, I'd call it "The Secret of Living to One Hundred and the Way it Looks from the Bottom of a Well." The memory of the good day starts with Juan Carlos the Costa Rican poet (who you might remember from past letters) and me taking a bus up a winding road onto the green shoulder of a volcano. The whole way there Juan Carlos is telling me how disgusted he is with Costa Ricans, even though he is one. He says they don't care about anything but *electrodomesticos* like blenders and fry pans and stereos and how to get to Panama in order to buy crap for cheap. He says he needs to read books, that's all, to read books and to write poems. He says he explored the war in El Salvador and found it distasteful. He was with a group of students when one hundred were shot on the steps of the university during a student strike. He says he has a bullet wound in his belly. Right there on the crowded bus he lifts his shirt and shows me the scar. (This was before we roomed together and I saw all of the stripes on his back as well.) The scar looks like a pink star the size of a quarter on his smooth brown belly. I'm impressed and a little envious.

"It's painful to try to write about what matters," he says. "Not to mention how much it hurts to get shot in the belly."

We get off the bus in front of his parents' house, a little two-room shack surrounded by coffee shrubs as far as you can see. His dad is asleep in a hammock on the porch. When he wakes,

I can see how bent over and old he is. His name is Don Joaquín and the first thing he tells us is how the neighbor dog ate one of his chickens. At least that's what I gather. He doesn't have any teeth and so I can't really understand him. He offers me a couple of green plantains to take with me, and he makes a fist and flexes his arm and says, For strength! Up high on the mountain here the air sparkles with sunshine. Juan Carlos's mom's named is Marci and she keeps smiling at me and bowing and saying how happy she is to meet me, how glad they are when their son brings his friends. Then she and Juan Carlos go outside and she shows him some plants in the yard. A man comes into the yard and don Joaquin and doña Marci greet him and they talk about a neighbor who died yesterday. The heat, dust, the whistle of bugs. The neighbor finally leaves and Doña Marci fires up the wood stove to do the cooking and it's suddenly so hot and smoky in the kitchen I can't believe it. Don Joaquín tells me Marci won't use the electric stove (a brand new one, next to the wood stove) because she'd have to learn to cook all over again. Doña Marci waddles around the kitchen and makes us tortillas and coffee. Then she makes us scrambled eggs. The stove smokes and we all wave our hands in front of our faces between bites. Out the window, the chickens that the neighbor dog didn't eat drink the waste water from the sink, where it drains out onto a little patch of gravel.

Afterward, Juan Carlos and I caught a bus back to San José and stopped by to see Black Chepe's place. He's kind of a happy hustler we know from pickup basketball games down on the Sabana. He's from Limón and speaks English and works the Plaza de Cultura helping tourists. We sat at his kitchen table and his wife Lupe made us ice cold *horchatas*. Not his wife, but the mother of his children. She seemed all right. I kept thinking, Chepe sure made the right girl pregnant. Twice! He couldn't marry her because he had nothing and when you have nothing, hey, who can make that kind of promise? But they seemed to like each other. He liked how she took care of his children, and she liked how he stopped by when he could and brought money or papayas or mangos or something. He never came empty handed, and he liked to sit with his daughters on his lap, and I think with Lupe on his lap when the girls went to bed. They had something okay. Not great, but I felt envious again so what does that mean?

In the city, the air was even hotter and we were upstairs in a two-room flat, and after a while both the little chocolate girls were tired of sharing their parents and started crying so we said our good-byes and headed to the casino where Juan Carlos had to pick up some money for plants he'd delivered last week. In the meantime, I sat at the blackjack table and watched all of the rich people, specifically the ones at my table, a beautiful blond woman, high on something, gambling, waving her arms, talking like a duck, and her muscular companion with the sleeveless denim shirt, also blond, not-quite as high, and a little embarrassed. They were both from South Africa and he'd lost all of his chips in ten minutes and would have split already if she hadn't kept winning.

When Juan Carlos came back into the casino where all of the rich people were, it was like I saw him for the first time. His face unshaven, eyes dark and youthful, wearing green overalls and a loose flannel shirt over the top, he looked vulnerable and sad. We went across the street for some spaghetti. Even though he just got paid, I bought. Bad deal because the chairs were so hard they hurt my ass. And when he started talking over the roar of the traffic, an unending monologue about the rise of paramilitary organizations in his country, the storing and shipping of guns, the importation of well-armed "traffic" helicopters, the politics getting uglier and uglier, I had a terrible sense of foreboding. I looked at the pretty flesh of his mouth moving and cold death seemed to walk in the door and sit on my lap. To distract myself I looked over his shoulder to the women passing by across the street. The nice looking young women in their yellow and pink and white, their short shiny haircuts and cute shoes, and I said *desesperado* because I liked how the word felt coming off my tongue, *desesperado*, desperate, and it's also how I felt in my gut, just dying for something.

I don't know if any of this has a point, Dad. Maybe you

know now, seeing as you're already dead, but to us, the living, it was just another late night of drinks and snacks. Juan Carlos had stopped talking and suddenly couldn't seem to eat fast enough. "*Sí sí*," he agreed, his mouth full of spaghetti, *la situación está muy desesperada*, the situation is very desperate.

Hugs and fishes,
Toe-Moss (-Me) Con-Con

four

vice is a good thing

Stepping into the bar is like stepping into a druggy dream. I see a giant green parrot and a black bear but the parrot is moving and the black bear is stuffed. Also a stuffed mountain lion and coyote and a tall man wrapped in Ace bandages with a slit for one eye and a slit for his mouth. I think he's supposed to be a mummy. I feel the warm air on my face, so warm I wonder if I'm flushing. The bar smells of beer and booze and hamburgers and French fries. There's a man with a pumpkin—a real hollowed out pumpkin—over his head, looking out through cut triangle eyes and talking to a very tall geisha with a whitened face and a little blossom of red lips and a yellow silk robe that hangs open to reveal a hairy chest, so maybe he's dressed as a cross-dresser and not a geisha. There's a warrior in camouflage, or is he a hunter? There's a baseball game on the big screen but nobody is watching because it's a Halloween party, and I didn't even know it was Halloween. Talking to the mummy is a woman with bare legs below and mostly-bare breasts above a sparkly purple cheerleader outfit, and another woman with a doughy face topped with Marge Simpson hair and a plastic tiara balanced on top. She's wearing a very tight, very low-cut nurse outfit. Actually, most of the women are dressed in mostly skin, a Halloween costume that pushed me right out of the Halloween party circuit about a decade ago. Call me a prude, but after a certain age I didn't think it was fun to dress like a slut anymore. It's a kind of grumpiness that I know Mark got tired of but I couldn't dress like that without feeling ridiculous and predictable and, well, even when I was young I didn't feel I had the body to pull it off. Mark said Halloween was supposed to be ridiculous, and what was really predictable was my attitude. I guess we had a few fights about it.

I stand in front of the stuffed bear for a long time, then make my way through the crowd feeling invisible. Instead of ordering a beer I ask for a whiskey, a double Jameson's with one ice cube. I hope my destination isn't the bear's stomach. It's not that I'm feeling more fragile but more as if I'm suddenly transported and glad to be transported to whatever fair la-la land this is. I lean against the bar and pay for my drink and turn and am about to take a sip when a leprechaun at my elbow says, "Harold Bong."

His eyes are green and his cheeks are flushed and even with his green hat on, I'm at least a couple inches taller.

It's loud. It's hard to hear. I incline my head. "What?" I say.

"Bong," he says, and extends his hand. "Harold."

Which makes me laugh. I repeat his name. "Bong?" I say. "Really?"

He shrugs. I take his hand. It's big and rough.

"McBean," I say.

"McBean?" he says.

"No," I say. "Not really. It's Janine. "

"Janine McBean?"

"McCarthy."

I'm looking out over the crowd for Bart. It's not that I want to talk to him, but he's the only one here I expect to have met. I don't see him. I turn to Bong, who's still looking at me, confused about the name.

"I didn't even know it was Halloween."

"It's tomorrow," he says. "But tonight's the party."

We both lean back against the bar. Bong isn't touching me but almost. I have my elbows back and my drink in my hand. I sip the whiskey. I forgot how much I like whiskey.

"Who are all of these people?"

"They come every year."

"You all know each other, then?"

He nodded thoughtfully. "Most, I guess."

"I'm an old crone," I say.

"A what?"

"A crone."

"Is that some kind of bee?"

"That's a drone," I say.

"A what?"

"A pilot-less bomber."

He's staring at me in his leprechaun costume and I'm laughing again. "An old woman," I say, and one of the reasons I'm laughing is the irony of what's going on, what I'm feeling even as I say this. After four months without it, my period is coming. I haven't had other symptoms of menopause but at my age when my periods stopped (coincidentally, soon after Mark's death) I thought, oh, *et tu*, friend?

Bong looks amused by something as well, or is merely trying to share my amusement. I think about what his face would do if I told him why I'm smiling. An unkind little fantasy. I didn't used to think this way. I used to be socially generous, with plenty of room for other people's stories but lately I've almost gotten used to these mean little thoughts bubbling out of my brain's soup and my Husband Recently Died story leaves little air for others. Somebody walks past with some kind of marshmallow treats on a platter. We each take one. I think of the story Mark used to tell about organic marshmallows. Actually, Tommy mentioned the phrase in a letter but Mark took the phrase and made up a story for the kids. I suppose I've inherited it.

"Do you know where marshmallows come from?" I ask.

Bong looks at me. The music is loud and I don't think he can hear me any easier than I can hear him. Maybe he's too short, but that doesn't make sense. His ears are just about my mouth level. Anyway, he shakes his head and moves on. Maybe he did hear me and that's exactly why he left. Just as well, as into the vacuum caused by his exit slides the mummy. He's drinking a beer through a straw in his mouth slit. His one eye is very dark, almost black, and the other is covered. He looks at me and without any facial expression to judge him by, I get the creeps. I contemplate walking away but I like the whiskey and I'm close to the bar and I order another and I think hey, you don't just walk away from a mummy. What if he's somebody you once knew?

"Hey," he says, "somebody just asked me the purpose of a mummy."

I don't know what to say to that and doubt I've heard right anyway. His one eye looks at me. Regards me. For some reason I think I should be home sleeping rather than here. I think of the geese down by the river sleeping in the tall grass—is that where they sleep? Or floating in the river, in an eddy. I think of the horses sleeping standing up in the wind all bunched together. I think of the chickadees sleeping wherever they sleep at night, fluffed up against the wind that I can't hear inside because of the sound of music and so many voices and can't feel in here because of these thick log walls that separate this warm light and still air and from the black cold of forever outside. I think of Tom Connor and his thirst and think I feel it too. I order another whiskey, my third. The mummy speaks again. I can't hear him so he leans down to speak close to my ear. I can feel the wind of his breath coming though the beer-wet slit of his mouth.

"I told him I don't know," he says.

"Don't know what?" I yell back.

"The purpose of a mummy in modern society."

I wasn't sure what to say. I finally said, "Who asked that?"

He shrugged under his wrap of bandages.

"The purpose of a mummy?"

He nods, one eye twinkling.

"People died," I say. "They made mummies out of them."

"We do?" he asks.

"The Egyptians. The Maya."

"What about nowadays?"

"What?"

"In modern society?"

I shrug. He does too.

"Halloween," I say.

"What?"

"Costumes."

I think he's laughing under all of that bandage. His one eye continues to twinkle, anyway. I can tell he's still looking at me even though I was focused on paying for the whiskey. I still want to tell the marshmallow story but it's so hard to talk I'm not going to try. I take out a cigarette, light it. The mummy is still looking at me.

"Want one?" I ask.

He fingers a can of snoose from under his bandages at about waist level and takes a dip, slips it into the mouth slit. Then suddenly I'm dancing with the mummy, who's taken my hands and has me whirling around. I have to put the cigarette between my lips, and that's how I'm dancing. I can't believe it, not only dancing, but with a dangling cigarette! We do one or three or five songs. Me and the mummy. We dance around and around the stuffed bear standing on his back legs in the middle of the party. It's okay because although I don't really get to enjoy my cigarette, the dancing takes me away from my drink, so it's there when I get back, and the mummy kind of pats me on the small of my back and says something I can't understand and then wanders off in the direction of the men's room. I get a comic picture of him digging for his do-jiggy (a medical term) between layers of Ace bandage. I find my drink and sip, and lean back. From inside the warm barroom, with the rock and roll music and the laughter and the big screen showing the baseball game that nobody is watching, you can't hear the wind. And you can't hear when the wind brings the snow and how it swirls down in big flakes. People start coming in from outside with flakes in their hair and on their shoulders. Suddenly Bart is standing next to me. He's dressed in a big green garbage bag, through which he's torn a head hole. He wears it as a poncho.

"What are you?"

"Green slime," he says. "And you?"

"A widow."

He tilts his head back, lifts the big red eyebrows, looks me over with eyes so green they seem electric. "No black?"

"Passé," I say.

He gestures to the bartender to bring me another of what I'm drinking, then says, "How's Puppy?"

"In the car," I say. "I didn't know there was going to be a party."

"Halloween," he says. I glance at him and see that yes indeed he is trying to be a smart aleck.

"Really?" I say.

"You threw together a pretty realistic widow costume anyway."

"How did you ever get the idea to come as slime?" I say.

This amuses him and I realize we are flirting. He touches his head with his forefinger and raises his big red eyebrows, as if to indicate brains. I give him a quick smile for his cleverness but I don't want to flirt and I need a tampon. I take the new whiskey, and pour my old one into it, then excuse myself and make for the ladies room. The quiet there is a relief. I didn't know how loud the music was until I closed the door. I feel my shirt pocket for my two cigarettes. No tampon machine but two young women leaning toward the mirror—let's call them I-Dream-of-Jeannie One and I-Dream-of-Jeannie Two. I think I've stepped into one of Mark's adolescent fantasies, surrounded on each side by beautiful, mostly bare-breasted twins. Suddenly I love them anyway, as they both have what I need. Ah, sisterhood. I take one from each and duck into the stall, do my business and but stay right there on the toilet and drink my whiskey. I feel my chest pocket for a cigarette and I light one up. I haven't done this since high school, sat in a toilet stall and smoked, and I find it more pleasant than it seems possible for something so banal to be. One of the discoveries of grief is the places I've found unexpected pleasure—absolutely stunning pleasure. Peeing outside. Starting my period. Smoking on the toilet in a public bathroom. *Ah, whiskey!* and I take another sip. Vice is a good thing, I think, and suddenly it's very fun not to be a doctor in Wisconsin anymore but instead to be a grieving widow on the edge of the wilderness. I want to sit here forever and I wish I'd brought a book but then I realize I do have some letters in my handbag. I sit on the toilet and sip whiskey and inhale tobacco smoke and reach into my bag and get one. Why not? Nothing like an almost twenty-year-old letter from an ex-lover to complete the bathos. When the two I-Dream-of-Jeannies leave I can hear the music get loud again through the open bathroom door and I imagine dancing with the stuffed bear, holding its hairy paws and kicking up my heels like a happy bride. I suppose I'd have to lead. I love the way nicotine focuses my mind, but you'd never know it because even as I unfold the letter and start to read I'm thinking if Tommy were here I'd ask him…Ask him what? I had a question in mind but it slipped away. So instead I'd just ask, *What's the purpose of a mummy in modern society, Tommy?* Maybe I'd ask, *Do you want to hear a story about where marshmallows come from?* The whiskey's making the inside of my head start to glow and the scary thing is I'm still thirsty and thinking that before this Crossing-The-Great-Plains-In-My-Grief thing is over I just might throw myself face first on the ground and start calling for a witch doctor.

maybe they'll see I'm mute

Dear Wencheen,

Last night I met an un-shaven kid from California who's lived in a skiff for five months in the estuary and is trying to get out of the country. He fishes from the skiff to support himself and when he sells enough fish he comes here and buys beer and tries to flirt but there are no English speaking women here and he speaks Spanish with a club tongue. He looks at me and shrugs and says he's not hard up yet, which is almost comical because he looks like a kicked dog. He has trouble keeping his eyes open when he talks. *How did you get here?* I ask him. He looks at me. *How did I get here?* I nod, *Yes, how did you get here?* He shakes his head, looks at the floor, which is planking with gaps between boards so we can see the water of the estuary below us or smell the mud when the tide is out. He seems intrigued by the question. He seems to want to answer but is stumped, as though I asked him to recite the periodic table. He can't stop shaking his head and his confusion is frankly too similar to mine to be interesting so I move down the bar to where three men are clustered, red-faced, arguing about soccer.

I went to the big game yesterday and it was very hot in the sun but the sky was blue and the grass green and each tiny breeze a lovely, lovely thing. Whenever a player got even a charley horse during the game he writhed around as though he'd been shot. I was sure he'd never walk again, then in about two minutes, after everybody got a little rest, he'd hop up and play would resume.

Hijo de puta! I heard shouted a half dozen times a minute, *Hijo de puta!*

After a while I stayed seated when everybody else stood so I could get a little shade. If you stay seated when everybody around you is up and cheering, you see some stuff. You should try it. For instance, an over-fed thug was standing in front of me and he had a gun tucked into his belt under his shirt and I could see it easily when he stood and cheered, and I could also see how he had this habit of touching the handle of the pistol with his right hand and at the same time casually dropping his left hand and tenderly cupping his balls. Just to make sure they were there. In fact for the duration of the game I would say he was very attentive to his gun and to his balls, or—as the men down here sometimes call them—his *muchachos.* After we won, the crowd (except for me) ran down on the field and stripped the players. It was the championship game after all. *We won, we won we won!* Everybody danced, boiling bodies, a spontaneous bacchanal. I watched a man moving his hips like a woman striper and touching himself like a woman masturbating. Not just for a moment or two but for a good five minutes and everybody around him laughed and laughed. A woman bent over at the waist and bounced her hot summer buttocks against her boyfriend's crotch—the boyfriend stood with his hands clasped up over his head, prisoner style, grinning like a frog. The crowd carried banners, whistles, drums.

Women unbuttoned their blouses and their skin glowed in the heat. Men driven mad at the sights pissed joyfully over the grandstand. Walking timidly in this chaos were the players— they'd been stripped by the crowd down to their jockstraps— and they wandered around looking slight and a little scared, stunned with joy. The whole wild scene gave me a feeling of contentment I can't easily describe or explain, but as I drift- ed away, on the way back to my *pensión,* still floating in the love but just around the corner from the madness, I passed a door opening into somebody's home. Actually just a big room lit only by a bare light bulb in the back and crisscrossed by shadows and a clothes line on which hung sheets for privacy walls at night. It was quiet and smelled of damp fabric, food, bodies, breath, and coal smoke. I stopped for just a moment to breath it all in. It looked terribly cozy and I wanted to step in and lie down. There's a lot of love down here and I feel it in such odd and varied places. First the game, and then alone like this outside an open home. On a crowded bus, sitting down or standing up and pressed on all sides by people as if I'm just one part of a benevolent mass of living flesh, and we're all going somewhere. I feel it where I'm sitting now in a café where they don't just serve instant but fresh brewed and refills if you want them. I hear it in the sound of the boys in the street singing ¡*aguacates!* and ¡*tomates!* and also in the mufflerless street traffic loud as a moto-cross track, the narrow sidewalks and the pickpockets, all the people in line for buses; the way they tolerate hunks of scrap metal on the streets, piles of sand, dogs everywhere, kids sitting on the curb, breakdowns of all types, crowds, flies, gross smells, bad paint jobs, near miss- es, loud music in crowded places—things that make gringos grumpy they dance their way through down here, or endure patiently on a crowded bench or in a pool of shade at the side of the road. I love the old saggy buildings, shacks, and news- paper headlines announcing storms battering coasts, rich girls turning fifteen, masked gunmen shooting unknown victims, bejeweled couples visiting from Buenos Aires or Madrid, cars crashing, bombs exploding, warlocks gathering—there seems

to be love love love bobbing along in the river of ongoing tragedy, love in the taste of imminent death, love in loud color and
bright sound, love even in the bus exhaust billowing in across
the tables of the café as I sit writing. Across the street is a movie theater and no matter the movie—Mary Poppins or Bruce
Lee—they stand up the same big promo sign on the sidewalk
every day (translations mine):
   ¡Acción! (Action!)
   ¡Violencia! (Violence!)
   ¡Sexo Fuerte! (Strong Sex? Hard Sex? *Good Sex*)
   Which brings me to something else I love. I've been thinking about women's body parts lately: necks, shoulders, breasts,
hips, thighs, etc. Before you start rolling your eyes as if you
know this already, as if you know me, let me explain that the
parts seem to hang in my mind, an image behind the eyes,
not with clear edges like in a photo, but more like a feeling,
an essence, a shadow. I mean you couldn't quite draw what I
see because there's also a scent and a taste. It's driving me a
little crazy. I woke in the morning unrested and bothered and
couldn't connect my night dreams with the actual world I live
in, with the actual women I see everywhere. I have an ache
in the upper part of my chest, or at the base of my throat, as
if I have something I want to say but can't speak, can barely
breathe. Women by the hundreds pass me on the sidewalk like
fish in an aquarium—beautiful and untouchable and moving
in a medium I can never know. They are dressed in every and
any color, every and any shape, all ages, rich poor young old,
and as I watch them go, their faces impassive and eyes bright
and alert, strides firm and loose at the same time, I wonder
can they really be inspiring such dreams? I like to watch them
pass and wonder if they have lovers or husbands or both, I like
to wonder if they are happy or feel like I do. I like to guess
by the way they walk what they want and need and if they
need like I need, and I wonder if they have dreams as vivid
and hopeless as mine and what they think, if they think, when
they look at me. Nobody speaks to me. Maybe they can see I'm
mute and couldn't answer back if I tried. I look at them with

my bottomless private yearning and they look back with theirs (they could burn down small buildings with their eyes) our bodies bumping past each other on the crowded sidewalk and good bye forever but hello, here comes another one! I cross the street and hide in a café and find a place at the counter and while waiting for my order I take a book from my bag and I try to read but can't get past the first paragraph. So I take out a pen and paper and write to you. What I'm thinking is it's like the way the top and the bottom come together in an hourglass, the way people, strangers come together. The places we touch are small and the immensity of our solitude expands forever outward the farther we get from the actual point of contact. I don't like that image, don't think it's quite right. I wish I understood more about black holes because the vague idea I have of them seems a better metaphor for the depths of a person's solitude, for the mystery of desire and personality. So I guess this is a letter that says *I'm lonely, I'm lonely, I'm lonely!* I hope you're not. You are married. I don't know what that means. Part of me thinks it must be wonderful. Mr. and Doctor Farmer Family, backbone of America types, two kids and a cool motor boat and all the cheese curds and bratwurst you can eat, all the Fox Deluxe beer you can drink. I think it would be great fun, and I'm not being ironic. Somebody to bitch and whine to, somebody in my bed who claimed—or once vowed, we'd have evidence, we'd have pictures—to want to be with me forever. Part of me wants badly badly badly to have a missus to love me madly madly madly and part of me thinks (knows) it would be torture to be loved like that and only be able to love her halfway back. I mean, do you really have to give up all the others? The men down here rarely do, and rarely seem to feel bad about it, so that probably makes it bearable to their wives. I think to a woman a hang dog is even more contemptible than a promiscuous dog, and I'd probably be both. Of course the women complain endlessly about their dog-men but I ask you this, who is it the dog-men are fucking? So I can't quite figure out why women claim moral superiority in that game. I suppose we all need to tell ourselves a story that helps. We men tell ourselves we are strong and brave, and you women tell yourselves you are strong and virtuous and other women are sluts or dupes. Why not? People who insist on honesty can't be trusted and, frankly, without illusions we are all just un-inflated balloons.

Hey, but what do I know? I know women are neither as virtuous nor as slutty as they think they are, and sometimes I think only a man can know women as only a man can know what it takes to please one (knows her needs and caprices even better than she's able to know them herself) and sometimes I think the only universal truth I know about women is after they get to know me, to really know me, as I've said before... they lose interest.

Give me this much credit at least: I do try to embrace the mystery—particularity if I'm sleeping alone, and I'm pretty certain marriage is just another thing I wouldn't be any good at.

Yet is that any reason not to try?

Never at least to try?

Never never never?

I am your very own stranger in very strange land,
Thommy McNorCon

where marshmallows come from

Do you remember when I was telling about my wise father who, after reading the memoir about the messed-up Irish family, announced he'd never known any Irishman who drank like the father in the book? Remember how hearing him say that made me wonder what my own blind spots were? I mean, if a man as wise as he was could be so blind, what must I be missing?

When I read this letter I saw it—or at least I saw what one of my blind spots kept me from seeing for years and what must be obvious to you by now: Tom Connor's letters to me were love letters.

I'm not saying he was trying to woo me. That's a narrow idea of a love letter—a declaration of the writer's love for the reader and a plea for the reader's love in return. But suddenly it was clear to me—especially in this most explicit letter—that Tommy's letters were his way of making love to the world, which included me, of course, his reader. I felt as if a veil had been lifted, the scales fallen from my eyes. He loved crowded buses, voices in the streets, truck exhaust billowing into a café. And despite his vivid, hopeless dreams, he loved women, too. I was being loved in these letters. A man with more love in his heart than he could stand was sharing it with me. Not to seduce me, but to seduce the world, or maybe to seduce himself into surrendering into the arms of this strange world. To love and to be loved. To love his unsteadiness as well as his steadfastness. His disloyalty and his ever onward, brave and never-ceasing loyalty. Always love—and love all ways. Love bigger than I could have imagined or seen or known with my own dark, weak, narrow eyes. And by confiding in me that despite the hopelessness of his cause—*without illusions, we're all just un-inflated balloons*—he was still determined to inflate himself and float away, and wasn't that a surrender? Wasn't he giving himself to the wind? And in showing me his tricks, wasn't he giving me something—*we all need all the encouragement we can get*—wasn't he giving something to me as well?

But what could I do with it? I mean, what he gave was something so big and beautiful and impractical that when my life was indeed full—when Mark and I were Mister and Doctor Family Farm, two children, et cetera, I'd had no place to put it. What would you do if on your birthday your old friend sent you as a present Michelangelo's Pietà? Beautiful, sure, but where's the sense in it? Mainly you're just thinking, *Where am I going to put it?* And before you ever get a chance to really look at it, you've got it stored in the shed draped in a sheet to keep the pigeon shit off it, behind the old Harley your husband never rebuilt and the deflated raft you bought because once on the way to work you drove over the Wisconsin River and saw a man drifting by lying in the bottom of a raft, spread eagled, looking at the sky, and you thought you had to do that at least once before you died…. (But you never inflated the raft. You didn't have time, and everybody knows it's dangerous and dumb to float down a river without looking where you're going.)

In the bathroom stall, I fold up the letter and put it back in its envelope and then I close my eyes. I can see Mark's eyes. I can feel Mark's heat next to me. I feel my anger at his leaving me and I feel his heat on my body and the coldness of his death and the coldness at my core, and I feel like a failure and I know I've had a wonderful life and I don't know what any of that means. I'll do what Tom did and embrace the mystery, especially since I'm sleeping alone. Embrace the mystery, especially since that's all there is left after any of us have come and gone.

When this backbone-of-America type (me) comes out of the bathroom, my drink empty, my cigarette smoked, my letter read and replaced in my bag, there's Bart waiting for me in the same place the mummy and I had been standing, and because I'm suddenly self-conscious about how long I've been in the bathroom, I shrug an apology and apparently he takes that as an invitation to dance because out we go. He's short and graceful, and I like his light touch, how his fingers feel on my waist and how they let me spin away. While we are dancing I get this picture in my head that the dance floor is crowded not just with our bodies but with our memories and our dreams and also everything and everyone who has ever been here before—and not just this indoor space, but this place on earth, this canyon, they are all here, crowded in. The natives who lived here before us, the ghosts of the dead. Mark, is he here? I look for him. Maybe he's the mummy, although the mummy was a better dancer. I think of Tommy's hourglass image—all of the mystery—and all we can manage to touch comfortably are the few square inches of skin on our hands, which is just fine with me. While I'm dancing I'm filled with these kinds of crazy feelings, and also I'm still thirsty and I forget about not drinking and dance back to the bar two or three times to finish yet another whiskey Bart has bought me. I don't know how long we dance but I begin to work up a sweat and lose myself in the music and swirl of the party, and after a while I need to rest so as we happen to be dancing by the door, I spin off and step outside. I immediately regret how much I've drunk, because I have to hold onto the log wall to keep from being blown over by the wind. Snow blows horizontally across the parking lot and has begun to accumulate in the tall grass. I step back far enough to light my last cigarette. I watch the storm and endure the cold long enough to wake up and to be anxious to go back inside again. Just inside the doorway, I see Bart, as though he's waiting for me. He steps outside and joins me instead.

"You know where marshmallows come from?"

He laughs.

"No," I say, "really."

"How they're made?" he asks.

"Yes."

He shrugs. "They're jet-puffed, right?"

I shake my head. "They are not really jet puffed," I say.

"What's that even mean?" he says.

"It means jets puff each of them."

"But they haven't?"

"What?" I say.

"The jets." He looks at me, confused. "Puffed them?"

"Myth," I say.

He shakes his head and smiles. "What can you believe anymore?"

"Believe this," I say, and I wait a beat, two beats. I feel his eyes on me. I'm trying to tell this like Mark would, and I'm better at it than I thought I'd be. I guess I've heard it told many times. "Believe that marshmallows are organically grown," I say. "They come from the marsh."

"Well, sure," Bart says.

"Young men walk ten days through waist-deep, snake-infested, croc-infested marsh water to get to where they grow."

"Where's that?" Bart says.

"A marsh on the other side of the world."

"China?"

"Near China."

"Then no local marshmallows?"

I shake my head. "It's a rite of passage for the boys. They wear thick leather gloves and sleeves to part the razor sharp leaves of the mallow plant—layers of them, like artichoke leaves, only five feet wide and ten feet high. The pickers pry back giant leaf after giant leaf as they make their way toward the delicate stalk at the center of the plant, the stalk that every seven years produces just one ripe mallow."

"Amazing."

I nod. "These stalks are fifteen feet high and pencil-thin, and each one grows one perfectly white and soft mallow."

"No jets, then?"

"No," I said. "They're puffed with marsh gas, and when they're ripe they appear glowing and balanced on the top of the fragile stalk, a piece of holy fruit. They're only ripe for a few hours before they begin to rot, so the boy has to be there at just the right time, and he has to jiggle the stalk just enough to send the mallow tumbling (and not so hard as to break the stalk, crippling the plant forever)."

"Wow," Bart says. "One marshmallow per plant every seven years?"

I nod, take a moment to let the profundity sink in, the extent of the sacrifice required for us to eat just one marshmallow. "And if that doesn't sound hard enough, walking ten days to the middle of the marsh, squeezing between giant leaves that will cut your flesh like butter, jiggling a stalk just hard enough, but not too hard, there's something else."

"Something else?"

"The marsh-gas puffed mallow must not get wet—you can imagine how that would destroy it. So the boy has to try to catch a tumbling marshmallow before it lands in the marsh water."

"Which I suppose is not easy?"

"No, especially in the high winds that coincidentally hit the marsh every seventh autumn when the mallows are ripe."

Bart shakes his head in mock amazement. I can see by his eyes he likes the story.

"How old are the boys," he asks.

"Old enough," I say, which is just exactly what Mark used to say. Old enough.

"For what?" Bart says.

"Well," I say, explaining. "If the boy makes it back with a

mallow—"

"Just one mallow?"

"Yes, one per boy."

"Wow," he says. "Labor intensive."

I nod. I am mimicking Mark's gestures exactly. I think Mark's spirit has come into me while I tell this story. I raise my eyebrows. "Rites of passage produce cheap labor," I say. "It's also the way wars are fought."

Bart looks at me, head turned, puzzled by the political turn. Mark was always sure he was going to be shot by a firing squad of right wingers who called themselves patriots. He'd say, *Some day the patriots are going to shoot me. Don't worry about this cancer.* But the patriots never came.

"Each boy must catch one mallow and tuck it into a dry pocket and bring it back to the tribe as proof he made the journey."

"Proof of the journey?"

"For the *journey* is the object. Not the mallow. The mallow is simply proof of the journey. And each boy who makes it home with a dry mallow will be rewarded as a man."

"How's that?" Bart asked.

"With many cattle."

"That's good," he says.

I shrug. This next part was what Mark added when he was telling the story to adults. "And abundant sexual opportunities."

Bart grins and opens his eyes wide. "That's very good."

"So he has to be old enough," I repeat.

"Sure," he says, "Of course." Then he says, "Marshmallows. Who would have thought."

"Yeah," I say, and I think, Mark did. Mark thought about these things as if they were real. Tom wrote me love letters for thirteen years and three months and in one of them used the phrase *organic marshmallows* and Mark liked that and turned it into a story he could give me and our children.

The snowstorm is blasting the parking lot, the snowflakes swirling in the floodlight from the front door. I shiver and wonder at my ridiculous effort to protect my cold little self in such a wind. Who cares if I crack? And what happens if I do? My little adventure, I suppose, my little mystery. I fall back and Bart holds me, and I let him hold me for a moment, then step away, and he lets me step away, and I know things will be okay between us. I'm relieved. I mean, I'm not worried he's going to be weird, or any weirder than I am.

"Are you coming?" I ask, heading in again. "My mind is blown."

"Mine, too," he says, and follows.

The mummy is standing just inside the door. Looking with his one brown jealous eye, he asks, "Did she tell you the purpose of a mummy?"

The music is loud and Bart says, "The purpose of *what*?"

"Mummies," the mummy says.

"No," Bart says. "She told me where marshmallows come from."

"Where *what* comes from?"

I slip past them both to find my whiskey. I still have a few sips left and feel as if I'll die if I don't find it.

proof of un-intelligent design

Before dawn I dream the cabin door is open and the bear has come in with the snow and brought a bad smell. I dream he's eaten the dog or chased him away, and I can't get out of bed or even turn my head because I'm afraid of his growling.

I blink awake in the morning to a sharp headache and roll over to see a partially wrapped mummy with a bare shaved head lying on his back on the floor in front of the woodstove.

And snoring like a—like a what?—like a strange man with sleep apnea.

And the smell? Him.

"People who say they're never lonely or bored and have no regrets," Tommy wrote me once, "are either too busy or lying. And if they're too busy to feel their loneliness or boredom or regrets, they're too busy to feel much of anything. Except *Yip-pee!*...followed by fatigue. If one of them came into the ER, and I had your job, Doctor, I'd say: *Let's get some vitals on this patient! Somebody roll out the code cart!* Or, even better, *Forget it—just call hospice!"*

Nevertheless as I lie in bed looking at the sleeping man, his smooth head nestled into a pile of Ace bandages, I have to acknowledge that there are dangers both ways. Because if you are never bored or lonely, and you have no regrets, you've probably never drank too much and had a mummy drive you and your puppy home through a storm. You probably wouldn't remember how his bold brown eye made the skin of your neck tingle when he asked if you could drive, and how your legs felt weak and your mouth dry so you answered the only way you knew how, by falling down flat on your face in the snow.

That dull ache of regret I have in my chest right now? Yours—you without regret—yours would be heartburn, and there are pills for that.

Thank goodness I'm still dressed in my widow costume when I throw off the covers, but I'm cold and my hands are shaking as I work around the sleeping mummy in front of the stove to get the fire going without waking him. I'm afraid to look at him very closely but I can see that despite his bald head he's younger than I thought, mid-thirties, and every time his breathing pauses, the thought passes through my mind that maybe he's dead. Then he starts again—a kick-start, like a motorcycle—and I'm relieved. If he died I'd have to deal with my children hearing about a young man coming home with me and dying and it shames me to think about how if this were to happen—if this man really does die in his sleep in my cabin—all I anticipate feeling is embarrassed.

After stuffing wood in the stove over the mummy's body until the fire is roaring, I go outside and pee. I don't like how I leave a mark in the snow, and so I use my boot to kick snow over it and decide I'll have to shovel a trail out farther away from the cabin. I brush six inches of dry snow off my car window and see the dog and let him out. I can't believe I left him in the car. More regrets, but he's happy to see me anyway and runs circles in the new snow. It's the deepest he's ever seen, and as he runs the snow sprays up in front of him and he snaps at the air. He runs tighter and tighter circles, snapping the air, stopping, burrowing his nose and rolling, then up to his feet again and back in the direction he ran. Watching the puppy is exhilarating and for a moment I forget that I have a headache and a strange man in my cabin. There are ravens in the yard and magpies—did something die around here?—and soon the puppy is chasing them. They rise just in time and glide out into the meadow, where the blond grass sticks out of the new snow. The tan-and-white puppy matches perfectly the field he's running through. I look up high at the cliffs and the gray rock is broken by horizontal strips of white snow and the pine and fir clinging to ledges look darker green trimmed with white than they did yesterday, and the sky above the cliffs is so bright blue suddenly it makes my heart ache. It seems this would be a problem, but the day is too nice to see it that way, and if I escaped last night without incident, I don't see that I have to worry too much about this morning. To have a man-mummy sleeping on the floor in front of your woodstove on a cold Halloween morning seems for a moment almost normal.

I need to change my tampon so I make my way back behind the house to the outhouse. Even though I can't see any bear tracks, I call for the dog. Thinking about the bear makes me remember how I saw him on the stump, how I have this memory of him waving good bye to me. He yawned and covered his big mouth with one hairy paw and waved with the other, as if he were going to bed. *Nighty-night!* he called. I know he didn't say that, but that's what I remember. Or did I dream it? Do dream memories and other memories get stored in the same place? And if you forget which memory is a dream and which is a waking event, does that mean you're insane?

Now what?

Until the cabin warms, I get back in bed with the puppy, and this time, just to be safe, with my precious canister of pepper spray as well. The young mummy is still on the floor sleeping and who knows what he will be like when he wakes. I don't understand the appeal of the shaved head—a little hair, I always think, is better than absolutely none—especially because at this angle, the way he's lying, I suddenly get a comic image of his head as a giant penis. Then, as though to spare me, the perfect gentleman he must be, he rolls over and I see his face and his un-bearded cheeks are clean and they show his strong jaw, and his lips are full and the muscles of his neck thick and the skin of his throat smooth. I'm intrigued by the beauty of his young, masculine face. I lie in bed with the puppy and roll onto my back and stare at the ceiling and at the smoke-darkened pine paneling and listen to the young mummy snore and snort for breath, and I assess things. When a bear hibernates he breathes less than ten times a minute, and his heart beat drops to about the same. In order to keep his muscles from atrophying during the long months of inactivity, he does a series of isometric exercises. After Pierre, my friend Lisa married a born-again Christian, and then went that way herself, and the last time I talked to her she kept giving me semi-scientific facts about the natural world and then saying, "If that's not proof of intelligent design, what is?" I just shrugged, I wouldn't argue. But I think, why design an animal that has to sleep at all? What sense is there in that? I could slit my mummy's throat or he could die just trying to breathe when his airway sags shut between snores. Even if he doesn't die, he subconsciously starts to feel he's suffocating and so gets a shot of adrenaline to make him explode into breath again, and his heart has to absorb this stress all night long. Why didn't God make us either better sleepers or more energetic so we wouldn't have to sleep? I think of the word *sleep*, as in *sleep with a man*, and then of that story about my daughter when she was in high school wanting to sleep with her boyfriend even when she told me she wasn't ready for sex. I wonder what she would say about me bringing this man home, or him bringing me home. Proof of *un*-intelligent design, I'd say, but at least I didn't wake up to find him in my bed, which would be proof of really, really dumb design. Small blessings.

No. I look at him, the long size of him stretched out on the floor in front of the stove. *Large* blessings.

Suddenly he bursts into another round of snoring and rolls over onto his side, and then back again onto his back. Noth-

ing like a handsome, young mummy almost suffocating in his
sleep at the foot of your bed next to the woodstove to get you
thinking. But to show how far I am from being ready to be
with a man, what I begin to think about is my medical training, particularly what it is I learned in those sleepless years
while I was learning to be a doctor. I know there are people
who want to limit the number of consecutive hours a resi-
dent works, comparing the work to truck driving or piloting a
plane, but here's a second opinion. During those many hours
we worked, we saw conditions in patients that we would never
have seen if we weren't at the hospital, at the clinic, and all of
those consecutive hours allowed us to see a crisis through with
a patient—we didn't just admit him or her and then go home
and read a report but see him from the time he came into the
hospital, his series of treatments for twenty-four hours, maybe thirty-six hours, and we'd see how the treatments affected
him. Even more importantly, we learned that we could do it.
That we could push past what we thought we could endure. If
we were tired and didn't think we could deal with one more
problem, well, we learned we were wrong, we could deal with
one more problem, or two, or ten. And we could do it profes-
sionally, that is, as the problem asked to be dealt with, not as
we would like to deal with it. It's a little habit of thought, but
it's a crucial one. Also, working at your limit teaches you dependence on others—you can't do it alone, you need the team.
I could never have taken care of my babies without Mark. He
was home in those years and I was not, so I both resented my
dependence and was envious of all the time he spent with the
twins, but ultimately I was too tired to hold all that and had to
surrender to the team. I did what I could. If I wasn't sleeping,
I was nursing the babies, or holding them, or feeding them, or
changing them. Frankly, I don't remember much more. The
days and weeks and months of those first few years are a blur
to me. I remember the smell of my babies' breath, and the feel
of their little mouths and their eyes coming alive in the first
few months and their mouths beginning to smile. Mark talked
about their words. He loved hearing them learn to talk, but I

can't say I remember that much. I remember being tired, but time is a beautiful anesthetic and I don't remember much of the unpleasantness. Mark and I didn't argue except occasionally about the frequency of sex—I think he felt like he had to be a monk, or that most of the time he had to be his own best sex partner. I did what I could; we did what we could. We helped each other as we could, and there was a lot of tenderness, I seem to remember. He remembers going to sleep rigid and twisted in turmoil—he told me this much later, but I don't remember that. I remember going to sleep with him wrapped around me, his warmth, his tenderness, the way he loved me, the feel of my babies against my body. I remember going to sleep feeling hollow and empty but hollow and empty in a good way. It was not a pace we could have maintained, but we could endure it for the three years of our marriage corresponding with my residency corresponding with the first three years of having the twins. I remember holding them on my lap, both of them, and reading books, their little fingers touching the pages. I remember falling asleep as I read. I remember Mark putting all three of us to bed and one very good thing we had going for us was that we weren't counters. Almost all of the counting couples I knew—*I have the baby for five hours on Tuesday, and he has the baby for two hours on Thursday, so he needs to take the baby for either three hours on Wednesday or one on Wednesday and two hours on either Monday or Friday, and if he gets to go bowling on Saturday I get to go running on Sunday*—counting couples were doomed, it seemed to me. I don't know what it is that makes people's brains that way, but ours weren't and so we were lucky. During our twenty-four years we fell in love, I mean, really tumbled hard, three or four more times after the first time, and each tumble more miraculous than the last. There was Chile after the earthquake and when I had to let go of *the idea* of breastfeeding. Nothing like too many *ideas* to fuck up a marriage, Mark used to say. Breastfeeding for a long time is a good idea, but if it makes you angry at your husband, or puts him in a box in which he can only be angry at you, then I suppose it isn't. And the way I felt when I let go of that, a surrender, a vulnerability, a dependence—feelings I fought all the way—were exactly the right feelings on the right path. Which is odd, I mean—and why I say the secret to a long marriage is good luck, because the fact is I fought the path over and over again. I stayed in love with my husband almost despite my efforts to the contrary. Maybe if I'd been less tired or a better fighter, we'd never have made it. If I'd been more successful at what I was trying to do, which was to *not* sink lower and deeper into dependence—to *not* fall, and to *not* keep falling all over again into Mark's arms—we'd never have made it until death do us part. Because each time we surrendered more fully than we thought we could, each new surrender brought with it the same panic and wild joy that madness brings, that love brings, too. For a little while when the kids were in grade school we went to church, and our pastor had a saying, he'd say, if it pulls too hard, just let go. All of your efforts are futile and it's probably for the best if you fail but the paradox is that you still have to try hard and you still have to try hard not to fail. How does that make sense? You have to believe things are important, and you have to feel these important things ripped from your hands, see them float away, feel yourself a blind and lonely animal on earth. Only by failure can you get past panic and on your way to humility and the joy of love.

"Paradox is the door," he used to say. "We have to walk through it—and giving up trying to make sense is the first and bravest step."

I look at the sleeping man wrapped in Ace bandages at the foot of my bed and try to let sense float away like a balloon. Tommy seemed instinctively to know how to do that, and maybe that's where his real courage lay, his naked striving—almost embarrassing to read sometimes, his semi-polished Pietàs arriving in my mailbox once a month. I look at the table and the fourteen stacks of letters and realize that somewhere in the deepest part of my wounded heart I knew what I'd find if I read them again: his way of loving the world, a place where a mother might hold her crucified son across her lap, where a father might drop dead of a heart attack in front of his thirteen-year-old son, where a mother might lose interest in her own son and flee, where men with guns joyfully massacre villagers, and where a dear, kind man, the one I loved and married and made children with, might die for no good reason.

(If that's not proof of un-intelligent design, what is?)

The mummy snorts, stops breathing, snorts, stops breathing again.

Yet is that any reason not to try? Tommy asks. *Never at least to try?*

as good a purpose for a mummy as any

Finally the mummy wakes. What a relief. His breathing had me more on edge than I knew. Because when he wakes and I no longer hear the breaks in his breathing, I feel suddenly calm and my crazy thoughts come back to earth again, back to the practical stuff, like, *Who is this guy?* And, *Is he going to hurt me?*

I hold the pepper spray under the covers and watch him sit up and rub his face. I find the trigger with my forefinger and the safety with my thumb. He doesn't seem to notice me. I wonder if he was very drunk when he drove me home. Not as drunk as me, but too drunk to drive. He stares at the wood stove crackling in front of him. The light from the window behind him puts his face in shadow. I am very still and quiet and my splitting head is wondering how long before he looks at me. Because he is so young I don't like thinking of what I must look like to him, and then, suddenly, I look at the disaster that is the kitchen and I feel embarrassed and ashamed.

"Good morning," I say, and my voice startles him. He turns suddenly and looks at me. He has that one dark eye and, surprisingly, one yellowish green eye. He blinks. He pulls a can of Copenhagen out from between his bandages and dips a pinch into his lip and smiles.

"What did you tell me was the purpose of a mummy in modern society?"

"You're still asking that?"

He hunches forward toward the woodstove and spits. I hear the hiss. "It's a good question."

"It's your only question," I say.

Outside I hear the wind pick up. The blue sky is framed in the window and the snow blows off the roof of the cabin past the blue sky. The mummy is sitting with his legs straight out in front of him on the floor, settling his weight back onto the heels of his hands and staring into the fire. Maybe he's lost interest—who knows what he's thinking about—why he's here? How he got here?

"Mummies drive people home," I say.

He rubs his eyes. "I remember driving."

I let that sit for a moment. The way he says it sounds not all that convincing that he remembers anything else. Me, for instance, or this place. I'm embarrassed. I suppose I was hoping that he'd been sober. I was hoping I might have acted responsibly even though I drank so much I fell on my face in the snow.

I sit up. I turn and let my legs drop out from under the covers and onto the floor, but I keep the blanket over my lap hiding my hands and the pepper spray.

"Mummies remind us that there's nothing new under the sun," I say. "That we've always been afraid of dying, and that everybody who ever lived on the planet is going to die, or is already dead."

All of that kind of pours out. Too much alone time has made me socially inept. He opens the woodstove and spits again.

"Like your car," he says. And then nothing.

"My car?"

"It kind of died last night."

"What?" I sit on the bed and watch him stare at the fire.

"Just as I'm coming in the driveway," he says. "It stalled and then I couldn't start it again. You have any tools, in case it won't start this morning?"

"Tools?"

"Yes."

"Whatever's in the closet," I say, and point. "There's no screwdriver though. Or not the right kind."

"What?"

I nod through my disaster of a kitchen at the back door held shut with a stuffed chair, stool, and end table.

He gives the whole absurd scene a long, glazed look.

"The top hinge came out of the wood and I can't get it back in without a screwdriver."

He gets up—he's very tall—and strolls untouched through the mess in the kitchen, leans over the barricade and fingers the dangling top hinge and the smooth, dry spackling. "Got any coffee?"

Relieved to do something, I stand up and put water on the stove to boil.

After a while he says, "That's not going to hold a screw anyway."

"What?'

"Not if the wood's rotten underneath."

I don't know what to say. Now he's poking around in the closet and gets out the toolbox. "If I get your car started, will you drive me home?"

"Sure," I say. "But where is home?"

"Town," is all he says, and he's out the door with my keys and a toolbox. I see him try to start the car and then get out and open the hood and look at the motor. I see his breathing in the cold air, the dog running around him. He talks to the dog and bends over the motor. Pretty soon he's back in the car and I see exhaust coming from the tailpipe. He's got it running. He's coming back to the cabin. I panic at having done nothing but watch him. He bursts in looking healthy, especially for a mummy. It's funny to me that over what looks like a union suit, he's still wearing mostly just Ace bandages.

"Aren't you cold wearing only that?"

He smiles and pulls the union suit away from his chest. "Actually, I'm hot."

"What was wrong with the car?"

He shakes his head. "Loose cable."

"What did you do?"

"Tightened it."

I turn toward the counter and pour the hot water through a coffee filter. I realize I don't even know his name. He probably told me last night and now I've forgotten and I'm suddenly embarrassed.

"Will it be okay?"

"Should be. But I'm going to leave it running for a little bit."

"Can I make you some eggs?"

He rubs his eyes. Puppy is all over him now. He fends off the dog with one hand. "What?"

I repeat the offer but suddenly he's standing right behind me. I think he's come over to see what I have to eat but he puts his hands on my shoulders and I jump. "Oh," I say, and he laughs behind me and takes his hands off but before I can say anything else, or even turn, he puts them back on. His touch is gentle and this time I stay still for just a moment—don't ask me why, for even as I write these words, I think, how could I? Why didn't I scream? Turn and hit him with something? Because a warmth spread from under his cold palms all across my shoulders to my neck and up the back of my skull and even though I know this is not what I'm interested in—him, his body, sex—even though it's not what I'm interested in, I also seem uninterested in stopping it. Almost out of curiosity I let him turn me. *Almost* because I think of curiosity as a question in the mind, and this was more like a quickening of the flesh— if not quite desire, then an unexpected physical eagerness. I'm not trying to split hairs here but what's mysterious to me is how I've been huddling under a blanket with pepper spray and now seem to have no fear. I think of these lines from a poem, *In me a man has come/everywhere a man can go* and although they aren't exactly what I have in my head, I have that feeling of experience and calm, a feeling like a breathy *Hey,* like a deep *Oh,* like a curious and interested *What is this?* That and the simple fact that I can't actually believe a man-not-Mark is going to try to kiss me. It's just never happened in more than twenty-four years. I don't know what weird waves I give off, but when it comes to resisting temptation, well, I haven't had much. I can pat myself on the back and praise how loyal and virtuous I was while I was married—and of course I know if I'd thrown myself at certain men, or even just offered, they would have obliged—but no man ever took me by the shoulders and turned me to face him and lowered his face to kiss me.

So I let him. I smell his skin (good) getting closer and then before I can think or speak I feel his lips on mine and his invisible mustache on my lip and I can't help it, I'm kissing him. He must have eaten some mints when he was outside because there's no tobacco in his mouth and mint is what I smell and taste, and I close my eyes afraid to see this strange mummy-man's face right next to mine, his dome head and boyish cheeks, and one hot brown eye and one yellowish green. I feel his hands move down my shoulders to my back. I feel my legs get weak and my weight begin to be absorbed by his arms, and I hear his breathing and taste his minty tongue and he's a surprisingly good kisser, or maybe he just seems good because of the length of time it has been for me. How long since I've been kissed? And how strange and odd it is to be kissed, to have another's mouth on yours, and to like it enough to want to open your mouth as far as it will go and your head falls back and you lose your breath and soon have to break away only to breathe, to catch your breath, and then there is the face of the stranger too close to your face and you see the delight in his eyes and you can't believe there is a strange man's face so close to yours, especially this mummy-man who slept on the floor and who started your car, and who drove you home last night when you had no business driving. And you don't even know his name. The thought freezes you. *You think, what am I? Who am I to be in this strange mummy-man's arms?* And

then you stop thinking, stop trying to make sense and kiss
him one more time to see if you can find that first feeling that
has slipped away, and this time his mouth feels different, tastes
different even, and his hands drop from your waist to your
hips and you feel suddenly a little trapped by his arms and you
break away, spin away, turn away, and squeeze your eyes closed
when you feel the last of his touch drop away, and suddenly,
damn you, you're crying. Jesus. Like a child, tears have sprung
to your eyes. You hope he hasn't seen but he's so silent behind
you that you know he has. Also, your body is quivering as the
silent sobs shake your frame, and you keep your eyes closed,
and your back turned, and you can feel him there behind you
like you could feel the bear. The heat of him, the smell of him.
You feel humiliated and angry. You hear him moving behind
you. You hear him say, "Hey, I'm sorry, I couldn't help it." You
struggle with the desire to reassure him but what comes out
is your doctor voice telling him he needs to go and you'll give
him a ride. You ask him to wait in the car, please. You tell him
you'll be right out.

"Will you at least bring me a cup of that coffee?" he asks.

"Yes."

"Cream and sugar?"

"Go outside now."

So this is what mummies are for: they drive you home when
you can't, they fix your car, they kiss you. They make you cry
mysterious tears. Well, no more mysterious than anything
else, say, than the sunrise, or the wind, or the fire in the stove
that keeps you warm. No more mysterious than the laws of attraction or the certainty of grief. In fact, tears are quite banal,
really, everyday kind of stuff, old stuff, *Georgie Georgie, puddin
'n pie, kissed the girl and made her cry.*

Out the window I see the mummy has dutifully gotten into
the passenger side of the car and shut the door. I can see his
young, shaved head through the glass. He's waiting patiently,
but I need to wash my face first. I need to put on some lipstick.
I need to comb my hair, at least. For the time being a mummy
has given me a purpose. This one at least needs a ride home—

and what else was I planning on doing this snowy morning? He needs his coffee. I pour him a cup, add cream and sugar, pour myself one, black, and carry out the steaming cups in my bare hands.

We drive east on the unplowed gravel heading away from the mountains. Our coffee makes the car smell good. Up out of the river valley, the land extends wide and white as far as I can see. The road is slippery and the snow is six inches deep and my compact car slides around and once even slides off the road. Mummy pushes it back up onto the road—another purpose of a mummy—and we're off again. It's twenty miles and when we get inside his little reddish house on the edge of town, I see a woman sleeping on the couch. When she wakes, she barely lifts her head. Her face is yellow green, and at first I think what I'm seeing is make-up from her own Halloween adventure story, but as I get closer I see her eyeballs are very yellow as well. There are three empty bottles of wine on the coffee table and the television is on the shopping channel and the house smells bad. Mummy introduces me to his wife, who doesn't respond. She's closed her eyes and apparently uninterested.

"Your wife?" I mouth the words, looking distressed.

Mummy raises an eyebrow at me, and shrugs apologetically. Then he offers me the use of his truck to get back out to the cabin. His offer distracts me. He says he doesn't have to go anywhere for a few days, and when the road is plowed, he'll drive out in my car and get his truck back. He says he's grateful, but I want to punch him for putting me in this situation and I want to get out of there as fast as I can before his wife opens her eyes again and starts asking questions. He gives me the key to his truck. He walks out with me and tells me how to put it in four-wheel drive. He has a tired way of moving that lacks bullshit, somehow, and I can see now it's why I trusted him. He's a married man who just kissed me and yet he moves honestly. Does that make sense or am I justifying myself? Probably both. He asks if I've ever driven a truck and I tell him yes. He's still unselfconsciously wearing the Ace bandages wrapped around most of his body from the waist down and when he smiles I can see he's a kind man, a tired man, thirty-something and already middle-aged. I get in the truck and he closes the door for me. He says okey-dokey through the window. He pats the metal door as I drive away.

As long as I'm in town I figure I'll get groceries. Even pushing my cart around in the store I can smell the mummy's house on my skin. I think of that woman's jaundice and her liver most likely in N-stage failure. I should have said something but I wanted to get out of there so fast I didn't. When I finish shopping, I go back. My squeamishness—my petty embarrassment over my soiled virtue—seems suddenly immature. Another balloon I just watch deflate and fall on the ground at my feet. I don't care if I kissed her husband, and for all I know she doesn't care either. I knock on the door. The mummy answers. He looks different not wrapped in an Ace bandage anymore but dressed in a sweatshirt and jeans. He looks as if he hasn't slept for a week, yet my reappearance seems to have amused him.

"Haven't we met?" he asks.

"I need to see her," I say.

He steps aside. I hear his wife ask, "Is it her again?"

I walk into the dark and smelly living room.

"Open the drapes," I say.

"No," she says.

Mummy spreads the drapes and the room floods with the bright light of snow and clear sky. His wife covers her face. I step carefully closer.

"Please," I say. "I'm a doctor."

"Please," the woman says. "You're a whore."

"You're very sick."

"No shit."

"Have you been to a doctor?"

She laughs into her hands.

"What's your name?"

"That's a personal question."

"Please," I say.

"Fuck you," she says, and takes her hands off of her green face, and laughs. "And my last name is Bitch."

I touch her head. It's cold and clammy. I'm struck by how young her face is, how smooth her green skin. She smells very bad, though. I look at the mummy and swallow my embarrassment. "What's your name?" I ask.

"Alex."

"How long has she been this color, Alex?"

He shrugged. "A week? Two?"

"Is she being treated for anything? Has she been to see a doctor?"

"She won't go."

I look at the empty bottles on the coffee table. There are more on the floor next to the couch. "She needs to go to the hospital right now," I say. "She needs to go to Great Falls. She's very sick. I don't know how sick but she needs to be examined. Can you take her there?"

I notice that his hands are shaking. He turns to look out the window.

"Take her to the emergency room. Can you drive her there?"

He nods. "If she'll go."

"She needs to go."

"I'll need my truck back."

"I can get back to the cabin in my car."

"Get some chains first," he says. "It's getting cold out there."

I watch him pick her up. She seems as light as a feather in his arms. Mark used to pick me up like that as well, with ease, with a jolly joy. I think about how much of the relationship between men and woman can be explained by the simple fact that a man can sweep a woman up into his arms and carry her away. A woman, well, it's hard to lift a man. We usually have to drag him. Or get behind him and poke him until he moves.

I follow behind them and carry the groceries from his truck to my car, and after they leave, I drive to the hardware store and buy chains and practically freeze my fingers trying to put them on. Then I realize I've put them on the wrong tires, the back tires, and my car is front-wheel drive, so there in the hardware store parking lot I take them off the back tires and put them on the front tires. This is just the kind of thing Mark would have done, and the chore of it, of having to do it, makes me feel suddenly sorry for myself, and while I am on my back in the snow, reaching behind the tires to try to hook the frozen metal chains I cuss and I cry again, which makes me angry as well. My fingers are freezing and I can't see past my tears, but finally I get the chains on and I climb back into the warm car and dry my tears and rub my hands together until I have some feeling again in my fingers. *Goddamn Mark!* I think, and pound the steering wheel in melodramatic agony. *My goddamn freezing cold hands!* Then I get an idea that gives me solace, or at least distracts me. I get out of the car and jog past the hardware store to the grocery store across the street, where I buy pack of cigarettes. It's not as if I don't deserve them. I put the pack on the seat next to me and look forward to sitting calmly back at the cabin where I can smoke and think and get it all figured out.

I head out of town. The sky is still crisp blue but the wind is blowing and the tire tracks we made on our way into town have already been erased by drifts. The chains make a lot of noise and I drive slowly. Although we are theoretically on the plains, the road isn't flat or straight. Up and down hills and then curvy along the river. I don't see another car or truck, and I have a sudden panic in my stomach that if I went off the road, I'd be here for a long time. The temperature has plummeted and I don't have adequate clothes to walk for hours to get help. I grip the steering wheel and lean forward to see through the defrosted glass just above the dash. When the road climbs up onto the bench there's the Eastern Front of the Rocky Mountains lit up cold and wild in the angled light, jagged peaks like old dreams hanging between heaven and earth. The Indians thought the gods lived up there—or if they didn't think that, they should have. Because the gods must live up there, just as they also live in that living room with that sick, drunk woman. I think of my bear sleeping—I hope—somewhere in all of that ice and rock. I think of Mark, of Tom Connor, and I think of

Alex and his yellow wife, and suddenly the land and sky are so beautiful I want to cry again. What's wrong with me? I'm coming apart into a thousand little pieces and I want to say I hold them all together, I pull them all back together, but I don't, not even close.

When I get back to the cabin I bring in some wood, stoke the stove, heat water for tea and sit down with a cigarette and another letter to read. Just holding the paper in my hands calms me. It's dated January 1990. When I read it the first time I was in residency in a county E.R. and immersed in long hours of work, up to my neck in what results from poverty and violence and drug and alcohol addiction and the inadequacy of medical care and inadequacy of love and inadequacy of everything. In addition to the day-to-day drama of my work life, Mark and I were trying to figure out how to get back to Wisconsin. I was applying for jobs in smaller hospitals. We wanted to buy a farm. Mark wanted to raise livestock and grow vegetables and set up a woodworking shop. We were starting to think about our life together. Obviously we'd begun our life together—twins in a 500-square-foot apartment. But we were starting to think about how it could be, how it should be, how we wanted it. Our house. Our farm. My job. How we'd raise the kids. I mean, we would be making choices about the place they would come to consider their hometown. Mark wanted to go back to his, and that was fine with me. I just wanted to work close by. I didn't want to have to commute into Madison. I remember that was important to me, and I'm sure we had some real blow-out fights, but what happened anyway was I commuted forty-five miles each way for twenty-one years and listened to hundreds of books on tape and thousands of hours of beautiful music and we had a good life.

The cabin is warm and everything feels lighter and brighter, especially when I look at the floor where the mummy slept last night, there and not with me. I'm grateful, for that, and also for his helpfulness and good nature. Alex the mummy. He kissed me—he couldn't help it!—and I kissed him back. *Dead men are my weakness.* I laugh. His wife looked like she was in acute liver failure. Soon she'll be dead, and I know it as suddenly and clearly as I know anything. Does Alex know this? Part of him must. And so he came home with me, to leave her temporarily before she left him. To kiss me, a woman acquainted with grief. I must smell like it. He kept asking me the purpose of a mummy. As though he needed the answer to a riddle, and it didn't even matter what the riddle was.

Have I stopped making sense yet? A mummy drove me home last night and now his sick wife to the hospital. I sip my tea, his kiss still on my lips, and even bigger than shame is the strange and sudden pleasure I feel wandering around in the big windy gaps between the thousand pieces of me. Which— not to make too much of it or anything—which is as good a purpose for a mummy as any.

descriptions of lovely mountain treks to follow

Dear Doctor,

This was nine years ago and something I got thinking about this morning after I squeezed between a couple of helmeted big-gunned soldiers into a corner café and ordered *gallo pinto* with a scrambled egg, and the waitress asked if I wanted bread or tortilla and she brought me a flour tortilla (from a package) that tasted like paper. The pinto and egg were good, filling and cheap. While I ate I read a translated Raymond Carver story in the newspaper—I love how they have things like Raymond Carver stories in the daily newspaper. The same newspaper that reports that a *duende* (short, mythical demon) was seen leaving a parking lot after four men and a woman, suspected rebels, were found dead and mutilated in the central park last night also prints a Carver story. Well, I guess these newspapers are just literary magazines with large circulations.

My Spanish is good but not terribly precise and I think what happens in the story is a man leaves his wife and steals an ash- tray, or she kicked him out and he stole it but he didn't really *steal* it because she knew he took it. It was Christmas in the story, or right after. As far as I can tell the story was about stuff you want to say and you need to say but don't. Important Things. We feel like something inside us is missing, has been taken, maybe, and we try to make up for it by taking a fuck- ing ashtray. Anyway, no ashtrays here so maybe that's why this morning I started to want to tell you about this thing nine years ago—not that I haven't wanted to before but it seems more urgent, suddenly, and if I don't get through it all in one letter, well, forgive me, but I'm going to try to give it a try. I'm going to start at least. I've been working on a novel for years but in some ways most of what I've written has been talking around it, dancing around it, or maybe just dancing around trying to understand what *it* is! Regardless, now I do know, and rather than steal an ashtray again, get you thinking about that, mad about that, distracted by that, I'll try to start to tell what I want to tell. I think it ends with the abyss. I've been reading a lot—lately Václav Havel, and he's helped me under- stand my own writing—and I think I've done a wonderful job of dancing around the abyss in all of my letters but I've never taken you by the hand and led you right up to the terrifying edge—made you see what you see when you get to the lim- its of finite experience. Because however wonderful making love and reading and eating and traveling might be, when you arrive at the glorious edge of worldly pleasure, there you are, staring into the darkness. Think of those moments when you are at one with the world, when you feel sunlight on your skin and it reminds you of a day long ago at the lake with your fam- ily or your friends, when you smell hay or cottonwood pitch and are bathed in good feeling and the rightness of the world and the life you've lived, when you see sunlight on the tree out the window and the indescribable pattern of shadow and color makes you weak at the knees. Havel says that at precisely these moments of greatest possible fulfillment you also feel a vague

anxiety, a faint echo of infinite yearning, the strange under-
tone of a deep, and inconsolable sense of futility, as though
your happiness were nothing more than a tragic mirage with
no purpose and leading nowhere. In short, it is during these
moments of ultimate fulfillment that we also feel (or smell) the
breath of infinite non-fulfillment.

I always wondered why I chose our glorious road trip to try
to kill myself. I think now it was because from the joy of utter
comprehension—our love, our bliss, our intoxication—from
that ecstasy bloomed the terrible mystery. In my supreme happiness and harmony with the world, I thought, *What's next?*
What else? What more? And because I was standing on the
high cliff edge of fulfillment, I could see there was no farther
to go! Only to the abyss. Only there. And so I felt the despair
as well as the ecstasy, do you understand? The ecstasy led me to
the edge and I knew I knew nothing, and for a terrible moment
I knew I never would.

"Oh, Janine, do they teach you about this in med school? As
long as we're breathing we have to keep exploring—and once
we reach ecstasy, we know that no matter how hard we try,
how far we push it, all mortal experiences end at this place, at
this glimpse into the dark *Unknown*, into the abyss, toward a
place beyond which we can neither go nor understand—yet
paradoxically, this cold darkness is the only place we *can* go
to find the answer. The place of absolute mystery is the place
we *need* to go in order to understand. Understand what? Why
nothing less than the meaning of our life! Remember when I
was staring out the window of the jet plane smelling Zochee
on my skin? Remember how Bach guided me out into the
darkness? But only so far…only far enough to see the abyss.
What exquisite torture!

So my writing has partially evoked it, like Carver's character taking an ashtray evokes a kind of mute and petty revenge
for some unspeakable sense of loss, and partly my writing *is* it.
I mean, this trying, trying, trying, this writing, writing, writing *is the meaning.* But I know I need to go further. And at
the same time I'm getting ahead of myself, trying to tell you

where this story is going. I'll start again. I'll start with where I am—the here and now. Ass on a café bench. Fork in my right hand scooping rice and beans into my mouth. Eyes reading Carver. Loving the food, loving the story. Loving it despite being back in this bloody city where it all started nine years ago. Putting the fork down and picking up a pen, a clean sheet of paper, and writing you. My forearm sweating on the table top as I write. I have some notes about that day, those days. I have them back in my room so I know I'll have to go back there to finish the story but even without the notes I remember walking along this same street in the late afternoon and stepping past a couple of goons guarding a fancy car into a bar to watch a football game. The bar was full of Texans and Guatemalan whores, and the Texans were rooting for Dallas against I don't remember, Philly, maybe, and the whores were passing time getting their assess palmed and mooning over their drinks while one of the Texans kept trying to explain in pitiful Spanish the rules of the game. One of the women in particular had a lovely shape under her clothes and just so you don't think I've gone all smarty pants, I kept picturing her naked with her long curly black hair hanging down and curling around her breasts. I think that means I felt sorry for her and wanted her, too. There's a non-sequitur for you. I'd come from Costa Rica just a day or two before and my mom was on my mind. This was only a few months or so after you saved my life, remember, and I did find Mom, but I thought it would be melodramatic to tell her I'd tried to hang myself in Helena, Montana, although frankly I couldn't think of much else to say. Which was okay with her because she'd found a hustler guru down there and was too orgasmed out by their *sessions* and by what she kept calling her *new metaphysics* to have a real conversation or even to focus her eyes. I'll get into all that some other time but for now let's just say I was a little melancholy with the journey. The Cowboys had fourth and a yard, and all the drunks yelled go for it. I hate the Cowboys and am not that partial to Texans, so when they made the first down and everybody cheered I couldn't stand it anymore and walked out and down the street to find another bar that didn't have a big ol' red convertible Mercedes parked in front of it with big ol' Texas plates. I now think if I'd only been a Cowboy fan I might have stayed and then who knows what my life would be like? I might be a doctor like you or on my way to a life of ease and bounty in the import-export business, who knows? I might be the kind of fellow who knows how to wait until the cloud passes and then go on living in peace and delight without asking troublesome questions. I might never have written you even the first letter, much less this hundredth. But the Cowboys did make the first down and the Texans did cheer obnoxiously and so I ducked out of one bar and into another, where I stood next to a tall, blond, surfer-looking fellow wearing a cowboy shirt and a red bandana pirate-style over the crown of his head. Turns out he spoke with a slight accent, and I asked him where he was from and he said, Curaçao. Like any good Dutchman he could speak five languages, yet he condescended to be very impressed with me because I was the first American he'd ever met who knew where Curaçao was. He was a talker. He entertained me with his opinions. He said war wasn't evil, he didn't believe in evil! He said the elves are not bad and they are not good, either! They are just elves! He said everything in declarative sentences like that, with exclamation points, and he didn't waste time on connective phrases. Here are some of the things I wrote down later that evening: "I'm talking to you because if I spoke to the German on the other side of me, my father would break my knee caps!" Or, "I hate governments! They create a system of order out of chaos, and I thrive in chaos!" Or, "The empires of the world were built by second and third sons of the nobility!" And, "My older brother got all the family titles but I'm making truckloads of money!"

He fascinated me. He got me out of myself and we got drunk together. "I laugh until my eyes water every day! All I care about are my mates and surfing and my hammock and campfire! Get a bit pissed at night! Sleep till noon! I am completely and utterly focused on myself! I will never love a woman and I will never have children!"

While he talked, beautiful prostitutes kept approaching and draping themselves across his shoulders. He ignored them. Well, he ignored them until he noticed that I couldn't. A particularly beautiful one stood next him and he reached up and put his hand on the low neck of her knit top and pulled it down, revealing her bare breast. My eyes must have popped wide open but both he and the woman seemed only mildly amused. He covered her again.

"You Americans think a bare breast is sexy! You get all adolescent and weird about it!"

"I am a writer!"

His language, and the woman's breast, had made me bold. It just popped out! It was the first time I ever told anybody I was a writer. After which he said, "No American writer has ever written literature!"

I said, "What?"

He laughed and said, "You will never understand because you are American and so cannot understand!"

I didn't disagree and I'm sure I kept nodding my head like a fool. "I've never really been sure I ever understood anything about literature except I love to read it!" I said. "And because I love to read it, I want to write it!"

"Literature is like the Great Pyramid!" he said. "It's an astoundingly beautiful human creation that is thousands of years old! All you have to do with your life as a writer is spend every waking moment trying to drag your rock up there onto the pile!"

I liked that. The writer as a worker. The writer as an ant. The writer as part of a grand human enterprise. It felt less lonely. It felt less scary. I raised my glass and I was probably smiling from ear to ear. I downed my beer, wiped my mouth.

"I'll try!" I said, continuing our exclamation point conversation.

He gave me that all-knowing European smile. Arrogant, of course, but I've come to understand that it's an earned arrogance. I mean, Europeans do know something we Americans don't. While we were driving our Chevy to the levy drinking whiskey and rye, they were been busy destroying and rebuilding their whole fucking civilization. Twice just this century—and how many times before that?

"You'll *try*," he said. "What a charmingly delusional and optimistic thing to say. And very American!"

Here end my notes from that night.

So how do I continue? As simply and straight-forwardly as possible.

He told me his name was Van Dyke—"I got it from that Mary Poppins chap!"—and he told me that because of this deal or that (I think now he was trying to tell me without telling me he was in the business of selling arms) he had some contacts among the guerillas. As I writer, would I like to go up in the hills? Make a scoop for the *New York Times*. Get famous? Haul my stone a step or two closer to the Great Pyramid?

At the time I figured he liked me. And as delusional and optimistic as that sounds, it also might have been true. He had a way, despite his condescension, of making you feel that he liked you. But it was more than that, it was a kind of neediness he had—this tall handsome aristocrat with long blond hair under a pirate bandana, dressed like a surfer, who right after telling me how rich he was getting, told me he liked to laugh until he cried and all he really cared about was drinking with his mates around a beach campfire. I know by offering me this opportunity, he was showing off how connected he was. But just below the puffed up surface I could see him as a lonely little Dutch boy growing up in Curaçao, wearing his proper wooden shoes and watching the natives run barefoot on the beach. He wanted to be just one of the boys! He wanted the rest of us boys to think he was jolly good fun!

But who can speculate? I never saw him again—or I did, just once—but what happened that night was I said yes. The next morning, he sent a car to pick me up at a park. The car drove me to the edge of the city, where I waited for a cattle truck that drove up a dirt road into the mountains. I was squeezed in the back with fifty other people. I'll bet there were five bodies touching mine as we jostled over bumpy dirt roads, climbing, climbing. All the men carried machetes, many of the women had baskets. We rode for an hour or so, standing up, holding on and looking over the high sides at the forest and the mountains. Feeling the warm sunshine and then the glorious shadow. The mountains here invent new colors of green, from the bright glowing greens of sunlit leaves that give you goosebumps on your neck to the deep shadowy greens that make you feel a weight in the pit of your stomach. It's odd, all of those colors, only one word: green. After a while I began to notice that somebody behind me was tugging gently at my shirt. I glanced back and nobody was looking at me. I felt the tug again, and reached behind me but the hand was gone. Then the truck stopped. We were in the thick of the forest by then, surrounded by giant tropical trees I can't describe with any precision, only to say they were strange and odd and wrinkled, and I wouldn't have been surprised if they'd started talking like the trees in the Wizard of Oz. I felt the tug again, and only then did I understand that somebody was telling me to get out; somebody was telling me that this was my stop. I grabbed my bag and jumped out the back and the trunk took off. I stood alone on the side of the road. After the sound of the truck died out, it was very quiet. Quiet except for a hundred birds and my heart beating madly. I stood there in the dirt road for I don't know how long. It was probably only a minute or so but it seemed like forever. I turned around to look for a place I might be able to sit on my bag and wait, and that's when I saw Jorge, and seeing Jorge, here's the first thing I learned: Just one man with a machete on the side of a deserted road is more frightening than many men with machetes packed into the back of a truck.

He said something I didn't understand, and I nodded. I know that doesn't make sense, but I could barely speak any Spanish and had not brought an interpreter so was going to get very used to not making sense. I was also going to have a problem as a reporter. How could I write a story about the guerillas if I couldn't talk to them? Jorge didn't seem to care. He ducked into the woods next to a giant tree whose roots he had to climb over, and he signaled me to follow. It got instantly cool in the forest, and I shivered. Maybe it wasn't the temperature. For the first time since I'd left my *pensión* that morning I thought maybe I'd made a mistake.

I'm going to stop now. This feels like a serial and that wasn't my intention but the drama of the story in this form might help me get through it, help me push onward. I mean, I can break it down. I don't have to tell the whole thing, I don't even have to know the whole thing. I can just sit down and write the next part for you. That's something I can manage. And now that I've left you hanging, *I have to manage!* I am not merciless, after all. I can't leave my poor Dr. Wencheen McBean waiting and waiting and waiting....

So I know I have to tell you the rest of the story.

But not today.

Stay tuned. Descriptions of Lovely Mountain Treks to follow.

In the meantime, if he's curious tell your studly hubby I am your little gold-hatted, high-bouncing lover, sending you long-range leaps and smooches on the cheek befitting our appropriate platonic status,

Tom

Only phantom floozy courage passing

I need some fresh air. I get up from the couch and walk outside. It's cold and getting dark and the only bit of color—pastel pink and yellow—is in the sky. The trees and rocks are gray-to-black shadows on the white snow. I shiver, but cold is just what I need. I step toward the corner of the cabin to look up at the cliffs but instead see something in the snow at the side of the house that keeps my eyes down. I walk over and take a look, bend over like some old woodswoman. Bear tracks. I've never seen one before in my life but it's clear what they are and they lead along the side of the cabin past the kitchen window. The cold air on my skin goes right through to my bones. I go back inside and get the pepper spray and a headlamp and go outside again. Were the tracks there when I got back from town? I didn't notice them. So the bear must have been right outside while I was reading the letter. What was the puppy doing? Sleeping near the stove. I stand still and listen. The wind in the trees. In the canyon. It reminds me of the sound coming from Soldier's Field when my dad took me to Bears games as a girl. We'd always get there late. We'd always have to walk the last half mile, it seemed, in the cold wind. We'd hear the roar of the crowd rise up and it'd make our blood run hot. Had the Bears scored? I loved watching them, huge men in black, and I had the idea when I was very young that the Bears were somehow really truly bears. I loved sitting close to my father in the stands on cold days and drinking hot chocolate. He smelled of` wool and pipe tobacco and he put his arm around me and I felt protected by him and also swallowed by the immensity of the stadium, and the crowd, and the sound of the crowd. Like the wind here, but all of that goes silent and disappears when I step around the corner of the cabin and I see the bear scat. I shine the light at it still steaming in the cold snow. I turn the lamp off and look around me. The trees and huge fallen rocks are still and black and frozen. I listen. I feel my heart beating a panic. I try to stay still like that. Try to take it all in through the skin but suddenly feel like prey, like I'm being watched, and I run back inside the cabin, close the door and lock it. Puppy knows what I found. He's running circles again, around the stove and into the kitchen and around the table and then back around the stove.

I go to the kitchen window and spread the drapes, put my hands up to the sides of my face and look out. The glass is cold and the night is darker and stiller from inside. I look for movement and see nothing. I'm still choking on my beating heart. I drink a glass of water and then stoke the stove with wood. I pick up the broom and sweep up after myself, and I sweep the wood crumbs into a pile and then into a dust pan. I don't know why I sweep the floor but leave the table and the kitchen a mess. I don't know why I open the front of the wood stove and toss the floor sweepings into the flame and watch the sparks. I don't know why I pick up the letter again. Yes I do. To distract myself, to see if I can disappear again in the wilds of Central America. Mark thought the last line of that letter hilarious and he started teasing me about my gold-hatted, high-bouncing lover. Neither of us knew it was from a poem made famous because it was used as the epigraph for *The Great Gatsby*. To us it was just a funny image, a comic picture of Tom Connor's relationship to me. A way to laugh at the natural tension the letter created. Sometimes when I left to go to work, knowing I'd be gone for thirty-six hours, Mark, the children on his lap, might say, "Long range leaps and smooches as befitting our appropriate platonic status!" And then that got shortened to just "long-range leaps and smooches," and we'd both say that to each other whenever we'd leave to go somewhere, and that got shortened to just "leaps and smooches," which was one of the last things Mark said to me before he lost consciousness, or tried to say, his eyes sparkling with love. He was asking forgiveness, I know, and I gave it to him, forgiving him for dying, for leaving me. I gave it to him, but after he was gone I felt less generous. Why is that? Does that mean I was just faking it when I smiled and held his hands and kissed him when he said leaps and smooches and asked with his eyes, loved me with his eyes, asked me with his eyes to let him go?

No, it wasn't a lie then, but it's not something a person can do just like that, in the blink of an eye. It's a gift I'm still paying for. *Be generous,* I tell myself. *Be kind. Get rid of the anger.* Easier said than done. For instance, I not only do not want to go back to the farm at Thanksgiving, I resent that my children want me to. A family gathering without Mark is too excruciating for me to contemplate, so I guess all of this running around with bears and mummies and letters from gold-hatted, high-bouncing lovers is my way of not thinking about it. Not surrendering into forgiveness, total forgiveness. But the issue is still on the table. It was a promise, after all. *Will you forgive me for dying?* What a hard-hearted bitch to hold that against him! I resent what I think of in my smallest moments as my children's attraction to the maudlin sentiment of our family gathering at Thanksgiving from all parts of the world. How dare we face that family time without Mark, without the person who had really been the center of our family? He used to hold my hips in his hands and say, "Your ass, the center of family." But in all seriousness, he was the center. His humor and good nature and the simple fact that he was home more than I was. Yet how do I clear my heart of the crap and let the light inside, the fresh air inside? Just when I start to feel I'm almost there, I'm not again. I feel the hardening, the closing, the heavy flesh of my face, the frown, the dark pall over my eyes. I think of Mark fucking me and fucking that gypsy and fucking whatever else he might have fucked when he had the urge to stick it in and I said no or was stuck at work taking care of, say, a young Honduran woman whose kidneys were failing but who had no insurance and was sending money home to her children and so came in only when she got too weak to work and with a complication that would kill her within a week. Fuck. Then I think of Mark in bed that night near the end leaning over my curled up body and licking my shoulder, tasting my skin when he thought I would be asleep and I think, he got all of it. All of it. All of what I am, all of me…and he took it all away.

Okay, now I'm a mess. I've got the dog calmed down and on my lap but I'm still shaking. Did all of my surrenders take place in bed? (No. Just the important ones. Ha ha.) Oh, I know they took place in my heart but they played out in bed. That's the truth. And I'm still struggling with this one. I don't want to let go of the anger. Because beyond that is what, the abyss? The Bear? And then what. Who is going to want me ever again? (Don't say the mummy!) Who is going to lift me up in his arms and carry me away and touch me like that again? And how do I manage this surrender without it? I'm humiliated by all of my tears. I keep thinking, okay, I've cried enough, and I think I'm maybe done, and then suddenly I'm crying again and I think I might never be able to stop. I know there are women whose children have been devoured by monsters. Women whose children are dying one by one of starvation right in front of them. Women who are hauled off in the middle of the night and raped by soldiers. Women who've been hurt more than I have. Rather than consoling me, making me feel good to have had my good life, the thought of those women makes me cry even more, as though my ache connects me with their ache. I rifle through the stacks letters on the table until I find one I remember. A poem he wrote about a woman he saw from the rooftop of a Tegucigalpa hotel when perhaps he was feeling as vulnerable as I am.

I stand up to look out the window again and the snow in the yard and the scattered trees and the house-sized rocks and the cliff beyond. The world as it has been and will be long after I'm gone. I sit down again.

"Dear J-Bean,

The hiss of dark, the music of concrete, the smell of horns
rise in a breeze to the rooftop of a Tegucigalpa
hotel. Oh, and I should mention the melancholy.
I'm smoking to get the taste out.
The lives of the dead are only the beginning.

I saw a woman late at night walk alone, heard her heels
tap the secret even the rock street buckled and cracked and broke
            windows and tilted signs.
This was not a natural disaster but the natural way
things are after laughter from the pool hall dies.

The clump of boys go home, the shutters close, girls on the stoop
dissolve into night, even the pimp who backhands
her across the face slams his car door and drives away.
She stands alone on the curb, with a hand raised to her cheek.
Oh, and have I mentioned the melancholy?

She waits a long time still as a rock or a rabbit,
and then she drops her hand from her face and walks around
            the corner and leans
against the wall and from here I see the bare
tops of her titties as she talks to someone
I can't see. Just so you to get the picture

I'm on a rooftop four
stories up leaning on the brick wall smoking a cigar and drinking
rum from a plastic cup. Rebar sticking out of the wall and out of
    the roof and the low
clothes lines make walking and drinking even harder so I lean
my elbows on the concrete and lean out over the city like
    a dumb king

with my friends also drinking and smoking and wobbling over
    this wild
city on the night—oh, and have I mentioned the melancholy?—
    on the night
before we are to fly away again which is when we hear the tap-tap
    of her high heels.
We look down lean over to see
her start to walk down the middle of the street,

tight pink tank top and blond hair on brown skin shoulders and
    more leg—
she has no pants on,
only a thong and her round buttocks are bare flanks like
    a magnificent horse
she's riding toward the corner of the broken street or the
    next corner or the next
where she'll stand to flag a cab—more

leg and hip and bare bottom than anybody
has ever seen in the history of the world.
Catching the cab won't be hard
or maybe it will if they know her and know she never pays
except with skin, skin to the night and city like a dare

or a gasp—nothing will be nothing, blessed be nothing,
dust, death, but not tonight for her—
her bare legs and high, bare saying *hey! hey!* like the call of
    ravens with each
scrape of her heel and each quiver of her high, bare—each
step says LIFE, says take me but be warned for I'm brave
    and bad and soon

I'll be gone—each quiver of her high, bare—
gone. And then she was—did I mention?—around
the corner and even the sound—did I mention?—gone and
        all of us
blinked sex and talked, hey—the melancholy?—and we felt it,
felt her high bare gone hollow like a shadow of only

phantom floozy courage passing, her high, bare
unguarded womb and me without a thought.
Whose mind can get that big anyway? Something has to break
when a woman walks wearing no pants late at night down a city—
did I mention?—a city street wearing no pants.

We saw her from the rooftop of a Tegucigalpa hotel. We slid
        back our drinks
and blinked our bent selves back from the wall. We leaned
        toward the stairs and our safe
beds and oh, sure, yes, listen—did I mention yet
(her steps, her steps, I will, I will)
—the morning?"

When I finish the poem letter I lower it to my lap and I close
my eyes and I hold the image of the woman walking away and
turning the corner and the sound of her heels. I stay like that
for a long time with my eyes closed. I feel her enter into me
and I feel as if I were there on that roof and I feel as if I've
been there on that broken street walking with her, and I will
never forget her, although I know I've read this letter before
and somehow—until now, until reading it again—forgotten
her. I swallow. I'm thirsty. I want to stop drinking tea and start
drinking wine. I think I'll smoke and drink until I can't keep
my eyes open. I think I'll read this poem over and over again.
I think I'll think of this woman for a long time. But first I need
to open my eyes, and I'm surprised at how dark the cabin is.
Only the light over my shoulder illuminating the pages of the
letter and casting a cozy orange light over the rest of the room.

The wind is still blowing. There's an encroaching chill that I know will require constant feeding of the stove with wood to keep at bay. This is the work of the living: keep the fire going. Then I hear something against the glass in the window above the sink and when I look into the darkened kitchen I can see the bear looking at me. A bolt of heavy fear passes through me and fuses me to my chair. I sit stunned for a moment in disbelief. Then the fear passes, or it lightens, anyway, I don't know, but I stand and walk over to the window and we look at each other, the bear and I. He's up on two legs in order to see in and I do not know what possesses me but I look at the bear and the bear looks at me with his black and stupid eyes and for a moment he turns into Mark smiling, and then into a mummy winking, and now he stands with his paw on his hip like a young Tom Connor and he blows a bubble off his tongue.

"Happy Halloween," I say, but it's too late, because when I blink again Tom's turned into the bear again, nostrils inches from the window and exhaling steam that spreads a mist on the glass. I feel a new fear in my chest so heavy and hot that I struggle to breathe, struggle to stand like that for who knows how long, stand with only the sink stacked with dirty dishes and the glass and the dog running circles again at my feet to keep me upright, that and my phantom floozy courage, my anger, I shout.

"This is my house, Mr. Bear!"

Miraculously, he turns his head and lowers himself from the window and he disappears into the dark and I drop my head and close my eyes and feel such a sense of relief I think I'm going to cry but don't, for once I don't. I don't pee in my pants or curse or cry or get drunk and wake up with a mummy on the floor in front of the woodstove, no sir, none of that. Instead I go over to the lamp and I turn it off and I lie down on the couch that has never and never will again feel as soft and comfortable and I close my eyes and cover myself with a blanket and before I can think another weird thought I escape this crazy dreamland for sleep.

five

blah-blah, blah-blah, blah-blah, I'll be back

End of July Something,

Dear Ja-*nine*, Ja-*ten*, Ja-*eleven*, Ja-*twelve*, Ja-*thirteen* years of writing you, Ja-*fourteen* years since we last saw each other in Helena, Montana, where I tried to hang myself and you got both of us beat up in the bus station—

Darling, at least we'll always have Helena! You went home to finish high school and I bet you thought I was only trying to catch up to my flaky dying-of-cancer mom. I bet you thought I only carried a backpack. You never really knew all the rest. But how would you? I never told you how heartbroken I was, how I missed you, how in that short time I fell in love with you, and how ashamed I was to have plunged into such despair when I had you, when I had you in my world, in my life, in my bed! It made no sense to me, and I have spent years trying to understand it. So I never told you that, and I never told you that in addition to my backpack full of shame and heartbreak,

I carried a little black suitcase that fit both a portable type-writer and all of the ambition in the world. Well, I know I told you something, but only a little bit. What I wanted to do was write novels, and as far as I was concerned, novels were the most amazing of all human creations. They contained worlds I could walk into, people I could love and care about. They could make me see the world more clearly; they colored it, framed it, gave it order. And not for a couple of hours like a play or a movie, but sometimes for weeks. Because even after you set a book down and go about your life, you feel as if you are still in the book and you see the common things of your life different-ly, you see your dog, your girlfriend, your car, your job, your body differently. The air smells different. The sky looks differ-ent. The earth under your feet feels different. Even in suffering, there's the beauty, the beauty, the beauty! My god! Aaaaah! I wanted to write novels like the novels that made me feel this way, novels like *The Brothers Karamazov*, like *Ulysses*, like the *Grapes of Wrath*, *Heart of Darkness*, *To the Lighthouse*, *Gats-by*, *The Sun Also Rises*, *Absalom, Absalom,* and yes, just lately, *War and Peace*. I wanted to be in that conversation, the what-is-a-human-being? conversation. The how-do-we-find-mean-ing-and-dignity-despite-certain-suffering-and-certain-death? conversation.

You didn't know because I never told you. I suppose I thought I'd be famous by now and that's how you'd know. I thought that after a few years I would begin to publish short stories that got the right people's attention. It would be a brief and sparkling apprenticeship, and within a few years, certain-ly before I turned thirty, I'd sell a novel that would be pub-lished to mad raves, a novel that would light up a new part of the heavens. It would establish me as the voice of my gen-eration, a voice that all others would compare themselves to, a voice that our children's children would be still be reading, loving, hating, rebelling against. But that didn't happen. I'm thirty-five now. (You must be thirty or thirty-one? Wow! And beautiful, I'm sure, and a doctor, now, and a mother. What wonders you have made of the time, a real live wonder woman, turning yourself into wonderful things!) Not so with me. On the outside I'm still, these fourteen years later, the same as I was: An aspiring novelist. No different. I've sold four short stories to literary magazines for a total of two hundred dollars and a dozen free copies, and I've never heard one word from a reader, good or bad. I was very excited to get the acceptances but publishing the stories has been no different than putting them in a bottle, corking the bottle, and tossing the bottle into the ocean. Maybe somebody, somewhere read the stories I published, but certainly not the right people, and if the right people read them, they were unimpressed.

Okay, I told myself. That was disappointing but it didn't de-rail me. Because even if short-story fame didn't pan out, I was still going to write a novel that would blow everyone's mind. A novel about love and beauty and death, about re-birth in the midst of decay, squalor and revolution, hope and despair. You know, the regular stuff of masterpieces. But the novel is a bull I apparently can't ride. Because every time I think I've got him in the chute, he breaks out, jumps out, and I've got to go round him up again. In the meantime he's grown so when I get him back, he doesn't fit in the chute anymore. So I go back to the beginning and build a bigger chute, but by the time I do the bull has grown even more; he's too big, and he jumps out again!

Now, rather than feel a dose of good, healthy despair—de-spair that might stop me—what I feel is admiration! I swoon looking at the way he struts across the grass, his big head in the air, nose in the air, his neck thick and sleek muscular flanks full of grace. So beautiful! I can't help it, I go after him again, and the whole thing happens again, and there's where I am, fourteen years later, looking at my beautiful runaway nov-el, my graceful beast, trotting away from me and my broken chute for the last time. Free at last, free at last.

Me too, I suppose, because I'm going to let him go now. I'm going to give up trying to get him in the chute and ride him. I know I'm not too old to be a writer—lots of great ones didn't publish until their mid-thirties and older, but I'm old for me.

I just don't have the gas anymore. Some days at night I can see so much change in my mind. And maybe I just sit around bored for a while, and it makes me think *real* hard. And that's tough. It's like I'm time factoring. Everybody's got a good/different idea—everybody's got a story. Why would mine be anything remarkable? Makes me sick thinking of all the time I wasted believing that. Gags me with a whopper. Lots and lots, tons really, of real things get traded away for shiny stuff. Poor Indians. Who's the fucking hero here anyway?

A bum I recently walked past on the street shouted out, *Hey, you gotta glow!* I agree. And I'm feeling my glow fade. Oh, sure, I could stay determined. Even idiots can make up their minds; they just blab out an idea and look around real nervously until they see the old bobbing heads. Shit, it's an epidemic of bobbing heads. Stay the course! Nod, nod, bob, bob. But I don't want to spend another season in hell, or season after season. I've been traveling around these countries for a long time on a dream and now I want to go home. Like Odysseus. Only difference is he won the war and had a pretty wife and a pretty Greek island to go back home to. Me? I've lost the war—and I don't have a home at all. But besides that, hey, we're brothers. We're both wanderers. And both of our journeys are post-traumatic stress induced. You see the real shit—on the battlefield of Troy or here in Central America—and hey, there is no fast and easy way home. That much we both know, Odysseus and me.

I'm going back to the States, not sure to where, but the one thing I know for sure is I'm going to make a difference. Maybe not until I die but then at least I'll quit thinking about what it is. I'm going to go back to college and then get a job that actually pays money. Wow, imagine that! And have an actual effect on somebody's life. (Okay, the metaphoric castaway on an island who read my stories? The stories I metaphorically put in a bottle and threw into the metaphoric sea? That guy fished the story out of the bottle that washed up on his deserted beach, and he read it, and sure, I admit, his metaphoric life was changed. His eyes were opened and he got a brief but fulfilling glimpse of beauty and God and meaning....)

But I've had it with metaphors. I want a bull to be a bull, a tree to be a tree, light to be light, and God to be God. I want a real woman with a real body that bleeds real blood to give me real children who eat real food that I need to do real work to get real money to buy. I figure I only get to breathe a finite number of breaths, and I don't want to keep breathing and writing about things that nobody but me feels particularly compelled to imagine. I want to do something that affects the world. I mean, well, you know what I mean. You're a doctor. You help people every day. Somebody comes into the E.R. with a broken bone or a spastic heart or a sliced hand and you help them. (Nobody says, *Gosh, Doc, I really admire your work but this particular piece isn't quite hitting home for me, so I'll have to pass on making an offer this time....*) Anyway, that's what I want to do—something real. So my plan now is to finish my MBA in Miami and then start a really cool business that makes something or provides some service that helps a lot of people. That gives them something that makes their life a little better, a little more endurable. Don't laugh. I know it sounds sappy but hey, you must know by now, I *am* sappy.

Speaking of business, I've got some unfinished business with you. With you and with that significant other of yours, that hunky love monkey of yours, Sir Mark the Farmer, as I know he must also be a big fan of my work and hangs on my every line. What I'm getting at, of course, is I have to finish the story that started all of this, the story of what happened when Van Dyke sent me up into the Guatemalan mountains to meet some rebels way back when, way back when I told him I wanted to be a writer, when I was brand new to this part of the world, could hardly speak Spanish, just wanted to learn and write something that mattered, and without even knowing it, without having a clue, really, Van Dyke gave me everything I needed, everything but the talent to do something with it.

So where did we leave off so long ago? Let me make myself comfortable here in the café before I begin. Here's the meta scene: me sitting at a pink-painted wooden table in the Soda

Castro Ling next to a screen-less window. There is no breeze
and the ceiling fan stopped working just a few minutes ago. A
motorcycle as loud as a helicopter speeds down the block and
I burst into a terror sweat. The wooden table top slides under
my wet forearm, so does the pen in my hand. A fat Chinese-ish
looking boy is trying to stomp a mouse he's got trapped in the
corner of the restaurant. Another Chinese-ish looking kid is
throwing a napkin at another who is singing some inane soccer song. These kids are "the help," and they've served me rice
and beans and brought me a cool tamarind drink. In the opposite corner of this little café from the boy trying to stomp
the mouse is a man on the pay phone quoting bible stories.
Two pretty women walk by the window talking, one of them
catches my eye and does a little obscene thing with her mouth
and eyes that the women do down here to flirt. It looks like
the faint beginning of an orgasm face, a quick little chin lift, a
little lip curl, a little pout, eyelids dropping halfway over liquid
eyes—all of that very quickly, but it makes me weak and I want
to chase after her, throw myself on the ground behind her and
take her ass in my hands and bury my face in the flowered
fabric of her skirt, smell her, die for her. Melodramatic? Well,
I guess. But we're talking about reproduction here, aren't we?
You'd die for your children, I know you would. What could be
more important? (Don't tell me *art*, or I'll bite you!) I look at
this woman walking away who dared to give me that casual
and obscene little look and I think I'd be satisfied, I'd give up
everything, just to be the breeze that touches her life-giving
skin….

No, I'm lying. Breeze-schmeeze. I want to empty myself and
flood her. I want to fertilize all of her eggs at once.

Hey.

Alas.

I want to follow her and love her but she's already down the
block and around the corner and here I am. Still in the Soda
Castro Ling. Writing. Tired, and I haven't even gotten to my
story.

I promise this is not a teaser. I need to write what I am going to write, but I am going back to my room now to lie down and see if I can take a nap. And if I need to knock on the door of Suyapa, the pretty, young buck-toothed prostitute who lives through the plywood in the room next door—so I can quiet myself, so I can rest before continuing this letter in the evening—be patient with me. One of the reasons I'm getting out of the Great Novel Writing Game, besides the poor pay and wretched living conditions (Suyapa's and my mattresses are stuffed with cornhusks and there are mice living in them), is I'm also always afraid I simply don't have enough warm blood in my veins to feel what I need to feel, to say what I need to say.

So. My blood has cooled and thinned. I must repose, recover, re-heat, return. (Iambic literary talk meaning blah-*blah*, blah-*blah*, blah-*blah*, I'll be back.)

Hasta luego and *hasta* kisses.
Tee-Con

not a pretty Greek island either

I put more wood in the stove and sit close while it clicks and hisses and the fire grows. I need a break myself before plunging onward into the second and third of the series of letters that arrived within a few days of one another, the last real letters he sent me before the fragments of the Elizabeth Bishop poem. I wedge in yet another piece of wood, and lean toward the flames—*repose, recover, reheat*—and when I'm warm enough I decide to go outside. I get up and look at the mess in the kitchen and the barricaded back door and have about a tenth of a second of an impulse to clean it all up, finally, the messy dishes and the scattered groceries, and maybe even call somebody who can fix the back door, but the feeling scoots on by like a bird past the edge of my vision. I bend down to pull on my big leather boots (untied), old navy blue puffy jacket with the duct tape repairs on the sleeves and back, a Green Bay Packer stocking cap and leather mittens—what I've come to think of as my old man outdoors outfit—and step outside. I had planned to take a walk but am suddenly lazy. I just stand in the yard and feel the sun on my face and listen to the quiet, the dripping of snow off the eaves. The setting sun lights up a pine tree across the river and makes the melting snow glisten on its branches. Tom's sentences are like a balm on my body, or something strange in the air. I feel as if I'm absorbing their cadence and moving though a new medium—swimming rather than walking. Maybe like living under water, certainly seeing the world through a new and different lens. More focused, less focused. Oddly, I feel suddenly optimistic and happy. The tree glows. It's just a tree, though. Just sky, just river, sun, meadow, cliff. Up high I see an eagle. Just an eagle. The bear tracks are disappearing in the sun but along the side of the house and up the draw in the shade they're still visible. I step inside one of them. My entire boot fits. I step inside another, and that boot fits, as well, of course. I think about following the bear this way, walking inside his tracks and I look up the draw where they lead and I stare into those trees and then, again, I see him.

He's sitting on his haunches looking at me standing in his tracks looking at him. I squint and wipe the wind-tears from my eyes and squint again. I stare. The bear doesn't move, and neither do I. I stand and wait and sweat breaks out under my clothes and soon I'm pretty sure that what I think of as a bear is not a bear but a bear-shaped something. A stump. A shadow. This is getting old. I am tired of bear-shaped somethings turning into bears and bears turning into bear-shaped somethings but nevertheless my heart beats faster and every cell of my body comes alive and my legs want to run away or at least retreat, take a step back, another, just a few and I'd be around the corner of the cabin. I could go inside. I could get the bear spray. I could stay inside. I could think about something else.

But I don't. In fact, just to be perverse, I do the opposite. I walk toward the bear-shaped darkness in the trees. I walk slowly at first and then faster. I touch my waist where normally I'd be carrying the pepper spray and it's not there, of course, but two things keep me going. One, I admit, is that a big part of me suspects that what I'm looking at is not really a bear at all—it hasn't moved, and with every step he looks more like a shadow than he does a bear. And two, if he is the bear, I'm tired of his bullshit.

How many times does he think he can come around and scare me? Whatever the number, he's exceeded it, and I'm tired. Tired of seeing bears that are bears and tired of seeing bears that are not bears, and tired of having to have the same frightened reaction every time, like a programmed machine. I try to keep my feet in the bear tracks headed up toward the draw, and whatever it is is a couple hundred yards up that way in the trees, and I walk toward it and I am getting closer and I am getting closer and I feel my stomach tighten but I know it's just a shape, and then of course I know it's the bear itself, and then it's just a shape. Three or four ravens watch me from the low branches of one of the first trees. They stare at me in their blackness, black bodies, black beaks, and I want to tell them to mind their own business but as though they sense my mood they fly off over my head, their shadows passing quickly over the patchy snow. I keep walking. I don't shout. I don't want to betray my nervousness. If I knew for sure what I knew, I'd say I was going to prove it to myself, prove what I know is true— but what I know keeps changing. Even the sky that just a moment ago when I stepped outside seemed to glimmer with the promise of a shiny yellow and blue day has dulled under a gray haze. Smoke? It's high and I can't smell it but it's changed the light enough to make perspective flatten and the bear or bear-shaped darkness in the trees harder to see. The only thing that stays the same is that with each wet step in the wet melting snow my determination grows. March-march, march-march. The trees get closer, the bear-shaped darkness gets closer, the bear does, too. I'm walking up a little slope and the exertion is making me breathe hard and I'm saying a nursery rhyme as I walk, "The brave old Duke of York, he had ten thousand men, he marched them up to the top of the hill, he marched them down again." Finally, when I'm about fifty yards away I wave my arms and I shout, and the shout echoes off the cliffs behind the bear or the bear-shaped darkness, which stays as still as a rock. Maybe it is a rock. The bear tracks I was following have veered to the right so I am no longer walking in the old prints, and the closer I get the more sure I am that the big bear is long gone and all I'm walking toward is a big bear-shaped stump—and of course this makes me braver. I shout and wave my arms, "Go away, Mr. Bear!" I yell, and I don't even care that I have no bear spray—who needs bear spray for a bear-shaped shadow? I stomp and walk and shout and wave my bare hands, and when I get about thirty yards away from the big bear-shaped something, it moves.

Oh god. I stop. I swallow. The bear-shape has turned and begun to walk away like a real bear. I think I forget to breathe. My heart is pounding in my chest. It is a bear. The bear. He looks back at me over its shoulder but keeps walking. I am close enough that I think I can see the gleam of his cinnamon fur and the movement of his shoulder muscles under his fur, and then his back is turned and all I can see is his moving round bottom and I'm overcome with what I can only call a heroic flush. I mean, I shout at him one more time. "Go away!" He starts to run and I can't help but take a few running steps after him. "Go on!" I yell. "Quit spying on me, you pervert!"

I quickly stop. I can feel my blood coursing through my neck. The sky is graying and the wind moves the tops of the fir trees through which the bear has disappeared, up the draw, between the steep rock faces. I stop and look back to the cabin and the puppy is running circles on the flat. I turn around and walk back. As soon as I turn my back on where the bear ran, I feel fear jump me again, jump on my back and dig its claws in my neck and shoulders. I want to turn around again and make sure the bear is still disappeared, hasn't come back down and isn't chasing me now, but I refuse. I make myself walk back to the cabin without looking and that takes way more courage than what I just did, actually, way more courage to coolly walk back than it took to charge after the bear when I was halfway sure it was just a black shadow and not a real bear. But the bear was a bear. The bear is still a bear.

Coming down the hill toward the cabin, the cozy-looking

cabin with smoke drifting out its chimney and still some snow in the yard, I see the silver curve of the river below where it comes out of the canyon, and I remember watching the twins sledding the big hill on the farm, their two bundled little bodies on the green plastic sled. Mark had set them on it and let it go and they were old enough to sit up and hold each other but the sled after going down the hill kept going across the flat and toward the cut bank over the creek, a five- or six-foot drop from the flat pasture down into the little watercress-choked creek. We watched the sled go and go and go, slowly, slowly, without stopping, and Mark and I looked at each other when we knew the sled was not going to stop before the cut bank, and we started yelling for the kids to roll out of the sled. It was going so slowly it wouldn't have hurt them to roll out, and they still had plenty of time, but they were too little to respond. They were big enough to sit up on a sled and hold onto each other but too little to see where the sled was going and roll off to avoid disaster. The sled kept creeping along the flat closer and closer to the cut bank, and when it got to the edge it seemed to hover for a moment as though it might stop. I was running and shouting for them to roll out but they didn't—couldn't—and just when I thought the sled might stop like that, on the edge, balanced, partway over, it tipped down and fell out of sight.

Mark and I were running as fast as we could in the snow, running and laughing and scared, laughing because of how slowly the sled was going, and those little hooded bodies holding on to each other and unable to respond as the sled crept closer and closer to the edge, but scared because after the sled tipped and fell we could no longer see them. When we got to the cut bank and looked down, they were fine, muddy from the mud on the edge of the creek, and cold and wet and crying, but fine. We each picked one up and carried them back to the house and stripped them and sat with them in front of the woodstove. I sat with Mark by the stove with our children on our laps and drank cocoa and they felt small and vulnerable in our arms and I thought, this is our family, this is our family, and Mark held my hand and later when the kids were napping we made love like we hadn't in a long time. I remember thinking *this is the last time, the last time,* thinking that I had nothing else in me and even my skin was gone by then, all gone, and how I must have been living behind a wall of fear and determination because as we sat by the fire with our children on our laps I felt it all fall down. My heart seemed to soften, to melt, not as a matter of will or any sense of virtue but more as a response to the laughter and the cold and now the warmth, and by the time we fell into each other's arms, raw and surprised, I felt as if I had nothing solid left and my waters had turned. I was a lake and my waters turned.

Mark, later, when he wanted that again, sometimes asked, just to make me laugh, should we put the children on a sled and send them down the hill toward the creek?

I see the little curl of smoke from the cabin. I'm still walking toward it and still not looking back over my shoulder to make sure the bear isn't chasing me. I'm being brave, I tell myself. "The brave old Duke of York." March, march, march, and as I march I think of my Cody's brave and earnest face when he played sports, his idea that if he just worked hard enough, he could make the team, his heartbreaking effort, and then of Kate and the way things came easy to her, school, languages, romance, and now she's far away and determined, and I think she might be unhappy, not the unhappiness that breaks you but the unhappiness that sometimes comes when you are doing something hard, trying to be married so young, trying to live in Kuala Lumpur, of all places. It can be miserable, the uncertainty, the aloneness, and then suddenly I feel how lazy I am, how lazy I've become. Even the memory of how hard it is to be twenty-five makes me tired and want to rest. Pathetic! Especially after having spent most of three decades working hard—and liking it. I mean, I loved my work at the hospital, loved being a part of a team in the ER, loved to work when it was busy, when we were getting slammed, because with every cylinder firing in my body and my mind I felt, often felt, as if yes, yes, yes, yes, this is how I am at my best, this is how I live best—there at the hospital and then home, sometimes into the middle of another work day, and I'd join the team driving tractor or cooking or whatever was going on, often tired but also enlivened by the activity, the hay wagons coming down the ridge road, stacked neat with square bales lined up to be unloaded into the barn, a fence crew from the swampy pasture behind the ponds back for lunch, there was usually a place for me to jump in and help, and I loved that kind of life, coming home to that kind of life. I'd think, this-is-me-this-is-us, this is *our* good life.

So we did have a home. We do have a home. It's not a pretty Greek island either, but it is, as Mark used to say almost daily, the most beautiful piece of ground on earth—287 acres of steep oak and hickory forest and narrow, deep soil hollows where the grass grows thick and fast and the clear springs feed the brook trout creek. Snow falls and drifts and the hills look naked white under crooked black trees and windless nights in the winter are as quiet as a coffin until spring and you can hear the hills seep water and the valley air begins to stir and hum and the calves grow and the air turns hazy in summer, you could eat it for the smells and the feel of it on your tongue, and on balmy nights fireflies and stars light the darkness and the morning fog on fall mornings burns away in the sun. The hillsides turn yellow and orange and scarlet, and I remember the rolling smells of soil and stalk, fruit and wood, and the changing shapes of shadow on the hills and the hollows, the green the blue the yellow the gray the white the black, the light, the light, the light, the light.

Kate needs to come home and Cody, too. They need to see each other and catch a breath of it. They are young and weary, and they need a gulp of the north wind coming off the river in the late fall and blasting into the valley carrying death and a promise, a big wind that says remember it all and then forget it all, that cools the dying and flames the warm blooded, that says get up and get ready, cut wood, seal windows, make applesauce, because everybody needs to lie down and rest, yes, you too, but not now, not now, not yet....

The sky above the canyon is eerily yellowish and flat from

the angle of the sun and high smoke. I grab an armload of wood and go back inside the cabin. When I pass over the threshold into the dark I have an image of being swept up in Mark's arms and carried. Suddenly I'm lonely, I just want my old life back. Where did it go? I feel grief like a weight in my legs. I stack the wood behind the stove, and I turn on a light. I take off my hat and my hair is sticking up with static and my face is sweaty from the walk. I take off my mittens and I put the hat and the mittens in a little pile next to the door. I smooth down my hair and then get the broom and clean up the mess I made coming in, the slush, the wood crumbs, and I sweep them into a pile and then into a dust pan, and I toss them out the door and close it again. Then I take the navy blue puffy jacket off and my boots off, and I slip on my sheepskin slippers and find the second and third parts of the letter.

They'd arrived on the farm in separate envelopes and sat by the radio on the kitchen counter with the bills and advertisements, and I tossed them in the beach bag on the way to the river. It was a hot summer day and I was looking forward to the river, and I probably thought something as casual as, oh yes, Tom was telling us the story of going into the jungle so many years before. He's decided he's not a writer anymore but still wants to tell that story. Mark and I had been surprisingly moved by how he told us he felt his glow fading, his ambition, such a huge ambition and we'd never really known it. Really, by his letters, we would have thought he was a complete, who knows what, fuck- up? Slacker? So the declaration of his ambition and how he was letting it go, had decided to come home, was moving. I had never met anybody who wanted to be a writer and so until reading this letter figured it wasn't really that much of an ambition. I mean, if you want to write, you write, right? It's not like you need to pass a test and then get into a school, and then pass a hundred tests, and then have a grueling apprenticeship. All I'm saying is while I felt sympathy for what seemed to be a tiredness, an early middle age, I also felt surprised that he'd ever had that kind of ambition to begin with.

So I must have picked up letters two and three of the story, and put them into the canvas tote with our towels and water, thinking they might be fun to read. And I must not have had time to read them at the river, playing with the kids, keeping them from wandering out into the current, because I read them in the car on the way home. I remember the children in the back. I remember the green hills at dusk, the pale blue sky, the world as benevolent as only Wisconsin on a summer evening can be when you are driving through it with your family and all of you are alive and healthy and floating on bounty. And isn't this the question, how to reconcile? Not just with each other—flawed and weak and untrue as we may be—but with the world?

I get up and put lotion on my hands, so shriveled and dry since I got here that sometimes when they catch my eye they scare me. I think, whose ugly hands are these? Especially because I've grown my nails longer than I've had them since I was a med student, but they're untrimmed and naked. I pour myself a cup of wine and get a cigarette out of my jacket and I sit down, collapse more like, with the remaining letters on my lap in front of the woodstove, with the weight of sadness in my bones. I'm tired and although I'm too skinny and need to eat, I'm not hungry and it feels like evening and I feel like drinking and smoking. I want to cry and I haven't even begun to read, because I'm thinking about Tommy's whole life, now. His life from the beginning to the tragic end, and I feel suddenly as if I know him dead in a way I never knew him when he was alive. He seemed to know plenty about me—seems to still know me—even though I was only wrote him a few brief notes in all of those years. I feel ashamed at how little I was able to grasp of his struggle, not really to *reconcile*, but to stay open, to love the world so full of suffering and evil, betrayal and injustice. And isn't that the work of it? I mean, for all of us? To be brave enough to spread our arms and open our hearts and fill our lungs with the terrible beauty of living? And isn't that what he was trying to do, tried so hard and for so long to do?

The light in the cabin has faded and suddenly it's too dark

to read, which is okay because then I can't see the papery dried skin on my hands when I light cigarette number what? Who cares. My mouth tastes like a chimney, so it may as well be one. I'm not counting anymore. I take a good drag and the nicotine settles my mind. I pull a blanket up over my lap and reach up and switch on the standing lamp next to my chair and begin to read.

I was beginning to think a lot about beer

Dear Woman,

(Sometimes writing or saying that beautiful word, *woman*, is like writing or saying *apple, pear, grape*—I can almost taste the fruit! Okay, I know it's *inappropriate*, as they say nowadays instead of *bad*, to talk this way to a married woman but try to be compassionate. Suyapa was not there, not in her room, and so I lay alone in mine thinking of her at the table this morning, how she looked down at her soft little bare arms supporting her and at her pretty breasts under her blouse, how she adjusted the sparkly little trinket I gave her, arranged the rest of her features—chubby cheeks with dimples, bud-red lips pursed over her teeth—into just the right expression of gratitude and smart-ass seduction…oh, yes, where was I again? Compassion. I was asking for yours. I'm bad, yes, but imagine if you had what I have growing in my pants four to eight times a day and shouting: *hey! hey! hey! hey! hey!*

Might not *you* be bad, too?)

Sorry. I'll start over and try being compassionate with you as well. Take a breath. Oh what the hell, take two. There's plenty of air. This time I'm writing from a breezy table in a kiosk on the beach. The sun is just down, the sky is full of wild pastels, the palm leaves are clicking in the breeze, *salsa* music carries across the wide beach from the dance club. I've napped, showered, and come here to write you. Isn't it funny how this is all about writing you? Maybe that's why I can't write novels. Or maybe that's how great novels are written, like this, like letters, like putting the face of the reader right there on the table, a little imaginary photo above the typewriter or notebook so I can focus on you, on you, on telling you, Janine McBean, Doctor, Wench, Woman, (Oh, yes, and I keep forgetting, your Sig Other, Hubby, Stud-Monkey, Very Best Farmer Friend—greetings to you, Sir!) so I can focus on telling you something, something, something I'm not sure how to say.

I'll start anyway.

You'll remember I met the outlandish Van Dyke, who arranged for me to get picked up at my hotel and dropped off where I could get a ride in the crowded back of a truck up into the mountains. I was poked and prodded until I dismounted alone, and there waited until a machete-toting stranger named Jorge appeared. I seem to remember leaving off when we were walking in the jungle, ol' Jorge and me...(In addition to Tolstoy, I've been re-reading *Catcher in the Rye*, and so forgive ol' Holden for breaking up my diction.) We're walking in the jungle and what does it do but start to goddamn rain. I told you I couldn't speak Spanish very well, and well, I didn't bring a rain coat, either. So instantly my pocket notebooks get soaked and so does the only pair of clothes I have, the ones I'm wearing. I don't know why I didn't bring an extra set or even a hat. I guess I didn't foresee the ordeal. This is interesting to me now. What *did* I foresee? Going up into the hills, having a meeting with a Fidel Castro-type and his brother in a hut. Smoking a cigar, having some of the local brew. Maybe shooting guns for target practice? I was not by nature a hip revolutionary guy, but there was a certain glamour to being a revolutionary, wasn't there? Doesn't it all seem an innocent time? And only fourteen years ago? Or maybe I'm the only one in which these things have changed and now feel so long ago and cobwebbed, not the events, but the attitude of the man/boy who lived them. I followed behind Jorge in the Jungle and it rained so hard that even though he was only five or ten feet in front of me I could barely see him. The ground got slippery and I had much better shoes than ol' Jorge but I kept slipping and tripping and wiping my forehead so I could see, and ol' Jorge didn't seem fazed by the rain or by the slippery trail at all. I mean, he was like a duck carrying a machete, glancing back from time to time, slightly amused. I don't know how long we walked—mostly uphill—and I was getting tired and filthy from falling so much, I couldn't talk, I had nothing to write on, and it was starting to get dark and no sign of any revolutionary beauties or swaggering *bandoliered* young men who would tell me all and give me food and cigars and in short, treat me like a hero because I would *tell their story to the world!* I might have had a little bit of the young Russian in me, as well, the wild scribbler of *Heart of Darkness* who is captivated by Kurtz, who lives with him, takes care of him, who is transformed by him—*The man has enlarged my mind. He's made me see things!*—some of that going on, too. Who knows what faeries float in the minds of the young and innocent? I know I could see Jorge's shape in front of me. He was short and sure-footed on the dark, slippery, uneven trail. He seemed to see through the dark and the rain like a cat. He carried the machete in his right hand and he swung it occasionally at something in front of him. Jaguars, maybe. Could he be the man who would expand my mind? But all he wanted to talk about, if *talk* is the right word, as he couldn't speak English and I couldn't speak Spanish and it must have taken an hour for me to even figure out who he was talking about—all he wanted to talk about was Bruce Lee (Bru-leé) and Chuck Norris (Chew-Nóree), and then it took maybe another twenty minutes for me to eventually figure out he was interested in my opinion about which would win in a fight, if ever such a fight could be arranged.

I tried to explain that I'd never even watched one of those chop-chop movies all the way through so I'd never even thought about it. But what I was saying was so unbelievable to Jorge, so incomprehensible as to be un-hearable. And maybe unforgivable, as well. In other words, I think Jorge figured I couldn't possibly be saying what I was saying, because if I were truly such a moron, how could he justify coming all this way to get me? And walking all the way back with me? So he generously gave me the benefit of the doubt and attributed the impression of my ignorance to my garbled Spanish.

Finally, trying to talk when I was so tired became impossible, so I stopped trying. Jorge, however, chatted all through the night, the rain coming down so loud I could barely make out the sound of his voice. It had been only a week ago I was in Costa Rica at a country club pool sipping screwdrivers at nine every morning and ogling the staff, one of whom—a pretty eighteen-year-old, cat-eyed hunter—would reward my patient sad ordeal with imaginative sexual favors delivered every evening in her rooftop cot room, where I accidentally-on-purpose stumbled the first night I was there, taking the stairway up one last turn, opening the door into her little shelter, and finding her perched like a patient puma. Thinking about her made the walk with Jorge harder but I'm not one for the easy way, so I kept thinking about her all night long as we walked—walked all night long! I know people all over the world have walked all night long. I've read those words, I'm sure, in books, but to do it is different from what that simple phrase makes it out to be. We walked all night long. Short, simple, clean. So that's the first difference. Actually doing it is not clean and not simple and not short. A night is a long time. And walking in a rainy jungle means falling down and getting up and falling down and scraping yourself and feeling your hands caked with mud and your clothes grow heavy with rain and begin to chafe, yes. I feel a little gay using that word regarding my clothes, but after about two hours...hours...that's the thing about walking all night long, there are *hours* in there, but nobody counts them.

They don't matter. All that matters is the dawn. By dawn you will have made it all night, and hence, completed the phrase *all night long*—but a few hours into it I found myself saying to myself in rhythm with my walk, *my pants are chafing, my pants are chafing.* That inane chant was oddly accompanied by pornographic images of me and Clemencia, my rooftop lover, the images like taunting reminders that there did indeed exist a world of physical comfort, and I'd left it voluntarily.

Why didn't I stay there with the eager fauna of Costa Rica? Sure, mom had left for the beach with her new happiness guru and there was nobody to pay for it anymore, so I guess there was that, but Clemencia and I could have run off to a shack somewhere up on the shoulder of the mountain and picked coffee and lived in happy state of arousal and satisfaction, arousal and satisfaction, for the rest of our days!

Unrealistic?

Perhaps, but no more so than what I was doing now, walking and falling down and walking and falling down again in the slippery forest—rain pouring down in what? buckets? sheets? pissloads?—to visit the guerillas and to write about them.

My pants are chafing, my pants are chafing

What I am getting at with this by-now tedious description of how *me wee bit-o-flesh suffered*, why I'm lingering on this is to show the childish mindset with which I began my excursion. I went into the forest a twenty-one-year-old boy and even as I was walking that night I kept thinking of the line from *Death of a Salesman*—the uncle goes into the wilderness with nothing and comes out with diamonds, or something like that. He says, *It takes a great kind of man to crack the jungle!* And so I'm sure I thought I was—or thought I might yet become—*a great kind of man.*

But in truth, I did not. I came out…I came out a…I guess I'm still trying to figure that out. I didn't come out wealthy or great, however. I came out broken, but broken *open*, broken *bigger*, if you know what I mean. In the depths of the horror I found a reason to live and it didn't have to do with anything but what was inside me. There's a thin line between hope and despair and in addition to learning I could walk all night long, I learned I could balance on that line—not by will or by strength but by some act of surrender, maybe. At my core is a coldness as deep as the earth and that's exactly the place the fire started. I'm not trying to brag, because I have failed at this, feeling this—I have failed at feeling this way more often than I have succeeded—but something happened at the bottom of a well up there in the mountains, something both horrible and wonderful, and I could not have missed it because as I huddled in the darkness I learned how to love. Or I learned I *could* love. Because I don't mean to say I can love better than you or better than anybody else—I stumble along in that pursuit I'm sure more poorly than those around me. But just like everybody else on earth, everything I know I know because of what I have suffered and what I have loved. We all have our crooked trails. Mine led me up into the mountains and then down deep into a well (don't laugh) where I saw God's face and heard his voice, and somehow led me back again.

Back again to here, fourteen years later, sitting in a clean, well-lighted café in Guatemala City—yes, I've left my beach kiosk and my cornhusk mattress and my mercenary heart-breaker, the plump Suyapa, and two days later continue this seamless narrative back in Guat City, where I started it, where I began writing the story in a letter to you. I had hopes for a Marlow-like jungle experience. I wanted to be transformed, to have my mind expanded, blown open—and I suppose that's indeed what happened—only I think it was my heart that exploded. Nobody tells you how much that experience hurts, though. Or maybe I wasn't listening when they did. You have to understand that when I was twenty-one almost everything in my head came from a book or a movie, and I'd only imagined those experiences partway. I mean, I'd read about walking all night long, but never imagined how tired I'd get walking all night long in the rain. Or how the fatigue would make me cry like a baby in the dark. Feel sorry for myself, so wet and muddy and tired.

We didn't even stop at daybreak, either. The rain did, but

the forest was still wet. We walked up the side of a huge mountain, and although I didn't trip and fall quite as much as I had in the dark, I was beginning to get very thirsty and hungry. I began to grab wet leaves from along the trail and lick them to keep my mouth moist, and when we came to a muddy hole, I wasn't afraid to get down on my belly with Jorge and drink.

Finally, at dusk, after walking more than twenty four hours we arrived at a village. I was fed and watered like a beast. I don't really remember what I ate but I'm sure the same as I ate the entire time I was there, corn tortillas, a little salt, and beans. I surrendered my filthy clothes to my hosts, an old bent-over couple, Eusebio and Olimpia, washed the mud off of me, and slept soundly on corn stalks on the ground in a dark little leaf hut that smelled of smoke. I lay in the dark that first night and thought of my mom, wondered if I'd ever feel like seeing her again, and well, the answer after fourteen years is no, but I didn't know that then. Her story, if you've forgotten, is that my dad, Tom Connor, Sr., had died eight years before—and after that she just kind of floated away on gin—which was nothing new to her, she'd been floating on gin long before his sudden death. But once he was gone, she had nothing to anchor her, not me or my sister, certainly. (My sis was off at college anyway, and I went off to spend my teenage years in my aunt's garage. She was good to me, let me do whatever I wanted, fix up the garage like a bachelor pad extraordinaire, never bothered me between nine p.m. and noon, and generally let me run like a wild dog. Yippee!) So anyway, back to Mom, eight years after Dad's death, she's gone out to Glacier Park with an old friend, and the next thing I know she's dying in a hospital in Helena. That's why you and I hitchhiked there, if you recall, but when we arrived she'd apparently been miraculously freed from killer disease and flown south to Costa Rica, a place neither of us had even heard of back then, and after you left I went down to find her, which wasn't hard. With Mom, just find where the rich people hang out getting high or drunk, and she'll be there. She had a great excuse this time, as she'd been magically freed from cancer, so she suddenly got "spiritual" and hooked up with an ex-priest who had expensive taste and she lived with him in his house, exquisitely appointed with plenty of booze and bowls of ecstasy like bowls of peanuts, which made Mom super happy and friendly, and made it seem like we were all really good friends, indeed. I was put up at the country club and began passing time with my rooftop lover Clemencia—and like that we might have all lived happily-ever-after, but after a month or two, Mom called me over for dinner one night because she said she needed to tell me something. I got there and the ex-priest was gone, and she'd had the cook make me a nice dinner of roast lamb—the only lamb in Costa Rica, she told me—and she sat me down and licked her lips and finished her sixth drink and said she had a surprise for me. She folded her hands like a good girl—do you remember how beautiful she is, was? How she could make her angelic face look like a...well, like an angel? Then, as though she's giving me a long-withheld gift, she told me my late father, Tom Connor, Sr.—this is what she called him to me, had always called him to me, Tom Connor, Sr., as in *Tom Connor, Sr., will be home late for dinner tonight, so, hey, I was thinking a cocktail or two to pass the time*—she told me Tom Connor, Sr. was not my real father.

"What?" I said.

She lifted her arms in a grand gesture as though she was talking about the beautiful house we were sitting in, the beams and windows and tiles and grand ceilings. "This man," she said, "Scott Sullivan. He used to live and preach in Lake Forest. He is your real father."

I didn't know what to say. Mom waited, opened her big eyes. "It's been my secret," she said. "Even Tom Connor, Sr., didn't know. And I've only just recently told Scott."

Apparently the lie had gotten too heavy for her and she finally needed to rid herself of that burden and tell me the truth. I still didn't know what to say. She got tired of waiting for me to speak and began to cry. Her blue-sky eyes made tears I couldn't quite believe. What is odd is how the whole scene made me feel. Not like I'd gained a father, which is what, in her drunken illusion, she'd hoped. Tom Connor, Sr., rest his soul, was still my dad, and always would be my dad. But what happened was I saw my mom clearly for the first time, saw her as a pathetic bullshitter whose revelation of my parentage was calculated to make me feel sorry for her and the terrible burden of her guilt.

Rather than feel as if I'd gained a father, however, I felt as if I'd lost a mother. My best idea of who she was—a sad widow, ever-grieving my father—had been shattered, and this new freak had emerged from the cocoon. Frankly, I didn't know what I felt about her, and my ambivalence freed me. I could let her go. Just let her go. If she wanted to drink herself to death with this man—and she seemed to want to—then that was okay with me. I had some pretty heavy drinking to do myself, by golly, after which I started breaking my new father's lovely furniture—you've seen me in one of my break-the-furniture moods, and after subduing me with not one, not two, but three *watcheemen* (I'm proud of that!) Mom decided she'd punish me by no longer paying for my room at the country club. Also, she and her (s)ex-priest—I won't say his name again—decided I'd harshed their mellow for the last time, and so they headed off to an unnamed beach, guessing rightly, that I wouldn't stick around.

So I went to Guatemala? So I met Van Dyke? So I'd taken this little hike into the mountains? How much sense does it make that I ended up here? I was thinking that one night as I lay on the ground in the dark listening to people talking outside in some Indian language I couldn't even name, much less understand. While I slept in a leaf hut that was used as a kitchen by the bent-over couple who lived in a little stick and mud hut next door. The man had been digging a big hole in the back yard that I grew to understand he wanted to make into a bio-digester. Did I know anything about bio-digesters? No. They were disappointed. What good was I? First I'd disappointed Jorge with no fresh knowledge or worthwhile opinion on the Bruce Lee-versus-Chuck Norris question, and now, well, frankly, I didn't even know what a bio-digester was. No matter. The next thing I know I'm shoveling all day long with ol' Eusebio, who has this ambitious plan that he is going to use organic wastes to produce methane to produce power, but so far the only tool he has is a shovel—and a second one he borrowed from a neighbor for me. A bio-digester. That killed me, that he wanted to make that. He'd seen drawings somewhere. He knew he needed concrete and tubing and lot of other things but this part he could do himself, the digging. Well, with me, too. The hole was big already. He'd been at it for days—a bent old man, shoveling away. It was almost a meter deep by two meters in diameter, round, and he made me understand he wanted it three meters deep and three meters in diameter. Nice vertical walls in the clay, nice flat bottom. And because it was the rainy season, about six inches of water on the bottom as well. In other words we were digging mud. And *shoveling all day long* is another string of words that's easy to say but harder to do. My mind kept racing around thinking of how we could drain it, get a pump, something like that, or how we could wait until the dry season, or find somebody with a backhoe, but the old man just kept digging, and that was the difference between us. He stood in that water and shoveled steadily—slowly, as you can imagine, I mean *very* slowly, his back bent, he must have been seventy years old—burying the shovel in the muddy water, lifting it, half the time the mud would slip off the shovel before he got it up over the wall, but half the time it didn't, so he got about one small shovel of mud out of the hole for every two strokes, but on and on he went, cheerfully, wordlessly. Didn't he know he should have been on vacation somewhere rather than standing in water digging mud? And me, young and strong and healthy in comparison, it was much harder for me, because not only did my hands blister terribly, but I carried the burden of self-pity and the knowledge that we were lacking something—a pump, a backhoe, etc.—that would have made the job so go much faster. I also had other questions, such as *once we get this hole dug, how were we going to get the concrete and the tubing, and whatever else was necessary?* So without that stuff, wasn't it a waste of time to be doing this?

That made it a lot harder, my absurd idea that we were wasting time. Time that could have been better spent. Doing what, I don't know, but anything would hurt less than this....

And the rebels—how I loved the rebels now! Whoever they were, I envisioned them coming out of the forest and freeing me from my tedious task of shoveling, shoveling, shoveling. Hurry, I thought. Where were they?

All of that thinking wore me down until, finally, I'm sure I was a worse digger than even old Eusebio.

But the days passed like that. A week, two weeks, and what I know now is that I learned a little bit about misery in that hole, and what I learned is that misery is bearable. I learned that re- gardless of the physical pain I was strong enough to dig all day in the mud. Just as I'd learned I could walk all night through the rain. And I learned that most of the misery we feel is mis- ery we bring on ourselves with concepts such as time—as if it's truly possible to save or waste time. Also I learned that because there is never any escape from it, suffering is no reason in itself to quit anything you really want to do. Kind of a basic lesson in growing up, so nothing to brag about. Only, maybe to be ashamed that I was learning it at twenty-one and not at nine, or ten, or eleven, like this old man must have learned it. And like the children in the village seemed to already know, haul- ing water, hauling wood. I mean, slow as we were going, Eu- sebio and I were making progress. We were making progress a lot faster than we would have made progress had we done nothing. He had a shovel, he knew how to use it, and I was learning, and after many days—I lost count after twenty—we about had it, three meters deep, three meters across, vertical sides in the red clay, about six inches of muddy water on the bottom. We climbed out—we'd built a ladder so we could—we climbed out and looked at the hole, looked at each other, and the old man smiled for the first time, and I did too.

What I remember after that was doing nothing, the long days of waiting and not knowing what I was waiting for, and everybody leaving me alone. Even after all of that digging with Eusebio, people were suspicious of me. I remember it being hot in the morning, so I stayed in the shade a lot and retreated to

my little leaf hut when it rained in the afternoon. I remember I
searched the skies in the openings between trees as though expecting something to appear. I thought it ironic that I'd been
in such a hurry to get the hole dug, and yet there it was, done,
vertical clay walls and muddy water on the bottom, and still
we had plenty of time. For what? I told you I was worried about
how I could do a story on these rebels if I couldn't speak Spanish but so far I hadn't seen any rebels, no armed rebels anyway,
and mostly the people I was with spoke Indian and instead of
learning about the insurgency and the revolution against the
forces that have fucked these folks over and over again since
The Conquest—and actually, since way before that. I filled
my journal—dried finally after the rain almost turned it to
mush—with ideas I had for a kind of revolutionary love story,
like *For Whom the Bells Toll*, which I'd read recently. I was
looking for my Maria, my little rabbit that I could make the
earth move with, but none of these girls wanted anything to do
with me, wouldn't talk to me. Gave me tortillas but didn't flirt
like the girls I'd gotten used to in the city. I don't know what
they thought of me as, but a sex object I wasn't. It didn't matter,
really. I had my journal. Which I lost and so can't quote from
but even if I had it I wouldn't. I have my pride. You might get
an idea of how bad, how raunchy, how bogus. How even after
all of that walking, all of that digging, I was still full of either
self-pity or self-aggrandizement. One or the other to get me
through the night. I call it my *before* writing. Everything after
what happened there is my *after* writing. And I don't think I
started writing you letters—I know I didn't—until after.

Finally, I'd pretty much forgotten about the rebels. I was
bored and tired and I was beginning to think a lot about beer.
It was morning. A pretty morning, yellow sunshine, sparkling
dew on green leaves. Have you noticed these horror stories
always start that way? Since Stephen King, at least, nobody
starts with: *It was a dark and stormy night.* Instead, the day
started out normal, everything recognizable as the world you
know and love. Birds singing. The smell of cooking fires. The
murmur of women's voices as they walked by with water, and

the men disappearing into the trees to their fields with their machetes and heavy hoes. And the peace of it, particularly poignant that day because I had decided I was going to leave, felt almost blissful. I was going to go around and say my good-byes. I'd already arranged with Jorge to walk me out. I was going to eat a good breakfast and then we were going to go on our long walk. No rain this time. Plenty of daylight. By tomorrow I'd be down in the city. I'd be drinking beer and feeling special for my special adventure. Feeling very superior to the other tourists. Already anticipating using this special experience to write a really good story, and also to impress some eager-to-be-transformed (eager to shed her clothes like a skin) hippie girl on a Central American adventure. All of this was swirling wildly through my head as I ate sitting on the dirt floor of Olimpia's house, which is where we were when we first heard the shooting. It was coming from the valley, and the shots were muffled by the forest. Curious, we walked outside to look. It was coming through the trees from down across the meadow. We weren't afraid, or at least I wasn't. I think maybe I was expecting the wild rebel boys to come up the valley shooting joyfully. I don't know. We walked down that way through the trees to get a better look and what I remember seeing first were the cows, staked in pasture overnight on the far hillside, shot dead.

Then we heard the helicopters, a growing buzz in the distance and then a sudden roar as they burst over the closest hill, flying low and already on top of us. The chop of the rotors filled the valley with a sound more terrifying than I'd ever heard. They hovered over the village in the draw below, and the sound shook my bones. Then we saw soldiers running through the trees down the far hill toward the village, and we could see them shooting into the huts, and from where we stood, a couple hundred yards up the hill, we could see people running away and the soldiers chasing them. It's a story we've all been told so often, the story of a massacre—Sand Creek, My Lai, the Romans in Carthage, the Japanese in China, Genghis Khan, and have you heard of what is going on right now in Yugoslavia and Rwanda? On and on, *ad infinitum*, with a thousand and one named and unnamed massacres in between. It's hard to make it real, hard for anybody to make it real with words. People with weapons chase people without. The victims fall, flop, crawl, get chased down, raped, stoned, beaten, chopped up, or shot. You hear the whoops of the killers, the horrid shrieks of their prey, a burst of shooting, a single shot, you smell the wafts of gun smoke and helicopter exhaust. Hear another lone shot. Then a burst of five, ten. Silence. Screaming. Three more shots. Wails of horror. Moaning. A shout or two. Directions, orders. I'm trying to recall the specific chaos and all that is coming out are words describing a generic massacre. The wild, unreal quality of the human shapes moving through the trees. You blink and breathe and think you can't really be seeing what you are seeing. All of that, I don't know how to write it so it's new, and I almost feel as if even to try is a lie or a sacrilege. Because this kind of slaughter is not new. It's old. It's simple. There is nothing so banal, it turns out, as running up to somebody and killing them. There is nothing so common and understandable as—really, in our bones we all understand evil—as the strong destroying the weak. There is probably a story to be told from the point of view of each unique killer or victim, but I was just a witness, somebody who watched it for a while—what, 30 seconds, a minute?—frozen, before Eusebio and Olimpia grabbed me and ran with me up the hill through the trees to the well above their house. They lowered me into it. Four meters? Five? Smooth clay walls, shin-deep water on the bottom. I do not know, and never will, why they didn't get in it themselves.

I have to stop now. I'll sleep. I'll get up tomorrow to finish this. I promise.

Love,
Tom Connor Junior

one good thing considering I've a guest

I dream the bear is pulling me out of my bed—not hurting me, but pulling me, his slobbery mouth wetting my shoulder but his teeth gone or at least not painful. It feels as if he's gumming me, but the strength he has and the smell of his breath are powerful and I'm holding on to my covers but being pulled out anyway. I say *leave me alone, leave me alone,* and then he does. Suddenly he lets go, disappears, and I hear Mark's laughter.

It's very cold when I wake. The fire in the wood stove has all but gone out. There is a heavy frost on the inside of the windows. The puppy is curled up on a chair with his nose under his tail. I'm shaking as soon as I get out of bed. The water in the bucket by the sink has a thin layer of ice. I pull on my big leather boots and clunk to the door and then outside without the pepper spray. A few steps past the corner of the cabin I pee, hugging myself, kicking snow over my yellow spot and bit of toilet paper when I'm finished. I'm assuming the paper will disintegrate in the moisture of the snow and the melting snow because it would be embarrassing to see come spring. Next time I'll bring enough that I can wrap and carry back inside to burn in the stove. Too late this time, though, and I kick the snow again, stomp the spot with my boot. I look at the sky and the pin pricks of stars and the paling in the east, and in that light I scan the snow for the bear's tracks leading away from the window, and I can see how my boots followed his tracks up the draw and where I stood when I chased him from his spying perch in the woods.

He hasn't been back. Or maybe he has. Even awake I can feel him breathing, I can smell him breathing. I think somewhere is a bear looking to find a place to bury himself alive and he's calling me, beckoning me. I look at the cold rock and the cold trees and fallen stones and I see him in every stump and every bear-shaped dark spot on the rock, on the cliff, and in the trees. I blink. I look. I stand shivering. It must be time to hibernate. I think of my children and their faces and their faces are blurry and unrecognizable, I can't make them clear. I know they want me home, they want me home, they want all of us to be home by Thanksgiving but all of us aren't going to be there. They're far away and I am far away and Mark is even farther away. It's three weeks until Thanksgiving. Of course I think all of this while I'm loading my arms with wood that's covered with snow and scratching and freezing the skin of my arms and by the time I get back inside my toes are cold, too, these unlaced leather boots uninsulated and not made for winter. I put some more wood in the wood stove and the rest I stack behind it and in that dim light I take my clothes off and crawl back into my bed, the sheets still warm. I curl up and I can feel the bear curling into a ball under a log somewhere, half covered with dirt, half covered with branches. I can feel him close and see through his weak eyes how the world goes fuzzy until spring.

I wake in the full yellow light of late morning shining through the window and the slam of a car door. When I sit up I can see Bart's truck parked in the snow. I get out of bed and pull on jeans and a green sweatshirt. I want to go outside to greet him rather than have him come to the door and look at the squalor, but I'm freezing so instead I squat in front of the stove and blow on a little pile of kindling and red coals. He knocks.

"Come in," I say.

He steps inside. "Hope I didn't disturb you."

I hate what I'm wearing, but something about having last seen each other at the bar, him dressed as slime and me a drunken widow has made us old friends

He doesn't look at me anyway but at all the letters on the table, then at my trash, the black plastic bag stuffed with my partial clean up and the counter covered with dirty dishes and groceries and the ridiculous barricade against the back door. I blow into the stove and the coals brighten but cold ash makes a little cloud that I can taste.

"You okay?" he asks.

I wipe my face. "Do I look worse than I think I do?"

He shrugs. "Got any coffee?"

"None made."

He walks over to the kitchen counter. "I'm glad you made it home safe," he says.

I'm still squatting, still blowing. I'm not home and I'm not so sure I'm safe. I can hear him pour water into the tea kettle and set that on the propane burner. The flame in the stove catches. I sit back on the floor and hold out my hands to warm them. He's stepped toward the back door, reaches over the barricade to touch the smooth and worthless spackle-repaired door-frame.

"Alex drove you, right?" he says.

"The purpose of a mummy."

I wait for him to tell me the spackle can't hold a screw, but he doesn't. He's back in front of the kitchen window again.

"The bear looked in there last night," I say.

He turns, looks surprised. "Here?"

I nod. "We stared at each other through the glass."

He's seen something out the window and now walks toward

the front door.

"Where are you going?"

"Look at its tracks."

Once he's outside, I get up and go into the kitchen and look at myself in the little round mirror and my hair is a beautiful not-blond not-brown not-gray color. Even though it's longer than it's been in years, it still doesn't even come to my shoulders. Not long or short. I'd brush it but I can't see my brush, so I try to flatten it at least so it's not sticking up. Hopeless, so finally I just tie on a scarf. My face is awful, eyes puffy, but I manage to put on lipstick at least. It's light—too light to really notice but it helps. Then I pour ground coffee into a filter and balance the filter and plastic holder over a metal coffee pot. The teapot clicks as it heats over the flame. I can see Bart out the window. He's bending over the bear tracks and Puppy is next to him, looking up at something in the trees. The bear tracks are the same ones I walked in. Bart must see my boot prints as well. He stands and turns and walks back around the front of the cabin. He knocks politely, then opens the door and steps in, Puppy at his feet. He's a short man, but strong, and he moves gracefully.

"It's a grizzly," he says.

"Then it's different than the one I saw before?"

"Was it?"

"You saw the tracks," I say. "The first one, too."

"I couldn't tell in the dry dirt," he says. "These are in snow."

I try to think. I don't know. I remember its face changed from the bear's face to Mark's face and then back to the bear's face. I don't tell Bart that. And I don't tell him how I don't even know how many bears I've seen that turned out not to be bears at all, so how can I possibly be expected to keep track of all the bears I've seen that are actual bears? I assumed they were all the same one. Why would so many of them be interested in me? I don't tell him I saw the bear yesterday in the draw behind the cabin, and I don't tell him how I went after him like a crazy woman and chased him away. Instead I say, "How can you tell it's a grizzly?"

"The size. And the claw marks."

"So what's that mean that he's a grizzly and not a black bear?"

He shrugs. "Hard saying."

"No," I say. "What?"

"I suppose it means they're harder to scare," he says. "I mean, once they come around, if they want to come around."

"I scared this one off."

He raises his eyebrows. "He was probably just curious."

I pretend I'm just curious. "Why would he keep coming around? Does he want something?"

"You're probably on his circuit. He's looking for food."

"Puppy?"

"Maybe," Bart says, but his eyes glance at my garbage and my kitchen counter.

"He's a criminal. Peeping in at a woman like that? Waiting to eat her little dog."

Bart laughs. We both sit down and watch the fire in the woodstove grow, feel its warmth. He pets the puppy, which seems suddenly starved for attention.

"You don't mind that I stopped by to visit? I'm on my way to town."

"No," I say. The tea pot begins to whistle.

"You sure?"

"It's okay," I say, and I get up to pour the hot water through the coffee.

"How long you going to be around?" he asks.

I watch the hot water settle over the grounds in the filter and listen to it begin to strain through in a trickle onto the bottom of the metal coffee pot. "I haven't decided."

"How's Alex?" he asks.

"Alex's got a very sick wife," I say.

"He does."

"You know them?"

"I do."

I look out the window at the green trees and the snowy meadow. The sun is breaking out from behind a thin layer of clouds. "It's going to be sunny," I say.

"The snow'll be gone by afternoon," he says.

I pour him his coffee and take it to him and then pour mine and go over by the stove and sit down. He looks at me out of the corner of his eye.

"I'm married, too," he says.

I know why he's saying it but it still feels odd and I don't like the assumption that something's possible between us, which it is, of course, it's just embarrassing to admit when you're dressed in a dirty green sweatshirt and dirty jeans and an old scarf to cover your dirty hair. I taste cigarette and lipstick and suddenly feel foolish. I almost panic and say something harsh. Instead I say, "Married?"

"My wife lives in Minneapolis."

I don't say a thing.

He says, "The dam is no place to live, it's just a place to be for a while."

"This too," I say, meaning the cabin.

I know he wants to ask what I'm doing here, where I came from, why I'm here. I can see he's assessed the basic mess of the place, the old food, the stuffed garbage bags—it must smell in here, I suddenly realize—the letters on the table, the letters on the floor next to the chair, the empty boxes of wine, the saucers with cigarette butts and ashes, and how I must look. I touch my scarf. I look at the fire. I wonder what's brought him here. I wonder how he ended up living by himself at a dam on the edge of the wilderness. I don't ask. Neither does he. We just sit like that in front of the stove and finish our coffee. I'm about to offer him something to eat when he puts the cup down and stands up.

"I should be going," he says.

I don't disagree. I stand up with him and he starts walking toward the door, but turns toward the kitchen and the mess. "Can I take your garbage into town?" he asks.

"I'm still cleaning. I have more food than I can eat, and it's all going bad." I tell him I'm going to clean out the fridge and take it all down to the canyon lodge and use their dumpster.

He shrugs. "Okay."

"Okay what?" I say.

"Last time I came you'd had a bear at the door. This time a bear at the window."

"You think he's here for a snack?"

Bart shrugs again, and it irritates me.

"It smells in here?"

He shrugs again. I have to look away. It does smell, and he's embarrassed to tell me.

"Bears have good noses," I hear him say.

Who cares. It's not as if I invited him over.

"Thanks for the coffee," he says.

"You're welcome," I say, and I look back at him and he smiles and his smile is suddenly reassuring and handsome in its shyness.

"At least you've got your bear dog. Puppy, right?"

"Bait, I should call him."

Bart laughs and bends to pet the dog one more time and then turns to go out the door. I feel the cold coming in and with it a sense of panic. I don't know why I do what I do next, but it just happens. I just feel something and so I put my head out just before the door closes.

"When are you coming back from town?"

He turns and looks back. "This afternoon sometime."

"Stop by then," I say, "On your way back. I'll feed you."

He raises his eyebrows. They look alive on his mostly hairless head. "Can I bring you anything?"

I nod toward the kitchen. "Is it that bad?"

"No," he lies. "I just thought—"

"Don't worry." I think for a moment. I try to assess what I have in the cupboard and fridge and what has gone bad and what I need: details. But my mind is a blank. I have a feeling as if I'm terribly under-prepared for a visitor. Also, it might snow. I could be here a long time. But I've bought way too much already, more than I could possibly eat.

"Good bread and good cheddar cheese," I say.

"Okay," he says.

"If you can get it. And some soup, if you want it."

He smiles that shy smile again. "Lettuce? Cucumber? Do you have dressing?"

"If you like blue cheese."

"Do you have ranch?"

I shake my head.

"I'll bring some," he says.

"Oh," I say, calling after him, "One more thing." He pauses but doesn't turn. "Will you check in on Alex and his wife? Let me know what's happened."

He lifts his hand to show he's heard and gets into the truck and shuts the door. He rolls down the window. "On one condition."

"What's that?"

"That you promise you'll take that garbage bag to the dumpster, plus anything else that needs to go."

"Deal," I say.

When he drives off I see his head in the back window of his truck under the gun rack and the rifle and when he's gone I go outside and bring in more wood and fill the wood box next to the stove. I stack more split wood next to the box. Then I sit down. I don't think it smells so bad, really. I mean, I am going to clean the kitchen and take the garbage, but first I'm going to read some more, and before that, I decide suddenly, I'm going to do my nails. They are longer than they've been in years, since I started doing rotations, third year. When you are putting your fingers on and in people's bodies five, ten, twenty times a day, well, you don't want nails.

I sit down and first I file my nails and push back the cuticles. I take my time. Then I get out the bag of polish—not mine, I found it here. A treasure of twenty, thirty little bottles of color. How many? I line them up on the table and count twenty three. I look at them all, read the names. Sky Blush. Clay Blue. Canary Song, Seawater, Glacier Lake. Apple Tart, Grape Lady. A little checking and most of them have hardened, but I find a few I can still use, like Raspberry Nights, which goes on smooth and blood red, and I dab the tips with white—actually with Whipped Cream. When I'm finished I spend a lot of time just looking at them. Whose hands are these? I can't believe it. I have so much fun doing it, I take off my slippers and socks, and I wash my feet my feet in a basin, dry them, and then I do my toenails as well. I sit by the fire as the morning passes painting then drying my nails. I imagine getting a phone call—imagine Mark calling me up. *Hey,* he'd say, *What you doing?* Drying my nails, I'd say. *That's good,* he'd say. *Somebody's got to dry your nails and it may as well be you.* Right, I'd say. *A wet nail may not be an altogether bad thing,* he'd say, *but it's certainly not as good as a dry nail.* No, I'd say, a dry nail is better than a wet nail. *So you stay right there,* he'd say, *and just keep on drying those wet nails.* I will, I'd say, I will.

The stove warmth feels good on my face. It's making me sleepy. I know I have to get up and clean but for the time being I decide to stay put, on the couch. I wish Mark could see me. I think maybe he *is* seeing me. I wave my hands in the air to show him how I'm drying my nails. I can see—no, I can't see—but I can feel him smiling, if that makes any sense at all. Mark never saw me doing anything like this, just sitting in front of the stove, drying my nails, and I wonder why I never did, and I'm sorry I never did, and I think he likes seeing me do it now.

I laugh at myself. At least I find myself amusing. That's a sign of sanity, I suppose, which is one good thing considering I've a guest coming for dinner. I think I should probably clean up and I do clear the table of the stacks of letters, arrange them along the shelf at the base of the big front window. I sweep the floor and pick up some of my clothes and straighten my bed, and while I'm doing it I'm feeling more and more ashamed that I've invited Bart for dinner. Another woman's husband, again. The mummy's wife was dying and this one's wife fled across the plains. Why? Because maybe Bart's a maniac after you get know him. I can't believe I asked him to get groceries, and for what, to make what? Grilled cheese, canned soup, and a salad? I'm a mess and my cabin stinks and I'm sure he must be so weirded out that he'll never return, which suddenly is all I'm hoping for, that he won't return. I don't need any food at all. I have more food here than I can possibly eat—so maybe I'll make some eggplant parmesan or ratatouille because I think I have everything I need for that, but even as I think of this cooking plan I know I won't do it.

I sit down on the couch in front of the stove and take a deep breath. What the hell. I take another one. As a doctor, I heartily recommend breathing, one hundred percent, and I can tell you I never had a patient come to the hospital suffering from excessive stale food odor. I take another breath and I listen to the wind pick up outside, rattle the glass of the window. The fire hums in the stove and a draft of air rushes up the chimney and the heat has me suddenly sleepy. I pick up Tommy's last letter but I'm too tired to think, too warm and comfortable to keep my eyes open. I lay my head back and doze off, wake, doze off again. Even grizzlies need to sleep, don't they?

When I finally wake for good I can see by the clock in the kitchen that it's only one o'clock. Who cares? As my mother used to say in her subtle Polish accent, *What's time to a hog?* Out the window the sun is shining, the snow is gone, and the afternoon stretches ahead of me like an empty meadow. The fire has died down but not the wind, yet I'm not cold. I stand up and get a big glass of water, and while I drink it my pretty red nails surprise me. I can't believe how good they make me feel. I put the glass down and turn my hand this way and that to better see them in the bright light from window.

Okay, I'm ready, I think, or as ready as I can be to go back down into that well. I light a cigarette and sit down on the couch to read the last letter.

common as flies and as beautiful

Dear Doctor,

A well. Lichen? Moss? Green living things. Spiders. Dark.
Cold. Wet. A round sky straight above. Panic—what if somebody comes by and pulls up the rope and bucket? How am I
going to get out then? And what if all the villagers are killed,
who will walk me down the mountain? (Shameful, I know,
but I thought that, too.) Doctor, this ache I have in my heart?
Perhaps I've a piece missing. As though I am filled with space
and I am empty. Don't send me to a specialist. I don't need
their instruments and tests. I know there is no cure except the
fire. Which perhaps is the same as to throw myself into God's
hands. I'm standing shin-deep in water in a well, I'm feeling
scared, weak, hungry, cold. It's not a metaphor I'm looking for
here, it is actually God's hands I need, arms to give comfort,
warmth, rest. I'm also hungry, so could use some real lamb
flesh to eat and some real lamb blood to drink—like my mom

fed me in Costa Rica the night she became my not-mom. Still, it was good. I loved the gravy, the mint jelly. Again, no metaphor, here. There is flesh and blood and hunger and cold and thirst, earth, sky, water, light, fire.... I look up at the round blue sky above. I'm both hiding and trapped. I feel the slimy clay sides. Wonder about snakes and bugs. Wonder how long the vertical walls have stayed vertical and not collapsed, and wonder if that's any evidence that they are not going to collapse again today. I give the rope a little tug to make sure it's secured. I give it another. I wonder if will support my weight. I think about climbing up just to see. I hear the shooting get closer and decide not to climb, not to peek my head over, because what if when I put my weight on the rope, it comes loose up there? What if when I put my weight on it, it pulls down? Do I really want to know that now? Or would I rather hold the still hanging rope as a possibility of escape?

Also, the shooting is getting louder and I'm getting colder. Wet almost to the knees and shivering madly. Villagers from down below having run up the hill are being chased and shot. I hear shouts. I can't tell if they are the shouts of killers or of victims. More shots, very close. What if the shooters look down and see me? I'm in a hiding place with no place to hide! Cold irony, cold water. When you are in the bottom of a well, there is simply nowhere else to go. I mean, you can rest. What else are you going to do? Here I'm feeling the temptation of another metaphor. That the descent into the well was a descent into the subconscious—and like many great mythological heroes, I had an internal battle raging, and only through a subconscious experience, a journey into the earth's womb, the cave, the underworld, only an experience like that will give me the knowledge and guidance and perspective to know better truth when I'm walking again on the surface of the earth. All of that is true for me, I mean, it really happened, so I reject its truth as metaphoric truth, as faux truth, as kinda-like truth. No, the real truth was a dark wet well that I kept feeling snakes in. I kept imagining one slithering past my stomach, my thighs, my balls. All this while I listened to the shrieks of murder above me. The scream of a woman who must have been being raped, because after a while her on-and-on again scream was muffled, and then grew into a kind of a hoarse breathing, like an animal gasping, moaning quietly, and then nothing. All day long. All day long.

And then it was night. And the stars came out in my little round sky. And then the flicker of fires on the one tree branch I could see. I breathed the smell of smoke. I sat in the water in the dark and felt my body grow so cold I thought I'd die of hypothermia. But I stayed conscious and I kept my head above the water, and I thought about the mystery of death—how mysterious could it be when everybody did it? How hard must it be, if even the clueless morons of the world did it? These thoughts kept me amused, as I remembered a man I met in San Salvador on my way to Guatemala. After dinner we wandered around the capital and whenever he'd see a street dog—and I tell you, on every street in Central America is at least one skinny, mangy, trotting street dog—whenever he'd see one he'd ask the closest kid—and on every street in Central America there's at least one ragged kid—so he'd ask the kid, *Where's that dog going?*

The kid would always shrug. He'd wipe his snotty nose and say, *No sé.* I don't know. Or he'd say, *No se sabe.* Nobody knows. This made us laugh very hard. We were drunk but we loved the idea of all of these streets stretching out in all of these directions, and stray dogs loping along all of them, going places, and nobody knew where! The mystery multiplied by un-countable number of street dogs on an uncountable number of streets going to uncountable, and unknowable, destinations!

And that's just the dogs, my friend said. So imagine all the rest of the mysteries, like where we go when we die.

No sé. No se sabe. A million, billion times.

Nothing like hiding from murderers at the bottom of a well to focus the mind. Or un-focus it. I look up at the sky above me that's not the sky anymore but an eye looking down at me. But it's not the eye of God, conscious, loving, warm; it's the eye of nothing. Starry nothingness and nothing else. It's an eye that doesn't see. The eye looking down is the eye of nothing—there's nothing in the eye, and then, when I blink, even the eye is gone and my last little metaphor slips away, and all there is left is nothing, *nada*. No eye at all, only a small, round, empty sky. Our *nada* who art in *nada, nada* be thy name. I was in a deep, dark, cold well. That was it. And the cold had me shivering uncontrollably, the cold and the fear because suddenly I didn't know how long I could endure it. But even the question *how long?* had lost its meaning because by then even time was gone. There was only suffering, and the faint light of stars on the water, and I felt a heaviness in my bones I knew immediately as death. I welcomed it, because death slowed and then stopped my shivering. Death coaxed me to slump down finally in stillness, to rest.

Then I heard the voice of the old woman, Olimpia, above me. I heard Eusebio as well. And I heard soldiers speaking Spanish. I heard a brief struggle, and two crisp gunshots, and then some grunting near the well's opening above me. I lowered myself into the water so as not to be seen, and then I heard, felt, the explosion of two bodies landing on top of me and splashing in the water and I hoped I'd made no sound because I could hear soldiers laughing some more. Then I heard the sound and smelled their urine raining down as they peed over the edge of the well into the water where I hid and where Olimpia and Eusebio now floated. And when the peeing stopped, the sounds above me grew quiet, the voices withdrew, and I thought for I don't know how long that I'd have to kill myself as well. I'd have to make a noose of the rope and climb partway up, and I'd have to destroy myself as well. I knew this time I would not fail. This time I'd succeed, as there was no *you*, no Janine McCarthy to rescue me, no angel, no arms of God, and I knew soon I'll feel death's full embrace and be glad.

But then Olimpia, floating there in the dark water next to me, spoke.

What?

She was floating on her back, face up, and I reached for her, pulled her close. I held her head in my arms. In the faint light from the stars I thought I saw her eyes move. And then she spoke again, in Spanish, mind you—why hadn't she spoken to me before in Spanish?—and she said, ¿Qué hacemos? What do we do?

Wait, I said, wait. I probably said it wrong, because she whispered again, ¿Qué hacemos? I kept saying nothing, rest, nothing, cradling her head against my chest, whispering so nobody up top would hear, and as I said it, *wait, rest, wait,* I felt something change inside of me. I cannot explain this. But somewhere in that cold dark horror with her living head against my chest, I felt a warmth growing around my heart, a heat I can only think of as a fire, a spirit, and the only word I can put on it is love. I felt the heat quite literally coming out of her body and into mine, warming me, and I felt a growing love for her, and for Eusebio. When I glanced up, I saw a soldier, a boy really, his round Indian face under a helmet, and he looked tired and shocked, like he needed sleep, and he was looking down at us. I don't know what he could see, but he must have heard because he stared down into the well to where I held Olimpia's warm head against my chest. Then he blinked and pulled his head back. I'm telling you the truth here—he blinked and pulled his head back, disappeared, and in that moment I loved him, too.

Janine. I'm asking you to try to imagine how I stopped shaking. How I stayed warm with a dying woman's head in my arms, how I watched all night until I saw the sky lighten and turn blue and when the sun had risen enough, the yellow light landed high on the well wall and lit a spider's web and the layers of soil, and how it lifted all of the terror of the night, even as I felt Olimpia die in my arms, smelled her last breath, how it was beautiful. More beautiful than anything I'd ever seen before. And I knew that no matter what happened to me, that I would live, even if the walls collapsed and I was buried with Olimpia and Eusebio, I knew I'd felt something that I could carry forever, something that could never be shot or buried or frozen. Why be afraid of what every other person who has ever lived on the planet has done or will do? It's as common as flies and as beautiful, the dead, the dying. They glowed in the light of morning. In the same light I imagined the soldier sleeping. I imagined his eyes closed and his face smooth. I hoped he was. I hoped he was warm.

Love, again,

Tom

P.S. Oh, yes, I waited all day, and then when it got dark, and the stars again appeared in the hole in the sky, I put my weight on the rope—it seemed a miracle that it was still there—and I kissed Eusebio and Olimpia and lifted myself out of that grave. I kissed the heads of the dead and I put my weight on the rope and I climbed up. It's funny, but I think the last time I climbed a rope I was in junior high and I was pretty good at it, so I was surprised at how hard it was. The rope was slippery and my hands tired and weak, but I made it, and I climbed out of the well, young Lazarus blinking alive again in the world. There were still some soldiers down in the village, I could hear them talking, see lights from a fire. I walked up the hill and around, and came out below them, where I stumbled on newly turned dirt, dark and rough in the night, and it was probably the third time I tripped that I understood I was walking on the newly turned earth of a mass grave. I walked all night long in the dark and in the morning kept walking, and by afternoon had come to a road where I flagged down a truck. The city was just beginning to light up like a jewel box when we came around the belly of the mountain and the road made its final descent. I got off at a semi-familiar place and made my way down dozens of streets past dozens of stray dogs and barefoot children to the *pensión* I'd been staying in before all of this started, and I didn't have any money but the owner gave me a room on credit, and when I lay down on that mattress I disappeared into the dark. As I have many times since, I dreamed I was back in the well holding the woman's head in my arms as she died. I could see still the smooth shadows of her features, still smell her breath and feel the last beats of her heart in my hands. I still hadn't bathed, hadn't washed the soil off my skin and I lay in my room in the *pensión* holding that tenderness in my flesh and hearing her words like a bell. *¿Qué hacemos? Qué hacemos?*

I wanted a drink; I wanted a shot and a beer. I wanted to eat and be drunk. But safe there in the *pensión* I again lay holding her head against my chest and I closed my eyes and imagined the light on the water and the circle of sky and—*What do we do? What do we do?*

Love what's mortal, hold it close to your bones—I try to do this, I really do. But then what? What else but give it all out to you—this love, this broken beauty—as though it might even be enough.

                                                        —TC Junior

six

when the moon is full, you idiot

This is the letter we read in the car. I must have read the other one at the beach because I don't think I would have had time to read them both in the car between the river and the farm. I remember I had to lean over my thighs and put my face in my hands—but now I remember the twins were not bickering in the backseat. In fact, they weren't even with us. We must have dropped them off with a sitter and decided to finish out this lovely day with dinner out. So we weren't even coming from the beach because I suddenly remember I was wearing a black skirt and a light blue top with spaghetti straps that tied on top of the shoulders, and I remember Mark reached for the letter and took it out of my hands. He'd pulled off the road into the shade of the pin oaks along the fence line and he read the letter, too. We were parked on the shoulder of a county road on a balmy Wisconsin summer evening, and there were no children in the car and I was wearing a black skirt and that blue top—why?—had we come from something?

Were we going to something? We must have gone out for an early dinner. We must have been driving home when I'd fished the letter out of my purse. It was August, the evening sky like cotton candy over the dark green, wooded hills. Maybe it was my birthday? I read the letter first and I remember how after I finished reading I stayed bent over my thighs with my face in my hands and I cried, and how Mark, curious, pulled over and held my head in his lap while he read the letter. He stroked my hair and wet cheeks. He held my head like that and I let him hold my head and I don't know, it must have been dusk already when we stopped because now it was dark, or almost dark, and when he finished the letter he told me he loved me, he loved me, and I said okay, okay. I remember listening to the peepers in the dark out the window and I began what would be a long process of forgiveness, which was really as much about forgiving myself. This was a year or so after the gypsy had left, and something was changing, I don't know. By self-forgiveness I don't mean his transgressions were my fault but you can't be married to somebody if you think he is wrong and you are right. Or you can't be married happily for very long because not only is being right unimportant but it's also impossible. Even needing to be right is not right, or needing to be *more* right. So right is irrelevant, and even if it were, I wasn't anywhere close. What I was crying for as much as for Tommy with the dead in the well was how even as I'd expected Mark to love me, love me, love me and only me, I'd forgotten to love him, forgotten to love loving him. So maybe I was feeling the terrible inadequacy of my love, the inability of my heart to open wide enough to love it all, and that's about when I could feel Mark getting aroused. It's the kind of thing that might have made me disgusted some other time, might have made me sit up and say, *Jesuschrist, does it always come down to this?* Which is of course exactly what I mean by not right. Not exactly cruel but cold, or even better, unkind, yet this time I felt as if his response was logical, as if something like that could ever be said to be logical. It was just right and normal and a way for us to be intimate, if that doesn't sound too clinical, I mean, I unzipped him. I reached in and felt his heat even before I touched him. I heard his sharp intake of breath, and I felt as if I'd passed through a door and was now inside looking out. I felt his fingers untie the straps on my shoulders and my top loosened and fell. My god, I was a married woman, thirty-one years old and the mother of twins, but somehow when it came to sex and my husband I could feel almost new, which is the mystery over and over again, isn't it? Not where is the dog going, but why does this touching sometimes feel like nothing, and then suddenly back from the abyss, it can make us feel all over again as if we've never lived, never really loved, not until now.

It's getting to be late afternoon. I smoke another cigarette in the darkening cabin. I haven't done anything to prepare for Bart or to clean up my garbage and bag it and take it to the canyon lodge. I go outside to pee, then back inside and wash my hands and stand in the kitchen and think about dinner. Because I don't know what else to do and it feels like a good way to start, I take a survey of what food I have. I've got milk that's gone bad, that smells. Also moldy feta and cucumbers gone soft. I've got over-ripe tomatoes on the counter and hard hamburger buns. Peaches, soft and almost falling apart to the touch. In the cupboard I've got cold cereal and two loaves of whole wheat bread—moldy now—and sprouting potatoes and sour cream I'm afraid to open. I've got an eggplant I bought just a couple of days ago that's still firm. Italian sausage in the freezer and hamburger, too, and hotdogs. Why would I ever buy hotdogs? Maybe I was thinking how Mark used to train our puppies. "Why do the dogs like you better?" I asked him once, and he told me how when they were puppies he carried bits of hotdog around in his pockets so he could give them a piece when they came to him. "Oh," I'd said. It seemed like cheating. Like bribing. I'd look at the dogs, I'd say, "You sluts!" and it would make Mark laugh, but I remember thinking, Why didn't I know that? What was I paying attention to? Mark was like that until the end, telling me things about himself that I felt I should have known if I'd been paying attention. Like those spherical wooden balls he made. He told me he'd always wanted to try that, having seen them some place long ago, but I never knew that, never knew he saw them, never knew he carried the idea of them in his head. What else had he always wanted and never told me? That he loved digging worms and fishing for bullheads as a boy? Who knows. To go to Chile? At least we did that. That he was glad for the life we had together? No, he told me that. That he loved me? He told me that a lot of times. He told me that way more than I told him. I figured he ought to know. Just the thought that he might want or need to hear me say it hardened me a little, so I didn't say it, wouldn't say, never said, *Hey, you're a good man, a brave man, my hero.*

I look at the dog over on the chair watching me in the kitchen look at the food, at the hotdogs. "Poor Puppy," I say, "You'd have been feasting if Mark were here and not me." I slice open the plastic wrapper and pry loose one of the frozen dogs. I leave the rest on the counter to thaw and throw the one out the front door. The puppy scampers after it, thrilled.

I step back inside and close the door of the cabin. Ironically, except for how I felt about him, it was in my nature to announce what I was thinking and feeling—so often in fact, and so often out of context, that he probably had difficulty processing. I told him what flowers I liked (irises), what birds I liked (herons and meadowlarks). I told him when I was tired and when my ankle was hurting, or when I had a little sore on my arm and who did what little transgression at work that bothered me, and if a patient had gotten under my skin he knew about that, and if there was something wrong about the house, he heard that, too, or if I was troubled about something one of the kids was doing or going through, I talked that out as well. Perhaps he was good at faking it but rarely did I feel as if he weren't paying attention. When I'm with a group of women who are complaining that their husbands are clueless or don't pay attention—a common topic, believe me—I tend to keep my mouth shut. In fact, with Mark and me if there was a problem, it was probably the opposite. What irritated me was how too often I felt observed, like he was a dog watching me, watching me, and I'd say, stop watching me, why are you looking at me, and he'd say because you are the most beautiful thing in the room, or something about love, yes, he'd say, maybe it has something to do with love? and I'd say, I'd don't want to be loved right now, and it would be funny, I mean, it would be pleasant between us, but that's the way it was, mostly, him looking at me and thinking about me and me looking at him more when things weren't right. When I came home and things were a mess in the house—even though he might be outside working all day, I somehow felt entitled to come home and not have a mess to look at, and so of course on those days, he'd hear from me. Not that I'd scold—I was too proud to scold—but he'd know I was unhappy. I'd make sure he knew. He'd come in and he'd go into the kitchen, just the sound of my greeting a little edgy, maybe, and he'd stand in the kitchen and get something to eat out of the fridge, and that's another thing that bothered me, him standing in front of the refrigerator like a teenager to eat, to snack. Well, yes, I noticed that. And now I'm standing in front of the refrigerator looking at what I have. Butter. An onion. Green peppers. Celery. Carrots. On the counter is a bag of pasta and a bag—a bag!—of rice that I haven't touched, and the thawing clump of hot dogs. I've got the wrappers of four big dark chocolate candy bars still out on the counter. I pick up one and smell it. What else have I eaten since I've been here? Salad. Toast. Peanuts. A couple dozen eggs. I remember I liked to watch Mark eat eggs. I don't know why but it fascinated me to watch how he'd cut a fried egg in half, fold it over, and fork that half into his mouth. Then he folded the second half over and forked that into his mouth. Two well-cooked fried eggs, four bites. Fascinating. Maybe I didn't look at him enough.

Now I'm torturing myself and I decide to stop and the only way I can stop is to quit this pathetic attempt to clean up and go outside. At least the table's cleared off, the letters still stacked on the wide sill under the big front window. I pull on my boots and my jacket and my cap over my scarf, and I feel as if I'm a child escaping what I'm supposed to do, playing hooky, and I'm embarrassed that Bart is going to come back and see I haven't done anything with the garbage. Then he'll know I'm crazy, know I'm a mad widow, and he'll probably flee up the canyon to his dam, which is what he should do anyway, seeing as how he's married. I tell myself I'm doing all of this for his wife's sake, trying for her sake to repulse her husband but that only amuses me. Then I think of how hard it is for a woman, even if we don't want attention from a man, even if we want him to go away, how hard it is for a woman to purposefully make herself repulsive. I wonder what a person does to "run" a dam? Doesn't the dam just sit there? Maybe his job is only to call in everyday and say, *It's still up!* And if it cracks or breaks, he calls downstream and says, *Run for high ground! Here comes the water!*

Somebody has to do it. And of all the things people do, well, nobody could ever argue it isn't vital. Tommy would have liked that kind of job. Be prepared to be a hero but most of the days, well, most of the days you could do whatever you wanted. Visit widows. Hunch over bear tracks. Drive your truck into town to buy groceries with your rifle in a gun rack behind your head.

I grab the pepper spray and step outside into a fierce wind roaring out of the canyon. Puppy is instantly at my feet—he likes me! The Hotdog Goddess! I pull my hat down low and watch the wind toss a flock of ravens like black rags over the top of the cottonwood along the river and spill out and bend the fir and pine higher on the benches before pouring invisibly out onto the plains. Just looking out that way, east and homeward and forever to what's become a heavy pewter sky, a ready-or not-here-comes-winter sky, makes me I feel panicky. What if a storm hits and buries the cabin and I can never leave? What if the dam bursts today, when Bart's in town, buying groceries for me? What if behind that big wind comes the water? I imagine Puppy and me floating out into The Big Wide Open where there hasn't been a sea in a million years. Our bones would mingle in the gumbo with the fossil bones of dinosaurs.

I start walking and that feels better. I'm grateful for Bart's visit this morning, at least, for it helped me see my pathetic self and maybe that's the start of something, although not today, not today, thank you very much, not today, unless you consider painting my nails a start. I slip my mittens off so I can see them and again feel the pleasure they give me. I imagine telling somebody a year from now, two years from now, *It all began to change for me the day I painted my nails.*

I turn uphill behind the cabin heading for the draw between the cliffs where I scared the bear away. Since that image in my head of the canyon filling with a flood, I'm more afraid of the dam breaking than I am of the bear. Nevertheless I scan all the shadows in the meadow under the trees and farther up where the trail enters a draw and the beige grass turns to a pine needle forest floor, and all of the shadows stay shadows. The walking feels good, slightly up hill. The wind is so loud I can't hear anything else but it's at my back and it pushes me, so at least my scent is out ahead of me and I won't surprise anybody but myself.

The trail switches back a few times in the heavy woods and the trees are making so much noise bending and cracking I think they might fall over. The wind in their branches up high sounds like a waterfall. Puppy is running madly, not in circles like he does when the bear is near, but alert, his pointy ears pricked upward and his macaroni feather tail up and his eyes sparkling. Prancing and smelling and listening to the world's big breath. Who knows where it all started, with a butterfly's wings in China? Thank you butterfly, for I suddenly love the wind. Its power to push me up the switchbacks astonishes. The way it lights Puppy up. I think of patients who came into the E.R. suffering with an almost organ-deep malaise, really. Their eyes flat, their limbs heavy, a kind of dull ache all over their body. Some are coming to the hospital finally to die after years of suffering with no medical care. Others only need a place to spend the night, a bed, a roof, somebody to ask them serious and respectful questions. And others carry an unknown world inside them and walk stunned and confused and in pain— nothing fatal, but nothing fixable either. Like the old woman with the dull eyes who in Spanish told me her heart ached and something about the moon and then went on talking about her ankle and her knee and her hip. I wanted to slow her down and focus on the heart pain.

"When?" I asked the interpreter. "When did she say her heart aches?" The young woman interpreter repeated my question.

The old woman looked irritated at having to stop and go back and repeat, so she said, impatiently this time, "*¡Cuando la luna está llena!*" As if to say, *When the moon is full, you idiot!*

"I see," I said. "And how long has that been happening?"

The interpreter spoke, the old woman spoke. Then the interpreter turned to me and said, "Since her husband died."

"And how long ago was that?"

Again the exchange in Spanish. "A long time," the interpreter said.

"How long?"

More talk. I waited for them to finish.

"Thirty-two years," the interpreter said.

I looked at the old woman, who was looking down at her brown and wrinkled hands on her lap. I looked at the earnest young interpreter. I shrugged and I told her I was sorry but I was going to have to leave now.

The interpreter's big blue eyes grew very wide. "Should I translate that?"

I called a colleague to cover my shift, and when he got there I walked out of the hospital, and the next day I drove west across the plains to Montana for the first time since I was sixteen and running away with Tommy. The world is full of suffering but sometimes all there is left for comfort is more world. Thirty-two years of full moons. I wish I'd have asked the woman if there was anything that helped, anything she did or took that might have helped. I wonder if her relief ever came in doses of high gray sky and the feel of the ground under her feet and walking in a wind like this, on a trail like this. The air is free for the breathing and this much of it blowing makes every nerve in my body alert. Not that her heart wouldn't still hurt, but what's thirty-two years with a million-year-old cliff looming ahead and all the air in the universe rushing out of the canyon next to you?

Good medicine, amusing myself with nonsense, feeling my heart pump blood like it's supposed to, and watching a twitching puppy light up the trail like a...like a what? Like a who-cares-what. Like a pretty dog running in the woods.

We follow the trail up the draw away from the river through to the top of the bench, then walk back through a grassy field to where the edge of the bench breaks and becomes the cliff. Here I'm high above my cabin looking down at the boulders around it and the scattered fir trees and the beige meadow sloping down to the depths of the canyon where the river makes a silver S past groves of aspen and cottonwood. The long summer and sudden winter have turned their leaves from green directly to black. No gorgeous gold this year. To the west I see massive parallel ridges running north and south, with narrow valleys between, mountains beyond mountains. I can't believe I've been here weeks, almost a month, and this is the first I've been up here. My little cabin has a brown shingled roof and it looks so small I can't believe it fit me and those letters, me and all of that big beautiful sadness. And not just those things but all of my temptations to smoke cigarettes and to drink too much, and all of that food on the counter going bad, and bags of garbage and paranoid stacks of firewood, too. It seems just my confusions would need a cabin twice as big, or a whole separate one would do nicely as well. One for my resentments and one for my little vanities with a separate wing for the vanity that I don't have any vanities. And one for my self-pity, particularly the one that I am not like other people, and can't afford to feel sorry for myself. That's got to be the biggest of them all, poor me, can't even say poor me, so that would be a big cabin, indeed, or a small cabin with plenty of wings that I could visit as I felt the need. There'd be the I-have-to-take-care-of-everybody-else-who'll-take-care-of-me? wing, and even out here I feel as if I have to make sure Alex and his wife are okay, and Bart is okay, and I feel guilty for not cleaning the cabin, for not doing what Bart asked me to do, take the garbage out, ashamed for inviting somebody for dinner and asking him to get the food and then not doing the one thing he asked. Even standing way up in the wind on the edge of the cliff, I feel suddenly embarrassed thinking of him walking into the cabin this morning and how it must have looked and smelled.

Sometimes my feelings are so predictable I bore myself. Up here, standing on the edge of the world, you'd think I might be different. Up here with the Rocky Mountains behind me and the Great Plains spread out before me all the way to forever, you'd think I might have been transformed into something nobler. But pretty fingernails or not, I'm still the same person I've always been and it's nothing if not tedious. I know it's impossible to ever go back to where and when and how things were. Mark is gone forever—and suddenly it's as if I never knew what that word meant, *forever*, until now. I look out at the long horizon and feel the big wind getting cold, and I'm so lonely I want to die.

I lean into it. The wind is strong so I have to lean out over the cliff to keep from blowing backward. I'm looking down at my cabin and the river and the gravel road and a tiny truck heading this way from town, still a mile or more away.

I look past it and see the plains to the east and the curve of the earth and a clump of distant mountains past Great Falls. I imagine the grassland full of buffalo and elk and imagine walking across it. How far could I get before I go mystic? Before I throw myself face first on the ground and start calling for a witch doctor?

We don't deserve this land, that man told me years ago, my first time crossing the plains. *We stole it and don't deserve it.*

As if anybody could *deserve* the earth. And one thing I know for certain is I didn't steal anything. When this land was being stolen from the Indians, my relatives were being chased out of Russia to Poland and starved out of Ireland by the English.

What does any of that mean now?

Maybe only that I'm far flung. Maybe we all are.

Below me about fifteen feet, a stunted fir grows out of a crack in vertical rock. A chickadee clings to a twig on the top of the tree. A little bird in the wind.

Suddenly, a bald eagle—rising up the cliff face—appears hovering just a few feet in front of me. I can see its talons and its beak, its ragged white head and clear, sharp eyes. Surprised as I am, the eagle rises even higher. I watch him soar and I think, no, I'm not a little bird clinging to a branch. I'm that eagle!

Why not?

Seeing an eagle is a good thing, Mark used to say. It's always a good thing.

Look far, I think, look far!

I lean back, pull back from the edge, catch my breath, and feel the emptiness, the abyss below me and also in my stomach. I feel my skin and feel the wind, and feel nothing different between the inside of me and the outside of me. I look at the chickadee on the twig, balancing, balancing, and then again at the eagle soaring and the other—its mate?—much higher and beckoning. I watch how they relax and let the wind lift them higher and against my better judgment I open my coat, spread it, hold it open like wings and lean out over the cliff just a little bit more. I'm not trying to kill myself, or to fall, but I can't say I'm completely against the either idea. Mainly what I want is to feel is what it feels like to be held like this. I open my jacket all the way and spread it and feel the wind pushing me back, holding me. I lean into it a little more and my stomach and breasts and face are full of the wind, and my eyes are full of sky and they begin to tear.

Below me, Bart's red truck is coming over a rise and then dropping down to the river bottom on his way to my cabin, and then eventually back to his no-place-to-call-a home dam. I think of Tommy's poem about the woman without pants walking down the city street. Where is she going? When will she know she's there? How long will she have to walk before she's safe?

Then I see him way down below through my wind-wet eyes. He appears out of the same draw I walked up to get here. He comes into blurry shape in the grass among the boulders and scattered fir trees. He sniffs the air. He wanders around the clearing in front of the cabin. The bear.

I let the wind push me upright and close my jacket. I rock back onto my heels and hunch down and look. Bart's truck is getting closer and I can see that when he pulls in my little two-track drive, he's going to get a surprise. The bear has a hump between his front shoulders and I can see how big he is as he walks past my little white car. He pauses in front of the cabin, raises himself up on two legs and sniffs. He can't hear the truck coming, and can't see it yet for the bend in the road. I think he must be hungry and I wonder why I couldn't see him like this before. He doesn't care about me. He's just a hungry bear, smelling food, and my cabin is in his place, maybe just the place on earth where he thinks he belongs, my kitchen his kitchen, my rotten food his feast, because as casually as if he were opening the door, he swats the big front window. I can't hear anything except the wind, so it's like watching a silent movie. The glass crashes inward and the bear disappears briefly in a cloud of papers blowing out of the cabin and up and around him in a swirling corkscrew breeze, all the letters I'd stacked on the sill. The bear stands upright and rotates his huge head in what must be amazement at how the letters rise up around him like that, scraps of colored notebook paper blowing in a higher and wider circle until, one by one and then in groups they catch the main current of the big wind coming from the canyon and blow out across the flatland like a flock of mad tropical birds.

Then the bear ducks his head and goes in.

why do all puppies have the same breath?

I hear the rifle shots as I run with the wind at my back across the bench toward the top of the draw, and by the time Puppy and I have fought the wind back down the draw to the cabin, Bart has the bear's massive head and neck circled by a chain and is dragging him out the front door of the cabin with his truck. Speechless, and astounded by the strength of the bear's smell, I stand by the big broken window and look in at the chaos of garbage and shattered glass wet with blood. Bart gets somebody from Fish, Wildlife and Parks to deal with the carcass, and he takes care of the paperwork, and even hauls off the garbage while I sleep on the couch of the dam house that night and the next listening to all the air in the universe pour through the canyon. Here's where it all speeds up—here's where it all slows down. I have a sense I'm to blame for something, but also, for some reason, I don't seem to care. I hear Bart come and go at owly hours but don't see him much, don't see much of anything. I can barely open my eyes much less move. You'd think I'd been the one who'd been shot. For the first time in a while, I'm floating on something bigger than any particular feeling of mine. I don't know what it is—and I don't know anything more than when the wind slows and finally stops, I get up in the eerie quiet and drive the few miles out to the cabin. Bart has even found somebody from Great Falls to come with new glass for the window and fix the trim and re-hang the back door. I do the final cleaning, though. I scrub the blood off the ceiling and floor but don't think it's possible to get all the bear smell out. I pack the rest of my things— they smell of bear, too—then call and leave a voicemail with my friend that there's been an incident with a bear but everything's going to be all right. That's all I say. That and also that I'm grateful for the use of the cabin but am going home again.

Bart comes by just as I'm leaving. He gets out of his truck and we stand for a moment in front of the cabin and look at each other. It's cold and cloudy, and his playful eyes aren't so playful anymore. He's tired like I am, and not happy about killing the bear and we both know who's to blame but what we feel is also more complicated than blame or shame and neither of us knows how to say any of it. We stand under those massive cliffs and above the river lined with cottonwoods turning black and we shift our weight from one foot to another, just a couple of dumb humans. Finally I say good bye. He smiles, wishes me luck, and we shake hands and I get in my car and drive away.

In town, I decide to visit Alex and his dying wife, or at least look in on them. I step up to the door and knock, and Alex answers. I say hello and ask if I can see his wife. He steps aside and I walk in and she's on the couch again. Even through the smell of cigarettes and booze I can smell she's dying. I part the drapes just a little bit, enough to see. I kneel down on the carpet next to her and she looks at me with a blank face and says, "Hi Doctor."

"Are you in a lot of pain?"

"She is," Alex says.

"Doctor?" Her eyes are too big for her sunken face.

"Janine," I say.

"I don't want to die ugly."

Her name is Sadie and she's near the end and it occurs to me that I don't have to be helpless. I'm not licensed in Montana so I visit a local doctor who tells me he knows her. I ask him to prescribe morphine and assure him I'll take care of her. He does, and I buy it for her, go back to their place, move her to the bed and set up an IV. I teach Alex how to give it when she needs it. I stay in a hotel but Puppy and I are over at their house for as long as I have to be each day. I buy food. I cook. Alex and I eat. I wonder where her family is. I wonder about her friends but I don't ask. I know from Mark's dying that people don't know how to walk into a house like this. What can they say, what can they do besides sit and wait? With Mark, the three of us took turns, and the plan was that when the end came the one who was sitting with him would call the others. The morning he died Kate was supposed to spell me after midnight but she didn't and I sat and listened to Mark's breathing and I thought, let her sleep, let her sleep, and then before I knew it, I slept. When I woke Mark wasn't breathing anymore. I lay down on top of him and kissed his cooling face. I felt his rough cheek against mine for the last time, and I curled up next to him and laid my arm over his chest and looked past his stillness out the window at the pink dawn growing over the new green hills. It was springtime. I could smell it through the window. I thought my heart would explode, and then I think it did.

¿Qué hacemos? ¿Qué hacemos?

When I get to Alex and Sadie's house the last morning, Alex opens the door for me with a telephone to his ear and his red and watery eyes tell me it's over. It's been less than two weeks since the bear was killed, and I'm exhausted, but what else is new? Tired is good, as my mom used to say, because when you're no longer young, tired is how you know you're still living. I walk past him to see Sadie lying in bed peaceful at last and almost start to cover her face but I don't want Alex to come back into the room and see her that way. He's on the phone with her relatives, I can hear, or with his, but I don't wait to find out. Before I leave I step up close to him, stand on my tiptoes and kiss his cheek. For some reason, I'm too tired to cry, but his cheek is damp and I can taste his tears.

In the car, I let Puppy into the front seat and he's excited about it. He helps himself to my lap, licks my face, and I pet him under his chin. I wonder why all of the puppies I've ever known in my life have had the same smelling breath. One of the mysteries, I guess. Where's the dog going? Where do we go when we die? Why do all puppies have the same breath?

A couple of days later I'm sitting outside my motel room in North Dakota in a pool of dim yellow light from the window over my shoulder. Two leisurely days of driving and I sit under a blanket and look at the night sky and smoke a cigarette. I've got just a few left in the pack and I'm going to smoke one an evening, and on the fourth evening, the day before Thanksgiving, I'll be home. The night is cold and the stars are painfully bright. In the mess that was the cabin I only saved one of Tommy's letters, or a part of one, and even through the cigarette smoke when I bring it up close to my face it seems I can still smell the bear.

"I love this place," he begins. There's no date. No place name. It's anywhere. It's yesterday. "Partly because of the fishermen mending their nets in the shade of the almond trees. And the pair of pink pigs that walk out onto the beach every morning and roll in the black sand and shallow surf. And the hungry donkeys, their hammer heads buried in the overflowing garbage cans, and even the mad dog I saw yesterday walking tighter and tighter circles in the hot sand and the kids who noticed and threw rocks at him until finally he lay down to die. It's all here, the great carnival, the whole beautiful disaster. You can imagine how fond I am of the young mothers in their t-shirts and underwear bottoms sitting in the damp sand with their children, their smooth brown legs shiny when wet. And of course the older girls whose blood quickens and eyes stray to watch the big gleaming boys playing soccer on the beach. Hey, I'm even fond of the two dwarfs, Chepe and Consue, who push an ice cream cart during the day and sit with me on the porch at night, and soon drunk, tell tedious self-mocking stories interrupted by obscene gestures at any and all women of childbearing age who are unfortunate enough to—"

It's the only a fragment of clear writing that's left on the page but it's enough to remind me of the way one beautiful man lived in the world, loved the world, made it shimmer and shared it with me. And it ends, as his life did, suddenly—torn and, not unexpectedly, stained with blood. So I need to tell what I know about that as well.

my head that far up my ass

After he gave up writing, Tom Connor moved back to the states and got his MBA in Miami. For a few years he worked selling custom yachts, which gave him an opportunity to travel. He met his wife in Monaco of all places—Adriana was his limo driver—and he tried to get Mark and me to come over for their wedding. We couldn't. It was too short notice and not where we really wanted to go if we were going to travel abroad. But Tommy was thrilled to have found Adriana. He seemed very happy on the phone. They bought a house in Seattle, I think. The yacht job ended and some other job started. They had two children, a son and a daughter, in about a year and a half. Occasionally he'd call me, so that's how I kept track of his movement from job to job, state to state, the birth of his children, Adriana's longer and longer visits home. Eventually I asked him to stop calling me when he was drunk, and the phone calls ended for a long time. That made me sad when I thought about it, but I didn't think about it very much. I had a full and busy life. We had a full and busy life. Mark was doing less and less farming, raising only a few grass-fed steers for restaurants, and doing more and more cabinet making. I was either working my shifts in Madison or I was home running the kids from here to there, going to their recitals and athletic events. Mark and I would look at each other long enough each day to pass some logistics back and forth, and then, frankly, speaking for myself, I didn't really care to look at him anymore for fear of more logistics, something else he was going to tell me I had to remember, another detail to pass on in our tag team parenting. It wore us down. I see it in the faces of parents who have children in those middle years, a weariness that kills marriages. Even if you wanted to slip back to the house with your spouse and burn it down with *sexo fuerte*, well, once one of you notices the oil stain on the driveway and gets thinking about the last time the oil was changed, and the other begins to wonder if the laundry is ready for the drier, or begins to calculate that if the pork chops are taken out of the freezer now, they'll be ready to cook for dinner, well, after you get past some of that, if you ever do, you might sit on the edge of your bed with a desire like a big wind turning and turning in the hollow of your stomach, but your skin gone numb, your skin where you touch the world, where you touch each other like some thick layer of leather guarding all of that anxiety. Even if you try to kiss, especially if you try to kiss, you can feel the nothing there. You know what you need but you look at this person needing the same thing—a little comfort, a little rest, a little space to tumble—and after spending every waking moment trying to stay upright, stay on your feet, stay sane, well, you have no idea even how to begin to fall.

So I guess I was there. It was evening after work. I remember a storm cloud appearing over the hill. I remember Mark coming toward the house quickly to get in before the rain. He was wearing his wool plaid haystacker hat, tennis shoes, shorts, and his tan Carhartt jacket. I'd just come home from work, showered, and was sitting on the couch trimming my nails. I missed my mom. She'd been gone a number of years by then—died suddenly from a stroke—but there were still plenty of times like this when I wanted to call her. Just to hear her good cheer. Just to hear her say my name. My hair was wet. It was touching my neck and making me cold. I was thinking I needed a haircut and thinking Mark would say he liked it the way it was, and I was thinking I'd get one anyway. He wouldn't complain but he'd be a little disappointed. I'd do what was right on principle, I thought, cut my hair the way I like it—but there'd be little pleasure in it, and no joy at all.

Mark ate in the kitchen standing up, said he didn't feel well and went to bed. I poured myself a glass of wine. I wanted to go to sleep as well but didn't want to go in the bedroom until he was asleep. I didn't want to hear about his aches, his stuffed nose, and make sympathetic sounds. I didn't feel so well myself. The phone rang.

"Janine McBean?"

I could tell right away he was drunk but it had been so long I was glad to hear his voice. He started right in as though we'd talked last week. His job in the state of Washington had ended but he got a great teaching job in Idaho. He'd been playing a lot of golf, and loved it. He just got a new dog and a new truck.

"How's Adriana?" I asked. I could never remember his kids' names.

"They live in Orlando," he said.

This was the first I heard that he no longer lived with them. She'd taken the kids to Monaco last year, he said, and when she moved back to the States, she moved to Florida.

"She likes Florida," he said. "She's happy there."

"And you?" I asked.

"They're all trilingual. I'm *try* lingual, too. I guess I'll try anything."

Despite the goofy joke, his voice was sad. I tried to attach the sound of it to the man who wrote about the bottom of the well. The man who wrote about Zochee—and suddenly I saw those letters as similar. The cold and empty universe he saw through the airplane window and the cold and empty nothing he saw looking upward from the bottom of the well, and how he tried to fill them both. I stood up and looked out the rain spattered window into the dark yard and pasture, at the black outline of the wooded hills beyond. I told him I still thought sometimes of the letter he sent describing his experience at the bottom of the well. I told him I remembered how he said he'd had a deep coldness inside of him—and I felt that too. Too often. So could he still conjure the heat, I asked, the fire, the warmth?

There was a long silence after I asked that, and I was stirred to remember his revelation about love, something I never forgot, because I used to feel it profoundly when the children were little.

"Love what's mortal," I said into the phone. "Hold it close to your bones."

He giggled and I could hear the ice in his glass, hear him swallow.

"That's Mary Oliver," he said, his voice kind of sliding around the words. "I stole that shit. Think she'll mind?"

I told him I didn't care if the words were original or not. They'd stayed with me. Did he ever think about them?

"Oh, I guess I do," he said. "Especially the part I left unwritten."

"What's that?" I asked.

"The third part?"

"Yes."

"And when the time comes to let it go, let it go." He laughed, flat and dry.

I sat down in my dark living room. I heard him drink again. I drank, too.

"Tommy?"

"What?"

The twins would have been teenagers, and they were upstairs on their phones or computers. Mark was in bed. Maybe I heard a horse whinny. We still had cattle, so I might have heard some bawling in the pasture. I don't know. I know it had stopped raining and I was sitting in a house among the mortal. They were breathing all around me and I suddenly had a premonition: the house an overgrown hole in the ground, our own lives long forgotten. Wind, weeds, stars.

"Nothing," I said. I poured myself another glass of wine and tried to catch my breath.

Silence on his end.

"I'm glad you called, though," I said.

"Maybe I'll come by."

"Oh?"

"I might just let go of my job here in Idaho. It's nice, but I'm kind of looking elsewhere."

"Well, come visit," I said. "I mean, if you're ever in the neighborhood."

THEN SPRING, JUST A year and a half ago, and an old friend of his called one Sunday morning and introduced himself as Bernie Harris. He told me he was driving Tom from the West Coast to Orlando, where Adriana and the kids lived. Tom had lost another job—his third in three years. Crashed his truck and let the bank take back his house. Bernie apologized for not calling earlier, but was it okay if they stopped by that evening?

"Yes, of course," I said, "Stay for dinner. But Tom—he's with you?"

"He's not feeling that great."

"Is he sick?"

"Not really He just asked me to call.

Suddenly I remembered something. "Bernie," I said. "Bernie. Are you the one that was in the Olympics?"

"Yup." He laughed. "That's me."

They got to the farm in the late afternoon. Tom was still handsome, still smooth-faced and boyish, his body shape remarkably unchanged from the lithe 20 year old I'd said goodbye to in the Helena bus station. But he was so drunk he could barely talk. Or walk. In fact, he walked with a cane, and a yellow service dog stayed right by his side as though he were a cripple. If you didn't see him drinking, didn't smell him, didn't get too close and see how alcohol had thinned his skin, you might think he had Parkinson's or had had a stroke. His dog's name was Moncho, which Tom said with a Spanish accent. It picked things up for him. It sat by his side. It was a big dog and he used it to steady himself. He perched on the edge of the chair and sipped whiskey he'd brought in a briefcase. He offered some to us. Mark said sure, Bernie and I said no. Tom couldn't keep up with the conversation so we talked around him. It was terribly awkward. When Mark and Bernie went outside after dinner, I wanted to go with them but couldn't leave Tom all alone. So I stayed in the living room. He kept drinking, and I talked out of nervousness. About the Olympics, about gymnastics, the things we'd been talking about at dinner that had nothing to do with anything. He was going back to a wife, an ex-wife now, who was only taking him in to keep him off the streets. But how long would that last? I didn't want to scold but here he was, thirty years since I'd fallen in love with him, sixteen years since his last letter, wobbling drunk in my living room, with nothing to say. I was mad. He finally told me to shut up and come over and stand next to him.

I was wearing a knee-length, navy blue wrap skirt, a print, and when I got close enough, he put his hand under the hem onto the back of my knee. Why would that surprise me? But it did, and I jerked back suddenly and almost slapped him.

"I want to touch you," he said, and the words seemed to roll around in his mouth before falling out a little misshapen.

"I guess you do."

"Come here."

I stayed where I was.

"Please." He stretched out his arm.

"Tom." I stepped farther away. "I don't want you to."

"Okay," he said, and folded his hands.

"Don't pout," I said.

He sipped his whiskey. Out the window I could see Bernie and Mark standing in the yard talking.

"I'll talk to you, though."

"How sweet," he said. "But I can't talk with you way over there."

I looked at him. He blinked his little red, drunken eyes and wobbled even as he sat. Maybe that's what did it, his helplessness. I stepped up close to him again, next to him, and I took his right hand and I put it on the back of my knee where he'd first touched me. It was cold and small. His breathing changed immediately with his hand there. He sat still.

"You're a Wonder Woman."

"No, Tom, I'm not. I'm trying, though."

He sipped his whiskey again. I reached down and took it out of his hand and took a sip myself. He nodded and smiled crookedly. "Did you have a subject in mind, madam?"

"Your last letters," I said.

He reclined his forehead against my hip. He breathed deeply. I had the feeling my body was temporarily keeping him from drowning. Mark and Bernie had moved away from the window. I looked down at Tom's head, his thick hair still a beautiful brunette.

"That well," I said. "I've never forgotten. How you felt so cold, and then warm."

"Oh, Janine," he said.

"Was that true?"

"I'm sure I was trying to write it just like it was," he said, and I could feel his moist breath on my skin through the thin fabric of my skirt. "But what I remember most in that well is wanting really badly to get out of there and get drunk. Hell, I probably would have settled for staying right there with the dead if I'd had something to drink."

"Did you really hear that woman's voice?"

"I don't know anymore," he said. "It all seems a hypothermic dream, doesn't it? In my less generous moments I think a better question would be: did I really have my head that far up my ass?"

He turned so his cheek pressed against my hip and we stayed like that for a while. A minute? It seemed like a long time listening to each other breathe.

"Did you ever love me, Janine?"

"Tommy."

"Did you?"

"Yes, but—"

"Do you still?"

My knees had been quivering and I was fighting back tears, but his questions made me unexpectedly irritated again. That and the fact that he was petting his dog with one hand and me with the other. After all these years, drunk, pitiful, and on his way home to his ex-wife and children, he asks what I feel. Had he ever cared before? Ever asked what I felt about anything?

"Well?" he said, and if I wasn't angry enough, his hand began to move up the back of my leg.

"Don't."

My voice was sharp and his hand stopped. I spun away and stood by the window and straightened my skirt. The door into the kitchen opened and Mark and Bernie started to come in but instead they got talking about something else and stepped back out. Tom had collapsed over his knees, his face in his hands, but I stepped past him to the kitchen. I watched Mark and Bernie out the window as I rinsed the dishes, my stomach contracting around a stone. Tom stayed in the living room and I stayed in the kitchen, but with my hands in the sink I could still feel his cheek against my hip and his moist breath on my skin through my skirt. These were our lives, the only ones we'd ever have—but what could I say? What could I do? I felt tender, righteous, foolish, ashamed, resentful, and sorry for myself—in that order. Why didn't I run in there and wrap my arms around him and hold him, tell him something, tell him anything. To quit drinking, sure, but if not, then to take a long walk on a cold night, but not to go to Florida and ruin his children's lives. I wanted to tell him that I loved him, but with what kind of love, and with what words? Helpless inside my hard little shell, I looked out the kitchen window at the round hills flush with spring and it began to sink in that I'd never see him again. I was relieved when the door opened and Mark and Bernie came back in, and I felt exhausted when the evening ended and we all headed out to the car. Tommy and I kissed each other on the cheek in the driveway. He hobbled the rest of the way to the car with his cane and his yellow dog. He sat in the front seat and looked at me and blinked. I wish now I had bent through the window and given him a long kiss on the mouth, this one, who loved me enough to leave me, in front of the one who loved me enough to stay. I don't know why I didn't. I don't know why it mattered. It was the only night of my life I'd be with these two men, when they both were still living and for some reason still in love with me.

I stood with Mark's arm around me and we waved as the car backed up, turned around under the gas tank and mercury lamp, then drove past the barn and out the driveway to the county road.

"I'm sorry," Mark whispered, as he kissed the top of my head. "The poor fucker's fucked, isn't he?" Then he went back inside, leaving me alone to watch the red tail lights of the car get smaller and smaller down the valley until they finally disappeared.

I'm a sap, but look, there's fire
in the belly of the world

I'm still sitting outside my North Dakota motel room under a blanket with Puppy on my lap. I'm looking north into the star-bright sky, the flat land going all the way to the arctic, and I'm waiting for something. I debate whether to smoke another cigarette and then I do. My hands get cold, so I take turns smoking with my right hand, then with my left. The hand I'm not smoking with I warm up under the blanket against Puppy's belly.

Six months after Tommy's visit I woke up in a cold sweat thinking about him. It was fall on the farm and every breath carried with it the big-gulp promise of winter. I'd dreamed Tommy was lying on the sidewalk outside the hospital and as I was stepping past him, he reached for me. Before he could grab me, I ducked into work and during my entire shift I kept expecting he was going come in but he didn't. I knew he was outside dying but I didn't go out for him, and when my shift was over he was gone.

When I woke, I called his ex-wife's house in Orlando. A man answered. I assume now he was one of Adriana's relatives, her father, perhaps. He spoke French. I spoke English. I asked if Tom was there.

Il est mort.

I don't understand French and the connection wasn't good. I asked again if Tom was there.

Il est mort.

I don't know how many times I asked this same question—more than two, less than five—before I finally understood.

Il est mort.

I was stunned and full of questions but he couldn't understand me and I couldn't understand him. That evening I called back and talked to Adriana. She had what I would have called an Italian accent but her voice was flat. She told me Tommy had been dead for a month and was already buried.

"How?" I asked.

His living in the house became unbearable, she said. She kept giving him deadlines that he ignored. He drank heavily and made their lives miserable and frightening. He lived in the basement and shouted upstairs when he needed things. Their 9-year-old son Marco, especially, tried to be attentive, bringing him food and beer, but he could never do enough. One day Adriana and Tom argued bitterly. Tom was waving his pistol around. He was very drunk and shot the pistol twice into the wall. Adriana ran upstairs and gathered the children and they fled to the driveway. They got in the car and Mariana, their 11-year-old, dialed 911. That's when they heard another shot from the house. Adriana told me she went back in to investigate. She said her children begged her not to, but she had an idea and she had to find out. She made her way down the stairs into the quiet basement. Too quiet. She looked around the corner from the hallway and saw his body on the couch he rarely got up from.

"It was very ugly," she said, "but it was over."

I told Adriana that I was sorry, that I felt partially responsible, that I should have done everything I could to keep him from going home. At first she didn't answer when I said that, and I realized she didn't know me at all. I was just a voice on the phone to her. Then she said Mariana felt responsible as well; she thought dialing 911 from the driveway caused her dad to shoot himself.

"Poor girl," I said.

"And my son," she said. "He thinks if only he took better care of his father in the basement."

"Okay," I said, "I understand. I just—"

"No," she said. "I don't think so. Or maybe. I don't know. I don't know who you are or how you knew my husband. I think he meant something to you but, you know, I'm not... interested."

She didn't say it in a mean way. Just very matter of fact, and sad. I could hear her breathing. I could hear in her voice she had nothing left. We hung up.

I spent a few days feeling bad for Tommy's kids, and angry at him for ruining their lives, for giving them that nightmare, and regardless of what Adriana said, I still felt angry at myself. But that didn't last long because only a week after getting that grim news, I got some more. Mark was diagnosed with melanoma. I could go into the medical details but instead I'll just say the cancer had already spread. This was just last October and by May he'd be dead. So it was a busy time, and I had a lot to do, a lot to be mad and sad about, and no room left to grieve for Tommy.

Now, sitting on the sidewalk outside my North Dakota motel room, I hold Puppy on my lap and again I read the scrap of letter I saved. It's all I have left, this piece of notebook paper stained with bear blood, this beach scene with donkeys, pigs, and children stoning a sick dog, young mothers with wet, shiny legs and bitter dwarfs selling ice cream. It's all here, hope, despair, life and death, tragedy and comedy—and despite his ugly end—love.

At the beginning of this story, I said that all I'd done for too long was keep myself intact, that perhaps I was looking for a place where the shell of my body might crack and the cold dust inside blow away in the wind, and I wondered if that would get me home again.

Now I have new questions. Not will I get home, but can I spread my arms wide enough? Can I stretch my heart big enough? That man who loved from the bottom of a well…nobody could do that forever. No living man or woman could maintain that for long without feeling bitter from time to time in the bright light of day, too sad anymore for words, and perhaps even crave the abyss. A mad dog needs killing, after all. Life is never neat and clean and the road home is treacherous and dark. Okay, you've heard these things before. But sometimes it takes a wonder woman or a mummy to guide you. A dead poet—Blah-*blah*, blah-*blah*, blah-*blah*, *I'll be back*—or a bear. Some things you can't understand until you break, and what I find tragic now isn't my effort to protect my dusty essence, my cold self—there's a little quixotic comedy there—but my urge to make the carnival understandable, to force it to fit neatly inside my rigid little skull when it is only with my broken heart (that aches when the moon is full) that will ever have the chance to hold it, to hold it, to hold it….

Now, as if on cue, as if to show me that the world still does sometimes reward the patient, the northern lights begin to flare up from the horizon in wild blue-green flames that eventually spread over half the sky. This is what I've been waiting for, why I've been sitting outside on a cold November night with a blanket around me, throwing off my tobacco ration plan and smoking a second and even a third cigarette. The motel desk clerk told me he'd heard on the news this was expected but I still can't believe my good fortune. I suddenly want to cry with joy. Okay, I'm a sap but look, there's fire in the belly of the world!

I want to tell Mark, hey, it's *not* all gone, not even close, it's still here—*everything*—and my blood quickens.

Both of you, I say, and suddenly I'm thinking of my son and my daughter, as well, my babies, traveling from far away, flying in jet planes through the glowing heavens. They're coming home, of course they are. They're coming home to the farm and to their father and to me. I hold the scrap of letter to my chest, *both of you, all of you, yes.*

into the pool of it the door opens

The next morning I leave early but I am not in a hurry. I take my time and drive blue highways the rest of the way across the prairie and into the forest, winding around countless small lakes and into Wisconsin where Lake Superior stretches north to a blurry horizon. That evening and morning I walk the rocky beach outside my hotel, climb over driftwood clumps and scatter wild winter birds. I'm stunned by the beauty, by the cold liquid smell, and by the emptiness. There are so many people in so many places, it's hard to conceive of how many places there are none. Maybe I just can't hold the idea of *many* with *none* in my head at the same time. I don't know why I'm here but am beginning to think the question itself is suspect. I wear my wool stocking cap, mittens and my navy blue puffy jacket and I wear my fleece pants and I put my pretty nails in mittens and Puppy and I walk until dark and then walk even farther and I find a dry place to sit and smoke my second to last cigarette. The wind picks up and I'm cold and a moon lights our way back along the beach. In the morning, Puppy sleeps while I drive south over a big shield of leafless forest mixed with pine and hemlock that slopes upward from the lake for a long way, and then tilts and slopes down the other way toward the middle of the state. I could easily make it home today but I don't want to. I have not called my children and they have not called me, and I'm tempted a couple of times but I resist, I don't want to know and I don't want them to know, and I know that sounds ridiculous, but ridiculous is maybe just fine for this kind of thing.

I stay at little log lodge on a lake in the woods. The lodge smells of rusty water and clean sheets, propane and pine needles, and I think about all of the lakes in the woods, and all the log lodges, and how a person could do this forever, go from one to the other, all the same but each as quirky as the people who run them.

Because of the season, I'm the only customer, and being there makes me unreasonably happy. Especially because I eat dinner with the owner, a bent-over old man named Morton, who raised six sons here with his late wife, and now is the cook and the maid and the fix-it man. He makes me a beautiful homemade spaghetti sauce with his own tomatoes and basil and garlic. All alone there, and with few guests even during the peak months, he tells me he reads a lot, and he shows me his library of books. Nobody shows you their books anymore. He tells me about the loons on the lake and the fishers in the woods, and then he wants to talk about medicine, government health, private insurance, the nature of empire and economic systems, and even the way our brains work. When I ask him if I can smoke a cigarette after dinner—my last one, but I don't tell him that—he seems delighted and gets out his pipe to join me. We sit at the table surrounded by books and log walls, and beyond them by miles and miles of forest, and we smoke over our dirty dishes and coffee and it feels so civilized I almost want to cry. And then I do cry, and he sits silently for a while and doesn't say anything, and it's not even awkward at all. I want to ask him how he manages the loneliness—*how? how?*

how? I want to say like child—but when I finish crying I notice he's poured us each a little brandy, and we drink that before I go to bed, and I think maybe he's just shown me how.

In the morning we say a fond good-bye. He wishes me good travels. Then I drive the last few hours home.

I stop in the village and get the newspaper, the Weekly Home News, and a front page article is about a bear spotted in the township, so far south, so late in the season to be wandering. It's even been seen south of the river where our farm is, and there's concern about pets and small children that I find humorous. But a bear awake this late in the season must be a little mad, a little sad and lonely and lost, and I should know. Alert, I look for it on the drive south of the river through the slough and on into the hills. I don't drive directly to the farm. I take turns and follow county roads through narrow hollows past broken barns, past the places of people I know. I pass a dead deer on the side of road covered with ravens that fly up in front of the car like a black cloud. Soon it starts to snow, big wet flakes that stick on the ground and swirl in my headlights. I pass the Wood brothers shack, and I remember Mark and I coming to neighborhood potlucks here, and I don't even know who lives there anymore. I drive by the Johnsons' hilltop farm and memories of a hundred visits come to mind. I could stop in now and be welcomed. I don't. I feel I am driving thorough a landscape of ghosts. My youth. Our youth. Our young children. Where are they now? Where is that young woman who was me? Gone like Mark, here like he is. I am flooded by memories I may just drown in. But I relax and let myself rise to the surface and I'm floating in a hot, poignant pond on this snowy November evening. This is it, I think, this life, this feeling, and you can panic and sink or relax and float but it's love that will hold you up or kill you. It's all there is, and all there isn't. It's everything and nothing, the void and this are the very same thing. It's Tom Connor's gift, and I'm bringing it home.

By the time I get near the farm I'm ready. It's not snowing anymore but the hills have been dusted white so they look like giant marshmallows, lovely curves, high and steep and flat on top, and covered with naked black trees. Marshmallows covered with quills. I turn between two of them down our long driveway and see the house past the barn. But I don't see any lights and for a moment I think that maybe my children aren't there at all, that they've not come home, and the thought sends a terror of loneliness through my bones, but also, I admit, strangely, a kind of relief. I drive across the ten-acre front field where I remember sitting on the fender of the tractor while Mark planted corn. I slow the car on the little bridge where summer evenings Mark and I sat with a beer, our bare legs dangling over the edge, feeling the cool air from the creek while Kate and Cody dropped stick after stick over the upstream side then ran to the downstream side to wait for the sticks to drift out. I remember the first time Mark and I sat here watching the trout rise at dusk and knowing we could buy this place, not imagining all the living we had to do to make it our home but doing the living anyway.

I drive up past the barn with its big white letters that say Kraemer Family Farm in an arc, and past that to where my headlights pan the house and the yard, close now. I stop. I don't think I can get out of the car. And I don't think anybody is here anyway. It's almost dark. I turn my headlights and the car off. Then I see smoke rising from the house chimney, a faint light in the kitchen through the darkened living room, and then the light turns on above the front porch, yellow and warm, and into the pool of it the door opens and my daughter steps out. I can't see her face but I recognize her form, and she's looking across the yard at me and at the car, and behind her I suddenly see my son. It's supposed to be cold—it is cold, I can feel when I open the door of the car—but next to the house under the eaves is still a big stack of firewood. It's cold and dark and will get colder and darker as we head into the middle of winter but after that, as Mark used to say, after the solstice the six-month forecast is warmer and brighter, high summer, which for a farmer is about as much as he'd talk about the weather. I think about that as I walk toward my children up the snowy walk, my children who have stepped off the porch and are walking toward me. When we meet, we embrace, the three of us, quietly, outside in front of the stoop under that yellow light, and it turns out we all know what to do, how to hold it close, how to endure the burn of it, the undiminished glow, how to spread our arms wide and to breathe each other in.

We step back, and even though they tell me the wood box inside is full, I insist that as long as we are out here we each carry in an armload of dry oak that Mark split and stacked in his last months of strength. I think about this, and I think they might be thinking about it as well, but none of us says anything except to exclaim over Puppy, who is scampering along behind us, under us, almost tripping us. They tease me for my obsession, and though our faces are shiny with tears we're all laughing as we carry the wood inside. I smell the house again for the first time and it smells of something good cooking, my son's wet shoes, my daughter's hair, and even still of Mark and Mark's disease—the great carnival, the whole beautiful disaster. Through the living room windows I see the same view, the bottom pasture, white now, under snow, and cut by a curving creek lined with naked box elder and cottonwood. We fill to overflowing the box in the corner, then stack what doesn't fit on the brick floor next to the stove, a few sticks to keep us warm until morning.

acknowledgments

Thank you to Mike Patrick for his long friendship—and for his support through *Novelas Americanas* while I finished this book.

CPSIA information can be obtained at www.ICGtesting.com
Printed in the USA
BVOW07s2238180714

359069BV00002B/24/P

9 780962 378959